Praise for *The Good Thief's Guide to Amsterdam*

'A stylish and assured debut that introduces the fascinating Charlie Howard. Let's hope Charlie's as much of a recidivist as Highsmith's Ripley, 'cause he's a character you'll definitely want to see more of' Allan Guthrie

'A thoroughly enjoyable first novel. I look forward to more of Charlie's adventures as he indulges his penchant for travel and burglary' *Mystery Scene*

'This impressive debut owes much of its charm and success to its compelling anti-hero, Charlie Howard ... The detection is first rate, and Howard is a fresh, irreverent creation who will make readers eager for his next exploit' *Publishers Weekly*

'Ewan's pacing is spot on, doling out the information in just the right quantities to keep his readers zinging along with the story ... With such wonderful writing, readers are sure to be hopeful that Ewan decides to take on other cities, other mysteries' *reviewingtheevidence.com*

By the same author

The Good Thief's Guide to Amsterdam

About the author

Born in Taunton in 1976, Chris Ewan now lives on the Isle of Man with his wife Jo and their labrador Maisie.

His acclaimed debut, *The Good Thief's Guide to Amsterdam,* won the Long Barn Books First Novel Award and was shortlisted for CrimeFest's Last Laugh Award for the best humorous crime novel of the year.

Visit www.thegoodthief.co.uk

THE GOOD THIEF'S GUIDE TO PARIS

CHRIS EWAN

POCKET
BOOKS

LONDON • SYDNEY • NEW YORK • TORONTO

First published in Great Britain by Long Barn Books, 2008
This edition first published by Pocket Books, 2009
An imprint of Simon & Schuster UK
A CBS COMPANY

1 3 5 7 9 10 8 6 4 2

Simon & Schuster UK Ltd
1st Floor
222 Gray's Inn Road
London WC1X 8HB

www.simonandschuster.co.uk

Simon & Schuster Australia
Sydney

A CIP catalogue record for this book
is available from the British Library

ISBN 978-1-84739-359-3

Typeset by M Rules
Printed by CPI Cox & Wyman, Reading, Berkshire RG1 8EX

For my family

ONE

The moment I'd scanned the outside of the building, I turned to Bruno and said, "First impressions, it looks straightforward."

Honestly, I'm not kidding. *Straightforward*. That's what I said and I guess it's fair to assume I happened to believe it too. Looking back, I can't help but wonder what I was thinking. I mean, put that line at the opening of a crime novel and it's practically a guarantee that everything is about to get complicated. And there I was, a crime writer myself, saying the self-same sentence. What I should have done, if I wanted to complete the picture, was wear a T-shirt with the words "Catastrophe Here" printed across my chest.

Poor Bruno, though, knew none of this.

"Excellent," he replied.

I held up a finger. "But first impressions can be misleading. And this isn't something you want to rush into."

"So what do we do?"

"We case the job. Find out what we're up against."

Bruno nodded, concentration etched into his features. I could see the glint of excitement in his eyes, something I recognised from my own first outing as a thief. Otherwise, it would have been hard to guess he had criminal ambitions. He looked every inch the respectable young Frenchman: close-cropped hair, a dusting of stubble, jeans, a polo shirt, scuffed trainers.

"There's plenty we can tell from over here," I went on. "I can see the buzzers beside the door and I count eleven of them."

"Twelve."

"You think?"

"One is hidden towards the bottom, where the light is not so good."

"Huh," I said, and wondered how much the booze in my system was affecting my focus. I was tipsy, for sure, but I didn't feel drunk. "Okay, so twelve apartments. And I count, what, two sets of lights at the front of the building?"

"That's right."

"Normally, I'd allow for the same at the rear, meaning we should assume at least four apartments are occupied."

Bruno's brow tangled. "These people could have gone out and left their lights on."

"It's possible. But let's be cautious. And more importantly, you said the apartment is on the third floor, front-facing, and there are no lights on there. At least, I can't see any."

"There are none, you're right."

I gestured towards the window we were concerned with. "And the curtains and those shutters aren't drawn either, so unless the person who lives there has gone to bed at, what, a quarter to ten in the evening without blocking out the glare from that street lamp, we can assume the place is empty."

"We could find out," Bruno said, turning to me.

"How?"

"Press the buzzer."

"True," I told him, "but you're forgetting the night concierge."

I pointed through the glass double doors at the front entrance of the building towards a plump, balding gentleman who was sat behind a polished wooden counter. The man was swivelling from side to side on a high stool, meanwhile glancing down at a folded newspaper. There was a pen in his hand and a puzzled expression on his face and I felt pretty certain he was working on a crossword. Not that it mattered. All that concerned me was the fact that he was there.

"Think about it," I said. "If you go up and press that buzzer and nobody answers, and then afterwards you try and make your way inside to visit the owner of that apartment, the concierge is going to know something's up."

"I had not thought of it."

"Well, that's why I'm here." I placed a hand on his shoulder. "Now, you said the front doors are always locked. My thinking is the lock could go one of two ways. Chances are it's old – maybe it's been there as long as the building itself – so it could be rusted up and tough to open even if you happen to have a key. On the other hand, the pins could be so worn down from everyone coming and going all the time that we'll be able to pop it in less than a second. Either way, we can't have the concierge watching, especially with you being a beginner."

Bruno squinted at me, as though I was a distant figure on a far-off horizon. "What do you suggest?"

"A diversion, to get him away from his desk. Here, help me collect some rubbish."

Oddly enough, finding litter wasn't difficult in the Marais. As desirable as the area might have become, filled as it was with pricey boutiques, exclusive galleries and très chic brasseries, there were countless green plastic litterbags dotted around. We both collected a bag from inside the colonnaded archways of Place des Vosges and then I led Bruno back to Rue de Birague.

I jutted my chin towards the darkened service alley running alongside the building we were interested in. A wheelie bin was stationed there, looking as if it belonged to the late-night green-grocers situated just to the right

"For you," I said, handing Bruno my bag of litter and wiping my hands clean on my trousers. "Now, follow me."

"But the concierge – he will see."

"Not if we're quick. He's reading his newspaper, remember."

Before Bruno could challenge me any further, I darted across the street, grinning at the absurdity of what I was proposing. Never in a million years would I try this on one of my own jobs. It was really just for show, something to make Bruno feel as though he was getting value for money. I mean, any professional thief will tell you that the simplest solution to a problem is nearly always the best and, given a few days, I dare say I could have come up with a dozen easier ways to bypass the concierge. Odds were, a quick check of the rear of the building would reveal a service entrance or a fire exit that could make the whole issue redundant. It might even be possible to gain access through the greengrocers or the two-star hotel on the other side of the building. So sure, Bruno struck me as a nice guy, but he had to be a little short in the brains department to buy into my litter stunt.

I entered the service alley, raised the lid on the wheelie bin and peered inside. It was empty, though it reeked of over-ripe fruit. I lifted the bin clear from the floor and carried it to a square of ground adjacent to a side-entrance to the building. The smartly painted door had a laminated notice tacked to it that read *Poste*.

"My guess is this door backs onto the concierge's desk," I said.

Bruno nodded.

"So the plan is, we put the litterbags in the bin and set light to them, then we knock on the door and head back to the front of the building. While the concierge is busy putting the fire out, we pick our way inside."

"You do not think he will be suspicious?"

"Not at all," I said, waving Bruno's quite valid concern aside. "He won't have time to think. He'll act. And while he acts, we'll act. And once we're all through acting, you and me will be upstairs in the apartment we're after."

Bruno hefted the litterbags. "Do you think this will burn okay?"

"Sure," I said, freeing the bags from his hands and stuffing them inside the wheelie bin.

"Because I was thinking," he went on, "we could maybe use your book?"

Bruno grinned at me, revealing a set of perfectly aligned teeth, and then he stooped down and removed a book from the backpack he had with him. He held it before my eyes. I smiled back as if he was a regular comedian but really I wanted to smack him in the windpipe and split his nose with my kneecap for good measure. Why? Because the book he was so casually suggesting we should burn had taken me more than a year to write. It had been the hardest thing I'd ever worked on. I'd sweated every sentence, every damn word, and here was good old Bruno, someone I'd known for a little under three hours, cracking funnies about torching it.

"Not a good idea," I said, as calmly as I could.

"You think maybe the cover will not light? Should I rip it?" he asked, gripping the hardcover as if to do just that.

"No," I said, grabbing his wrists. "I think we should apply a little logic to what you're suggesting. You wanted me to show you how to break into this place without getting caught, right? Well, lesson one, Bruno, is I think the idea of burning a book with my name on it, a book I've personally inscribed to you, might be just about the dumbest thing I ever heard. Suppose we knock on this door and the concierge comes out before the book has burned right the way through? Or suppose the book doesn't catch properly? It's going to look kind of fishy, isn't it, if an apartment gets knocked over on the exact same night a charred copy of my memoir is found by the concierge?"

Bruno grinned again. "It's okay," he said, squeezing my arm and then caressing the cover of the book. "I am just joking with you, Charlie."

"Hilarious."

"Look, I put the book away," he said, returning my novel to his backpack. "It is safe. So, can we light the fire now?"

I muttered dark thoughts to myself, then reached inside my jacket and pulled out a cigarette packet. I lit a cigarette, took a calming draw and tossed my lighter to Bruno, watching as he leaned inside the wheelie bin and triggered the flame. Moments later, curls of blackened smoke emerged.

I exhaled, meanwhile rooting around in my trouser pocket until I found a short, flexible plastic implement. To the untrained eye, it might seem at first glance like one of those throwaway drink stirrers you find in coffee houses, but someone looking just a bit closer would notice a single row of plastic bristles at one end of the shaft. The bristles give the device the appearance of a very small, very painful toothbrush.

"You'll need this," I said, handing the tool to Bruno and taking another lungful of smoke.

"What does it do?" he asked, turning it in his sizeable hands.

"It's known as a rake. You slip it into the keyhole on a lock and brace it against the pins that are preventing that lock from opening. Meanwhile, you insert a screwdriver into the base of the lock and exert some sideways force." I passed him one of my micro screwdrivers – the one with a red, hexagonal handle. "Then you whip the rake out. With a simple lock, the plastic bristles'll jog the pins up to the exact right height so the lock can turn."

"And you think this will work on the front door?"

I took another draw on my cigarette, held the smoke in. "I think it'll work on the lock on the front door, but you'll need to turn the door handle to get all the way inside." I threw my cigarette into the litterbin. Already, the flames had taken hold and I could smell burning plastic and the scent of warm, rotten bananas. "Normally, I'd wear gloves. But we should be okay without. You ready?"

He met my eyes and nodded solemnly.

"Well alright then," I said, and rapped loudly on the wooden door.

I knocked three times, then gave Bruno a shove, pushing him in the direction of the street. He lurched forwards, caught his balance and broke into a run. I followed close on his heels. At the end of the alleyway, Bruno shaped as if to veer right but I reached out and yanked him back by his collar.

"Not so fast," I cautioned, pushing him against a display of fruit belonging to the greengrocers. "We need to check he's gone first."

I crept forwards and craned my neck around to peer through the glass windows in the two front doors. I caught sight of the concierge's brown cardigan sleeve as he disappeared into the back room behind the service desk and then I motioned Bruno over to where I was standing.

"Rake first," I said, watching him insert the rake into the lock and then seizing his wrist and moving his hand firmly upwards so that the bristles were forced against the pins inside the locking cylinder. "Good. Now add the screwdriver. Excellent. Now, whip the rake out and turn the screwdriver clockwise at almost exactly the same moment."

"I just pull this out and turn?"

"Yep. Just whip and turn and go for the door handle."

"Wait." He peered up at me. "I have to turn the door handle too?"

"I'll do it," I grunted. "You just focus on the lock. Okay?"

He nodded once more.

"Go ahead."

And blow me, he did.

"Superb," Bruno said, as the bolt snuck back and I twisted the door handle at just the right instant.

"After you," I replied, and ushered him inside.

TWO

The night concierge reappeared just as we entered. He frowned, his hand suspended above a fire extinguisher that was mounted on the wall behind his desk.

"Bonsoir Monsieur," I said breezily, treating him to a casual wave and a friendly bow, meanwhile taking Bruno by the arm and guiding him across the foyer. Bruno's feet seemed to catch in one another. I glanced sideways at the concierge. He still hadn't moved.

"Quatrième étage," I managed, jabbing my finger towards the ceiling.

Finally, the concierge shrugged and murmured something under his breath, as though he couldn't care less where we were heading.

"Bonsoir," I added, pointlessly, and watched as he turned his back on us to heave the extinguisher from the wall and return to the alley.

At the far side of the foyer, Bruno pressed the call button for the elevator. I heard an antique-sounding chime and the whirring of hidden cogs and cables, followed by the muted ringing of the elevator bell as the single carriage descended towards us. From outside came the whoosh and squirt of extinguisher foam. There was a pause, followed by a second and then a third blast of the extinguisher, accompanied by one of the few French words I could recall from my school exchange.

The foyer itself was eerily quiet and the lighting subdued, as if to prepare us for sleep. The decor was stylish, though minimalist. Flecked marble tiles covered the floor beneath our feet and the off-white walls were hung with a handful of bold, modern canvases. Sure, the concierge might not have said anything, but he worked in a quality building and it was reasonable to assume he was suspicious about our arrival coinciding with the fire.

"This is taking too long," I whispered to Bruno.

"There are stairs."

"No – it'd look odd. I just wish the elevator would hurry up."

Bruno checked the dial above our heads. "Two more floors."

"Marvellous."

I contemplated my feet, noting that my shoes could do with a clean. It was a job I'd meant to tackle before showing up for my book reading. Mind you, my tardiness hadn't seemed to put anyone off. By the end of the evening, I'd sold more books than I'd anticipated and that happy state of affairs had a lot to do with how much wine I'd drunk afterwards, and the wine had a lot to do with why I'd agreed to show Bruno how to set about breaking into an apartment building. I guess if I was the type of chap to keep my shoes clean, I probably wouldn't have got involved in such a hair-brained scheme in the first place. It's amazing, really, how much trouble a good shoeshine can save.

If I'd had the time, I suppose I could have turned my mind to what other chores I might have better occupied myself with, but right then the elevator bell chimed twice more and the burnished metal doors jerked apart. We stepped inside the cramped elevator interior, the carriage bouncing with our weight, and turned around just as the concierge returned to his position behind the reception desk. I forced a smile and nodded, then glimpsed out of the corner of my eye that Bruno was reaching for the button with the number three printed on it.

"No," I snapped, lashing out and compressing the button for the fourth floor before his finger made contact.

Bruno turned to me with a confused expression but I maintained my fixed smile as we waited for the doors to shuffle closed. As soon as they were sealed and the carriage had begun to rise, Bruno asked me, "Why did you do that?"

I rolled my eyes. "Because I told the concierge we wanted the fourth floor."

"But the apartment is on the third."

"I know, I screwed up. I think maybe I should have passed on that last glass of wine."

Bruno shook his head in an exaggerated way, as though I'd just dinged his car on the Champs-Élysées.

"It's not a big deal," I said. "We'll just get out on the fourth floor and take the stairs down a level."

"We should maybe have used the stairs anyway."

I sighed. "Look, nobody takes the stairs in a building like this when there's a working elevator. And we don't want to do anything out of the ordinary to draw the concierge's attention."

Bruno gave me a stern look.

"Granted, this evening may not be the best example of that. But you have to respect the theory."

The elevator bell chimed, interrupting us, and then the carriage came to a sudden halt on floor four, tossing my stomach lightly upwards. The doors juddered open.

"Go ahead," I said, and motioned for Bruno to step out.

Bruno moved into the corridor with all the stealth of a high-kicking showgirl at the Moulin Rouge, triggering a sensor that caused a series of lamps fitted along the corridor walls to light up. The walls themselves were painted a dusky red to around

shoulder-height and a muted cream thereafter. Immediately opposite the elevator shaft was a rubber plant with large, glossy
leaves, and a low banquette upholstered in tan leather. I stepped
into the corridor behind Bruno and followed him beyond a pair
of identical apartment doors that faced one another, towards a
featureless cream door at the end of the corridor. A green fire-exit
lamp with the words "Sortie de Secours" printed on it was
glowing just above the doorway.

We passed through the door and found ourselves on a flight of
concrete steps. The air was noticeably cooler away from the serv-
iced part of the building and as we headed downstairs, our
footsteps echoed against the breezeblock walls in a dull percussion.
On entering the third-floor corridor, we triggered another set of
lights. The corridor was decorated in the same manner as the floor
above, save that the rubber plant had been replaced with an aluminium umbrella stand.

"I don't see any security cameras," I said.

"No," Bruno agreed.

"None in the foyer either?"

"Only the concierge."

"I'm surprised."

"It is an old building."

I sucked my lips. "Modern interior, though. And an expensive
address. Seems unusual these days."

"Perhaps in London."

I shook my head. "You know, there are no cameras in my building,
near Grenelle. But it's still a lot more secure than this place."

"Yes?"

"It's one of the reasons I chose it. For the deterrent factor more
than anything."

Bruno gave me a sideways look. "So, to find a safe place to live,
I should maybe see if a burglar lives there first."

"Absolutely. But what are you going to do, keep an eye out for a guy wearing a striped jumper and an eye mask, carrying a bag marked 'SWAG'?"

Bruno smiled crookedly and pointed towards a cream-coloured door numbered 3A. The door had a brass peephole at eye level and what looked like a regulation deadbolt a shade lower than my hip.

"Will this work?" he asked, opening his palm and showing me the rake.

"If we're lucky, it might." I closed his fingers around the tool. "But you're getting ahead of yourself. You haven't checked if the apartment is empty."

Bruno looked puzzled. "Because I know it already."

"Wrong," I said, wagging my finger. "You think you know. But you don't know one hundred per cent for certain. And if you want to do this like a pro, you knock first."

Bruno cocked his shoulders. "It seems a little silly, no?"

"To you, maybe. Not to me."

I pointed to the door. Bruno waved the rake in my face.

"You do not trust me?" he asked.

"I wouldn't be here if I didn't."

"Because I already paid you, remember?"

"That's not the issue."

Bruno shut one eye and peered at me with the other. It looked like a complicated gesture. Maybe it was something he practised at home in front of his mirror.

"The thing is," I went on, "we only just met, agreed? And what you've asked me to do is pretty unusual. And sure, you've paid me and I've gone along with it, but I still don't know you any more than you know that apartment is empty. And all I'm asking you to do is knock on the damn door and you're being kind of funny about it."

Bruno groaned and dropped his shoulders. He glanced at the back of his hands and shook his head. Then he rolled his eyes, balled his right hand into a solid-looking fist and knocked very deliberately on the centre of the door.

We waited.

"Knock again."

Bruno's eyes grew wide, but he did as I asked. I stepped forwards and pressed my ear against one of the bevelled door panels. I couldn't hear a sound from inside. I nudged Bruno out of the way and put my eye to the brass peephole without success.

"I told you, it is empty," Bruno said.

"Seems that way," I agreed, backing away from the peephole.

"So?"

"So alright. Just pop the lock and we're good. We really shouldn't hang around out here too long, you know."

I was yet to hear a Parisian utter the words "Sacrebleu" but I like to think I got close. Instead, Bruno grumbled to himself and crouched down to assess the lock, blocking my view with the back of his head. I watched as he inserted the rake into the locking cylinder and braced it against the pins as I had shown him. He slipped the screwdriver into position and exerted some lateral force. He took a breath, squared his shoulders and whipped the rake out.

And nothing happened.

Bruno grunted, reinserted the rake. He forced it up inside the lock a little harder, bending the handle a fraction. He withdrew the rake a second time, in a more deliberate manner.

"Too slow," I commented.

Bruno's shoulders tensed. He didn't look at me but I could tell he was riled.

"You have to be faster. If you just visualise the pins in your mind and . . ."

"Yes," he snapped. "I will do it."

Bruno slipped the rake into the lock a third time and removed it without success. He tried a fourth time, and a fifth. After his sixth failure, he cussed and threw the rake onto the floor.

"Easy," I said, resting a hand on his back. "That's not such a simple lock. If it helps, you're doing everything right. In all probability, the rake just isn't up to the job."

Bruno shrugged, much like a teenager who'd just been scolded.

"You want me to pick it? You're welcome to try yourself, only it takes practice and maybe it's best you watch me this first time."

"Show me," he muttered.

I moved towards the door, reached inside my jacket and withdrew an ordinary-looking spectacles case. I popped the case open and selected one of my more flexible picks and a screwdriver with a slightly larger blade than the one I had equipped Bruno with. Once I'd gathered the bent plastic rake from the floor where Bruno had discarded it and returned the rake to my spectacles case and my spectacles case to my jacket pocket, I knelt down on the floor and faced up to the lock. I eased the pick inside the locking cylinder, hung my tongue out of the side of my mouth and went to work.

And maybe three minutes later, I'd cracked the thing. The deadbolt drew back with a reassuring clunk, like the boot mechanism on a German sports hatch, and I reached up and turned the door handle.

And right then I heard the *pip-pip-pip* of a burglar alarm priming itself.

"Damn," I said, as Bruno brushed past me. "You didn't tell me there was an alarm."

"Maybe you should have checked first," he called over his shoulder, flicking on a light switch and hurrying towards the source of the noise. A collection of recessed downlighters illumi-nated the hallway, the hundred-watt glare rebounding from the parquet floor. I stepped inside and closed the door behind me, then focused my attention on the end of the hallway where Bruno was opening a floor-to-ceiling storage cupboard. He fumbled for a light cord hanging by his shoulder and flipped down the hinged plastic panel on the front of an alarm control box.

From my count, he had maybe eight seconds left to enter the code before the alarm would really begin to sound. I'd had that happen to me once or twice in the past and it was never something I chose to ignore. I mean, even supposing you can disable an alarm once it's wailing flat-out, why would you want to? The thing has done its job by then and alerted everybody in the vicinity. At least, that's what I've heard – I've never hung around long enough to find out.

Naturally, if I'd known about the alarm, I could have bypassed it. And in the normal sequence of events, I'd have checked the door for signs of an alarm before I got busy with my picks. But it was too late for that now. I'd blundered on in, caught up in Bruno's frustration and the sticky trap set by my own ego. And yes, the booze too. How many had I had? Three, perhaps even four glasses of that heavy Bordeaux? Too many to drive a car legally, but apparently few enough to feel just tickety-boo about a little impromptu breaking and entering. And that was the nub of what was troubling me – just how foolish I'd been.

As I watched, Bruno tapped the code into the alarm panel, interrupting the ongoing *pips* with four lower notes registered in quick succession. There followed a longer *peep* and after that, silence.

Bruno turned to me.

"What was that, a test?"

He blinked and shook his head. "I forgot. That is all."

I nodded, trying not to let it bother me. "Are you going to invite me in?"

Bruno directed me through an archway at the end of the hall, into an open-plan living room with an expensive-looking kitchen-dinette at one end. He twisted a dimmer switch and I found myself confronted by a sight I hadn't expected. There was hardly any furniture – only a wide expanse of bare, concrete floor, encrusted with paint. The paint was all different kinds of colours, a random spectrum, like a giant Jackson Pollock installation. Leaning against the walls around the edge of the room were countless canvases and works in progress, most of them abstracts, with one or two more traditional portrait pieces. Over towards the full-length windows at the front of the apartment were a pair of easels with canvases clipped to them, and between the easels I saw what looked like a wallpaper pasting table, sagging under the weight of the paint tubes and brushes and trowels and cleaning fluids that had been stacked upon it.

Being a perceptive chap, I turned to Bruno and asked, "You paint?"

"A little," Bruno said, with a curt nod.

He removed his backpack from his shoulders, undid the zip and fished my novel out, setting the book down on the granite kitchen counter.

"You would like coffee?" he asked.

"Sure," I said, and approached one of the nearby canvases. The paint-spattered floor gripped the soles of my shoes. Maybe it was just as well I hadn't cleaned them after all. "These are good, Bruno. Really."

Bruno didn't respond. He was busy reaching inside a wall-mounted cupboard, removing two striped mugs and a packet of coffee grounds. I watched as he pulled the coffee machine away from the wall and tipped some of the granules into it, then hit a switch on the machine that burned an amber colour. The coffee began to percolate and Bruno opened the fridge door by his side. He stuck his head into the lighted interior.

"No milk," he said.

"Black's fine," I told him, running my hand over the canvas. "Might help me to sober up a bit."

Oh, if only I'd had that thought just a few hours before . . .

THREE

"'I want you to steal something for me.'

It wasn't the first time I'd heard those words, though usually the person saying them liked to warm up to it first. Not the American. He got straight to the point, casual as you like . . ."

So began my most recent book, *The Good Thief's Guide to Amsterdam*, and as I glanced up from the copy I held in my hands and scanned the faces in front of me, I had to suppress the urge to pause and check that they really did want me to go on. A year ago, if I'd turned up at the Paris Lights bookshop and explained who I was and the type of novels I wrote, I'd have been shown the door before I could ask if they stocked my work, let alone if they'd welcome a reading. Now all that had changed. With one book, I'd been transformed from a little-known peddler of trash into a little-known author of a faked memoir that was threatening to make me credible. The few critics who'd reviewed *Amsterdam* had hailed it as a brilliant conceit – not only was the author of a series of pulp novels about a career thief pretending to be a thief in real life, he was also pretending to have written a book about his exploits. There was just one problem: it wasn't pretend.

Oh, I'd had to change some things around – names, locations, the nature of what exactly was stolen. But to my mind, my book still felt like more than just an approximation of the truth – every word I'd put down on paper connected me back to what had really happened in Amsterdam.

Not that the crowd in front of me knew that. Either they'd bought into the whole charade along with everyone else or they didn't have the faintest idea what my book was about in the first place. And why should they care? I was a writer giving an outdoor reading on a warm spring evening in Paris and that ought to be enough to make even the most cold-hearted soul pause and lend me their ear.

Perhaps forty people had done just that. Most were students or backpackers, slouched on the green park benches positioned around me. Many of the rest were from the makeshift staff of Paris Lights, a bedraggled lot who slept in rickety beds among the sagging bookshelves at night and who worked the shop floor in return for their board during the day. There were others too: a middle-aged British couple sneaking photographs over my shoulder of the view across the river towards Notre Dame Cathedral; a nun in a taupe habit who was really more concerned with the pock-marked façade of the church of St-Julien-le-Pauvre; and a pair of wizened old Frenchmen in blue dungarees who seemed to be willing us all to vacate the Square Viviani so they could rejoin a decades-long boules contest.

They wouldn't need to wait much longer. I was only planning to read the opening chapter of my book and afterwards I might find there was a question or two to answer and perhaps even the odd copy to sign. Then it would be off to a local brasserie with the crowd from the bookshop, where I'd no doubt end up buying enough drinks to obliterate any semblance of a profit I might have made.

All of which was fine by me, so long as Paige came along too.

It was Paige who'd invited me to read in the first place, you see, and by happy coincidence she was really quite stunning. Her eyes were what first caught my attention – they were hazel and glistening and ever so slightly too large, as if the manic goings-on inside her brain were almost too much for them to bear. I liked that about her: the feeling of energy she had and the dizzy vibe she gave off. And I liked her delicate frame and her pale complexion, so pale you could see the blue tincture of veins coiled up at her temple, and I liked the ringlets of hair that fell around her shoulders and about her face, and when she spoke, I liked her voice most of all. She was American, from somewhere in the Midwest I guessed, and her speech was flighty and spontaneous and punctuated with shrieks of laughter. And God, did I want to kiss her.

And you want to know something truly shocking? Turned out I wasn't alone. It seemed to me that half the customers inside the Left Bank bookshop at any one time were young men aiming to catch Paige's eye. An awful lot of them were American grad students, loaded up with textbooks from semester-long courses at the Sorbonne. They spent their time browsing through Beat poetry and striking bookish poses and glancing over the top of Émile Zola paperbacks towards the central cash desk where Paige tended to sit. And hell, I couldn't really blame them, because I'd spent more than a few days doing the same thing myself.

It was maybe my third visit before I decided I was ready to talk to her and my fifth before I actually did. At the time, she was chatting with one of the unwashed hippies who worked there – a guy with a whole culture of organisms living among his crusted dreadlocks and matted, bright red sweater. She was being loud and opinionated and not at all how one is supposed to behave inside a bookshop. And I thought that was just great.

"Hello there," I said, approaching the counter with a lop-sided smile and offering her my hand. "My name's Charlie Howard. I'm a local writer."

Paige paused mid-sentence and took me in with those swollen eyes of hers. For just a moment, everything was on hold. Then she treated me to a blazing grin and pumped my hand energetically.

"Well hello yourself. I'm Paige."

"Charlie," I repeated.

"Poet?" the guy stood beside her asked, in a gruff, Mancunian accent.

"Mystery writer," I confessed, and held up a copy of my book for their inspection.

Paige scanned the title. "Looks . . . interesting," she managed, meanwhile turning from me to weigh the Mancunian's reaction.

The Mancunian wasn't sure what to make of me just yet so he reached for my book, checked the spine and brazenly assessed the publisher. His eyebrows jerked up a fraction. "This really you?"

"Afraid so," I said, and worked a bashful shrug.

"I'm writing a novel," the Mancunian told me, from behind his dreadlocks. "It's an epic fantasy wrapped in a socialist dystopian nightmare."

"That's . . . great," I managed, and caught Paige winking conspiratorially.

The Mancunian sniffed, wiped his nose with the sleeve of his red sweater and offered me his hand. "Mike," he told me. "You want to sign some books?"

"Why not? You have a few copies towards the back, I think."

Paige reached across the counter and squeezed my wrist. "Oh, well we can order some more now we know you. And you'll do a reading, right?"

"Er . . ."

"Oh come on, say yes."

"Um . . ."

"Pretty please," she added, and batted her eyelids.

"Well," I told her, shrugging, "If you put it like that . . ."

And boy, was I was reaping the consequences. By now, I was almost at the end of the chapter and I found myself consumed by the fear that I'd lost my audience altogether. I'd done my best to make the reading as engaging as I could but who knew if it had worked? I'd modulated my voice, though that was easier said than done, and I'd even risked an American accent on some of the dialogue, which was almost certainly a mistake. And as thoughts like that occurred to me, I cringed and began to read a little faster, straining to reach the final sentence as soon as possible without sounding as if I was hyperventilating.

With only two paragraphs left, I glanced up and noticed Paige gossiping with one of the men from the store. She was covering her mouth with her hand, which was pretty dumb because it just drew more attention to what she was up to. I guessed that said it all – even my host had had enough. I felt my cheeks flush and stumbled across a word. Paige looked up and winked at me. I paused, composed myself, and lunged for the end.

When it was finally over, I received a smattering of applause and then I asked if there were any questions.

"Yeah, hi," said an English girl sat off to my left. I took in the girl's large reading glasses, her no-nonsense centre parting and the collection of pimples at the corners of her mouth.

"Go ahead," I told her.

The girl gestured at a collection of well-thumbed paperbacks by her side. "Um, will you be writing any more of your Michael Faulks novels?"

I nodded, surprised that anyone in the audience had read them. "I'm working on a new one at the moment, as it happens."

"Oh cool. And . . ."

"Yes?"

"Well, it's just the author picture in these books." She gathered the top novel on her pile and showed it to me, pointing a bitten-down nail at the inside page. "It doesn't look very much like you."

I grimaced. "That's because it isn't me."

The girl frowned and blinked at the black-and-white portrait image of a suave model wearing a dinner jacket. "But, um, is that normal?"

"It's pretty unusual," I admitted, rubbing the back of my neck and working a sheepish grin. "It was just something my publishers put together really. They thought I'd sell more books that way."

I was lying, of course. During the past several years when I'd been writing the Michael Faulks burglar books, I'd always managed to dodge meeting up with my publishers and even my agent, Victoria. It was easy, really, because I was often travelling to new countries, moving on whenever I'd completed a manuscript or carried out a noteworthy theft. Back when I'd submitted the image of the catalogue model for my first novel, it had been a spur of the moment decision, but the photograph went down surprisingly well with my female editor and later my readership, which was mostly women. Truth be told, I'd had some quite eye-watering fan mail over the years and I was almost sorry that with *Amsterdam* I'd insisted on having no author image at all.

"It's kind of . . . weird," the girl told me.

It was hard to disagree. I pulled an apologetic face, then looked away and found that I had a handful more questions to answer. Once I'd satisfied my final interrogator, I moved across to the folding card table Paige had organised and sat down behind a stack of hardback copies of *Amsterdam*, fully prepared to watch the crowd disintegrate before my eyes. To my surprise, a modest queue developed and I ended up signing books and making small-talk for a good twenty minutes.

Meanwhile, the staff from the bookshop stood off to the side, smoking hand-rolled cigarettes and talking among themselves. They were a peculiar bunch: literate and well-educated, widely travelled and drenched in existential angst, yet at the same time living in a building with no hot water or bathroom facilities, several of them wearing stained clothes that looked as if they hadn't been changed for days. I wasn't surprised they didn't buy my book. After all, if they had enough cash to spend on novels, they wouldn't be living in the bookshop in the first place. And of course, living in the store meant they could read any book for free whenever they chose.

I wasn't surprised they were hanging around, either. Half of them looked as if they hadn't eaten a square meal in weeks and they must have figured they could hit me up for more than just a few glasses of beer. I didn't mind that. If I was trying to get by on just the sales from my book, it might have been a different matter, but I wasn't and I didn't, and the income from my thieving was quite capable of paying for a few plates of hot food.

I returned my attention to the person stood in front of me. It turned out to be my fan with the pimples and the centre parting. She was the last in line and she wanted all of her Faulks novels signed without buying my new book. I sat there scribbling my name, aware that she was studying my face intently, and then I closed the cover of the final novel and wished her goodnight. I was just twisting the top back onto my fountain pen, turning my thoughts to what I would say to Paige by way of thank you, when a young, muscular man with a confident grin approached the card table. The man snatched the top copy of *Amsterdam* from the pile and tossed it across to me.

"Would you like me to sign?"

"Yes, of course," he said, his English laced with a strong French accent.

"Who should I make it out to?"

The young man flashed me his dazzling grin again. "I would like, 'To my protégé'," he said.

FOUR

My protégé was sat up at the bar alongside me. I was smoking heavily – it's a French thing – and I was drinking a dense red wine from a very large glass. And I'd had one glass already and I still wasn't getting it.

"So, just to be clear, you want me to help you break into your own apartment?"

"Yes," Bruno said, looking at me intently.

"Because I have to tell you, if you want to know how secure your home is, there are firms that can tell you that. You simply contact them and set a convenient time and they send round a guy with a clipboard and a handful of colour pamphlets."

"This is not what I want."

"Because what, you don't trust those people but you do trust a guy who happens to have written a book about being a burglar?"

"Well, I suppose, if you put it like this . . ."

"It sounds pretty crazy."

Bruno pursed his lips and shrugged. It was a good Parisian shrug. He must have been schooled on it since birth, along with every other French kid. Certainly the barman was a fine practitioner of the art. I watched him gesticulate and shrug like an

Olympian, meanwhile pouring a shot of absinthe for a middle-aged redhead sat towards the far end of the counter. I got the impression the redhead was a regular and the absinthe was her familiar companion. The barman set the bottle back on the shelf and wiped his hand on his starched apron. No money changed hands.

I took another lingering draw on my cigarette. I wasn't smoking Gauloises – I kind of value my throat – but I was definitely smoking a lot more than I usually do. And I couldn't put it all down to the general ambience in the bar. It also had something to do with my nerves. This was no standard approach, no common request.

"This really your apartment?" I asked Bruno, eyes narrowing.

"Of course."

"Because it occurs to me you could just be trying to get me to break into a place that doesn't belong to you."

"Look, I will show you."

And with that he rooted around in the backpack he had with him until he found a crumpled piece of paper. He unfolded the paper, flattened it on the bar and smoothed the page.

I scanned the document. My language skills were only basic but I could see it was a printed letter from a French high-street bank, addressed to M. Bruno Dunstan, Rue de Birague, Paris.

"And that's you?"

"Yes," Bruno said, and pulled a credit card from his wallet with his name on it.

I took a mouthful of wine, swallowed, then drained the rest of the glass. I motioned to the barman for a refill and returned the letter to Bruno.

"This protégé thing, is that just to make me feel good or are you serious?"

"Serious," he said, and looked it.

"So why not ask me to show you how to break into an

apartment that doesn't belong to you? We could both make some money."

Bruno shook his head and rubbed idly at his bicep. The muscle was bulging from the sleeve of his polo shirt, like someone had forced all the toothpaste into the middle of an oversized tube.

To my side, the barman uncorked the bottle of moderately expensive red wine I'd been drinking and splashed some into my glass. He gave me a nod and I returned the gesture, then peered at Bruno.

"You don't trust me?"

"Maybe," he said. "Perhaps you are just a writer, after all."

My jaw dropped, somewhat dramatically. "I have to show you my credentials now?"

Bruno waved his hand, dismissing the point. "It is also about me. I like this idea, being a thief," he said, whispering the last word, even though we couldn't be overheard because the waiter had moved away and the acoustic café music was quite loud. "But maybe I will be terrible," he said, rolling his 'r's with gusto. "Maybe I will see how it works and know if I can do it."

I raised my hand to my face and covered my eyes. I peered out from behind splayed fingers. "Breaking into your own place won't do that. The job's about nerve as much as anything else."

He demonstrated his shrugging prowess once more. "But this way, I cannot be arrested, yes? It is my home."

"I guess. So what's your plan, you want me to run some kind of course here? First I show you how to crack your own place, then someone else's?"

He pouted. "It would be up to you."

"Because let me tell you, it's not going to be as easy as you think. Picking locks takes practice. And there are all kinds of locks. Every manufacturer has something different going on. I mean, granted, the principles are the same, but still."

"I would like to try, even so."

I snatched up my wine glass and reacquainted it with my lips, meanwhile glancing over Bruno's shoulder towards a corner table where Paige was sat with some of her colleagues from the bookshop. Dirty plates filled the centre of their table, alongside empty bottles of wine. One of the men, an Italian-looking guy with shimmering, coiffed hair and a high, square forehead, was being awfully tactile with Paige. He was smoking a cigarillo and gripping Paige by the shoulder, clinching her towards him, and the truth was she didn't appear to mind all that much. Her cheeks had a boozy flush to them and every so often she would roll her puffed-up eyes and collapse at some wildly amusing comment the Italian made.

Mike, the dreadlocked Mancunian I'd met, was sat opposite them, pouring more of the wine I'd paid for. He had on the same frayed, red woollen jumper he'd been wearing when I'd first spoken to Paige and I noticed that the overstretched sleeves were brushing against the rims of the wine glasses as he poured. Beside him sat a man in a garish skullcap who sported a pointed goatee that was weighed down with a colourful glass bead. The final member of their group was a serious-looking young woman with very fine, jet-black hair, purple lipstick and perhaps eight studs in her ears.

"Why do you want to be a thief?" I asked Bruno, my gaze still focused on the table across the room and, in particular, the intricate movements of the Italian's fingers on Paige's neckline.

"Maybe it is the challenge," he suggested, spreading his hands on the bar. "It is not easy, as you say. Maybe I would like to learn something like this. Anyone can break a window, yes? Not so many people can find another way in."

"So it's an intellectual exercise?"

"For me, I think so," he said, straightening on his stool.

"Well, for me it's about the money. So tell me, how much are my services worth to you?"

Bruno seemed taken aback by what I'd said but he recovered soon enough and delved into the back pocket of his jeans, withdrawing a folded bundle of notes. I gripped his wrist and forced it below the counter of the bar, checking to see the barman hadn't noticed.

"You want it to look like I'm pushing drugs here? Keep the money in your pocket. How much?"

"Five hundred euros."

My eyes widened. "And you figure that's enough?"

"It is all I have. I could get a little more, only . . ."

I looked at him, shook my head and took another draw on my cigarette. I exhaled over his shoulder, towards the ceiling. Just then, Paige exploded with laughter, the outburst beginning in her nose with a loud snort. Her body buckled and she nudged against the Italian in a playful way.

I tried to ignore how things were shaping up between them and focus on what Bruno was asking me instead. I didn't need the job or even the hassle for that matter but I couldn't deny I was interested. I'd been around enough confidence men in my time to know just how crudely he was trying to flatter me but that didn't make the effect any less potent. It wasn't everyday I was offered the chance to demonstrate my skills. Usually, I was more than a little concerned to ensure I had no observers whatsoever when I was picking a lock. But Bruno was giving me the chance to showboat and offering me cash to boot. By my calculations, the money would easily cover the food and wine I'd paid for, and I guessed I could always treat the episode as a harmless bit of fun.

Fun was something Paige seemed to be experiencing. She was giggling again, looking up at the Italian with an unmistakable spark in her eyes. I finished my wine.

"Let's get out of here," I said to Bruno. "I've had enough for one night."

Together, we left the bar and crossed Place Saint-Michel and then Bruno led me along the Quai running beside the inky River Seine, in the direction of the Ile Saint-Louis. Notre Dame Cathedral loomed alongside us, the arachnid limbs towards the Cathedral's rear bathed by the spotlights of a passing Bateau Mouche. Cars and mopeds streamed by, a clamour of diesel engines above the city's background hum. I took a few deep breaths to clear my mind, as if a lungful of traffic fumes could counteract the wine I'd ingested.

The stretch of wall we were walking beside had a series of green wooden boxes fixed to it. During the daytime, the boxes folded open to form street stalls selling artistic prints, second-hand books, snowglobes, fridge magnets and other bric-à-brac. The closed stalls were protected by the cheapest of padlocks. I could have picked them open in my sleep. With one arm tied behind my back. And a whole squadron of gendarmes marching by. And ... oh, you get the idea.

"She is pretty, yes?" Bruno said, from nowhere.

"Excuse me?"

"The American girl."

I glanced sideways at him. "I don't know what you're talking about."

Bruno studied me for a moment, then did his Parisian shrug again. "I live not far away. Across the river."

"So focus," I told him. "You need to concentrate if we're going to do this right."

FIVE

There are times I wish I'd listened to my own advice. There are times too when I wish I'd listened to my conscience. Days when I regret not listening to either are usually the worst.

The morning after I'd broken into Bruno's apartment, I woke with a hangover and a head full of regrets. I also cursed the time on my alarm clock because I'd forgotten to set the alarm before falling asleep and I'd have to hurry if I was going to make my meeting with Pierre, my fence. Stumbling towards the handful of cramped units that formed the excuse for a kitchen in my apartment, I dropped two soluble tablets into a glass of tap water and necked the fizzing sludge. The bubbles seemed to percolate in my brain, as if trying to jump-start my grey cells. I wished they'd hurry up and do something about the dull, mushy ache around my forehead and the queasy, hollow sensation in my stomach. Sure, I know I hadn't drunk that much wine but the truth is I'd been drinking on an empty stomach, a stomach that had stayed that way before I fell asleep and, hell, sometimes there's no logic to hangovers anyway.

I groaned and circled my fingers at my temple, then looked at the stale baguette on my kitchen counter and pushed any thoughts of eating it to one side. I moved into the bathroom, twisted the hot tap on the shower and stepped beneath the steamy jet. No matter how hard I scrubbed, though, or how much menthol shampoo I applied to my scalp, I couldn't rid myself of the feeling that I was thinking and moving at something like half my normal speed. And I couldn't shed the concerns that were niggling away at me about Bruno, either.

In the light of day, it seemed like a really dumb thing to have got involved in. And no matter what I'd said to Bruno, I hadn't agreed to do it because of the money. Five hundred euros might not be pocket change but it would be scant compensation if he got caught trying to break into somebody's home and happened to give the police my name as the "brains" behind it all. And the sad reality was I had only myself to blame. There I'd been, moping at the bar while Paige made merry with her friends at my expense, and instead of showing just a shred of maturity and walking over to join them in a good-natured way, I'd allowed Bruno to feed my ego, playing the hotshot thief and jumping two-foot into a situation I didn't feel the least bit comfortable about. All things considered, I'd been a bloody idiot.

Ten minutes later, I left my apartment and began walking at a brisk pace towards the gardens of the Champ de Mars. Actually, it wasn't too far from where I lived, though I hadn't told Pierre as much when he suggested it as a rendezvous point. My apartment was just off Rue Duroc, on the edge of the seventh arrondissement, an area popular with lawyers, bankers and diplomats. There were several embassies nearby and on weekends in particular, it was something of a soulless place. But it was central, with half-decent transport links, and, most importantly from my point of view, it contained modern apartment buildings like the one I lived in, where the security was excellent. My building might not have had a CCTV system but it did have a concierge and quality locks had been fitted to all of the doors. Sure, that kind of security meant the seventh arrondissement wasn't an area where I was inclined to practise my darker arts, but at least I had the comfort of knowing that anything I stole from elsewhere in the city would be relatively safe in my apartment.

As I neared the dusty gravel of the Place Joffre, at the rear of the Champ de Mars, I put on a pair of dark aviator sunglasses. I realised the glasses might look slightly odd to Pierre, since the weather was overcast, but I figured it had to be preferable to having him stare at my bloodshot eyes. The truth, you see, was that I was very keen to make a good impression. By my reckoning, it had been over a year since he'd offered me a decent job.

Naturally, that wouldn't have mattered a great deal if I'd been sensible enough to hold onto the money Pierre had paid me for the merchandise I'd left Amsterdam with. As it happened, though, just days after I'd received my share of what Pierre had made (which, inevitably, was somewhat less than I'd hoped for) I'd been contacted by one of my old school chums, Miles. Nowadays, Miles works in the City and he's very good at what he does and we've always been more than a little competitive with one another, and so the moment I foolishly bragged about the rather large sum of money I'd supposedly made from my latest suspense novel, Miles had insisted on investing the funds at a very healthy rate of return. I had no reason to suspect he would fail to deliver the kind of profit he'd talked about but the truth was I wouldn't find out for at least three more years, since that was the remainder of the time my money had been tied up for. So although I was rather well-off on paper, I was currently experiencing something of a lean period in terms of cash flow, and I was really hoping Pierre might change all that.

I found Pierre some distance along the Champ de Mars, sat in a green metal chair within the perimeter of an outdoor café, adjacent on one side to a fairground carousel, a basketball court and a children's play area, and on the other side to a stretch of lawn where, on brighter days, families would be sprawled on picnic blankets. A china espresso cup was positioned in front of Pierre, a clean ashtray off to the side. As I approached, he caught the attention of a pretty waitress clearing a nearby table and ordered me a café crème. He stood to shake my hand, eyes narrowing as he registered my sunglasses.

"You are turning European on me Charlie, no?"

"It's infectious," I said. "Ça va?"

"Oui. And you?"

I let go of his hand. "I'm fine. I've been working on a new book. *The Thief and the Fandango.*"

"Ah, très bien." He gestured for me to sit down. "And where is the great Monsieur Faulks?"

"Currently, Rio. He moves to Cuba in chapter sixteen."

Pierre frowned. "Cuba? To steal something?"

"I don't know yet. But Faulks needs somewhere to hide."

"And a woman?"

"He usually knows where to find one."

I winked, said nothing further. For many years I'd only dealt with Pierre over the telephone so it still struck me as somewhat odd to be able to meet him in person. Part of me wondered if we might have been better sticking to the old routine, keeping things as business-like as possible. It's true, we'd always been cordial with one another, but recently I'd sensed we were on the verge of new territory, where friendship might enter the equation. In my experience, that tended to make things awkward because there was more pressure not to let the other person down.

Strangely, in all our years of conducting business over the telephone, Pierre had been one of those rare people of whom I'd never fashioned an image in my mind. He was just a voice on the end of the line, shrouded in mystery. So I suppose it's odd that I should have been surprised by his age when we first met – he was pushing sixty – or by the mauve birthmark that clouded the skin around his left eye. Like a permanent welt, the birthmark gave his face a disjointed appearance – as if the right side was coming towards you while the left side backed away into the shadows. If that makes Pierre sound sinister, it shouldn't. More than anything, the birthmark gave him an air of innocence. And a man who dressed like Pierre could never be thought of as threatening. Today he had on a lemon sports shirt with a blue silk scarf knotted loosely about his neck, a pair of tan chinos and some cream-coloured loafers.

I took a seat and, out of habit, checked the tables near to us. As it happened, there were barely any customers. I clocked a middle-aged French woman in Jackie O shades, surreptitiously feeding her lapdog morsels of croissant, as well as a stern, distracted chap with an expensive-looking digital camera. Closest to us was a gentleman sat perhaps five metres away. I say gentleman because he was dressed in a linen three-piece suit with a straw boater upon his head. Since he was facing our direction, I was able to glimpse the gold chain of a pocket watch when he lowered his *Le Monde* newspaper to turn a page. A compact radio was positioned on the table in front of him, beside a half-empty cafetière, and since he appeared to be listening to the radio through a pair of discreet earphones, I didn't think our privacy would be compromised.

"You have something for me?" I asked Pierre.

He nodded, sipping from his espresso. "Would you be interested? I thought maybe with your book . . ."

I waved his concern aside. "I'm interested."

"Good." He paused while the waitress set my coffee down. The coffee smelled dark and strong, even through the cap of foamy milk. "And your hand?" Pierre asked, screwing his face up as if he regretted the need to ask.

"It's fine," I said, instinctively moving my right hand beneath the table, then smiling at my mistake.

With a shrug of my shoulders, I raised my hand for Pierre to see and he beckoned for me to pass it over to him. I reached across the table and allowed him to turn my hand palm up, to feel around the swollen, inflamed knuckles on my middle and fourth fingers. The fourth finger had begun to take on a slight crook in recent months and the truth is the way it looked had been bothering me more than the pain of the gouty crystals beneath my skin. Pierre gently squeezed the distended tissue just above my knuckle and I tried not to wince.

"I have medication. Pills, an injection if it gets bad."

"Too bad to work?"

"Not yet," I told him, withdrawing my hand. "I can still type. And I can still turn locks. My index finger is unaffected, that's the main thing."

Pierre nodded, backing away from me again. He blinked, the movement fractionally delayed around his left eye. A fine pair we made – a fence with a blemished face and a thief with early-onset arthritis.

"The job is simple," Pierre said. "But my client . . . cautious."

"They don't want mistakes."

"*Exactement*. And you must take only one thing."

"Which is?"

"A painting."

I felt my eyes widen. It had always seemed to me that paintings were exactly the sort of item a professional thief should be hired to steal. Cash, for instance, could feel a little sordid by comparison, and I refused to get involved with drugs of any description. But good paintings, especially portraiture, appealed to me. And besides, stealing art was often a neat way of working. Either the client wanted the work of art for their own personal enjoyment, in which case it would never draw any public attention, or Pierre would be asked to sell the painting on his client's behalf, in which event he could call on one of the better-established and more trustworthy networks in the business.

"Which artist?" I asked.

"It is signed Maigny. Early twentieth century."

My excitement dropped down a notch. Everyone has ambitions, I suppose, and I hoped one day to take something really special. A Degas perhaps, or even a Cézanne. Well, not this time.

I let out a breath. "You have a description?"

Pierre reached into his shirt pocket and removed a Polaroid photograph. He slid the photograph across the table to me and I picked it up and had a good look. I couldn't see as much as I would have liked. The image of the painting had been obscured by the camera flash when the shot was taken.

"It is oils, naturally," Pierre said. "A street scene of Montmartre. There is a flower seller and a young woman with a parasol . . ."

"Looks awful."

"It is worth ten thousand to you."

I hitched an eyebrow. "Really?"

"Oui."

I whistled and glanced up over Pierre's shoulder. Behind him, above the roof of the café and the rows of quivering horse-chestnuts, I could see the uppermost two-thirds of the Eiffel Tower. The burnished ironwork of the tower looked lace-thin against the brooding grey clouds, the yellow elevators slowly ascending and descending like jaded commuters. I caught sight of a blur of people moving around the highest viewing platform, the spark of camera flashes into the gloom. I was confused by what Pierre was telling me and bothered by the money involved.

"What's your fee?"

Pierre reacted as if I'd insulted him, squaring his shoulders and puffing his chest. "The same as yours, naturally."

"So your client pays twenty thousand euros. For a nothing painting."

"It may be worth it."

I shook my head. "Not on the open market."

"Who is to say? Perhaps my client is a collector, n'est-ce pas?"

"And just who is your client?"

Pierre paused. He held my eye.

"Oh come on. You're kidding me, right?"

Pierre hunched his shoulders and showed me his palms. "They call on the telephone. They will not meet."

And didn't that sound like a great way to do business.

"A man?"

Pierre nodded.

"Know anything else?"

Pierre just looked at me again.

"How about the photograph?"

He pouted. "Sent to my post office box."

"And you're comfortable with this?" I asked, jutting my head forwards.

Pierre tapped the edge of the table with his fingernail. "Maybe it is not ideal."

I rolled my eyes.

"But what is, Charlie? You tell me. The business these days, it is tough. Competition, oui?"

I sighed and reached for my cigarette packet. I removed a cigarette and began to light it. Pierre motioned for me to hand the packet to him and I passed him the lit cigarette instead. He took a draw, then stifled a cough. The last time we'd met he'd been giving up.

I leaned back in my chair and thought some more about what

had been said. The feelings that were stirring in me had echoes of Amsterdam. Something didn't feel right about the money we were being offered and I didn't like that Pierre knew so little about his client. Sure, that wasn't exactly unique, but I don't know, I was having doubts.

And yet, I was tempted too. Tempted to the tune of ten thousand euros for just a few hours' work. Back in my apartment, pinned up on the wall above my writing desk, there happens to be all kinds of information about the latest Michael Faulks novel I'm writing. I have a time-line and a plot summary and a list of characters. The character list is broken down on another piece of paper where I've drawn up a table with a series of questions. "*What is their main goal?*" "*What is their main strength?*" "*What is their main weakness?*" Now, if I were to put my own name into that table, the weakness box would be easy to fill. "*Greed*", it would say. And maybe beneath greed I'd add, "*Risk-taker*".

Ten thousand euros. It wasn't a life-changing sum of money by any stretch of the imagination, but put it with the remainder of the cash Bruno had paid me and I'd have enough for several months' rent. And it sure as hell beat the advance I was likely to get when I completed my novel.

More to the point, I was reluctant to turn Pierre down. I didn't want him to start passing jobs to other thieves ahead of me. He already had doubts about the state of my fingers, that much was clear, and I wasn't prepared to give him another reason to look elsewhere. Over the years he'd provided me with a flow of income that was unusually steady for a thief and I wanted that arrangement to continue.

"I'd need the money up front," I said.

"I have only half of it."

"Half of my ten and half of yours?"

Pierre considered my words for a moment, perhaps sensing the intent in my voice. He nodded cautiously.

"If I'm going to do this, I want all of it before I begin."

Pierre took another lingering draw on the cigarette, cheeks bulging. I'd offended him, I guess, though the truth was I didn't mind all that much. He closed his eyes and when he opened them to look at me again, the eyelid lingered over his left pupil.

"Amsterdam, Pierre," I prompted.

He vented smoke through his nose. "You think maybe I will ever stop paying you for Amsterdam, Charlie?"

Pierre shook his head ruefully and ground his cigarette out hard in the ashtray. After a moment's pause, he leaned down to his side and retrieved a leather manbag from the floor. He unzipped the bag, delved inside and removed a bulky envelope. He tossed the envelope across to me without a word.

"This all of it?"

He threw up his hands. "I should count it for you too?"

"Just asking. And the fee is non-refundable, correct?"

"Of course. The client pays half to hire us. That is the deal. And now my half is with you. Because we are friends Charlie, yes?"

"Friends, sure."

Pierre crowded over the table. The birthmark twitched around his eye.

"Then remember, do this right. I want my money too, yes?"

I nodded, holding his gaze. Then I broke eye contact and picked up the weighty envelope, slipping it into my jacket pocket. I pushed my sunglasses up on my nose while Pierre raised his espresso cup towards his lips. I realised I hadn't touched my coffee but I sensed our meeting was drawing to a close and I wasn't eager to prolong it. Besides, I had ten thousand new ways to buy a drink on my way home.

"So what kind of timescale are we talking?" I asked.

Pierre lowered his espresso cup and dabbed his lips with a paper napkin. "Two days. We can meet here. At ten o'clock, say."

"Sounds reasonable. Why don't you describe the place I'm breaking into?"

"It is an apartment," Pierre said, as if that much could be taken for granted in Paris.

"And where's the painting located?"

"There is only one bedroom. It is on the wall."

"Alarms? Locks? Attack poodles?"

He shrugged, as if the details were of little consequence.

"You do have an address, I take it."

"Oui, but of course," Pierre said, removing a folded piece of paper from a flap on the front of his bag and sliding the note across the table towards me.

I opened the note and scanned the address. And in that instant, what had struck me at first glance as a less than perfect scenario suddenly jumped clear off the scale.

SIX

"Good morning," I said brightly, when Victoria answered her telephone.

"Good morning yourself. How was the reading?"

"It was fine."

"Just fine? Not splendid?"

I smiled. "Didn't you hear? Splendid is over for me."

"Ah, you bludgeoned the poor word to death. That's too bad. It gave you an air of something."

"It was a triumph, for a time."

Victoria laughed. "A triumph? Where do you get this stuff?"

"My trusty thesaurus. How's hubby?"

There was a pause.

"Charlie," Victoria said, "exactly how many times do I have to ask you not to call Adam that?"

"Raw nerve?"

"Or to say that? Really, I'm going to batter you in a minute. Believe me, if Adam does ever propose, you'll be the first to know."

I grinned to myself and glanced down at the backlit screen of my laptop. The cursor was flashing at the end of a line I'd written, prompting me to continue. The only problem was I couldn't think what to type next. I was blocked. And often when I was blocked I called my agent, Victoria, and we'd shoot the breeze for a while. Sometimes, the words I needed to continue my story would come to me right in the middle of a conversation we were having and I could bid her a snappy goodbye and press on.

There were other times, though, when I had to wonder if we knew each other a bit too well. Occasions when, for example, I teased her about her boyfriend for no other reason than because I was frustrated with my writing or bugged out by something that had happened to me in the course of my thieving. And I very much doubted the percentage fee she made from my books was adequate compensation for that.

"I'm sorry," I said, not for the first time. "How is Adam?"

"He's fine," she replied.

"I was only kidding, you know?"

"I do. So tell me, are you stuck again?"

I made a clucking noise with my tongue. "God, sometimes it feels like you can crawl down this telephone wire into my brain. How did you know?"

"Because," Victoria said, as if I was a dunce, "this is the third time you've called me this week. And each time you've been blocked. So I put all the clues together and I played a hunch."

"A hunch?" I felt my eyebrows knit together. "Have you been reading Americans again?"

Victoria waited a beat. "I have a new client. He writes about a PI in Miami."

"A dick?"

She groaned. "That was a joke, right?"

"Would I stoop so low?"

Victoria didn't bite but I was pretty sure it was a struggle to control herself.

"Are you going to hurry up and tell me why you're stuck?"

"Since you put it like that," I said, and went on to explain my problem.

My problem related to a scene based around the Rio Carnival. Michael Faulks, my series character, was in Rio de Janeiro with the intention of breaking into a bank vault loaded with money ahead of a rival gang, all while the bank staff were out of the way, enjoying the Carnival festivities. As I'd really got into the scene, though, I'd begun to have doubts about the plausibility of what I was writing. The thing is, I've seen countless movies where teams of finely drilled, heavily armed robbers burst into banks, tell everyone to hit the floor, disable every conceivable security device one after the other and then empty the safe of millions of dollars of untraceable notes. But whoever heard of one man breaking into a bank, foxing every single alarm and camera and lock, cracking a maximum security vault and getting away with the perfect crime?

"That's what you're worried about?" Victoria asked me, once I'd set out my conundrum.

"You don't think that's enough?"

"Honestly Charlie, I have clients who need their hands held from time to time but you can really push it. You're concerned about credibility in one of your Faulks novels? Next you'll be telling me Ian Fleming made a few things up."

"Ouch."

"Charlie, in *The Thief on the Run*, you had Faulks double-cross a mafia kingpin, dupe the FBI and the CIA, base-jump off the Empire State Building and bed the daughter of the President of the United States."

"I sense there's a point to all this."

"The point, as you well know, is that the Faulks books aren't about realism. Your fans read them because anything can happen. And believe me, if Faulks can take down the New York mafia all by himself, he can sure as hell carry out a simple bank heist."

I scratched my temple. "You think?"

"Yes. But unless you've had some kind of a lobotomy, you know that already. And that makes me think something else must be bothering you. And since I happen to remember you mentioning a meeting with Pierre this morning, I'm going to play another of my famous hunches and guess there's a problem."

I rolled my chair back from my desk and set it spinning, lifting my feet clear of the ground. "Seriously," I said, the phone wire coiling around my shoulders, "we should totally apply for that "*Mr and Mrs*" television show."

"Just tell me, Charlie. You know you're going to eventually. So why don't we dispense with the cavalier asides and get down to what's really going on?"

I untwisted myself, stood from my chair and walked across to the wall beside my desk. My framed first edition of *The Maltese Falcon* was hanging there, slightly askew, and I straightened it. The Hammett novel goes everywhere with me. It's my one essential, along with my laptop and my burglary equipment. The truth is I'm superstitious. *The Maltese Falcon* was on my desk when I wrote my first published novel and I happen to believe that anything I write without Sam Spade watching over me is liable to be terrible. I never told anyone that before.

"You have a tight schedule?" I asked Victoria.

"Tell me."

"Oh, if you insist."

And that's when I shared everything that had occurred during the past twenty-four hours. Well, everything aside from my attraction to Paige, that is, because past experience had taught me how much grief I'd be letting myself in for if I happened to dwell on her.

Instead, I focused on how Bruno had approached me at the end of my reading and what had been said in our conversation at the bar. From there, I described the break-in to Bruno's apartment and briefly summarised the regrets I'd had about the whole thing the following morning. Afterwards, I recounted my meeting with Pierre, and then finally I gave her the killer news, the twist that had almost knocked me from my chair when Pierre had handed me the address of the apartment I was to burgle.

"You're serious?" she asked, once I'd concluded my story.

"Cross my heart."

"Wow." She whistled. "And to think, you were worried about your novel being believable."

"I know. Some coincidence, huh?"

"I'll say."

"So what's your take on it?" I asked, dropping into my desk chair once again.

"You don't want to know."

"Listen, I wouldn't have asked if . . ."

"Don't do it."

I straightened. "What?"

"Something's not right about the job. You know that or you wouldn't have called me. So don't do it."

I reached for a pencil and nibbled the end. "See, I think that might be a bit hasty, Vic."

"There. I said you wouldn't want to hear my opinion. What would you rather I said? That it's just one of those weird quirks of life that no-one can explain but you shouldn't be put off by it, you should just press on regardless and stuff the consequences?"

"No, I just . . ."

"You just what?"

"Oh, God knows." I flicked the pencil across the room, marking the far wall with a dot of pencil lead.

"Charlie, if I was in your shoes, I'd have turned Pierre down the moment he said he didn't know who his client was. We've been here before, remember?"

I made a noise that was intended to convey uncertainty. "I'm not sure it's quite the same thing."

Victoria huffed into the receiver. "Who cares? The fact is you chose to ignore your concerns because of the money Pierre waved in your face. But what you can't ignore, what you'd be plain mad to close your mind to, is that the place Pierre wants you to burgle just happens to be the apartment you've already broken into with this Bruno guy."

"It's Bruno's apartment."

"So he says."

I threw up a hand, for all the good that would do. "He showed me proof of address."

"God Charlie, I have a certificate on my wall here saying I own an acre on the moon."

"Hey, that was a carefully selected gift."

"But it's just a piece of paper! You want me to send you a letter saying I live in that apartment too?"

I pouted. "Bruno's letter was from a bank."

"Easily forged."

"And the credit card?"

Victoria paused. "I don't know," she said, exhaling. "I suppose he could have faked an application."

"All of that just for me? I don't buy it. And you didn't see him when we got inside that building. The concierge recognised him for starters, or we would have been stopped. And Bruno knew that apartment, Vic. He knew where the alarm panel was located and what code to enter. Jesus, he even knew which cupboard the coffee was in."

"I'm not going to argue with you," she told me. "I'm not even going to try to explain it. All I'm saying is what you already know – something's not right."

I glanced at my Hammett novel again, reluctant to concede the point. "Maybe."

"But you'll do it anyway, right?"

"I thought I'd just take a quick look."

"You're crazy."

"Think of the positives, though," I said, trying to control the pleading tone in my voice. "I know the layout of the building. I know I can pick the locks I'll come up against. The only real problem I'll have is getting by the concierge."

"So why call?"

"Honestly? I was seeking moral guidance."

"Excuse me?"

"Well, I've been thinking," I said, marking a circle on the surface of my desk with my finger. "Say this apartment does belong to Bruno. The way I see it, he hired me to show him how to break in, right? He paid me in full, up front, and nothing went wrong. So, it seems kind of duplicitous, doesn't it, if I go back and steal his painting?"

I could almost hear Victoria's jaw tense. "I can't believe I'm hearing this," she told me, a note of laughter in her voice. "Charlie, you're a thief for goodness sake. Where's this noble streak been on every other occasion you've broken into somebody's home?"

"But I've never ripped off someone who hired me before. I mean, it wouldn't occur to me to rob Pierre."

"You have a history with Pierre."

"Even so. You think it's bad form to break in again?"

"I haven't a clue," Victoria replied. "And if this is really what's bothering you then I have to say I don't know what to tell you. It's not for me to give you the go-ahead, Charlie. I've always let you talk to me about this stuff in the past, that's true, but I can't justify what it is that you do. That's for your conscience."

I didn't say anything for a moment and neither did Victoria. I could hear her breathing, composing herself. She was right, I guessed, though it wasn't as if I'd asked her to come on the job with me. All I'd wanted was her take on the situation and she was usually more forthcoming with that.

Off in the distance, somewhere near Boulevard Garibaldi, I could hear the screech and drone of an ambulance siren. You hear sirens all the time in Paris – as if they form some kind of plaintive, background muzak for the city. They're so common that I often don't notice them, but when I really pay attention, I'm able to distinguish between the police klaxons and the sirens of the other emergency services. That might not sound like something worth bragging about, but believe me, it's easy to take pride in certain skills when your liberty might depend on it.

"Something wrong?" I asked.

"Nothing."

"You're sure? Because I have to say it seems as though something's bugging you."

"Nothing's 'bugging' me Charlie. I just have work to do. I'm kind of busy today. And on that note, I'm going to go now, okay?"

"Okay."

I set the telephone receiver down and looked sightlessly at the two-pin plug socket on the wall near my feet. What on earth had just happened? No matter what Victoria said, there was definitely something going on and I ran my mind back through our conversation to see if I could work out what it was. I replayed every word I could remember, every nuance, even going over certain passages again and again. And still I had no idea what exactly had set her off.

No, that's not true, I did have an inkling; I just wasn't all that keen to explore it. Because the impression I was getting was that maybe after all the years of absorbing the details of my scams, Victoria had grown tired of my behaviour. Perhaps she'd been waiting for me to reform and was only just beginning to realise that wasn't going to happen. Stealing was in my DNA. It might not be anything to be proud of, at least not on any rational scale, but that didn't mean I wanted to quit.

I glanced down at my laptop, fingers poised to tap a key and remove the screen-saver that had appeared. But my fingers didn't move. I growled and slammed the lid closed, pushed myself away from my desk and swore colourfully. I couldn't very well write now, could I?

SEVEN

The day concierge was a woman. She was hard-faced, with sallow cheeks and a hairdo that looked artificial – all blonde highlights and fixing spray. She was also attentive. So far I'd watched three people enter the apartment building and she'd made each of them sign the guest register. That wasn't necessarily a problem; I could always jot down a false name. But suppose it wasn't Bruno's apartment? If she asked me to write the name of the person I was visiting and I happened to provide one she didn't recognise, I'd be in trouble.

Some might say I already was. A half-hour earlier, I'd ducked along the service alley to the side of the apartment building and made my way to the rear. There was a fire exit there, just as I'd hoped, but it was wired into a localised alarm system and a closed-circuit camera was fixed above the double doors. The handles of the doors had been secured to one another with a metal chain and a combination padlock, something I guessed any fire inspector wouldn't be too thrilled about. From the security measures that had been put in place, it wasn't hard to deduce that other people had broken in through the fire exit in the past and, although I could pick the padlock open without too much trouble and there were ways to dupe the camera and silence the alarm, I couldn't pretend it was tempting. Even supposing I got in without a hitch, I had no idea what lay behind the doors. Sure, it was likely to be a flight of stairs, but there could just as easily be a store room with a caretaker inside or a laundry facility being used by any number of residents. There could even be a second security camera, pointed straight at me.

A ground-floor window was positioned some distance away from the fire exit but it was protected by a set of iron bars. And since I didn't happen to have a blowtorch with me or a guaranteed hour without interruptions, I wasn't going to be gaining entry that way either. The other windows were too high for me to reach without a ladder or a serious growth spurt and I already knew the delivery door at the side of the building opened onto the concierge's desk. And . . . well, that was it. Those were my options. And since none of them were viable, I was going to have to look elsewhere.

Like next door for instance. Not at the greengrocers but at the two-star hotel. From the look of the tatty curtains hanging in the rear windows and the flaking render on the back wall, it was in no danger of improving upon its accommodation rating in the near future and I guessed the security would be relatively lax. It certainly appeared as if I could get in through the back readily enough. There was a rear service entrance that appeared to be permanently unguarded and I didn't doubt that it would connect with a guest staircase before very long. But then again, it was mid-morning on a Wednesday and there was no compelling reason for me to risk getting caught. And besides, I'd already had a much better idea.

The gentleman I found behind the hotel reception desk might well have felt more at home swinging from the rafters in Notre Dame Cathedral. He didn't have a hunched back, but he did have a quite enormous belly and if he'd bothered to shave at all that morning, then his razor was in dire need of being changed. He hunkered down over my passport as he copied the personal details into his ledger, the filmy drool on his lips threatening to drip onto his handiwork.

I say *my* passport but actually that's a little misleading. The passport in question belonged to an expat lawyer called David James Birk and the truth was I'd relieved him of it during a visit to his studio apartment some months beforehand. At the time, Mr Birk had been unavailable, something I was fortunate enough to know because a mutual friend had invited us both to the same production of *Madame Bovary* at the Palais Garnier Opéra. I'd declined, feeling more in the mood for a spot of thieving, and I'd come away from the night with a respectable bundle of cash and a nifty new wristwatch, not to mention the passport. Normally, it wasn't the kind of item I stole, but when I'd flicked by chance to the back page I'd been surprised to discover how alike we looked. According to his date of birth, David Birk was just one year older than me and his hair was perhaps a shade darker and certainly cut in a more business-like fashion, but I still felt confident that anyone casting just a quick glance at the photograph was unlikely to challenge me. As it happened, I'm not sure the hotel receptionist even looked at the picture. He was really just interested in Mr Birk's passport number so he could claim back the relevant tourist tax.

My room cost a little more than I'd expected, and that surprised me because the interior of the hotel was far scummier than I'd been anticipating. The lino in the reception area was covered in a fine layer of grit and dust, and although the lighting was poor, it was difficult to ignore the grime that adhered to almost every surface. Even the tourist brochures on a nearby stand looked out of date, the ink on them faded as though they'd been stolen from an outdoor display at some point in the late eighties.

There may have been an elevator, but I wasn't directed to it when Quasimodo handed me my room key and returned my passport, so I hefted the empty suitcase I'd brought along with me and began climbing the stairs. The threadbare carpet was gummy underfoot and the banister was loose and shaky. I went up two flights and paused to see if I could hear anybody moving about. I couldn't. There was only the peculiar hum of a seemingly empty building and the stale, musty smell of its interior.

I climbed on. If anybody stopped me, I would simply act as if I was lost or senile or American, and allow myself to be directed back down to my room on the second floor. I might even stretch out on the bed for half an hour, if I dared, and try again later. But as it turned out, I had no need to concern myself with back-up plans because I reached the very top of the building without encountering another soul and, once there, I made my way through a flimsy, poorly hung door and out onto the mansard roof.

The view was quite something. I could see an entire world of haphazard rooftops and chimneys and television aerials and clotheslines and church spires and skyscrapers. It was one of those seemingly common spring days in Paris, when the light has a peculiar clarity to it that makes every edge and angle appear absolutely distinct. I lowered my suitcase and stood with my hands on my hips and took in the warm air, perfumed with the scent of freshly cooked pastries and ground coffee and mouldy cheeses, and enjoyed the weird super-focus my eyes seemed suddenly capable of. Way to the north, I could just glimpse the pimpled cream dome of the Sacré-Coeur and to the south-west I could see the glistening onyx windows of the Montparnasse Tower. Off to the west, the gold dome of the Invalides stood out in bright relief against the greys and whites and tans of the office buildings and apartment blocks, and nearer still the dark turrets of the Conciergerie were topped by a fluttering Tricolore. In that brief moment, I felt like I'd been gifted my own private city, and I must confess it was with more than a little reluctance that I finally turned from the scene to get back to work.

Fortunately, I didn't have to do my cat-burglar routine and use a rope to climb up or lower myself a couple of storeys because the hotel and the apartment building were both exactly the same height. There was just a lip of tarred walling between them and I had only to step over it. Well, that and tackle the padlock on the door that led to the stairwell of the apartment building.

So from the back pocket of my jeans I removed a pair of very fine, disposable latex gloves and blew into the gloves to open them. That done, I slipped my left hand into the left glove and, being an orderly type, my right hand into the right glove. And winced. Hell, even the weight of the sheer plastic was enough to torment my gouty knuckles. Very carefully, I lifted the plastic away from the inflamed sores on my fingers, aiming to give them some respite. It didn't help a great deal and part of me was tempted to ditch the gloves altogether and just give the padlock a good wipe clean when I was done. But the truth is I've never really believed in that approach. Why risk leaving a print at all?

No, I didn't like it, and so I persisted with the gloves and reached for my spectacles case, quickly selecting a rake that happened to be slightly more compact than the one I'd armed Bruno with. I rested the padlock on my thigh to give myself something to lever off and inserted the rake. And a few moments later, the padlock was open and I was able to remove it from the rusting clasp and set it to one side, where it wouldn't get lost. Then I opened the door and made my way into the same stairwell I'd negotiated just two days before.

And although it was quite literally a pain, I paused and removed my gloves. True, all I planned to do for the next few minutes was make my way to the apartment I was interested in, but if someone happened to pass me and spot my gloves it might look suspicious. For that matter, I don't suppose the suitcase was such a great prop to have along with me either. It was very large, certainly big enough to be memorable, but I hoped that if anyone did happen to run into me carrying it, they'd just assume I was visiting a friend or hawking encyclopaedias. And besides, I needed something to transport the painting away in.

Mind you, it was awkward carrying the case in my left hand and I kept accidentally bumping it against the walls or catching it between my legs. I'd tried switching to my right hand, naturally, but the weight of the handle had been painful against the build-up of crystals in my fingers. It made me realise I'd have been better off investing in a record bag that I could have slung over my shoulder, but then again I wasn't certain how big the painting was, and it would be just my luck to break in with a bag a fraction too small.

All of which thinking had distracted me from how many floors I'd walked down. I paused and tried to figure it out in my head. Then I leaned out over the banister and looked up towards the top of the stairwell but it didn't help in the slightest. I was disorientated. There was a door to my side and I poked my head through and triggered the light sensor in the corridor. I could see the rubber plant and the tan banquette so I was one floor too high. I shut the door, hoisted the suitcase once more and made my way down to the third floor of the building.

Once I got there, I stood very still and listened for any noise from the corridor I was interested in. Then I dropped to my hands and my knees and studied the quarter-inch gap at the bottom of the door. I couldn't see any light and I couldn't hear anybody moving about, so I cracked the door open and peered through. The corridor was in darkness. I stepped out, instantly triggering the wall lights, and blinked away the sudden glare as I made my way to apartment 3A.

Facing up to the door of the apartment, I nudged the suitcase out of sight with my foot, then straightened my clothes, patted my hair flat and knocked. There was every chance somebody was inside. If it was Bruno, I'd make up some nonsense about dropping by to say hello. If it wasn't Bruno – well, I'd deal with that if I had to. But it was beginning to look as if I was in the clear because my knock went unanswered.

I knocked again, just to be sure, and when there was still no answer, I slipped my gloves back on, wondering as I did so if there was some way to tear the plastic away from the two fingers that were bothering me without destroying the gloves altogether. I wasn't concerned about the cost of replacing them, you understand, because I had a whole box of gloves at home. It was just that I only had one set of gloves with me and after all the trouble I'd gone to, I wasn't keen to delay the job for the sake of one glove.

Then again, you could argue it was a bit too late to be worrying about gloves at all. The fact is I hadn't worn them when I'd broken in with Bruno, so my fingerprints were already on the locking mechanism and scattered liberally around the apartment too. Would a few more hurt? Possibly not. But I guess in some ways I was keen to a draw a distinction between the two break-ins. The first one had been a mess, the kind of poorly executed plan that might have earned me a grade E at burglar school. This time, I was aiming for an A-plus and since I didn't want to be marked down for inconsistency, I resolved to keep the gloves on.

Besides, there were adjustments I could make to minimise the pain as much as possible. When I removed my pick and got to work on the lock on the apartment door, for instance, I used only my index finger and my thumb. It took a little longer to do things that way, and it felt kind of weird, like writing left-handed, but I only set off the pain in my knuckles perhaps three times and it was worth it for that if nothing else. As soon as the lock had withdrawn, I pulled down on the door handle and opened the door.

You thought I'd forgotten about the alarm, right? Well, guess again, because I was ready and waiting for those friendly *pips* and they weren't going to jeopardise my A-grade in the slightest. I fairly glided down the hallway to the storage cupboard and casually flipped down the panel on the fascia of the alarm control box before entering the code. The truth is I'd paid attention when Bruno had typed the combination in, you see. Call it a talent or a curse, but I notice these things. Some people have to read every word in a newspaper before they can get on with their day, others have to wash their hands a certain number of times before they can leave their home. Me, if I chance upon a code, I have to commit it to memory.

So I entered the code and I listened to the long, pleasing note of the device disarming itself. Once all was quiet, I returned to the corridor and retrieved my suitcase. Then I wiped down the locking mechanism as thoroughly as I could with a lint-free cloth, shut the door to the apartment behind me and got down to work.

Unsurprisingly, I wasn't in the mood to waste time so I moved directly through the paint-spattered studio space in the main living area to the bedroom at the rear of the apartment. The first thing I noticed when I entered the bedroom was that the slatted window blind had been left partially open, casting bars of daylight across the neatly made double bed in the middle of the room. The second thing I noticed was the discoloured, rectangular patch of space on the whitewashed wall across from me. Above the patch of wall space was a picture lamp but there was no longer any picture for the lamp to cast its light upon. The other walls were bare. There was no painting whatsoever.

For a moment, I stood absolutely still, as if waiting for the painting to materialise before my eyes. Having seen it in the photograph Pierre had handed me, I felt I could even conjure it in my mind, if that would be of any help. But of course it wasn't, because the bloody thing was gone.

I dropped my suitcase to the floor, with a thud very nearly as dull as my mind. The dimensions of the greying space where the painting used to be told me it was perhaps sixty centimetres wide by forty centimetres high, frame included. And the electric picture lamp suggested the oils were every bit as dark and grotty as I'd imagined. But that was all I could tell because there was nothing else to see. Pierre's client had been prepared to pay twenty thousand euros for the monstrosity but someone else had swiped it before he'd had the opportunity.

Not that it really concerned me. Thanks to my agreement with Pierre, I'd been paid my fee up front, so I guessed it didn't matter that the painting was gone. But if that was true, what exactly was bothering me?

Well, Bruno was. I really didn't like the way he'd manipulated me. Because it seemed obvious now that Victoria was right and it wasn't his apartment after all – that as soon as he'd watched me drink my coffee and bid me goodnight, he'd come straight to the bedroom, removed the painting, stuffed it into the backpack he'd so conveniently brought along with him and made good his escape. I didn't doubt that he'd have sold the painting for a healthy profit over the five hundred euros I'd been foolish enough to accept and he'd probably enjoyed a good laugh at how easy it had been to con me too.

The other thing that was bothering me was what Pierre might think. There was no way I was going to tell him about Bruno, of course. I might have been dumb but I wasn't completely insane, so I wasn't about to say to the guy who'd hired me that I'd known from the moment he passed me the address that something might have gone wrong. But I would still have to convince him that the painting was already missing by the time I broke into the apartment. We'd worked together for many years, sure, but I was a thief and Pierre was a fence and mutual trust can only ever stretch so far in those circumstances. I'd already pushed things by demanding my fee up front so what was to stop him wondering whether I'd pocketed the ten thousand euros and sold the painting myself to cut him out of the deal?

Problem was, how could I possibly satisfy him that I was telling the truth? It would be like trying to prove the existence of a ghost – all I had were signs of the painting's absence.

I suppose if I'd had a camera with me I could have taken a photograph of the bare patch on the wall. But really, that wouldn't have helped a great deal. I mean, there would be nothing to say I hadn't just removed the painting from the wall and set it down on the floor before taking the photo. And if I'd had the foresight to bring a camera along with me, it would only have made it seem as if I'd planned the whole thing in advance.

So far as I could see, all I could really do was take something that would prove I'd been inside the apartment. It wouldn't be any kind of guarantee that I hadn't double-crossed Pierre, but it was the best I could manage in the circumstances.

With that in mind, I turned my attentions to the antique dressing table on my left. The dressing table had been crafted from cherry wood and it had a quite beautiful roll-top lid. I approached the table and rolled the lid open. Of course, I wasn't looking to take anything the owner of the apartment might miss – I'd been under strict instructions to take only the painting in the first place – but I figured there had to be something appropriate.

The first thing I saw was a framed photograph and the reason it drew my attention was because it had been turned face-down. I propped it up and found myself looking at a portrait shot of a man and a woman. The man appeared to be mid-to-late-sixties, with grey hair pulled back from his forehead into a greasy ponytail. The woman looked around ten to fifteen years younger. She was platinum blonde with a bottle tan and heavy eye make-up. The picture seemed like a holiday snap – the couple were sat on a sunny balcony and there was a sliver of green ocean behind the woman's nut-brown shoulder.

I set the photograph back exactly as I had found it. I had no idea what they'd done to deserve being positioned face-down like that but I did know that a personal photograph was likely to be missed. There was a fair amount of make-up and some hair bands and brushes scattered across the surface of the dressing table, as well as various lotions and nail files and tweezers, all of which made me even more certain that Bruno didn't live in the apartment. I opened a pair of miniature drawers and found that the first drawer was filled with balls of cotton wool and the second drawer was crammed with yet more make-up.

None of it was of any use to me so I stepped backwards and looked beneath the dressing table and right then I happened to notice a plastic accordion folder down by my feet. I reached for the folder and popped the clasp and the insides fanned open to reveal a well-ordered collection of personal effects. I found store cards and video membership cards, insurance policies and credit card bills, general correspondence and medical prescriptions. There was also a driver's licence. All of the items belonged to the same person – a Madame Catherine Ames – and the pixelated image on the driver's licence matched the platinum blonde woman in the photograph. At first, I thought about pocketing one of the cards, but only the driver's licence had an address on it and I wasn't about to take that.

I went back to the accordion folder and riffled through the

various sections until I found a series of bank account statements. I paused and absorbed the details of the first statement I came across and then I worked backwards through the pile until I found a statement from many months beforehand that I thought it would be safe to take. I removed the statement, checking the name and address once more, and then I slipped it into my pocket, set the folder back down on the floor and closed the roll-top lid on the dressing table.

I hadn't been inside the apartment all that long but I was beginning to feel uncomfortable. This wasn't one of those jobs where I knew when the apartment was likely to be empty and how long it might stay that way. There was no guarantee I wasn't about to be disturbed at any moment and as far as I could tell, there was no emergency exit or alternative way of leaving the apartment other than the front door. But still, I didn't feel entitled to leave quite yet. Despite logic telling me that Bruno had the painting, it would have been remiss of me not to conduct a quick search of the apartment to make absolutely certain it was gone. After all, it wasn't completely out of the question that Madame Ames might have suspected that someone was after her painting and had hidden it.

So I looked at my watch and I told myself that I would search every possible hiding place I could think of in the next fifteen minutes. And that's what I did. I searched the bed and the mattress and the wardrobe. I checked behind the dressing table and I searched the adjoining bathroom (though only very quickly, because I couldn't imagine anyone hiding a painting where it might get wet). I poked my head inside all of the kitchen cupboards as well as the storage cupboard out in the hallway. Lastly, I went through every single one of the paintings in the main living area in an orderly fashion, including the canvases that had been clipped to the easels. I even checked the wallpaper pasting table for hidden compartments, of which there were none.

And once I was done, once I was absolutely sure the painting was nowhere to be found within the apartment, I shrugged my shoulders, collected my suitcase, primed the intruder alarm and relocked the door behind me. Then I retraced my steps up onto the roof and down into the adjoining hotel, even letting myself into the room I'd paid for with a novel device known as a key. Once there, I flushed my disposable gloves down the toilet and I stashed my empty suitcase inside the wardrobe. Finally, I walked downstairs to the lobby, returned my room key to Quasimodo, bid him a snappy goodbye and made my way outside.

EIGHT

Paige was sat behind the makeshift cash desk at the front of the Paris Lights bookshop when I entered. Her hair was tied back from her pale face with a black ribbon and she was holding a paperback novel in her right hand, her gimlet eyes scanning the pages. The book had a dark, foreboding cover and it was written by one of those Russian guys I've never been able to get to grips with. She seemed engrossed, her pupils jittering from left to right and back again, like miniature typewriter carriages imprinting the words on her brain.

I approached the cash desk and cleared my throat. Paige glanced up from her book, then did a double-take when she saw it was me.

"Hey there stranger," she said, setting the book down and tucking a stray curl of hair behind her ear. "Where did you disappear to the other night?"

"An appointment," I told her. "You have a good time?"

"Sure. Missed you, though."

"Looked that way."

She frowned, and the veins at her temple pulsed beneath her skin.

"Italian guy – has a long arm," I said.

"Paolo?"

I shrugged.

"Silly," she told me, reaching out and squeezing my hand. "You know, I read your book. It's fun."

"You sound surprised."

"Truthfully? I was. But I sat here yesterday and I read it between customers and, yeah, I liked it a lot."

"Well, that's something, I suppose."

"I even put my main guy on hold for you," she added, and lifted the paperback for me to see.

"Dostoevsky? Really?"

"You don't like him?"

I curled my lip. "I happen to think it's pretty obvious whodunnit by the end of the first chapter."

Paige rolled her eyes and blew a raspberry at me. Then she pointed beyond a group of customers towards a chipped trestle table on the other side of the room. The table was situated below a dusty candelabra and I could see a few copies of my novel displayed on it, beside a smouldering incense stick.

"I talked to Francesca. She's the owner of this place. She said you could have the table for two days."

I hitched my eyebrows as elaborately as possible. "That many, huh?"

Paige nudged me. "Hey, that table's a big deal. You should thank me."

"With dinner?"

Paige smiled and shook her head, as if I was a hopeless cause. Then she crossed her arms in front of her chest, assessing me with narrowed eyes.

"There is something I wanted to ask you, as it happens," I told her. "At the bar the other night, after my reading, I was talking with a guy. Name of Bruno." I glanced around the shabby interior, on the off chance of seeing him. "I don't think he works here but I wondered if you knew him at all?"

"Bruno?" Paige scrunched up her face. "I'm not sure. What does he look like?"

"Bit taller than me, maybe," I said, raising my hand an inch or so above my head in the direction of the rotted ceiling beams. "Kind of muscular. Short, brown hair. Unshaven. He was wearing jeans and a blue polo shirt. Had a backpack too."

"No," Paige said, shaking her head and chewing her lip. "I know a Bruno, but he's black."

"Not the same Bruno."

"Sorry."

"Not to worry. It was a long shot anyway. But now I think of it," I went on, knocking my temple with my knuckle, "could you do me a favour and ask the others who work here?"

"Sure," Paige said, uncertainly. "You lose his number or something?"

I smirked, wagged my finger. "Nothing like that. He mentioned he can sometimes get tickets at Paris Saint-Germain's ground. I was thinking of going to a game."

"Oh, fine," she gushed. "I'll ask around. And say, can I ask you something in return?"

"Sounds reasonable."

"It's just, all that stuff in your book," she began, "about picking locks and all. Can you really do that?"

I met her gaze. It was a question I'd been asked more than once over the years and I was yet to come up with the perfect response.

"I've practised a bit at home. Character research, I guess you'd call it."

"Oh, swell," Paige said, releasing a breath and then finding her feet. "Come with me?"

I did as Paige asked and followed her to the rear of the store, beyond a compact single bed that had been covered for the day in a moth-eaten quilt and upon which a selection of Keats' poetry had been displayed. The books we passed along the way were crammed into every available space, packed one on top of another on uneven wooden tables and bowed shelves, piled precariously on the tiled floor and stuffed into plastic crates and cardboard boxes that showed signs of water damage. There was a staircase on our right and countless paperbacks had been inserted beneath the treads and between the banister rails. The staircase shook as Paige began to climb and I wondered whether the whole thing would one day come crashing to the floor if a customer happened to remove the wrong book in the wrong place.

I went up behind Paige, distracted from the books scattered haphazardly on the treads by the swaying of her bottom in front of me. She was wearing a long skirt that hugged the contours of her body in a quite understandable manner. Below the skirt I could glimpse her ankles; bare and slightly chaffed and tantalisingly close.

Paige turned at the top of the stairs and walked along a narrow corridor, again lined with books of every conceivable size and shape and colour, as well as a cramped writer's nook with a battered manual typewriter. She passed a doorway on her left and sang out a "Hey" and I looked in as I passed to see a dusky parlour room furnished with a threadbare couch and a scattering of pastel-coloured cushions and frayed rugs. There were four people in the room, reclined in various positions, reading books and scribbling on foolscap notepads. There was also a silver tea urn and what looked like a very old and unsanitary bong on the floor beside the guy with the skullcap whom I'd seen in the bar-café with Paige. He was reciting poetry but, from what I could tell, it didn't appear as though anyone was listening.

At the end of the corridor, Paige climbed a new and altogether more dicey staircase. The treads were much thinner than before and we stepped on dirt-encrusted paperbacks for most of the way up. When we reached the top, Paige checked over her shoulder to make sure I was still following her and then she led me into a large room with a stained, unplumbed toilet bowl positioned in the far corner. There was nobody else in the room and from the lack of cushions and chairs and tables, I assumed the space was rarely used. The area behind the doorway was filled with yet more crates of books. There was an unmarked door on the opposite side of the room and Paige approached it and rattled the handle.

"A woman from Estonia was working here until a little while ago," she explained. "Her name was Sophia. When she left, I think she took the key to this door. And no matter what I say, Francesca refuses to pay for a locksmith to come around or to allow any of the guys who live here to kick the thing through."

"Just as well," I said. "Kicking a door through isn't as easy as it seems. And in here, well, you might bring half the building down with it."

Paige smiled and looked up at me from beneath lidded eyes. "You think maybe you could get us inside?"

I swallowed. "I could try."

She stepped aside and hovered over me while I assessed the lock. It was one hell of an old thing. The keyhole was so large I could almost see the internal pins with my bare eyes. I glanced around and screwed up my features in what I hoped was a bashful way.

"Would you mind giving me a few minutes?"

"Stage fright?"

"Something like that."

"I guess I can wait out in the hall."

"Actually," I said, "do you have a city telephone directory I could borrow?"

"You need a phone book to pick the lock?"

I grinned. "Nope. I was just hoping you might have one and I forgot to ask before."

"Downstairs," Paige said, with a heft of her shoulders. "I'll go find it."

While she was gone, I reached into my jacket and removed my trusty spectacles case and then I selected a likely pick and the largest screwdriver I carried. I could have done with a can of spray lubricant too, something that's always handy on a lock that hasn't been turned in a while, but I didn't have one to hand and, since I couldn't face the prospect of heading downstairs to ask the wannabe poet if there was any cooking oil in the building or the Italian if I could run my fingers through his glistening hair, I decided to press on with just my tools and my own innate talent.

I dropped to my haunches and peered into the lock, then inserted the screwdriver blade with my left hand and started to probe away with the pick in my right. By the time Paige had returned with the city telephone directory, I was in a whole new space.

It was a small room, perhaps the size of your average family bathroom, and unlike the other rooms in the bookshop it had some semblance of order. There were three genuine, well-crafted bookshelves, each neatly stacked with a collection of hardback and cloth-bound books. A leather-inlaid desk faced the opposite wall, and an electric spot lamp and a vintage telephone with a rotary dial were positioned on it. The final item of furniture was a soft-sprung reading chair beneath the narrow window. The window was partially obscured by a grimy rug that had been pinned up as a makeshift curtain. The room smelled musty and dank.

"Francesca's study," Paige said, in a hushed voice. "Isn't it awesome?"

"It's certainly unique."

Paige inhaled deeply and stretched out her arms, turning on the spot. "I think it's special, you know? There's a vibe."

"There's a smell."

Paige gave me a skewed look. "You always have to do that? Try to be funny?"

"Just try?"

Paige thought for a moment, casting a quizzical gaze back towards the door furniture and the lock I'd picked open. Then she moved towards me, coming real close. She lifted her face. I checked her eyes – she had them shut.

I kissed her, aware of the muted silence and the ghostly stillness all about. I put my hand to the back of her neck, felt the heat beneath her hairline and the softness of her skin. I reached my hand down towards her bottom but she backed away, shaking her head and placing a finger against my lips.

"Didn't you want to make a call?"

"A call?"

"That's why I brought you the telephone book, right?" She lifted the directory into my line of vision and stepped away from me some more. "Cos, I kinda have to go back downstairs, and all."

"Right now?"

She giggled. "Right now," she said, handing me the directory and running her fingers over my hand.

I tried not to flinch as she hit my busted knuckles.

"Does this phone even work?" I asked, hoarsely.

"Guess so," she said. "And hey, when you're done, you can figure out where to take me for dinner."

NINE

Once I'd closed the door behind Paige, I took a moment to familiarise myself with the study. It was cold, despite the spring sunshine outside on the street, and it was almost too silent – like some forgotten inner sanctum where a luckless person could get stuck and might not be found for months on end. I had no idea how many more floors the bookshop went on for but I was confident I wouldn't be disturbed. After freeing the telephone wire from behind the desk, I carried the telephone over to the sagging reading chair, gathered up the directory and sat myself down.

I opened the directory on my knees and meanwhile I dialled Victoria's office number. I heard a series of clicks, then a pause, and finally the prolonged international ringing tone. I wet my finger and turned the delicate pages of the directory.

"Victoria speaking," she said, after perhaps the fourth ring.

"It's your favourite client," I told her.

"Ah. Well, they all say that."

"This one means it. How've you been?"

"Fine. You?"

"Preoccupied," I replied, flicking further through the directory.

"With Faulks? Hasn't he knocked off that bank yet? I would have thought he'd be tackling the Pentagon by now."

I shook my head, as though weighed down by regret. "He's still at the planning stage."

"You mean you are."

"I suppose I do," I said, and sighed. "Thing is, it can sometimes be hard for me to tell us apart. It's almost as if I've become such a skilled practitioner of my art that I'm no longer able to separate myself from my characters."

"Sheesh."

"Sheesh? Really?"

Victoria exhaled into the telephone but she didn't say anything further. I didn't mind. I'd just found the page in the telephone directory I'd been hunting for and, after running my finger downwards, I was able to confirm there wasn't a single listing for a B. Dunstan in the whole of Paris. Of course, that didn't necessarily mean he'd made his name up, but it did mean I couldn't find his address all that easily.

I flipped a chunk of pages and began scanning the 'A's.

"Aren't you supposed to be saying something here Charlie?" Victoria asked. "After all, you called me, so unless my mobile just cut out, this is in danger of becoming an uncomfortable silence."

"Oh, sorry," I told her, pausing for just a moment in my search. "I was checking something. How come you're on your mobile – I thought I dialled your office line?"

"My phone's on divert. I'm on a train."

"Ah, that'll explain the background noise. You have a good seat?"

"I've just moved between carriages. People were staring at me."

"Bastards. You can't help the way you look."

Victoria groaned. "I'm struggling to believe I left my seat for this. But since I already made that mistake, tell me, are you calling because you ignored my advice and broke into that apartment and everything went wrong? Or are you calling to gloat?"

"Not everything went wrong," I replied, returning my attention to the directory.

"Oh God. You haven't been arrested, have you?"

"No, nothing like that. Everything went like clockwork, in fact. Only, the painting was already gone."

"Aha! Just like I said. I bet Bruno took it. And I bet he didn't even live there."

I pulled the telephone away from my ear and frowned at the receiver. "Looks that way," I managed.

"Well, I told you."

I didn't respond straight away because I was looking down once again at the telephone directory. There was a C. Ames listed at Rue de Birague in the Marais. Maybe, I thought, I could give her a call and ask her if she had any idea where her painting had got to? Perhaps I could even offer her a share of my fee.

"Told you," Victoria said again.

"Oh, yes. Sorry. Stupid me – I only made ten grand from the job, I suppose."

"But something wasn't right about it. You have to admit that."

"If it'll make you happy."

"Very."

I glanced up from the directory and stared at the back of the door. A knitted cardigan was hanging from a rusty nail and I could see a cigarette packet poking out of the cardigan pocket. I considered lighting up for just a moment but then I dismissed the idea. I wanted our conversation to remain private, so it was best not to do anything that might draw attention to myself.

"Then, yes, something was wrong," I said. "But I couldn't very well turn Pierre down without a good explanation. And, as it turns out, there was no harm in me going back to the apartment."

"Hmm. So what are you going to do now?"

"I'm not altogether sure. It's not exactly a scenario I'm familiar with."

"Failing?"

"No-o. Finding that someone else got there first. Especially when that someone else was me."

Victoria began to say something but I could tell from a change in her tone that it wasn't intended for my ears. It sounded as if somebody was trying to get past her on the train. I closed the telephone directory and sat with it on my lap, waiting.

"Sorry," Victoria said, once she was back on the line. "I'm trying to remember where we'd got to? Isn't this the part where I tell you to leave everything alone and count your blessings only for you to try to convince me there might be some reason why you should stir things up?"

"Wow. It's almost like you don't need me for these conversations any longer."

"Maybe I don't. Maybe I'm all too familiar with your next move."

"Ah, like my nemesis."

"Indeed."

"Except, I'm not going to try to convince you of anything," I said, resting my chin on my fist. "Because really, there's not all that much I can do. I did think I might try to find Bruno, but I have a feeling that won't be terribly straightforward."

"Because Bruno won't be his real name."

"Most likely. And if that's the case, I can only think of two possible options. The first is to find out if anyone at the bookshop knows him."

"And the second is the letter from the bank."

I nodded to myself. "I think so. If, as you so brilliantly speculated, it's a forgery, there's a chance he has some connection with the bank, which would explain how he was able to get the headed notepaper and the credit card. And it might explain something else."

"Oh?"

I made a humming noise deep in my throat. "I found some personal documents in the apartment in the Marais," I confessed. "The place belongs to a woman called Catherine Ames. She happens to keep an account at the same bank."

"Wait – there's only one branch?"

"No, it's a multinational – the Banque Centrale. So it could just be happenstance."

"Or it could be a clue."

"Or even a red herring. Which would you prefer?"

Victoria took a deep breath. "I'm not altogether sure," she said. "I like red herrings, if I'm honest, but I have to say they're not your strongest suit. So I guess I'd plump for it being a clue. But if it does turn out to be coincidence, and your leads don't pan out either, what are you going to do?"

I paused. It wasn't something I'd considered just yet. "I guess I'll just have to tell Pierre the painting was gone when I got there."

"And you think he'll believe you?"

"I hope so. But I figure I can always share my ten grand with him if he doesn't. It would seem a bit unfair for him to miss out, given the circumstances."

"Ah, there's that new-found morality again. Careful Charlie – you're in danger of creating a believable character here."

"Ouch."

"Oh, come on. That was nothing. Like one of your hubby jibes, right?"

"See," I said, trying to keep my tone as light as possible, "there is something wrong. I knew there was. What is it?"

"It's nothing."

"Oh come on. I can tell I've upset you. The other day on the phone, you were kind of weird and now you're –"

"What?"

"I don't know." I threw up my hand, as if grasping for the right word. "Antsy?"

"Antsy?"

"Uh huh. You've been pretty direct about some of my writing just recently and you've never been that way before. I'm really not sure what to make of it."

"Well," Victoria said, and I could picture her squaring her shoulders. "As my client, perhaps it's something I think you should hear."

"As your client?"

"Yes Charlie. I happen to rely on you and when –"

"Wait a minute," I said, crowding over the telephone receiver. "You don't think you can rely on me? Since when have –"

"Enough," Victoria said. "I can't do this now. I'm going."

And with that she hung up the telephone, something she'd never done to me before. I cradled the receiver, then put my hands to my face and rubbed the back of my neck. I lowered my hands, drummed my fingers on the telephone directory and idly scanned the books on the shelf by my side. Barely any of the spines had any text on them, so I had no idea what exactly I was looking at. I thought about setting the phone down on the floor and devoting a couple of minutes to one of the cloth-bound volumes, then changed my mind and picked up the telephone receiver again. I dialled the number for Victoria's mobile.

She answered with a hushed, "Yes?"

"It's me. Tell me what's going on."

"I'm back in my seat," she whispered. "We can talk later."

"I want to know now. I must have done something and I'd like to straighten things out. I don't happen to think it's fair –"

"Hold on," she interrupted. "Let me get out of this bloody carriage again."

I waited, listening to the muffled noises of Victoria rising from her seat and passing down the train aisle. I heard her mumble a few apologies on the way and every now and again there was a rustling sound, as if something was rubbing against the speaker on her mobile. Finally, I heard her voice.

"I'm coming to Paris."

"*What?*"

"I'm on Eurostar and I'm coming to see you. And I don't care what you say, Charlie, because it's ridiculous we've never met. I'm not prepared to listen to a single one of your excuses. We're meeting, and that's the end of the matter."

My eyebrows jerked up. I reached above my head to retrieve them from the ceiling and shook my head vigorously.

"But I'm right in the middle of a book," I said. "I could really do without interruptions just at the moment. It's in your interest that –"

"Charlie, enough. I don't know what it is you're afraid of and I don't know what you think I might do. But that's bull and you know it. If you can spare the time to break into someone's home, you have more than enough time to eat dinner with me."

"Vic, be reasonable. I'll come to London when the book's finished."

"You won't, though. We both know it. And I honestly have no idea why."

I swallowed hard, conscious of a buzz and a click in my ears. "That's a bit unfair."

"No, it's not. This situation has gone on too long already. If you want me to continue acting for you, then you'll meet me. Simple as that."

"But Adam," I began.

"What about Adam?"

"Won't he mind?"

Victoria paused, as if fighting to control herself. "Adam's a mature human being, Charlie. He's not the jealous type."

"I didn't mean –"

"Yes you did. But I really don't care. I couldn't give two hoots. I'll be in Paris in under two hours. I'm staying at the Hotel Moderne. Meet me there at seven and we'll find somewhere to eat. Agreed?"

"Um."

"Good. Then we'll speak later."

Victoria cut the connection and left me gaping at the receiver. I shook my head wordlessly, gripped my hair by the roots and wondered what on earth I would do. I called her straight back.

"Victoria, listen, I really don't think –"

"Adam and I split up," she said.

"*What?*"

"We split up."

"But you just said –"

"I know. But we broke up. Five months ago."

I became aware of my jaw grazing my knee. "And you didn't tell me?"

"No, I didn't. You kept going on all the time with that hubby nonsense of yours and I couldn't bring myself to talk about it when it happened. And then all those months went by and the truth is I've felt bad about not telling you for quite some time. But there, I've told you now."

I was silent for a moment. "I don't know what to say."

"You could say you forgive me and you're sorry it didn't work out."

"Of course I'm sorry. Christ, I'm even more sorry you didn't feel able to tell me."

"Well, me too. So listen," she went on, "is there anything you want to get off your chest before we meet? Call it an official amnesty. Speak now – tell me anything at all."

"There's nothing," I muttered, and put my hand over the telephone receiver. *Only the fact that I don't look anything like you imagine*, I thought.

TEN

Following my conversation with Victoria, I flicked through the telephone directory until I found a switchboard number for the Banque Centrale. I dialled the number and between my awful French and the passable English of the woman who answered, I was able to obtain address details for the three branches of the bank situated closest to Catherine Ames' apartment. The first branch was on the fringes of the Latin Quarter, the second was near the Bastille and the third was not too far from Les Halles and the Pompidou Centre.

Before leaving the bookshop, I returned the telephone directory to Paige and told her that I was going to have to pass on dinner for a day or so. I said that opening the door to the cramped study upstairs had given me an idea for the book I was working on and that I wanted to write the whole thing out before it slipped from my mind. I wasn't sure if she believed me or not but just at that moment I didn't altogether care. The fact was I was still trying to come to terms with my phone call with Victoria. I suppose I'd always known that one day we might have to meet and that when we did I'd be forced to confess to the deception I'd been guilty of. But I'd also assumed I'd have time to prepare for it and perhaps even find a sensible way to go about things. Now, I wasn't so sure.

As I walked in the direction of the Latin Quarter, I tried to come up with possible explanations for my behaviour that might sound credible. Sadly, the only excuses that occurred to me were quite obviously flawed. And somehow, I had a feeling this might be one of those times when a good-natured smile and a humble shrug wouldn't quite cut it. To make matters worse, I kept getting distracted by fantasies about avoiding Victoria altogether. I'd picture myself lying low in my apartment or even catching the train to London and pretending that I'd become confused about where she wanted to meet. It was nonsense, of course, but I just couldn't help myself.

At the same time, I was feeling bad that Victoria hadn't told me about Adam. I'd been making dumb remarks about him for well over a year, almost from the moment they started dating, and I could only imagine how crass it must have sounded when they broke up. Sure, I hadn't known any better, but why did I have to say stuff like that in the first place? Now I just felt like an ass. Worse, an ass who'd been lying to his best friend for years.

And I guess because I felt so ill at ease, I was really quite glad to have the distraction of searching for Bruno. Otherwise, I'm not altogether sure I would have persisted, especially when my hunt didn't begin all that well and I drew blanks at the first two bank branches I visited. The same was true of the third branch, which was located inside a grand, Art Nouveau building on Boulevard de Sébastopol. The haughty, impeccably dressed gentleman I spoke with at the customer information desk shook his head dismissively when I mentioned Bruno's name and he point-blank refused to consult with any of his colleagues. I raised my eyes to the vaulted glass ceiling and tried to think of a way to convince him otherwise but when I looked back down and met his unflinching gaze, I knew it was hopeless.

I turned from him and scanned the faces of the cashiers. They were sat behind dated-looking iron bars that were supposed to protect them from armed robbers of the kind Faulks was trying to outwit in Rio. I wasn't sure how the bars were meant to achieve that. So far as I was aware, most bullets are small enough to squeeze through two-inch gaps, and if I was a hard-nosed bank robber, the first thing I'd do would be to point the barrel of my sawn-off at the forehead of the nearest cashier and ask them very nicely to give me all of their money.

Fortunately, I only imagine these things, and perhaps I don't imagine them all that well, because it occurred to me now that the bank I'd been describing in my novel might be more than a touch unreal. It was very modern in appearance, you see, filled with high-density safety glass, panic buttons, silent alarms and multiple security cameras, not to mention guards who happened to be armed with Taser guns. And if that kind of facility could feel misjudged in Paris, I could only imagine how odd it might seem to anyone who happened to be familiar with Brazil.

But then again, I reminded myself, Victoria had made it all too clear that the Faulks books had little to do with reality. And truth be told, I was rather fond of the bank interior I'd described. It felt real to me, no matter how far-fetched it might be, and I needed a tangible backdrop to move my characters around inside. Plus, I'd invested a lot of time detailing the security devices in an effort to stack the odds against Faulks. I wanted my readers to think the task he'd set himself was impossible and then I wanted them to marvel at how ingenious his solution was. Of course, now all I had to do was work out how in hell one man could defeat everything I'd put in place.

But that was an issue for another day and I still had my current situation to resolve. In an effort to do just that, I walked along the line of cashiers, checking their intent faces, but I didn't see anyone who looked the least bit like Bruno. There were a handful of staff working at computer stations behind the cashiers but all of them were women. I turned around, searching for other possibilities, and my eyes chanced upon a featureless corridor some distance away that connected with a flight of stairs that appeared to lead down into a basement area. At the beginning of the corridor was a security desk that was manned by a stocky, shaven-headed guard in a dark blue suit. I could see a coil of flesh-coloured wire at his neck, connecting to a radio earpiece. I moved towards him and he stiffened, as if sensing a threat. I had no idea what was at the end of the corridor but I got the distinct impression it was off-limits to the general public. I could see an appointment ledger in front of the guard and a walkie-talkie clipped to his belt. I smiled awkwardly, then veered off in the direction of a pair of cash machines, as though I'd momentarily lost my bearings.

I didn't need any cash – I was carrying half of the money Pierre had given me – but I did want to spend a few more minutes in the bank for the sake of completeness, and using the cash machine seemed like my best excuse. So I removed my wallet from my pocket, inserted my cash card into the machine, entered my pin number and selected a modest sum. While the machine worked its magic, I looked up from the screen and aimlessly scanned the wall by my side. And that was when I saw him, staring back at me with a sightless gaze.

The photograph was only a little bigger than a passport image and it was in a smudged glass frame along with perhaps thirty others. I guessed I was looking at a set of photographs of everyone who worked in the bank. Bruno's image was towards the far right, fourth row down. His hair was a good deal longer and he had on a pair of wire-rimmed glasses, but it was unmistakably him.

"Bruno Chevrier" read the nameplate below his image. The row above contained a headshot of the bald security guard. Way over to the left was a photograph of the obstinate gentleman on the customer information desk.

I turned and scanned the interior of the bank once more, checking to see whether Bruno was in an area I hadn't spotted just yet. But he was nowhere to be seen. Perhaps he worked at the end of the mysterious corridor, protected by the hairless security guard. Or perhaps in a back room, answering telephones or processing mortgage applications. Hell, maybe he was even watching over me on CCTV.

For just a moment, I thought about returning to the customer information desk and asking if Monsieur Chevrier was available but I immediately discounted the notion. I'd already asked for Bruno by a different surname once and I didn't want to create suspicion. Besides, if he was working, he'd be unlikely to come down once he'd gained some impression of who I was. Another idea I had was to settle myself on one of the leather chairs positioned nearby and pretend to consult some of the banking literature in the hope he might appear. But that wasn't a plausible option either. The chap on the information desk already knew my French was basic, at best, and I got the impression I'd drawn enough attention to myself for the time being. If I sat down and flicked uselessly through some brochures, I'd most probably look as if I was planning a heist.

Just as I was considering all this, my money spewed forth from the cash machine and I slipped it into my wallet and made my way outside. I checked the time on my watch and found that it was nearing a quarter to five. I crossed the street and shuffled backwards into a recessed doorway between a sweet-smelling patisserie and a cramped tabac that gave me a good view of the front entrance to the bank. It occurred to me that I could wait until the bank closed and try to spot Bruno leaving for the day. Of course, it was entirely possible that there was a separate staff exit or it was his day off, but I figured I'd take my chances and stick with the front. If I was unlucky, I could always return first thing in the morning and try again.

Instead of just loitering, I decided I might as well pass the time by browsing in some of the nearby stores on Rue Quincampoix. If I was careful and didn't wander too far away, I could return at five and again at half past to keep an eye on the bank entrance. Besides, Rue Quincampoix was a regular haunt of mine and I felt confident one of the galleries or quirky design stores that lined the street would have something to hold my interest.

After consulting my watch once more, I stepped out from my surveillance point, walked to the end of the street and then turned left and left again. There was an American coffee house at the end of Rue Quincampoix, poised to ambush tourists on their way to and from the Pompidou Centre. The interior was jammed with people carrying frothy drinks away from the young, clean-skinned French students who worked there, towards the wooden stools positioned in front of the giant picture windows. In truth, the customers didn't have such a great view. A team of workmen were leaning on pickaxes and shovels in front of the window, talking among themselves, smoking cigarettes and scratching their backsides.

I skirted the spilt sand and loose bricks and walked on down the street, weaving between ornate metal bollards. Rue Quincampoix was a narrow, wavering avenue, permanently in shade. I passed a curio shop, then a cocoa-scented chocolatier, and paused in front of an antique store on my left. The place dealt mostly in furniture. There was a pair of half-decent, if garishly upholstered, Louis XV chairs in the window and a very respectable console table off to the side. A number of quite misplaced African artefacts were adhered to one wall and a few Tiffany-style lamps displayed on a central table. As I took it all in, the owner saw me hovering and raised his eyebrows optimistically but I gave him a polite smile and moved along to the adjoining store, which turned out to be a modern gallery space.

I stepped inside, and was instantly struck by the scent of fresh emulsion paint. The gallery hadn't been here the last time I'd come by and it looked as if it had only just opened. The brilliant white walls were hung with digital photographic prints. Several of the works were images of famous Parisian landmarks that had been superimposed onto one another. I spotted the Arc de Triomphe straddling the Canal Saint-Martin and the glass pyramid of the Louvre in the middle of Place de la Concorde. As I stooped forwards for a closer look, a young man in a white T-shirt with spiked hair and designer stubble emerged from a room at the rear of the gallery and gave me a discreet nod. He settled himself behind a smoked-glass table and began clicking on a computer mouse that was connected to a laptop. The man didn't ask me if I was looking to buy and I didn't bother enquiring about the prices. There were none displayed on the walls and that was warning enough for me.

Next-door again I found another gallery, though it was of an altogether different character. The interior was poorly lit and as I squinted through the thickened window glass, my sight was obscured by my own reflection. I cupped my hands around my face and peered inside, beyond the pleated, velveteen material that had been draped around the window. There were one or two Italianate mirrors resting on the velveteen and towards the back I could spy some marble busts, but the majority of the space had been given over to paintings. They were oils and watercolours mostly, and they were all, without exception, dreadful. The worst piece by far was the painting positioned nearest to me but I knew the instant I saw it that it had to be mine. Why? Because even from this distance, I could see it was the painting Pierre had hired me to steal.

Incredible, right? Well, maybe not so hard to believe. The way I saw it, Bruno had stolen the painting in order to sell it for a quick profit. The gallery was just a short distance from where he worked and it really couldn't have been much more convenient. From the look of the place, it wasn't the kind of establishment to ask awkward questions about the provenance of a piece of art and, besides, the painting really didn't merit that level of investigation anyway.

I entered the gallery and approached the painting for a better look. It was every bit as mediocre as I'd suspected. The glaze was grubby and could do with a clean but the real problem was the poor quality of the work itself. The composition was clumsy and outdated even for the early twentieth century, and the brush strokes displayed an alarming lack of skill. The flower seller in the foreground appeared almost cross-eyed, for instance, and her hand was grossly out of proportion. The woman with the parasol was even worse. Despite the supposed good weather, her parasol looked as if it had been caught by a rogue gust of wind, contorting her arm.

In all honesty, the most striking thing about the painting was the frame that contained it. The frame was oversized and very ornate, with elaborate mouldings and extensive gilding. It was the kind of thing I was used to seeing in museums, showcasing a dramatic sea battle or a dashing young monarch upon a stallion, and I have to admit it struck me as a shame that it had been paired with such an insipid work.

There was a paper tag hanging on a thread of string from the frame and I turned it over to discover that the asking price was four and a half thousand euros. I frowned. It wasn't an outrageous amount, I didn't think, but either I – along with the owner of the store – was missing something or Pierre's client had paid way over the odds to hire us. Maybe sentimental attachment came into it somehow. Perhaps Pierre's client desired the picture so much they were willing to pay more than four times its value. Or perhaps they knew it meant a great deal to Catherine Ames and they were prepared to shell out a generous sum to spite her. Whatever the reality, I had a decision to make. Did I buy the painting or did I steal it?

Stealing the painting was an option. Sure, the gallery was likely to have better locks and a more sophisticated security system than your average home, but that wasn't something that would necessarily get in my way. Whoever lived above the store might, though. From the looks of the building there were several apartments or offices in the upper floors and it would be logical to assume one of them might belong to the owner of the gallery. If I returned to break in after hours I'd need only to make a little too much noise to draw unwanted attention. And that was true of passers-by too. Rue Quincampoix was hardly the busiest of streets but it was close to the Pompidou Centre and if I was seen flashing my torch around inside the gallery after dark, I could soon find myself in trouble.

And why run the risk? The painting was priced at more than four thousand euros but that didn't mean I had to pay that much for it. If I could make a deal for a lesser amount, I'd still be clearing a tidy profit and I'd be maintaining Pierre's faith in me at the same time. After all, there was no reason I could think of to tell Pierre how I'd come by the painting. He'd just be glad to have it in his possession, ready to pass to his client. Yes, I'd be down a certain amount of my fee, and that bothered me to a degree, but it was something I could learn to live with.

A good deal of bartering and three thousand eight hundred euros later, the rather stern owner of the gallery was wrapping the painting for me in strong brown paper and parcel string. I was a little ashamed to be paying for such a poor piece of art in the first place, of course, and I did my best to explain as much to the gallery owner. Ultimately, though, I don't think she cared and neither did I. She'd probably expected to have the monstrosity stuck on her wall for six months at the very least, never anticipating she might be lucky enough to ensnare a witless Englishman. And I may have reduced my earnings to just over six thousand euros but I did have the satisfaction of a job well done. After a bad start, I'd used my brain to track Bruno down and, with just a little luck, I'd done far better than I had expected. I mean, even if I'd confronted Bruno outside the bank, what would I have achieved? He might have refused to tell me what had happened to the painting and then I'd have been stuck. I suppose I could have threatened to expose him as a thief, but there was no guarantee it would have worked. It's never bothered me all that much.

So the truth is I was feeling pretty smug as I left the store with the painting tucked under my arm and headed for the nearest métro station. I'd worked some angles and I'd followed my instincts and the only problem I had left to resolve was how to break the news of my real appearance to Victoria without losing her friendship for ever. And really, I thought, a chap with my skills and abilities ought to be able to pull that one off without too much trouble. It would all work out in the end. These things always did.

Or did they? When I got back to my apartment I wasn't so sure. For starters, the locks on my front door had been tampered with and the door was hanging ajar. Far worse, though, a woman was waiting for me there. And from the look of the clear plastic bag that had been taped over her head and the florid tone of her skin, I hadn't the slightest doubt she was dead.

ELEVEN

The woman was in the middle of my living room and her hands had been tied behind her back to the frame of the wooden dining chair she was sat upon. Her head drooped forwards, like a wilted tulip, weighing the upper half of her torso down and away from the chair. The bag that had been used to suffocate her was made of a thick, clear plastic, and I could see condensation where it was touching her skin. Her skin had turned a vibrant purple colour, almost as if it had been dyed with berry juice. The discoloration was at its most extreme in a fine band that ran around her neck, just above the lengths of electrical tape that had been used to secure the bag in place.

When I first saw her, I froze at the threshold to my apartment with the front door wide open. And if I'm honest, part of me was tempted to turn and flee. I'm not altogether sure what stopped me. Sadness, I guess. I've seen a man beaten close to death before but never anything like this. It wasn't just her lifeless pose or the brutality of what had been done to her; it was also the stillness in the room, the quiet all around, the funnel of dust motes twirling in the evening sunshine filtering through my window – the utter normality of everything else.

I stepped inside my apartment in a daze and set the wrapped painting down on the floor against the wall. Then I turned from her, dropped to my knees and took a moment to assess the dead-bolts that were flush with the frame of the door and the fascias of the locks themselves. The locks hadn't been forced or drilled – they'd been picked open. It wasn't the sort of thing I might have been expected to focus on, but concentrating on the locks felt oddly reassuring. I guess a psychologist might call it displacement activity but so far as I was concerned, looking at the locks was a damn sight better than looking at the body.

Frowning at my findings, I closed the door from the inside, then crossed the room to the kitchen, opened one of the cupboards and removed my box of disposable latex gloves. I slipped a pair of the gloves onto my hands, taking my time over the procedure, indulging in it almost. Finally, I took a deep breath, turned and approached the woman. Let me tell you, there are few things I've been as reluctant to do in my life as reaching out to touch her, and fewer still that have dashed my hopes quite so completely.

There was still a trace of warmth in her wrist when I placed my fingers against her skin but there was no sign whatsoever of a pulse. I released her hand and moved to the front of the chair. Crouching down and swallowing hard, I reached for her chin and tilted her face upwards. The bag rustled and the plastic became taut against the electrical tape around her neck. The face I found myself looking into was the most ghastly thing I've ever seen.

It was the eyes that did it – the desperation and panic in them. People talk about the sightless gaze of the dead. Well, not here. These eyes were full of knowing; a terrible understanding of what was about to occur. I looked down and saw that her mouth was formed into an infinite, aimless 'O', the plastic material sucked into a concave shape between her lips. Her lips were tinged blue and her cheeks and the skin around her eyes and nostrils had swollen dramatically, distorting her face in a sickening way. Blood vessels had burst all across the surface of her skin, as though her capillaries had detonated simultaneously. Threads of blond hair were congealed against her brow; the rest an unruly tangle on top of her head.

I lowered her chin back to its resting point and stepped away from her, crossing my arms in front of my chest. I felt my rib cage rise and fall, suddenly conscious of my own breathing. Closing my eyes, I tried my best to control the thumping of my heart and the curious whistling noise that had begun to form in my ears. My head swirled. I felt my legs buckle and I grabbed for my desk to steady myself before I lost my balance.

I recognised her. She was the woman from the photograph in the Marais apartment – Catherine Ames, the owner of the painting.

Quickly now, I moved into my bedroom and threw open the doors to the wardrobe. My holdall was stashed in the base, and some of my less incriminating burglar tools were packed inside, together with my real passport and driver's licence. I snatched up the holdall and added some clean clothes from my bedside drawers, then moved into the bathroom and scooped my arthritis medicines out of the mirror-fronted cabinet into the bag. I stood on the toilet seat and grasped for the top of the cabinet. My gloved fingers came away in a cloud of dust, gripping the remains of the cash Pierre had given me as well as a plastic pouch containing my spare set of picks and probes. I rushed back to the living room and stuffed my writing notes, my laptop and my framed Hammett novel into the holdall too. I checked the desk drawers for other essentials, then closed them and turned right around, scanning the room and trying to decide if there was anything else I needed. I didn't think so, at least nothing pressing. The room was beginning to spin and I raised my palms to my ears and bowed my head, drawing more air into my system. I squeezed my skull between my hands and growled deep in my throat. This wasn't the time to lose it, I reminded myself. This was the time to save my own skin.

Squaring my shoulders, I fixed my eyes on a random point on the wall across the room and strode past the body of the dead woman one last time, afraid to risk even the merest glance in her direction. Then I snatched the painting from the floor, hastily locked the front door to my apartment behind me and headed downstairs.

The concierge emerged from below the reception desk just as I reached the foyer. His sudden appearance made me jump clear out of my skin. I clutched at my chest and struggled to compose myself, my mouth opening and reopening and my eyes blinking furiously. The concierge offered me a hesitant smile. I swallowed my heart back down, cleared my throat and heard myself asking him in broken French if I'd had any visitors during the day.

The concierge shook his head no, brow furrowed, as if he'd picked up on my anxiety. I glanced towards the cluttered office area behind his desk, wishing that it contained a bank of CCTV monitors that could help clear my name. There was just one monitor, though, and it was screening a zany French game show. I looked back at the concierge and watched him eye my holdall and the painting while I tried to think if there was anything else I could ask. Nothing occurred to me, other than how suspicious I must have looked, so I did my best to smile casually, then thanked him and hurried out of the building and away along the street.

It was frustrating as hell that there was no CCTV footage and more than a little worrying that the concierge hadn't noticed anyone visiting my apartment, but I hoped there was still a chance he might be able to provide me with some form of alibi. I couldn't remember seeing him at his desk when I'd returned home no more than ten minutes before, but it was possible he'd seen me. And assuming Catherine had been dead for more than an hour, say, the timing of my arrival could put me in the clear. For just a moment, I thought about going back and checking with the concierge but then I realised it was a dumb idea. If I did that, it might make it seem as though I was trying to prime him for when the police investigation gathered pace.

And I had no doubt there would be a police investigation. Actually, I was surprised they hadn't arrived before I'd had a chance to leave. Because the whole thing reeked of a set-up – Catherine Ames had been killed in my apartment and I happened to have her painting in my possession at the time; my fingerprints could be found in her home if the police went looking for them; I'd even drunk her coffee, for goodness sake. It was all very neat, I had to admit. So it was odd there were no police sirens wailing or patrol cars screeching to a halt all around me, no officers demanding that I drop my holdall and lay spread-eagled on the pavement while they cuffed me. The only explanation I could think of was perhaps Bruno hadn't watched me go in.

Because that was who the murderer had to be. I mean, Bruno was the only person besides Pierre who was aware that I'd been inside the dead woman's apartment. He was the one who'd had me touch her things without my gloves on. I could remember telling him the area I lived in and he knew my name so it wouldn't have been all that hard for him to track me down. Christ, I'd even provided him with the skills he needed to break into my apartment.

How long ago had he killed her, I wondered? I racked my brain and remembered I'd left at around ten in the morning. It was close to half past six by now. Was she murdered while I was in her home? Judging by the warmth of her body, I guessed the answer was no. She couldn't have been dead for more than a few hours at the most, I didn't think, but then again, I was hardly a pathologist. But assuming I was right, that meant she could have been killed while I was at the bank or buying the painting. And that would make sense, because it would explain why I hadn't seen Bruno at work.

For a moment, I thought about calling the police myself. It occurred to me that I could place an anonymous call from a pay-phone and give them the name of the real culprit. That would save them time chasing after me and getting off on the wrong foot, but then again, might it seem as though I'd tried to frame Bruno? I had no idea. My brain felt overrun and my thinking confused.

I broke away from my thoughts to find I was at the end of Avenue de Breteuil, approaching the overland métro station on Boulevard Garibaldi. I hurried up the perforated metal steps, beyond the magazine stall where I normally bought my English newspapers, then fumbled a carnet of lilac tickets from my wallet and waited impatiently for the first train to come along, not caring where it was headed. A minute later, I was sat on a fold-down seat at the far end of a busy carriage, the holdall and the painting stowed between my quick-tapping feet.

I lowered my head between my knees and focused on my breathing once more. I could feel sweat on my back, sticking to my shirt, and the skin on my palms and face was clammy. My scalp prickled and I was conscious that I was trembling all over. In an effort to get my shakes under control, I clenched and unclenched my fists, meanwhile imagining that I was blowing into and out of a brown paper bag. I curled my toes up inside my shoes and tensed my entire body, willing myself to focus. Just then, I got the impression I was being watched and I glanced up from the dimpled plastic floor to see a teenage Goth studying me in a detached way, as though she was curious to see if I was about to have some kind of a fit. I offered her a weak smile and then, non-plussed by her blank reaction, I returned my attention to the floor and focused once again on my imaginary brown paper bag.

TWELVE

I rode the métro network for close to an hour before resolving myself to a new course of action. By then, rush hour had passed and the trains were less congested. When I stepped out at Pigalle, the flagstone pavements were almost deserted and I guessed most of the locals were at home preparing meals or enjoying a glass of wine in one of the neighbourhood brasseries. The tawdry signs outside the burlesque theatres and peep-show dens appeared faded in the weak evening sunshine, as though the colour contrast of the streets I was walking through had been minimised with the use of some giant remote control.

I climbed the steep, winding alleys and cigarette-strewn steps towards Montmartre with my holdall over my shoulder and the brown-packaged painting beneath my arm, aware only of the noise-lessness surrounding me and the sweaty fug that seemed to be clinging to my skin like a tight film. Blood throbbed at my temples and I began to feel faint. At that moment, I could have quite willingly tretched out on the grubby pavement, pressed my face against the cobblestones and closed my eyes for a time. I didn't, though. I kept on, throwing one foot in front of the next, working the muscles in my thighs and my calves, occasionally adjusting the way I was holding the painting or easing the strap of the holdall away from my shoulders.

The ascent was relentless and as I neared to the Sacré-Coeur, I found myself out of breath and tangled up in a morass of tourists, all of them moving too slowly and too aimlessly through the constricted streets in their bright T-shirts and baggy shorts and sunglasses, pointing their damn cameras and camcorders in my direction. Things reached a pitch at the Place du Tertre, a tacky square with all the authenticity of a movie set. Seedy waiters dressed in gaudy waistcoats did their best to entice passers-by to eat in their restaurants; caricaturists approached me with clipboards and speedy banter, while other "artists" offered to cut my silhouette from black sugar paper with a pair of nail scissors or encouraged me to watch them paint shoddy watercolours of city landmarks from memory. Side-stalls encroached onto the street, their display stands drenched in T-shirts, rucksacks and baseball caps with the word "Paris" printed over and over again in endless, varied scripts. I tripped on a blackboard sign for a café and almost stumbled into a busker playing a violin.

Eventually, by some quirk of good fortune, I forced my way through the crowds and shambled down a severe incline until I stumbled across the hotel I was looking for without having to ask for directions. Once there, I checked in to a room courtesy of David Birk once again, then I locked the door behind me, stepped out of my damp clothes and subjected myself to an ice-cold shower for as long as I could bear. When I emerged from the shower cubicle, the tiled floor lurched towards me and I had to grab for the toilet seat and sit myself down. Perched on the toilet, my face pressed into a white cotton towel, I tensed my jaw and told myself to focus. It was easier said than done. An hour passed and still I found myself in the same position, my body covered in goose pimples and my reflection in the bathroom mirror looking pale and disorientated.

Really now, I asked myself, where was this getting me? The answer was nowhere. The way I was going I was doomed to remain on the toilet seat until one of the cleaners happened to disturb me the following morning. And wouldn't that look like a fine tableau of guilt? I was being foolish. Running through the image of the dead woman in my apartment for the hundredth time wouldn't change a thing, other than drive me nuts. I couldn't save her. I couldn't alter the way things had turned out. All I could do was face up to the situation I'd found myself in and manage it as best I could.

And drink. A lot.

I eased up from the toilet seat, the muscles in my legs feeling tight as guitar strings, and wrapped the towel about my waist. The mini-bar was located inside a polished wooden cabinet and, given the circumstances I'd found myself in, I was cavalier enough to uncap a miniature of whisky without consulting the price list. I took a mouthful, then another. I swallowed and felt the warming burn deep in my throat. The buzz radiated out from my chest, like one of those TV ads for a flu remedy. I dropped the whisky miniature into the waste bin and selected a bottle of vodka to replace it. I took a slug from the vodka bottle, recoiled from the taste, then set the bottle to one side and removed some clean clothes from my holdall so that I could dress. By the time I'd laced my shoes and combed my hair and finished the last of the vodka, I felt just about ready to head downstairs.

The hotel bar was strikingly hip – if anything, it looked more Italian than French. The bar itself was an oblong cube of some kind of white Perspex and the spirits and wines were displayed on glass shelves that were back-lit with blue fluorescent lamps. There were a series of high circular tables and raised leather chairs around the edge of the room and perhaps six metallic stools in front of the bar. Only one of the stools was occupied. The brunette who was sat in it was twisting a mojito between her hands, avoiding the gaze of a handsome young barman who was drying glasses nearby. She was dressed as if for a night out: a summer dress with a floral print and dark costume jewellery. Her legs were bare and she wore strappy sandals.

I took the stool one away from the brunette and signalled the barman, ordering a bottle of lager. I didn't speak in my normal voice – for the sake of camouflage, I chose to adopt a Scottish accent instead. At least, I think it was Scottish. That was certainly my intention, but I was already half-cut, and who knew if it was anything like as convincing as I imagined? In my mind, I'd mastered a deep, Highlands brogue, my vowel sounds were perfectly clipped, my "r"s fully rounded, and there was an authentic cadence to my speech. Hell, so far as I was concerned, I might as well have been sat alongside my brother Hamish back in Inverness, wearing a kilt made from the family tartan and humming "Flower of Scotland".

While I admired my linguistic dexterity, the barman fetched me a lager from a see-through cooler and set it down in front of me on a jet-black napkin. I took a healthy swig. My head was swimming more than a little from the spirits I'd drunk back in my room but the lager felt good. I half-smiled to myself. It was booze that had got me into this mess and now I was hoping booze could get me back out.

"Looks like you needed that," the brunette said. She was English, kind of posh-sounding.

I lowered the bottle from my mouth and wiped my lips with the back of my hand.

"Aye, you could say," I told her, nodding sagely.

"Hard day at the office?"

"Och, just some wee things playing on mae mind."

"Oh?"

I smiled and pointed my finger at her drink. "How about yoo?" I asked, flattening my "o" sounds as best I could.

"Ah," she said, stirring the cocktail with a straw and arching an eyebrow. "I appear to have been stood up."

"I cannae believe that."

She snorted and gave me a sly grin. "Well, it's true. Although, if I'm honest, I'm not sure I really expected him to show."

"Aye? So are you looking for solace in your wee drink?"

"Nope," she said, shaking her head and taking a sip. "The mojitos are just really good here."

"Is that a fact?"

She waited a beat, then slid her glass towards me across the gloss surface of the bar. I reached for the glass, meanwhile shifting onto the stool alongside her. I sipped from the rim, ice crystals filling my mouth. The mint struck me first, then the rum. I set the glass down and nodded.

"Want one?"

"Aye, why not?"

The brunette ordered in confident French from the barman and he began filling a glass tumbler with ice. He was crushing the mint leaves with a pestle before she spoke again.

"My name's Victoria," she said, offering me a well-manicured hand. There was something very deliberate about the way she was looking at me.

"Michael," I told her, holding her gaze.

"Michael," she repeated, saying it slowly, as though she was just getting used to the sound of the name for the first time. "Really?"

"You dinnae like it?"

"No, it's not that," she said, frowning. "Would you mind if I ask what your surname is?"

"Birk."

She laughed.

"I dinnae think it's that funny."

"No," she told me, waving her hand. "It's just, for a second there, I thought this could have been a real karmic moment."

"Aye?"

She paused, as if debating whether to tell me anything further. Then her shoulders dropped, signalling that she'd decided to run with it. "Have you heard the name Michael Faulks before?"

I raised my hand to my chin, as though giving it some thought. "I dinnae think so," I said, at length. "Should I?"

"It would have been unlikely, I suppose. He's a character in a series of mystery novels. A burglar. I represent the author, you see."

"Is that a fact now?"

She nodded, contemplating me through half-lidded eyes.

"And are these wee books any good?"

She screwed her face up. "They're okay. In the past, they haven't sold all that well if you want the honest truth. But the guy who writes them, I don't know – I like to think one day he might write something pretty extraordinary."

"One day, you say."

"Perhaps."

I pouted, scratched at the stubble on my chin. I took another mouthful of my lager. I was just deciding whether to pursue the conversation when she went ahead and asked me something else.

"What happened to your fingers?"

I lowered the lager bottle and gazed at my inflamed knuckles. "Shut them in a wee door."

"Ouch."

"Aye. Lucky I dinnae break them."

"And what is it you do, Michael?"

"I'm a lawyer," I told her, once I'd swallowed some more lager.

"That's . . . interesting. What kind of work do you specialise in?"

"Och, all kinds."

"All kinds? Like mergers and acquisitions, or bank finance, or tax law or what?"

I looked at her sideways. "You ken about the law?"

"My father was a judge."

"Aye? Well, I'm in anti-fraud."

"Anti-fraud," she said, somehow drawing the words out.

"That's right."

"You know, I wouldn't have guessed it."

"Oh?"

"If I had to guess," she said, dipping her finger into her drink and bobbing the ice up and down, "I'd have said criminal."

"Excuse me?" I squeaked, forgetting my accent for just a moment.

She raised her glass towards her lips. "Criminal law Michael. Defending the guilty, that kind of thing."

"Och," I said, breathing again. "No. I was never one for all that courtroom stuff."

I broke eye contact and glanced up to find that the barman had finished my mojito. He set it down in front of me on top of another black napkin. I lowered my mouth to the straw and took a sip. The drink was cold and fresh-tasting, drilling straight into my brain. My very dumb, pea-sized brain. Why had I lied? Why had I put on such a crazy accent in the first place? I could have stayed in my room and avoided all this; could have checked into another hotel altogether for that matter. But there was no going back now. I'd just have to drink the mojito as quickly as possible and make my excuses.

"So," Victoria said, with a heavy sigh, "your name is Michael

Birk and you're a Scottish anti-fraud lawyer who just happens to be having a welcome drink after a long day at work."

"Aye, that's right."

She stared at me hard. "You really are pathetic."

I felt my jaw tighten. I wanted to look anywhere but at her. She leaned towards me, so close that I could smell the mint on her breath.

"I came to your damn reading, Charlie," she told me, through clenched teeth. "I was in Paris days ago and I watched you in that park and to begin with I really thought it might have been some kind of a mistake. Then I heard you read and I knew. You lied to me. You've been lying to me for years."

I gawped at her, completely at a loss. My mind grasped for something to say, a word to repair the damage I'd caused. "I dinnae know wha –".

"Don't," she said, a hard cast to her expression. She jabbed her finger into my bicep. "Just tell me, is there any reason you can think of why I should still talk to you after tonight?"

My mouth opened and closed, but I was unable to offer her a response. I leaned away from my drink, crumpled on my stool.

"I'm really sorry," I began, my voice sounding terribly proper all of a sudden. "I've had an awful day, Vic. I'm kind of messed up right now and . . ."

"I didn't think so," she said, interrupting me.

She reached for her purse and stood up from the bar.

"Vic," I tried again. "Let me explain. I'm an idiot. You know that. Please."

She shook her head, her neck muscles taught. Then she glared at me, lips colourless and pressed into a thin line. Finally, she turned and left me alone at the bar.

THIRTEEN

I went back to my room and slumped on my bed, staring at the wrapped painting leaning against my wall. I'd lost all sense of what my next move should be. I didn't know whether I should call the police and report the body in my apartment or call Pierre and come clean about everything that had happened. I gave some thought to leaving Paris altogether, for that matter, though I realised it might make me appear guilty. Had the body been found yet, I wondered, and if it had, were the police on my trail? It wouldn't take them long to learn my name – they need only ask the concierge – but they wouldn't know where I was staying or have any idea that I was using a false identity. I guessed I was safe for at least the night, barring some really bad luck.

So I had plenty of thinking time, even if, at that moment, I wasn't all that sure what I should be thinking about. Normally, I'd have called Victoria and talked the situation through. Oddly enough, though, I suspected that dialling her number and unburdening myself about Catherine's body might not be the best way to mend fences. And besides, part of me was reluctant to drag her into the whole thing. She'd made it plain recently that she'd had just about enough of being caught up in my criminal behaviour and I couldn't see how involving her in a murder mystery would improve her mood.

Without Victoria to bounce ideas off, I was left with only the bare wall that faced my bed. Strangely, the wall didn't seem to be coming up with anything particularly insightful. Maybe it was just biding its time, waiting to offer me the killer perspective when I thought all hope was lost. Or maybe the wall had just about as little to offer as I did.

I growled and threw a pillow at the wall but even then it refused to stir. I eyed the mini-bar once again and toyed with the prospect of oblivion but it didn't strike me as the most constructive of approaches. Unusual for that to stop me, I guess. After all, I was the same dum-dum who'd imagined a bad Highlands accent could trick a good friend into believing I was a complete stranger.

Alright, I told myself, *enough of the self-pity. Do something useful and imagine this is one of your Faulks novels. You've plotted yourself into this mess, you can't ask anyone else what to do and you need to come up with a plan. So, what is it?*

I scratched my head and stroked my chin and clapped my hands together. I clicked my fingers and drummed my nails on the beside cabinet. And . . . nothing. Nada. Not a clue.

I growled some more, then leaned over the side of the bed and reached for my holdall. My laptop was packed inside and I pulled it out and opened the screen. My intention was to make a quick summary of everything that had happened to me and try to work things forwards from there. It was what I sometimes did with my mystery novels when the problem I'd run into was too early in the book for me to trouble Victoria. And I really thought a methodical approach might help. I could see myself drawing up a series of bullet-points and short notes, and extrapolating from there until I reached a stage where my next move was inescapable.

Which it was, the moment the screen lit up and I was confronted with the following message:

BRING US THE PAINTING. WE ARE WAITING.

I froze, then glanced over my shoulder towards the window. The curtains were closed but even so, it was unsettling. I looked at the screen once again and read the message for a second time.

BRING US THE PAINTING. WE ARE WAITING.

Had it been typed while I was down at the bar, hamming it up as a haggis-eating Scot? No, of course not, I realised, because if that was the case the painting would be gone. It was hardly difficult to find in my room and nobody would have stepped over it to dig out my laptop and leave me a quite unnecessary message.

I thought back and remembered that my laptop had been open on the desk in my apartment when I'd headed out that morning, in sleep mode as I normally left it. So whoever had killed Catherine had gone to the trouble of typing me the message before they left. And that meant two things – one, they knew I had the painting, and two, they hadn't reported the killing just yet. How did I know that? Because if they'd reported the killing, there was a good chance I'd be in custody without access to the nifty little message they'd left me or the painting they were aiming to acquire.

And I also knew a third thing, or at least thought I did. They couldn't have been watching me all that hard because otherwise they would have seen me go into my apartment with the painting under my arm and they would have been able to confront me when I came back out.

But they'd killed a woman and I had no idea who they were, or even how they knew me.

I scrolled down, just to check that they hadn't written anything more. It was peculiar. How was I supposed to bring them the painting if I had no way of finding out how to get it to them? And why hadn't they left Catherine alive and waited in the apartment for me to return? They could have ambushed me, if they'd liked, and seized the painting without needing to kill anyone at all.

Maybe, I thought for just a moment, it was a smokescreen. Perhaps, as I'd first thought, the killer was Bruno and he was trying to throw me off the trail with the cryptic note and the misleading references to "US" and "THEM". But that didn't make any sense. I was a thief, not a detective, and so far as I was aware, Bruno had no idea that I'd managed to buy the painting he'd stolen. And if he wanted it that badly, why would he have sold it to the gallery on Rue Quincampoix?

Now I was really confused and no list of bullet points was going to get me out of the mess I'd found myself in. I closed the laptop and checked through the rest of my things for any other messages. There was nothing at all.

I glanced across the room at the painting. Everything seemed to revolve around the damn thing and I figured it was high time I had a proper look at it, so I crossed the room and retrieved it from the floor and set it face-up on the bed. The gallery owner had knotted the parcel string too tightly for me to unpick with my fingers, so I fished around in my collection of burglar tools until I found a small razor blade and then I used the blade to slice through the string and afterwards the brown paper, being very careful not to scratch the surface of the painting. I peeled the paper away in long strips, then lifted the painting and threw the torn paper onto the floor. I set the painting back down and looked once again at the miserable scene of Montmartre.

I didn't recognise the area in the painting but the scene had almost certainly been set among the tacky market stalls in one of the main tourist squares that led to the Sacré-Coeur. I could have gone out looking for the exact spot but I didn't think it would achieve very much. If the artist was so bad at rendering human beings then the chances of him accurately reproducing a specific location were slim. And besides, what could it possibly tell me?

As it happened, I was more interested in the artist himself. If, as I was pretty certain, there was no intrinsic worth in the composition, then something else had to be going on. The work was signed Maigny, as Pierre had told me, and though the name meant nothing to me, I had to admit that minor Parisian artists of the early twentieth century were not exactly my specialist area. Sometimes, an artist's story can give their work far more value than it might otherwise merit. So it occurred to me that Maigny could be famous in a way that had escaped me as well as the owner of the art gallery. If Maigny happened to be notorious, it might explain what all the fuss was about.

With that in mind, I reached for my laptop and connected to the wireless Internet service inside the hotel room, then called up a search engine and searched for "Maigny, Artist". But I found nothing significant. Several hits came up for a sculptor called Pierre Bontemps because he happened to have produced a statue of Charles de Maigny that was exhibited in the Louvre. But that didn't strike me as at all relevant to my current predicament and nothing else did either. On a whim, I called up a genealogy site and discovered that the French name Maigny derived from an old province of France lying to the east of Bretagne. Useful. I closed my laptop and returned my attention to the painting.

So, if the work was awful and the artist was a nobody, what else could be going on? I ran my fingers over the glaze and double-checked that the painting was definitely an oil. It was, so this wasn't one of those ruses you see in the movies where a valuable painting has been covered with some dreary watercolour to disguise its true worth.

Hmm. I picked up the painting and turned it over and found that a thin sheet of hardboard had been set into the rear of the frame to protect the canvas. The backing had a torn and faded sticker on it, discoloured with age, and the sticker bore the fragments of some handwritten French that I was unable to decipher. Very carefully, I reached for the metal brackets that were holding the hardboard in place and prised them away. I used one of my flat-headed screwdrivers to lever the hardboard up and remove it completely.

As soon as the backing was clear of the canvas, I looked down and a small charge ran through me. Resting on the canvas was a brown A4 business envelope. The envelope was unsealed and bulged very slightly in the middle. I was all set to reach for it and remove the contents when good sense took hold and I decided to slip on a pair of disposable gloves first. I dug around in my holdall until I found some and then put them on as quickly as possible, mindful of my fingers, yet eager to answer the questions that were hurtling through my head. At last, I reached for the envelope, parted the paper as carefully as I could and eased my hand inside.

My fingers emerged gripping a selection of papers and acetate cards. I checked the envelope for anything further, then when I was sure it was empty, I placed it back down on the rear of the canvas and carried my findings over to the small writing desk in the corner of the room. I flicked on a reading lamp positioned on the desk and started to sort through the documents.

I began with the acetate cards. They were a blue colour and largely transparent, which made seeing what was printed on them tricky. I angled the desk lamp upwards and held the cards against the light from the bulb. The images were still hard to pick out because they were very detailed but I was confident I knew what I was looking at: floorplans. There was no text to indicate what building the plans related to but there were three separate cards and each card contained a different layout of similar proportions, so assuming the plans were to scale, it seemed to me that they were likely to be from the same building and that the building had to have either a minimum of three floors or perhaps three wings.

I put the acetate cards down and reached for the square of paper that was next in the pile of documents. The paper looked as if it had been torn from a pocket notebook, of the kind that detectives are always carrying in television shows. Written on the paper in a rushed, slanted scrawl were a series of six-digit numbers.

45-98-90
45-27-81
60-21-56
77-70-09
16-30-78

I ran through the numbers in my head, as though reciting them might trigger something in my mind. Unsurprisingly, my attempt failed. No doubt they were codes but without knowing what the codes corresponded to I was pretty lost. They could have been scrambled telephone numbers or references to some kind of cipher wheel or even future winning lottery numbers for all I knew. But they were obviously worth something to someone.

The next piece of paper contained a list of names, written by the same hand as the six-digit combinations. I counted fifteen and all but three were for men. There were Christian names and surnames but no middle names or initials. I scanned the list but none of the names meant anything to me. I thought they were all French, though I couldn't be certain. Four of the names had two-digit numbers beside them and I guessed these numbers were the ages of the relevant individuals. I wasn't sure what significance this conferred on the names in question but I spoke them aloud almost without thinking.

"Henri Jetter, 51. Luc Murrel, 56. Jean-Patrick Deville, 39. Christian Fortin, 24."

The third name, that of Jean-Patrick Deville, had an asterisk beside it. Clearly, he was important somehow, though for what particular reason I hadn't the faintest clue.

The next item was a folded, photocopied document. It consisted of three sheets of paper that had been stapled together. Each sheet of paper contained a diagram of an electricity circuit of some description. The diagrams were very complex, full of a whole host of symbols that I couldn't begin to comprehend. I scanned them for any explanatory notes, of which there were none.

Next was a strip of photograph negatives. The strip contained six individual frames and I held each of the brown windows up to the lamp in turn to see if I could make out any of the images. It was surprisingly difficult. All I could see to begin with were a blur of sepia shapes, but on certain angles I could make out the interior walls of a room. Some of the images contained the tops of people's heads but they seemed to be incidental to what the photographer had been focusing on. I squinted and strained my eyes, twisting the negatives right around and turning them back to front, but I still couldn't be sure what I was seeing. To be honest, I wasn't too disappointed. I figured I could always get the photographs developed somewhere in the morning and if they contained anything useful, I'd be able to consider them in greater detail then.

Just two items remained. The first was an actual photograph – a zoom shot of a man and a woman in profile, holding hands across a café table and looking intently at one another. The man was middle-aged with a neat side parting and a handsome face. He wore a black roll-neck sweater and a chunky sports watch. The woman was much younger, early twenties at a guess, with blonde cornrows and a deep tan. It certainly looked as if the couple were unaware of the photograph being taken and the whole thing gave me an uncomfortable feeling, as though I'd trespassed on a private moment.

The final item was a flexible piece of laminated white card with a metal lapel clip fixed to it. I turned the card over and discovered that it was some form of nametag, perhaps a security pass. There was a quarter-inch digital image of the man from the photograph, this time looking straight at me. Alongside the image was the name Jean-Patrick Deville. Beneath the name was a barcode and nothing else.

The nametag at last gave me a few links. It told me the name of the man in the photograph with the girl and, of course, his was the only name on the list I'd found that had an asterisk beside it. He was important in some way, though quite how wasn't clear. But it was a start and it had felt like a long time coming.

I pushed the articles and papers around on the desk for a while, moving certain items alongside one another, overlaying them, trying to come up with connections. So far it wasn't happening but I had a feeling there was more to come. I held the strip of negatives up to the light again, trying to determine if Jean-Patrick Deville appeared in any of them. I didn't think so, although I couldn't be sure. Once they were developed, I'd know for certain.

Eventually, I grew frustrated and decided to put everything away and give my subconscious time to digest what I'd uncovered. So I collected the papers and photographs and blueprints together, put them back into the same order in which I'd found them and returned the lot to the brown business envelope. I repositioned the envelope on the rear of the canvas, slipped the hardboard backing into place once again and finally levered the metal brackets down so that the painting was just as it had been before I took it apart.

I turned and scanned the room, looking for a good hiding place. As a professional thief, I soon realised there were none. Every possibility I thought of necessarily meant that it was somewhere I would also think to look if I was searching the room. And I really didn't want the painting to be found. It was my trump card – the one item that everything connected back to. So long as the painting was in my hands, I had some control over my destiny. I needed to guarantee it would be absolutely safe, and there was only one way I could think of achieving that.

FOURTEEN

Under different circumstances, I like to think I would have been concerned by how readily the hotel receptionist gave me Victoria's room number. As it happened, I was just grateful for the break. Her room was on the same floor as my own, in the opposite direction from the central elevator bank. She must have paid extra for the view, which made me wonder whether I should have negotiated a little harder over the commission I was paying her. Not that right now was really the time to be bothered by such things. Now was the time to grovel.

I knocked on her door and awaited a response. When none came, I checked my watch and saw that it was closing in on eleven o'clock. I guessed she was in bed, which just made things worse. I knocked again, louder this time.

"Victoria," I said, in a low voice. "It's me, Charlie. I need to talk."

I heard a bumping noise, followed by footsteps. A floorboard creaked on the other side of the door.

"Victoria?"

"What is it?"

"Thank God, I was beginning to think I had the wrong room. I need to talk. Can you let me in?"

"I'm not in the mood, Charlie."

"I know that," I said, resting my palm against the door panel. "But this is important."

"Why don't you just go home and give us both some space? We can talk in the morning if we really have to."

"I'd like to go home," I told her, "but I can't. That's what I need to talk to you about."

There was a pause.

"What do you mean?"

"Please Vic, I don't want to discuss this out in the corridor. If you could just let me in . . ."

"Why should I?"

I swallowed hard and glanced down at the painting in my hand. Maybe this wasn't such a good idea, after all. Maybe I should have just taken my chances and hidden the painting beneath the chest of drawers in my room.

"Charlie, you tell me," Victoria went on. "Why should I let you in?"

"Because if you don't, I'll just use my picks?"

I laughed faintly but there was no response. I rocked forwards on the balls of my feet and pressed my forehead against the door.

"Vic, please," I said, squeezing my eyes shut. "I know I screwed up. I know you have every right to be mad. But I'm really in a tight spot here and I could do with a friend just now."

My words seemed to have no effect. I was beginning to think it was hopeless. I checked that the corridor was still empty before giving it my final shot.

"Listen, there's a dead woman in my living room," I whispered, and felt my shoulders sag. "She was murdered."

Victoria didn't reply. I really thought I'd blown it. Then, with a sudden thud, the deadbolt slid back and the door opened. I looked up to see Victoria stood in one of the hotel's monogrammed robes, her hand on her hip and her hair unkempt.

"I take it you didn't kill her," she said, mouth pursed.

I shook my head. Victoria gave me a stern look, one that instantly reminded me of the dorm matron at my old boarding school.

"Come in then," she said, at last. "We'd better work out who did."

A half-hour later, I'd apologised for my deceit at least three times more and filled Victoria in as best I could. My story hadn't been delivered in the orderly fashion she might have preferred, and I'd found myself looping back to prior events and repeating myself more often than I would have cared for, but as first drafts go it could have been worse. I thought I'd covered the main facts and my most salient interpretations and while some of my descriptions were necessarily rushed and a shade clichéd, I hoped that could be forgiven, even if my recent behaviour might not be. When I was done, I stopped pacing the floor and sat down in an armchair over by the floor-length curtains. I placed my chin in my hand and awaited Victoria's verdict.

From what I could see, she appeared to be caught up in the details already. I guess that shouldn't have surprised me. Despite the things she'd said in our last telephone conversation, I'd long been aware that Victoria took a kind of vicarious thrill from hearing about my criminal escapades. It was a sure sign of how big a murder mystery nut she happened to be. In fact, I sometimes got the impression the reality of some of the scenarios I found myself in never fully registered with her. Even now, I could picture her moving the facts and foibles of my latest scrape around in her mind, almost as if she was rolling a dice and nudging Professor Plum around a Cluedo board, peering archly at her suspect cards and trying to figure out exactly whodunnit in the modern apartment building, with the plastic bag and the roll of electrical tape.

And while we're on the subject, I guess I could be guilty of the same thing too. Perhaps it was a kind of survival mechanism – a way of enabling myself to think my way out of a predicament before I became paralysed by fear. And if that was the case, maybe it was no bad thing. It had worked in the past, so there was no reason to suggest it couldn't work again.

Just then, Victoria seemed to come round from her thoughts and she focused on me intently.

"You're sure she was killed?" she asked, for openers.

"Well, she certainly didn't have a pulse when I left."

"What I mean," Victoria said, in a controlled voice, "is are you certain she didn't do this to herself?"

"Absolutely." I straightened. "Her hands were bound behind her back with cable ties. There's no way she could have done it."

"Cable ties? You didn't say."

"Didn't I?"

"No," Victoria said, shaking her head resolutely. "You mentioned the bag that had been taped over her head but you didn't say her hands were bound."

"Oh. Sorry."

Victoria exhaled in a melancholy way and folded her legs beneath her on the bed, as though she was adopting a yoga pose. "I didn't think it could be suicide," she said. "I can't think of a logical reason why she would have come to your apartment to kill herself."

"Me neither."

"Could she have known who you were?"

"I don't think so. Our only connection is that I burgled her place and I didn't exactly leave a business card."

"Who did know?"

"Pierre. Bruno."

"And Pierre's client?"

I bobbed my head from side to side. "I hope not. The whole idea is that Pierre acts as a go-between. That way the client has no way of knowing who I am."

"And you have no way of knowing who they are."

"It's a flaw, granted."

"Have you been in touch with Pierre?"

I glanced at the carpet. "Not yet. I'm due to meet him tomorrow at ten. I figured I'd see what I could find out before then."

She peered hard at me. "You trust him?"

"I have to."

"So call him."

I shrugged, a little awkwardly. "Why don't we just see what we can figure out first?"

"What are you worried about, your reputation? Christ Charlie, there are bigger things going on here."

I just looked at her.

"You do remember Pierre's number?"

"Of course."

"So call him."

Victoria withdrew her mobile telephone from the pocket of her robe and held it out to me in a no-nonsense way. Reluctantly, I accepted the phone and entered Pierre's number. While I waited for my call to be connected, Victoria slipped her fingers into one of the gloves I'd abandoned on her bedcovers and reached for the zoom photo of the man and the woman I'd found among the bundle of papers hidden at the back of the painting. The painting was further away on the bed, resting face-down, with the hardboard backing off to the side.

I listened to the telephone ring eight times and then I looked up.

"No answer."

"Leave a message?"

"Best not," I said, and let the telephone ring out. I set the mobile down on the bedside cabinet. "Your number might have shown up his end. He could call back."

"Okay."

"Don't answer unless I'm here."

"Okay."

I smiled thinly. "You probably knew that."

She nodded in a non-committal fashion and put the photograph back with the remainder of the documents. She rested her gloved hand on the terry-cloth material covering her thigh and took a deep breath.

"Have you thought about going to the police? If you report Catherine's body before someone else does, there's a good chance they'll believe you."

I gave Victoria my most sceptical look, the one I reserve for the accordion players on the Paris métro system.

"It's an option," she said. "And it's one I think you should give serious consideration to."

"Hmm," I replied, stroking my chin and frowning, as though consumed by thought. "Nope, I don't think so."

"Why not?"

"Because this isn't one of your police procedurals, Vic. The cops here aren't the good guys. They don't necessarily have the sharpest minds; they probably won't work tirelessly to ensure justice is done. In all probability, they'll arrest me for murder and I'll never have an opportunity to clear my name."

"You don't know that."

"Sure I do. But more to the point, I'm not taking the risk."

Victoria studied me for a good few moments, as though she was weighing up if it was worth pursuing her argument. I adopted an expression that made it clear that would be pointless. After we'd traded one or two more meaningful looks, she finally decided to move on.

"So let's talk about Bruno," she said, with a shake of her head. "He's our number one suspect, correct?"

"I guess."

"What? You don't picture him as a killer?"

I shrugged. "Maybe, given the right motivation. But I don't know what that motivation could be."

"You said you thought he'd framed you."

"And I did. At first. But now I've had a chance to think about it, it doesn't make a whole lot of sense."

"How so?"

"Well, it doesn't fit with the way he behaved. Say I did get picked up for the murder, he'd have to know that the first thing I'd do would be to tell the police about him."

She frowned. "Really?"

"Well, maybe not the very first thing. I'd probably keep quiet to begin with. But say things were looking bleak for me – I'd much rather face a burglary rap than a murder charge. And maybe all I'd have to do is point them in Bruno's direction, which wouldn't be that hard because I had plenty of time to get a good look at him and I managed to find out his real name without a great deal of difficulty."

Victoria pinched her bottom lip with her gloved fingers and narrowed her eyes. "Maybe that would be your problem. It could look a bit *too* easy."

"What? You think it might seem as if I'd framed myself in a half-arsed way to conceal the fact I was really framing Bruno?"

Victoria screwed up her face. She waved her hand. "Forget I just said that. Way too complicated."

"I'm not sure I follow the logic."

"There isn't any." Victoria hitched her shoulders and began to remove the latex glove from her hand, one finger at a time. "What else about Bruno, though? You need more than a feeling, Charlie."

"You're right," I said, watching her fingers emerge. "I also have locks."

"Locks?"

"The ones on the door to my apartment. Whoever killed Catherine picked their way inside."

"You're sure?"

I gave her a funny look. "I like to think I'd be able to tell."

"Fine," she replied, tucking some hair behind her ear. "I'm just playing Devil's advocate here. So the locks were picked and you don't think Bruno could have done it."

"Not now I've thought about it properly. When I moved in, I fitted four new locks to my door," I said, showing her four fingers, as if to explain how numbers worked. "I don't always use them all and my best recollection is that I'd only engaged two of them before I went out yesterday," I went on, curling two fingers back into my palm, continuing to demonstrate my credentials as a mathematician. "But even so, they're top-quality merchandise and Bruno was an absolute beginner. He hadn't mastered the rake yet and those locks would require a lot more skill to be picked. Besides, I didn't leave him any of my tools."

"Maybe he was bluffing about being a beginner."

"So why involve me in the theft of the painting?"

"To frame you."

I squinted and shook my head. "We're going round in circles."

"Maybe because we have to."

"No. The framing scenario was just a dumb idea I had. If Bruno wanted to kill Catherine he could have done it in entirely different circumstances without the need to frame anyone. And besides, I'm beginning to think killing Catherine was more a way of threatening me."

Victoria raised her eyebrows. "Pretty extreme."

"I'm not arguing with you. But it makes sense when you factor in the message on my laptop. I really don't think Bruno could have typed it."

"Why?"

"Because he'd sold the painting to the antique store. My best guess is he had no idea what was hidden behind the canvas."

"But we don't know if any of this means anything," Victoria said, picking up a handful of the documents.

"It has to," I said, trying to ignore how she was touching the papers with her bare hands. "You're forgetting Pierre's client. Nobody pays twenty thousand euros for a nothing painting. Those papers are what this mess is all about."

"But if we discount Bruno, where does that leave us?"

"Stuck. Which is why I'm not discounting him just yet. I need to find him. And I need you to look after the painting while I'm gone. If I'm not back in time to meet Pierre tomorrow, I want you to go straight to the police with it."

"Charlie . . ."

"Come on," I said, finding my feet and giving her a tight smile. "You know how this works. I'm the lead character, the one who jumps into reckless situations and comes out the other end with the answers we need."

"Don't joke with me," she said, shaking her head as if in warning.

"I'm not. And you're the brains in the partnership, right? Which is why I need you to stay here and go through these documents to see what you can come up with. You're bound to find something I can't. Otherwise, this would all be a bit too real."

"It is real, Charlie."

"Hush," I said. "Don't spoil the illusion."

I clenched her shoulder. She looked up at me and I fixed on her eyes. I exhaled wearily.

"I am sorry about my jacket photograph. All my lies."

"So you've said."

"But you're not ready to forgive me just yet?"

Victoria moved her shoulder, freeing herself from my grip. "I'm pissed off, Charlie. That can't come as a surprise."

"I guess. But something you should remember is that I barely knew you when I sent that picture in. There was a lot I hadn't told you back then."

She nodded, unconvinced.

"Hey," I went on, "if it helps, you know more about me right now than anyone else in the whole wide world."

She gave me a half-smile. "Like how bad you are at a Scottish accent?"

I smirked, shook my head.

"That accent was a thing of beauty."

"You sounded like an Irishman with a speech impediment."

"I cannae believe it."

I grinned and held her eyes, relieved that there was a chance things might just return to normal between us.

"Go on. Scram," she said. "Before I get mad all over again."

"I will make it up to you, Vic."

"Oh, I know. Believe me."

FIFTEEN

The taxi driver I found shook his head and gave me a dubious look when I first showed him the address for B. Chevrier that I'd noted down from the telephone directory. Once we finally arrived at our destination, I could understand why. We were on the north-east of the city, overlooking a cluster of high-rise apartments in the very heart of the banlieue of Clichy-sous-Bois, the notorious Parisian district. The area was a ghetto in the vilest sense, a sore that had been left to fester.

My driver refused to take me into the banlieue itself. The best he was willing to do was to drop me on the hard shoulder of the route nationale situated nearest to the western boundary of the slum. He pointed me in the rough direction I needed, then took my money and drove away, leaving me in no doubt as to how foolish he thought I was being.

It was hard to disagree. Standing on the scrubbed asphalt and turning my gaze on the crumbling buildings looming ahead of me, I knew I would feel threatened if I happened to be there on a sunny afternoon, let alone in darkness at one in the morning. I could smell diesel fumes and scorched tyre rubber all around me, and my feet were mired in grit and tar. I checked over my shoulder, towards the headlamps of the moving cars on the main road, wondering if I should cut my losses and try something else. There was no guarantee the telephone listing I had was correct. It could relate to another B. Chevrier altogether but even if it was the right Bruno, he might have moved out since the listing was made. Looking at the buildings ahead of me, I felt pretty certain most of the residents wouldn't even have a telephone. For a moment, I thought about finding a phone box and calling the number, just to see if I could recognise his voice. But where would I find a working pay phone in the banlieue? And even if I did, wouldn't it cost me the element of surprise?

Reluctantly, I dismissed the idea, meanwhile stepping over the crash barrier at the side of the road and making my way down the steep, grassy verge. There were very few street lamps and fewer still that worked, so it was difficult to find my footing. I thought about using my pocket torch but I dismissed the idea right away. The torch beam would mark me out as an outsider, and if there was one place I didn't want to draw anyone's attention, it was here.

It took me almost an hour to locate the high-rise I was looking for. I guess that shouldn't have surprised me because the streets I found myself walking through formed a sinister maze, full of darkened alleys and corners, pitch-black underpasses and boarded up buildings. There were barely any street signs and the area didn't register on the maps of the city I had in my possession. So my only option had been to circle the zone the taxi driver had indicated, with my hands in my pockets and my shoulders hunched, trying not to jump whenever I heard footsteps or the high-pitched buzz of a nearby moped engine, always avoiding eye contact with the groups of youths I passed.

The high-rise had no security measures to delay me. There wasn't even a door on the front entrance. The hinges and the frame were there, but the door had been ripped free and discarded on the ground. I entered the foyer, broken glass crunching beneath my feet. There was an elevator, smelling bluntly of urine, but the switch-plate had been removed from the wall so that all that was left was a tangle of bare wires. The apartment I was after was number 71 and as I began to climb the stairs, I realised with a creeping dread that it was probably on the seventh floor of the building. I didn't relish the prospect of spending any longer on the stairs than I needed to. The further I climbed, the further I had to come down if I found any trouble.

When I finally reached the seventh floor, I sneaked through the wire-glass door at the edge of the stairwell and into the hallway beyond. The hallway was completely dark and when I tried the light switch on the wall nothing happened. I withdrew my torch and cast the thin beam ahead of me. The corridor was longer than I had anticipated and the light from my torch didn't penetrate far. Stepping forwards, I felt like a lure on the end of a fishing hook, woefully unaware of the dangers that lurked up ahead.

So far as I could tell, the hallway was empty. I say so far as I could tell because in the end I didn't walk down it for too long. The second door I passed was numbered 72 and the third was 73. I backed up to the first door in the corridor and found that the numbers had fallen off. Even so, it was reasonable to assume I was finally where I needed to be.

There was a combination lock in the middle of the door, so named because it had a spring lock that would engage automatically when the door was closed as well as a deadbolt that could be turned for added security. I cast my torch beam down along the gap beside the doorframe and saw that the deadbolt was engaged. I wasn't overly concerned. On closer inspection, the locking mechanism looked as if it had been refitted quite recently and whoever carried out the job hadn't cared about doing it right. For once, I thought I might not even need my picks – it looked as if I'd be able simply to prise the lock out from its housing with one of my screwdrivers, leaving the bolt to be manipulated sideways.

Before I tackled the lock, I pulled my gloves from my trouser pocket and went through the familiar ritual of easing them onto my hands, wincing as the sheer plastic snagged my knuckles. Those same knuckles would be pleased to hear that, for once, I wasn't about to knock on the door. Truth was, this was perhaps the first time in my career as a burglar when I actually wanted the place I was breaking into to be occupied. Or rather, I thought I did, assuming I had the right apartment and the right man.

With those concerns at the forefront of my mind, I pressed my ear against the door to see if I could hear any movement. Yet again the tactic failed to tell me anything useful. I was beginning to think the old ear-against-the-door routine was something I should drop from my repertoire – like a hackneyed magic trick that had lost its lustre. But I've always had faith in an orderly approach and I'm kind of superstitious about ditching any of my moves. Who's to say the one time I don't try it, there isn't someone with a shotgun on the other side of the door?

With a shake of my head, I pulled my spectacles case from my pocket and thumbed open the clasps, removing the largest screwdriver I carried. The screwdriver had an enlarged handle and blade, ideal for popping the locking cylinder out of the misjudged hole that had been drilled for it. I wedged the blade behind the exposed fascia of the lock and leaned all my weight onto it, using both hands, twisting the blade a shade to increase the pressure. Moments later, I felt the lock begin to ease outwards. I readjusted my grip, aiming for a smoother pressure, and readied my left hand to grab for the lock when it slipped free. I missed. The cylinder ripped away from the flimsy wood sooner than I'd anticipated, ricocheted off my grasping palm and bounced and rattled, making a seemingly endless tinkling noise on the tiled floor below.

I froze, the noise sounding a hundred times louder than I would have liked. Carefully, I backed off from the door and checked both ways along the corridor, straining my ears to pick up on any sounds. The darkness of the hallway seemed to thrum all around me. My heart skipped overtime and adrenaline flushed through my body. I looked again at the door and then lowered my eye to the hole where the locking cylinder had been. Beyond the rod of the deadbolt, I could see only darkness.

I waited a few moments more and, when nothing altered, I returned my screwdriver to my spectacles case and removed a pair of pliers. I used them to grip the shaft of the deadbolt and with a sharp tug and a grunt I yanked the bolt out of its socket in the doorframe. The door wobbled, then swung inwards, away from the toes of my training shoes. I tucked my pliers and my spectacles case away, wiped the sweat from my forehead with the sleeve of my jacket, tightened my fingers around my torch and finally stepped inside.

The first thing I noticed upon entering was the music. It was coming from the rear of the apartment: a regular, percussive beat – some kind of euro drum 'n bass. I wasn't a fan but right then I'd never heard anything sweeter. The way I saw it, the music must have smothered the racket of the locking cylinder dropping onto the floor and there was a good chance it would mask any other slips I might make as I moved forwards.

There was a definite smell in the place. I couldn't identify what it was to begin with but then I began to think it was probably the carpet. The carpet was sticking to my feet and it looked mildewed when I cast the torch beam down in an attempt to spot any low tables or units I might trip upon. As it happened, I saw only a sagging futon and a portable television balanced on a cardboard box. A pair of baseball trainers had been discarded on the floor in front of me, and a denim jacket thrown onto the stained futon cushion.

Ahead of me was a hallway corridor and somewhere at the end of that hallway was the source of the music. I readied myself, channelling the adrenaline in my bloodstream as best I could and squeezing my left hand into a fist around the dimpled shaft of the torch. I rolled my neck and gritted my teeth. I wasn't the world's greatest brawler but, based on how things had gone for me lately, I was more than willing to give it a try.

At that moment, I heard a muted scream. The scream was pitched above the noise of the music and it sounded as if it belonged to a woman. It came again – a pleading kind of yelp, as though the woman couldn't open her mouth fully. Oh God, as though she was being asphyxiated.

To my shame, my first reaction was to eye the front door of the apartment. It was hanging open, inviting me to leave. Another shriek. I could sense desperation this time. All of a sudden, I realised I had to act. I could stop him; save a life. Maybe even clear my name.

I moved down the hallway, the music and the muffled whines growing ever louder. I paused for just an instant outside the door of the room the noises were coming from, aiming to get my mind and my body in some form of order. A greyish-blue light emanated from around the edges of the doorframe. It made sense, I thought. He'd need light to see what he was doing but he wouldn't want it to feel too clinical. Another scream, feral-sounding and shockingly close. I raised my torch above my head, like a club, braced my entire body and kicked out at the door.

I bundled inside, then span around, poised to strike. There was a panicked, sudden yell, followed by an ungodly shriek. My senses grappled for order. I saw a blur of flesh and sudden movement, followed by a blinding light. Instinctively, I covered my eyes with my forearm, then blinked madly until I could just make out a splayed figure on the bed and a naked woman clasping a sheet to her body over by the far wall. The woman was very pale – her skin almost ghostly.

"Paige?" I said, over the noise of the music coming from the stereo in the corner of the room.

"What the hell are you doing?" she asked, not unreasonably.

I looked from Paige to Bruno. Bruno still hadn't moved. He was lying flat on his back on the mattress, wearing only a pair of underpants. For a second, I couldn't understand why he was just lying there, then I finally got it. He was handcuffed to the metal headboard.

"Kinky," I said, and received a sneer.

If he was embarrassed, he didn't show it. He did look anxious though, which was understandable given the circumstances. He cast a look towards Paige, as if expecting her to do something about me, and it was then I took matters in hand.

"Come on," I said, "night's over."

I crossed the room and grabbed Paige by her bare forearm, intending to drag her from the room. She twisted her body in an awkward manner, fighting to loosen my grip. I came at her again and then, right when I thought I had her, she threw her legs out from under her body and plummeted to the floor, tucking herself into a ball inside the sheet. I looked down, wondering what to do next, then instinct took hold and I snatched her ankles and began dragging her towards the door.

"Hey!" she screamed, as the back of her head hit the floor and her eyes threatened to crawl out of their sockets. She kicked her legs and twisted her body. I didn't care.

"Get the hell off me. What the hell are you doing? Stop, god-damn it."

I didn't stop. I kept on dragging her across the carpet, then out through the doorway into the hall, getting halfway around the corner before she reached for the varnished doorframe. She pulled against me and began to flail her legs more violently. I struggled for a while, imagining she'd relent, but I was underestimating her. Without warning, I dropped her legs, then lunged for her wrists. I prised her hands away from the doorframe, snagging her nails, then lifted her to her feet and manhandled her through into the lounge.

I gave her a final shove and she stumbled, falling flat on her face. She turned, clutching the sheet to her body.

"You said you didn't know him," I said, looking down over her.

Paige glared at me, violence in her large eyes.

"You do know he killed a woman, I suppose."

Something flickered across her face. Confusion, maybe.

"Catherine Ames. Did you know her?" There was no kind of a response. "Christ, I'm not sure why I'm even asking, you'd only lie. Here, get dressed."

I threw her the denim jacket and the baseball trainers. To begin with, she didn't move. Maybe she thought I was bluffing.

"Where are the rest of your clothes?"

Paige looked at me for a long minute. Eventually, she jerked her chin towards the bedroom. Her face was colourless, her jaw set hard. I could see the sharp outline of her clavicle through her skin.

"Wait here," I told her, and headed back down the hallway.

The stereo was still blaring when I entered the bedroom and I yanked the power cable out from the wall. The music ceased abruptly. I cast my eyes around the room, spying a skirt, a bra and a blouse towards the foot of the bed. There was also a pair of faded, striped knickers near Bruno's feet. I decided she could go without, then briefly locked eyes with Bruno, who still hadn't moved.

"Be back soon," I said. "Don't go anywhere."

Paige didn't take long to put her clothes on. Her movements were rushed and awkward, mainly because she'd worked herself into such a rage. I suppose I should tell you that I turned my back while she dressed but the truth is I looked. At the time, I told myself I couldn't be sure she wouldn't grab something and smack me over the back of my head if I was dumb enough to turn away. But if I'm honest, I think it also had something to do with wanting to make her feel as uncomfortable as possible. If that was my intent, I'm not sure it worked. Despite her fury, she had the presence of mind to put on her skirt beneath the sheet and to slip her blouse over her head before she let the sheet drop to the floor.

Paige gave me a spiteful look, loaded with bile. "You really expect me to leave? It's the middle of the damn night."

"You want me to call you a taxi?"

She held my eyes, as if waiting for me to relent. I wasn't in the mood. Yes, it was a risk letting her go – she might raise the alarm or even return with some form of weapon once she'd had the opportunity to think about it. And even though I was angry with her, I knew it wasn't entirely safe to send her out into the banlieue on her own. But then again, what else could I do? I couldn't talk to Bruno freely if she was in the room with us – there'd be too many interruptions. I had nothing to tie her up with and even if I locked her in the bathroom, there was nothing to say she wouldn't scream the place down. And considering I'd seen one woman dead from asphyxiation already, I wasn't all that eager to experiment with a gag.

And hell, the dead woman was really the point here. If she'd been found by now, it would have been in my apartment, and my name would be the only one the police would be looking for in connection with her death.

Paige was still watching me, as if sensing I was thinking the situation through. I didn't want to give her the impression she had any angles left to work. Hurriedly, I pulled a fifty euro note from my trouser pocket, then seized her by the shoulders, turned her in the direction of the front door and forced her all the way through. Once she was outside in the darkened hallway, I pressed the money into her hand.

"I'm shutting this door," I said. "And you'd better go. I'm not kidding about the dead woman, Paige. Really. Bruno's put my head in a noose and I intend to find out why. Take a cab back to the bookshop. And don't tell anyone I'm here. I'm not above killing people myself – not if it'll save my own neck."

I couldn't tell if she bought my last line or not and I had no way to make sure. All I could do was give her a final shove in the direction of the stairwell and shut the door behind her. I crossed the room and grabbed the edge of the futon, then dragged it all the way over until it was flush against the door. I stood still for a moment and sucked in some deep breaths, willing myself to focus. Bruno was waiting, silent in the next room, and I was ready for some answers.

SIXTEEN

As I entered the bedroom, I tossed the sheet Paige had discarded over Bruno's body. We'd need to talk for a while and I didn't relish the idea of doing that while he was virtually naked. Bruno didn't seem to care either way. Hats off to the guy – even hand-cuffed to his bed in a state of undress with a seriously ticked-off burglar watching over him, he still had the nerve to grin at me like he was holding all the aces. I guess that had a lot to do with Paige. He knew I'd been attracted to her and he must have felt pretty smug.

That changed when I saw the keys for the handcuffs on the floor beside the bed. There were two identical keys, both small, threaded onto a flimsy keyring. I picked them up and twirled them before my eyes, acting as if they intrigued me greatly. Then I opened my jacket and dropped the keys into my inside pocket. Bruno cocked his head and gave me a sceptical look.

"What?" I asked. "You think that's for show? I'll leave you like this, believe me."

He gave me one of his shrugs.

"It doesn't bother you?"

He added a pout.

"Yeah, you're a regular Houdini."

I turned and looked towards the corner of the room, where a straight-backed chair was positioned. I lifted the chair and tipped the bundle of clothes that were resting on it onto the floor. I carried the chair over to the side of the bed, sat down and put my feet on the edge of the mattress beside Bruno's shoulders.

"So. Shall we talk?"

He wet his lips. "I want to sleep with the girl you like."

"She's gone."

"Maybe she will come back."

"With the police, you mean? With reinforcements?" I shook my head. "She's not the type."

Suddenly, Bruno bounced up from the mattress, pivoting at his hips and lashing out at me with his legs, trying to connect with the side of my head. Instinctively, I rocked back on the chair so that his feet brushed off my chin. My skull and shoulders smacked into the bedroom wall. I put my hand to the floor, fighting for my balance, then looked up to see Bruno's body twisted on the bed, his hairy legs hanging over the side of the mattress. Before he could move again, I leapt into the air and dropped my elbow onto his back, forcing all of my weight down onto his contorted wrists. He yelled, sounding panicked.

"Did they break? I'll break them, you shit."

He tried to swing his body back around but I blocked him with my hip, then used both my hands to push down hard on his shoulder blades. I watched his right wrist bend unnaturally around the headboard railing it was attached to. Bruno screamed, though I still didn't think I'd broken anything. The skin near the handcuff on his wrist was pinched and very pale. I backed off, then snatched his ankles and threw his legs onto the bed. I set the chair on its feet again and sat myself down. I waited for him to compose himself.

"All I want is to talk," I told him. "Just answer my questions and that's it."

Bruno was staring wide-eyed at the ceiling, sucking in lungfuls of air. He rested his head in the crook of his armpit while his bare chest rose and fell in a fitful way. I wasn't sure how much his wrists hurt. If it was me, I knew the idea of the bones breaking would be playing over and over in my mind. He looked young now, much younger than me. I began to think he really was scared, and although that was useful it was also unsettling. I wasn't the kind of person to do that to people. At least, I didn't think I was.

"Breathe easy," I told him. "Stay calm. I'm not going to hurt you if you co-operate."

He rocked his head to the side and looked at me from over the curve of his bicep. I made my face as open as I possibly could. In any other circumstances, what I'd just said would be plain ridiculous. Bruno was far more powerfully built than me, and in a straight fight there would have been only one winner.

"I'm serious. Believe me?"

Bruno's eyes became plaintive. His cheeks flushed and I noticed a sweaty sheen on his skin. After a pause, he nodded.

"Good," I said. "So we just need to talk. And you're willing to do that, right?"

"Talk about Paige?" he asked, voice catching.

"What?"

He swallowed, the sinews in his neck standing out like cords. "That is why you are here, yes?"

"God no. I had no idea about that. She told me she didn't know who you were."

He smiled thinly, as though it didn't surprise him to hear it.

"How long have you two . . ."

"A month."

"Huh." I raised my eyebrows. "So at the end of the reading, you were what, pulling my chain?"

He shrugged, and the handcuffs rattled against the metal struts on the headboard. "I could see you liked her."

"I guess she's attractive."

"You guess." He smirked. "Me also. She knows it, yes? You can see it in her."

"She's confident, sure."

"She is good, you know?"

He winked and I shook my head as if I couldn't care less. I'd let us get way off track already. Perhaps it was because it was so late at night. There was a kind of background tiredness in my head, like a clinging mist. It was gumming up my thinking, making me sluggish. I needed to get down to it.

"I want to talk about Catherine Ames. Did you kill her, Bruno?"

Bruno's reaction was startling, as if someone had hit the pause button in his brain. His face went slack and his pupils became dark circles. I clicked my fingers until he refocused and stared at me, his forehead crinkled, eyes full of suspicion.

"She is dead?"

"Very."

He blinked, then swallowed. This time I must have convinced him. His jaw dropped and he shook his head from side to side, as though disorientated.

"How?"

"She was tied to a chair and suffocated."

Bruno began to shake his head more vigorously, as if trying to erase the image I'd put in his mind. Without a word, he lifted his arms and began to wriggle backwards on the bed, arranging himself in a more upright position. It still didn't look comfortable but it was a little more dignified. I wasn't sure how to read him. Either he really hadn't known or he'd been rehearsing what his reaction should be. I found myself wishing, not for the first time, that I was more like the characters in my novels – the kind that always know when a suspect is lying.

"When did she die?" he asked.

"Yesterday. The afternoon, I think. Where were you then?"

He stared at me, looking puzzled still. "At work."

"At the bank?"

He whistled. "How do you know this?"

"Never mind. Were you there all day?"

"Yes."

"What about a lunch hour?"

"There is a park nearby. I meet Paige."

"Convenient."

"It is true." He nodded, as if that proved everything.

"I didn't see you."

"In the park?"

"The bank. I was there around four-thirty. You weren't at any of the service desks."

"Because it is not where I work."

I paused for a moment, then let it drop. It wasn't something worth getting caught up in. These were questions the police might ask Bruno if they ever connected him to the murder. If they weren't convinced by what he told them, they'd have the means to investigate his story. For my sake, I needed to be sure they couldn't connect Bruno to me.

"Tell me about Catherine's apartment in the Marais," I said. "The one you had us break into."

His face tangled. "The apartment?"

"What, you're going to tell me you've forgotten about it?"

He blinked again, waiting for me to continue.

"You told me it was your place," I prompted.

"I lied."

"No kidding. But how did you find out about it? You'd been there before, correct?"

Bruno sucked on his lips, as if weighing his response. "Yes."

"I thought as much. That's how the concierge recognised you, and how you knew about the alarm code and where the coffee was kept. It's also how you knew the apartment was empty."

He nodded, warily.

"But how did you know Catherine?"

Bruno glanced down at his washboard stomach, as if it contained the answer.

"She was a girlfriend?"

He screwed up his face.

"A mistress then?"

"Hey," he said, as though offended.

"Well, what? You tell me, Bruno. I'm the one in the dark here."

"I sleep with her. Twice only."

"But she was what, fifty?"

"I do not know. Why does it matter?"

"Doesn't matter to me. Could maybe matter to Paige, I suppose."

He gave me an incredulous look, and I realised how misguided my threat was. They weren't in the middle of a romance, then.

"Go back a stage," I said. "You met at the bank, right?"

He screwed up his face, as though now he really was suspicious that I knew so much.

"I found out that Catherine had an account there," I explained, with a wave of my hand.

"How?"

I shook my head. I wasn't here to answer his questions and I wasn't eager to tell him more than he already knew. I didn't owe him anything, least of all a full explanation. And besides, it could be dangerous to join all the dots for him. Who was to say he wouldn't invent a few steps and give the police everything they needed to hang the killing on me? They already had the body in my apartment, once they got round to finding it.

"I want to know about the painting."

He held my eye, unwilling to commit just yet.

"Come on Bruno. I'm talking about the painting you stole, after I left you that night."

He still didn't say anything. I was surprised. He must have known by now that I'd put it together.

"Listen, you took it away in your backpack, right? Then you sold it to the gallery across from the bank."

"You have been following me?" he asked, squinting.

"No, as it happens. But the fact is I need to know about the painting, Bruno. I need to know why you stole it."

He blew air through his lips, as if he wasn't sure where to start. Before speaking again, he flicked his cuffed hands above his head, almost like he was wafting the issue away.

"For money," he said, gesturing with his head at the room we were in, as if that was answer enough.

"But you have a bank job. It must pay okay."

"Okay, yes. But I need a lot of money."

"You have debts?"

"Many."

"Who to?"

He chewed his lip for a moment.

"Just tell me, Bruno."

"There is a man who comes here, to Clichy. He will give you money, mais, it is expensive, yes?"

"You're saying he's a loan-shark?"

He nodded.

"Okay," I said, slowly. "And you stole the painting for money,

I get that. But what made you think it was worth anything? There were a lot of paintings in that apartment. Why take that one in particular?"

He smiled weakly, hitched his broad shoulders. "She told me, it is worth a lot of money. That is why it was on the wall, yes? The other paintings, she did them, but this one, it was different."

"In what way?"

"I do not know. But it was what she said."

"How much did you get for it?"

He smiled glumly. "Two thousand euros only."

"You expected more?"

He shrugged.

"How much more?"

"A lot, maybe. She had money, yes? It is why I knew her. At the bank, we have a vault. It is where I work."

"A vault. And Catherine kept some things inside it?"

"Of course."

"Like?"

"I do not know."

"Oh come on. You're telling me you didn't look?"

"I cannot," he said, insistent now. "Inside the vault, there are boxes, all locked. The customer, they sign a paper form and I let them into the vault. Then I take their box to a private room. They use a card to get inside."

"You mean like a swipe card?" I asked, gesturing with my hand as though I was passing a credit card through an electronic reader. "The kind with a magnetic strip?"

"Yes. I cannot see what is in the box."

"What did you think might be there?"

He stuck out his bottom lip. "I do not know. Money, maybe. It did not matter. I could not take anything."

"But the painting was different?"

"I think so."

"Because you had me."

Bruno held my eye, then nodded. "I did not have a key. Paige, she talked about your book and I thought maybe you could help me."

"Why didn't you just tell me the truth?"

He peered at me through narrowed eyes. "Would you have done it?"

"Perhaps. I don't know. I shouldn't have helped you as it was."

"But you did."

I let that one go. It didn't feel like a time to dwell on past mistakes.

"Tell me, how did you know the apartment would be empty?"

His face brightened, as though I'd asked him an easy question at last. "Catherine worked near Orléans, always from Monday until Thursday. On Fridays, she come to Paris for the weekend."

"What is it she did?"

"I do not know. She did not say."

I paused and looked about the room. The alarm clock on the floor near my feet read almost three in the morning. I had the feeling there was more I could find out but I wasn't sure how. The way I saw it, Bruno had no idea about the plans I'd found hidden inside the painting. When Catherine had told him the painting was valuable, he'd assumed it was because of the work itself, not what the painting had contained. And that's why he'd sold it to the gallery on Rue Quincampoix.

For a moment, I considered telling him about the plans to see if he could shed any light on them, but I didn't think it was likely. If Catherine hadn't told him what her profession happened to be, she'd hardly have told him something like that. And besides, keeping him in the dark might be more useful to me than telling him everything just now.

"Let me go?" Bruno asked, interrupting my thoughts and rattling the handcuffs.

I peered at him. "That depends. Where's the money?"

"Money?" He blinked.

"The two thousand euros you got for the painting. Where is it?"

Bruno began to look pale. "I need it."

"I get that, Bruno. In fact, I get the impression you need it pretty bad. The thing is, I could do with your help at some point in the next few days and I figure you might need some motivation. So what I'm going to do is I'm going to hold onto your money, and if you come through for me, I'll give it back to you."

"No," he said, sounding scandalised.

"Listen, it's going to happen. So either you can tell me where it is and save us both a lot of trouble or I can search until I find it. But I'm not leaving without the money."

"I do not have it."

"You're lying."

"It's the truth."

I sighed and got up from my chair. I stood with my hands on my hips and scanned the room. There were no obvious cubby-holes and certainly no safe. The pile of clothes I'd upended on the floor caught my eye and I crossed to them and went through all the pockets I could find. The bundle of notes was in the back pocket of the third pair of trousers I tried. I raised my eyebrows and gave Bruno a weary look.

"Surprise," I said.

He closed his eyes and shook his head, cursing his misfortune. I pocketed the money and made a clucking noise with my tongue.

"You leave me in something of a dilemma here, Bruno. I want to release you from those handcuffs, I really do, but how can I trust you now? I mean, what's to say you won't try and get this money back from me in an unpleasant way?" I scratched my head. "On the other hand, I might need your help and you won't be much use to me stuck here. So I wonder, what should I do?"

Bruno didn't respond. I guess he knew there was nothing he could say. It was all down to me now – down to how compassionate I was feeling. I have to say the cooling body in my apartment was making me feel less sorry for the guy that I might normally.

"Tell you what," I said. "I'll undo one hand and we'll see how you behave. If you keep hold of that railing, I'll be more inclined to trust you."

I met Bruno's eyes and held them, making sure he understood that I was serious. Then, when I felt he was ready to do as I said, I fished the handcuff keys out from my pocket and approached the edge of the bed. I checked once more on his position, making sure he wasn't about to try to kick me again or even bite me for that matter, then I flexed my arms, focused on the handcuff around his right wrist and inserted the tiny key into the lock.

"Stay still," I reminded him.

Bruno gripped hard on the railing, as if to prove that I could trust him. Very carefully, I turned the key. The handcuff popped open and I let it hang against Bruno's wrist. I stepped backwards, away from the bed, and looked down over him.

"Very good," I told him. "I'm impressed. Now, the bad news."

As Bruno watched, I pocketed the keys, then removed my spectacles case and pulled out the smallest rake I carried.

"You remember what one of these is, right? Well, if you're calm about it and you take your time, you'll be able to pop the lock on that second handcuff no trouble at all. But remember Catherine's apartment, okay? If you rush it, if you hurry to get after me, it won't work. I'm not going to hand you the keys; that would be too easy. But I will give you this rake, just so long as you keep your right hand where it is until I'm out of this room. Agreed?"

Bruno glared at me, real loathing in his eyes. His fingers gripped and regripped the railing, knuckles whitening.

"Hey, relax," I told him. "It'll work. Just don't drop it, that's all. And make sure you go to the bank as normal tomorrow. I'll be in touch and you'll get your money back. Okay?"

I stepped forwards and carefully placed the rake on Bruno's chest, keeping a watchful eye on his movements.

"I'm going to leave now," I said. "And hey, keep your chin up, protégé. Think of this as a free tutorial."

SEVENTEEN

My next move was a complete gamble and, to be honest, I was far from sure about it.

Let me tell you, I have a curious relationship with uncertainty. The writer in me fights it. I like to move my characters around in the scenes I devise for them, having them say what I need them to say and do what I need them to do. Sometimes, they'll surprise me and sure, when that happens it can be a good thing. The book I'm writing heads off in a direction I hadn't anticipated and I'm forced to think in new ways, hopefully keeping the story fresh. But I still need an overall scheme of who is going to wind up dead, who is going to be my killer and just how exactly Faulks is going to get away with the girl and the goods. I can handle some unknowns, a few grey areas for my characters to float around in, but I can't allow the big picture to become confused.

My thieving is different. Yes, I take a methodical approach to every break-in I commit, but I never know for sure what I'm going to find on the other side of any door I might choose to open. And, confession time, I kind of like it. What's the point in breaking some rules and, okay, some laws, if you don't get a buzz out of it? Some of the best moments of my life have been spent in other people's homes, uncovering things I hadn't expected to find. Believe me, it's a wonderful feeling plunging your hand into a sock drawer and coming up with a fistful of jewels. The downside is there's no overall scheme. I have a plan, and sometimes my plan might be detailed, but I'm not the one calling the shots. Anything can happen. I might blunder in on an ex-wrestler with a torture dungeon in his basement or a woman with a can of mace and a speed-dial connection to the local vigilante association. I can't control what the outcome of my thieving might be and the reality is it's just a small step from getting a thrill out of the unknown to receiving a sizeable prison term.

Factor in a dead woman, especially a dead woman who happens to be decomposing in your apartment, and the stakes just get higher. And here I was, long after four in the morning, facing up to the prospect of breaking back into that dead woman's home, without any idea if her body had been found just yet and, if it had, whether the authorities had sent anyone to watch her place.

It didn't look as if Catherine's building was under surveillance. There were no police cars parked in front of the lighted entrance and no plain-clothed detectives taking statements from the night concierge. Neither were there any signs of life in Catherine's apartment. The picture window at the front of her living room was in darkness and the curtains still hadn't been drawn.

The irony of being stood outside her apartment and planning to break in for a third time was not lost on me. Never return to the scene of the crime, right? Well, I very much doubt the originator of that piece of advice could have conceived of a burglar who would be dumb enough to ignore him not once, but twice.

At least there was one thing going in my favour – I still had the hotel room booked in my name and, by happy coincidence, I didn't even have to check out until noon. Yes, the front door to the hotel was locked and the handwritten French-English sign in the glass panel informed me that guests returning after midnight should ring the bell, but I couldn't see the sense in waking someone when I didn't need to. And I certainly didn't like the idea of drawing attention to myself just hours before a murder investigation might take hold of the building next door.

Pressing my face against the glass, I cupped my hands around my eyes to block out the glare from the street lamp over my shoulder. The hotel foyer looked deserted. It still looked that way when I was walking through it just a few minutes later, with my gloves on my hands and my pick and my micro screwdriver gripped in my jacket pocket. I stepped behind the reception desk and removed my room key from its numbered peg, for appearance's sake if nothing else, and then I crossed to the stairs and began climbing. If anyone challenged me, I would say that the front door had been unlocked when I tried the handle but I seriously doubted I'd need an excuse. The place was so quiet I could have heard a pin drop, if only there'd been somebody nearby to drop a pin in the first place.

I didn't visit my room, preferring to head straight for the roof. Once there, I glanced briefly at the yellow lighted windows I could see spread out across the city, drawing my eye towards the twinkling apex of the Eiffel Tower. Soon it would be five o'clock, and the tower would break into its hourly light display. Not many people would see it, I didn't think. Perhaps some clubbers staggering home from a late-night bar, or one or two of the homeless people who sheltered together in clusters of brightly coloured tents beside the River Seine. Hell, maybe even the odd burglar scaling a mansard roof somewhere else in the Marais.

Returning my focus to the task at hand, I popped my torch into my mouth and picked my way through the padlock on the rooftop door to the apartment building, then tiptoed down the concrete internal stairs. This time I didn't have a suitcase with me and I was concentrating pretty hard, so I had no trouble negotiating my way to the correct floor. My only real obstacle came when I readied myself to open the door to the corridor I was interested in. I couldn't hear anything, but I was still concerned that the area might be crawling with police. As it turned out, when the sensor light blinked on the corridor wasn't crawling with anything, except maybe carpet mites, and the relief I felt was enormous.

There was nothing to suggest that anyone was inside Catherine's apartment, and when I carefully tried the door handle I found it was locked in the same way I'd left it. An instant later my picks came into play once again, my tongue did its hanging-out-of-my-mouth routine and my two arthritic knuckles thanked me profusely for not involving them in my latest criminal escapade. Soon after, I was stepping across the darkened threshold and dashing for the alarm control panel in an attempt to cancel the arming blips before the occupants of the apartment across the way began to wonder what their neighbour was doing coming home at such an unusual time of the morning.

Once the alarm was silenced, I dropped my shoulders and released the breath I'd been holding onto. Then I spread my hands in my gloves and listened to the sound of the plastic crinkling. My eyes were becoming used to the darkness of the living room ahead of me and I was acutely aware of the murmurs the apartment was emitting – the noise of the fridge-freezer, the kitchen radio on standby, the hot water settling in the pipes – all of it registering as a background whirr in my ears, much like my laptop when I'm writing.

There were a pair of thin, gauzy curtains either side of the picture window at the front of the living room and even though they wouldn't block out much light, I drew them before turning on the main bulb. It seemed as though nothing had altered from my previous visit. There were the same paintings around the edge of the room and the same artist equipment was still scattered across the pasting table positioned between the two easels. I moved into the bedroom and found that nothing had changed there either. I closed the slatted blinds and turned on one of the bedside lamps. It must have been wired into the picture lamp up on the wall because that came on too, as if demanding that I acknowledge the spot where the painting of Montmartre used to hang.

I tightened my left hand into a fist, cracking my knuckles, and took a moment to compose my thoughts. I'd allow myself an hour. If I hadn't found anything by then, it was unlikely I'd ever find what I was looking for. Plus, I could be on my way before six, which would minimise my chances of bumping into any of the building's other residents when I left.

My self-imposed time limit gave me focus but it also made me acutely aware of the odds that were stacked against me. I was looking for something that might not be in the apartment in the first place and even if it was there, it could be hidden just about anywhere. An hour might sound like ample time but, let me tell you, when you're hunting in a methodical way, trying not to leave any signs of your presence, and all the while you're aware the police might show up at any moment, it's really not long at all.

Only eighteen months before, I'd found myself facing up to a similar task, searching a series of locations for three monkey figurines. Tough as that had been, I would have happily swapped assignments now because although they were small, the figurines were easier to find than what I was currently searching for. I'd also had a heads-up as to where two of figurines should have been located, but I had no such luck here. I was going to have to rely on my instincts and I was beginning to feel the pressure.

One fruitless hour later, after checking every single room and item of furniture and crevice I could think of, I broke my most sacred rule and gave myself an extra ten minutes. And boy, was I glad I did. Because as soon as I'd shaken off my frustration and my growing sense of doom and looked at the scene in front of me afresh, I locked onto something I'd been dumb enough to pass over the first time and knew right away it was where the item I was looking for had to be stashed. It was, and I allowed myself a moment to smile and shake my head at my own thick-headedness before reaching for the accordion folder of documents below Catherine's dressing table and removing the driving licence I'd found during my previous visit. Then I made like a peculiarly neat whirlwind and ensured that everything was back as it should have been before arming the alarm for what I sincerely hoped was the very last time and locking the front door to the apartment behind me with my picks.

I retraced my route to the roof, where I found that a dim, grey morning light had begun to form, and then I headed back down through the hotel. As I reached the second floor, I paused, debating whether to let myself into my room to snatch a few hours' sleep. In the end, I did go inside, but only to collect my empty suitcase from the wardrobe. It turned out to be a smart move because when I got downstairs I discovered that Quasimodo was just beginning his shift and I was able to return my key to him and heft my suitcase in a cheerless way, like a traveller doomed to an early-morning flight. Afterwards, I made my way to the nearest métro station, where I boarded a carriage with the first commuters of the day and did my very best to look like yet another respectable member of society.

EIGHTEEN

The bank was full of smoke. Alarms rang out in a piercing wail and sprinklers scattered water from the ceiling. Faulks was drenched to the skin, his clothes clinging to his body like webbing. He glanced up, letting the water flush the sting of the smoke from his eyes. Towards the front of the building, he could just see the glow of the green emergency exit lamps. Staff and security guards were fleeing, their heads bowed and their eyes screwed tight against the smoke and water. Faulks let them go, moving with determination towards the rear of the bank.

The secure area was deserted. Faulks turned and threw two more smoke bombs into the atrium behind him. Then he faced up to the steel gate and entered the override code he'd obtained from his hack into the computer system. Beyond the gate were four vaults. He moved immediately to the second one, inserted the master key and input the combination. The door dropped on its hinges and Faulks heaved on the outside lever until the mighty thing swung open and he was able to step inside.

Powerful overhead lights flicked on, illuminating the vault. Faulks saw bag after bag of cash – many millions of American dollars. There was too much for him to carry but he unzipped his canvas holdall and began to fill it as best he could. He had two bags stashed when he heard the high-pitched whine above the noise of the fire alarm system for the first time. The noise was plaintive-sounding, as if the vault regretted what it was about to do. Faulks realised too late: there was a back-up he hadn't thought of. The door began to swing inwards, gathering speed, and then it slammed closed with a definitive thud. Faulks swore. The vault was airtight. He got up from his crouched position and began to search for an internal safety catch. He couldn't find one. Chances were there wasn't one to find. Best guess, he had maybe twenty minutes before his air ran out.

Faulks banged on the door. He struck hard with his open palm, then drummed his fists. His movements became frantic and his banging louder, more insistent. It grew louder still and then there was a woman's voice from the other side of the door. "Charlie," the woman was saying. "Charlie..."

I looked up from my laptop, frowning. I blinked at the wall on the opposite side of my room, trying to pull myself out of the scene I'd been creating and make sense of what my fingers had just typed. I knew I was drowsy but something felt odd. Then I came round, and realised the banging was somebody knocking on the door to my hotel room.

"Charlie," Victoria said again. "It's me. Are you in there?"

Shakily, I got to my feet and crossed the room, rubbing my eyes with the heels of my palms. I had no need to put on a robe – I was still wearing the same clothes I'd had on the previous day. Originally, I'd planned to sleep when I got back from Catherine Ames' apartment, but I'd found I was too strung-out to relax, so I'd picked up my laptop and started writing instead. The scene in the bank had been surprisingly vivid in my mind, possibly because I was so tired that I'd been writing in an almost trance-like way, and in truth I was a little annoyed to be interrupted.

I yawned as I opened the door, fully prepared to ask Victoria to come back later. I didn't get the chance. She brushed past me into my room, heading straight for the television set.

"Thank God you're here," she said. "Have you seen the news?"

"What time is it?" I asked, stretching my arms above my head and rising up onto the balls of my feet.

"Around eight," Victoria replied, in a distracted way. She was pointing the television remote at the screen, thumbing the buttons.

"I haven't been back long then." I yawned again. "What's going on?"

A television image appeared, ballooning out from the centre of the screen, and Victoria pointed at some grainy footage of a ferry blockade.

"It's after this."

"What is?"

Victoria gave me an anxious look. "In a minute," she said.

A minute later, I was staring at myself. No, that's not quite true – I was staring at my author image, the one of the catalogue model in the dinner jacket. I heard my real name, though, and then I saw footage of the outside of my apartment building. The main entrance was sealed off with yellow crime scene tape and it was guarded by two uniformed officers with their hands behind their backs.

"What's being said?" I asked Victoria, aware that her French was a good deal better than mine.

"They found the body. They're looking for you in connection with it."

She turned to me and there was concern in her eyes.

"Anything else?" I asked, trying to keep my voice even.

"It's just a quick report. That banner down the bottom of the screen says 'Latest News'."

I watched as the banner disappeared and the newscast cut back to a female presenter with a sombre expression. Victoria killed the sound.

"So what now?"

I shrugged and yanked on the cotton material of the T-shirt I was wearing. "I guess I'd better not wear my tux today."

"Seriously. Don't you think you should hand yourself in?"

I ran my hand over my face. "Not at this rate," I mumbled. "They'd only think I was an impostor."

Victoria shook her head and sighed dramatically. She placed a hand on her hip, above the waistline of the dark blue jeans she had on. "Charlie, be sensible. It's not going to take them long to find out that isn't how you really look."

"You think? I'm not sure I left any photos in my apartment."

"Wake up. They only need to speak to your neighbours or the concierge at your building. Once one or two of them start saying it's not you, they'll know something's wrong."

"Oh. I guess." I covered my mouth with my hand, but the yawn I'd been anticipating failed to materialise. "Or maybe they'll think the guy who's been living in the apartment is someone completely different. Maybe they'll think he's assumed my identity."

Victoria looked at me as if I was mad.

"Could happen."

She exhaled and dropped her shoulders. "So you're not going to talk to them?"

"Are you kidding? To even try and clear my name I'd probably have to confess to breaking into Catherine's apartment, and where does that leave me? All I can give them at the moment is Bruno's name and I can't see that going very far."

"Did you find him last night?"

I nodded, then gestured for Victoria to sit down on the bed. I crossed my arms and rested my backside against a wooden cabinet. After a moment's thought, I reached into the mini-fridge to my side and removed a bottle of Perrier. I broke the seal on the lid and felt a puff of carbon dioxide against my fingers. I offered the bottle to Victoria but she declined and so I took a mouthful of the chill, fizzy water and swallowed it down before continuing.

"I'm pretty sure he isn't the killer," I told her, wiping my lips with the back of my hand. "He didn't seem to know Catherine was dead and I happened to believe him."

She turned up her nose. It wasn't a bad nose, as it happened. "Why?"

"Just a hunch."

Victoria gave me a withering look.

"Sorry," I said, and took another mouthful of water. "The truth is he was at work when she must have been killed. At least, I think he was."

"You think?"

"I only have his word for it. He says he was at the bank all day. Apart from his lunch hour."

"Well, there you go then."

"He met Paige."

I gave Victoria a helpless smile. She raised her fingertips to her temple and circled them, as if trying to ease a headache.

"Wait just a minute. Are you talking about the girl from the bookshop?"

"The one and same."

"Well that's a bit convenient, don't you think?"

I waited. I could almost see the thoughts turning over in Victoria's mind.

"Hang on, didn't you tell me she had no idea who Bruno was?"

"I did."

"But –"

"But she was there last night – when I got to Bruno's place. They're an item, apparently."

"Oh," she said, her lips still forming the shape of the word long after she'd finished pronouncing it. "I thought maybe you and her were . . ."

I wagged my finger. "Truth is, she's a little too wild for me."

"Wild?"

"She had Bruno all tied up. Kinky stuff. He was handcuffed to his bed, which is how come I was able to make him talk."

"She had him handcuffed? *And* she's his alibi?"

I set the Perrier down and held up a hand. "Listen, I think I know where you're going with this."

"Well, duh, it's pretty obvious. Catherine's wrists were tied to the back of a chair when she was suffocated. Bruno and Paige are into restraints. Same thing."

"Catherine wasn't naked and smeared in baby oil, though."

Victoria screwed up her face. "Oh come on, Charlie. What more do you want?"

I got up from the cabinet I was resting against and crossed to the window. "Motive, opportunity, maybe just the vaguest shred of proof."

"Humph."

"Now that's insightful."

Victoria scowled at me and crossed her arms in front of her chest. I took a moment to pull back the net curtain in my window and peer out over the side alley that ran beneath my room. There was nobody loitering suspiciously, not even a cat. All I could see was the gutter pipe of the building opposite and a moped that had been crudely chained to its base.

Victoria took a deep, audible breath and I turned around to catch sight of her shoulders jerking upwards. The collar of the plaid blouse she was wearing grazed the underside of her chin. She looked at me sideways and I caught a glimmer in her eye.

"What if I could give you a time of death?"

"That would be wonderful. But I don't happen to have my autopsy table with me. Or the body."

Victoria shook her head impatiently. "Pass me your laptop."

I returned to the cabinet I'd been resting against and handed the laptop to her, then watched as she smoothed her fingers over the track pad and clicked on an icon.

"What are you doing?"

"The message you were left," she said, distractedly. "It was typed as a new document in your word processor. Well, document properties should tell us when the document was created, so . . . bingo!"

"Go on."

"New Document 1 was first saved at 14.13 yesterday afternoon."

"Bloody hell."

"Impressed?"

"I am," I said, snatching the laptop from Victoria's hands and reading the information for myself. "I think my investigative skills have just been taken to an unprecedented level."

She grinned. "So that's lunchtime, give or take a half-hour. And it doesn't stop there, Charlie. I also have some ideas about the documents you found in the back of the painting. Hey, are you listening to me?"

"Sorry," I said, glancing up from the computer screen. "I was just thinking – maybe I've been a bit dim with this laptop. It could have the killer's fingerprints on it."

"Have you touched the keys?"

"Only a few billion times. But if you mean have I touched them since I found the message, I'm afraid the answer's yes."

"There still might be fingerprints, I suppose."

"I'm no expert, but I guess it would be hard to pull a distinct print off the keys when they're so smeared with my own finger marks."

Victoria winced, as though conceding the point. "You know what, the killer probably wore gloves anyway. But it is a possibility, no matter how slight. So I really think you should close the laptop and not use it for a while. And listen to my other brain-wave."

I met her eyes, and set the laptop down to my side. "If you're telling me not to write for a few days, this must be good."

"Well," she said, "you know the piece of paper with the six-digit codes written on it? I was thinking, they look like bank sort-codes to me."

Victoria gave me an eager smile, as though she'd just solved a particularly difficult anagram. I chewed on my bottom lip.

"You think?"

"Absolutely."

I rolled my lip between my teeth, squeezing the blood from it. "But do French banks even use sort-codes?"

A flash of doubt passed across Victoria's face. "I assume so."

I wrinkled my nose, unconvinced. "Listen, don't get me wrong," I said. "It could be you're onto something. But then again, the French might use a different coding system altogether."

"It's something to consider, though, right?"

"Sure. But where does it get us? If they are sort-codes, does that mean the plans relate to a bank job?"

"Makes sense to me."

"Does it? I think it might be the craziest thing I ever heard."

Victoria frowned.

"Not crazy on its own terms," I said, showing her my palms. "But you have to admit – it's stretching credibility a bit far. I mean, here I am working on a book about a bank heist and I just happen to get caught up in one in real life? It's kind of far-fetched."

"Not impossible, though."

"It would have to be the mother of all coincidences."

"But banks *are* linked into this thing, Charlie. Bruno works in one, for starters."

I nodded and pressed my fingertips together, wondering whether to say anything more.

"What?"

"You don't know the half of it," I told her. "The reason Bruno knew Catherine was because he works as a guard at her bank branch. She kept some valuables in the bank's vault."

"Well, there you go."

"I don't know, Vic."

"Come on. It's logical. It might be outlandish, given the circumstances, but banks are all over this thing."

"Meaning, what? Catherine was the mastermind behind a series of planned bank heists at the exact same banks that those sort-codes relate to, assuming they even are sort-codes?"

"Perhaps."

"And the blueprints and the electrical circuits and the photographs are the extent of this great master plan to rob six banks in the centre of Paris? And Pierre's client knows all about it, which is how come I was hired, and at least one other person knows about it, possibly Bruno and Paige, which is why they killed Catherine in my apartment and left me the message about the painting? Which doesn't make any sense, by the way, because it was Bruno himself who sold the painting to the gallery."

"Hey, I didn't say I had all the answers."

"And meanwhile it all neatly mirrors a book I just happen to be working on?"

"Alright," she snapped, throwing up her hands. "You've made your point."

I let out a deep breath and shook my head. Then I pushed up

from the cabinet I was leaning on and moved towards the bathroom.

"Where are you going?" Victoria asked me.

"For a shower. I have to meet Pierre soon."

"You're still going?"

"I am. And I need to think first. So I'm going to put my head under some hot water to see if I can clear it, maybe even reconcile this new stuff we've come up with. Then we're going to talk about the favour I need."

"Favour?"

"Yes," I said, reaching into my pocket and removing Catherine's driving licence. "Best practise your French. It could be you'll need it."

NINETEEN

It took me close to an hour to travel from the hotel in Montmartre to the École Militaire métro stop, at the rear of the Champ de Mars. Even so, I was a few minutes early so I did my best to slow my pace as I walked towards the open-air café where I'd met Pierre just two days before. I didn't know quite what I'd say when I got there. The idea of telling Pierre everything was certainly appealing, and might be essential if he happened to have seen the news report that mentioned my name in connection with Catherine's death, but part of me wondered if I should hold back some information. This was the second time he'd got me involved in a job that had ended up with somebody dead and my name heading the list of suspects and, just for a change, I wasn't too thrilled about it.

Now that Catherine's body had been found, I felt self-conscious about being outside in daylight. My apartment was only a short distance away, no doubt sealed off and overrun with forensic experts and crime scene photographers, and to all intents and purposes the French authorities were treating me as a fugitive from justice. I hadn't adopted any form of disguise because they were looking for somebody an awful lot more handsome than me, but all that could change in an instant. How long would it take them to put a more accurate identikit image together, or even to find a true likeness of me from some dark corner of the Internet?

I tried to shake the fear from my mind and told myself to stop hiding my face whenever a passer-by approached. I was behaving as if I was guilty and no matter how subtle the signs, I might draw attention to myself. Besides, thinking as though it was just a matter of time until I was caught was hardly the best way to stay focused. I had no idea how Pierre would react when he saw that I didn't have the painting with me and I needed to be alert if I was going to play things right.

Just then, I caught myself about to reach into my pocket for my sunglasses. I lowered my hand and shook my head. Pierre had commented on how unusual it had looked the last time we'd met and, if anything, the weather was even more sombre today. The sky was low and dishwater grey, a melt of formless clouds that threatened rain. There was a faint breeze but it was failing to make me feel any more alert. Sure, it's always surprising how capably you can function without any sleep, but it's never quite possible to shake the sensation that your brain is in danger of a misfire.

I was close to the café now and, shoulders dropping, I could see Pierre wasn't there. It hadn't occurred to me that he might not show but I supposed it made sense. If he'd seen the television news, he might have decided it was too risky to turn up for our rendezvous or that I must have fled Paris. I should really have tried calling him from the hotel. It was a foolish mistake because I could have saved myself the risk of coming out into the open. Why had I done it? Maybe because I wasn't thinking all that clearly. Maybe because I was overly confident in the police mix-up with my photo. I was beginning to think I might have to pay a price for my complacency and that was before a strange voice to my right said, "I'm afraid your friend won't be meeting you today."

I turned to find a smartly attired man sat on the park bench to my side. The man wore a tweed suit with a dark brown tie and he was folding a newspaper and smiling up at me in a relaxed manner, as if he'd been waiting patiently for my arrival. A group of pigeons were scavenging near his feet.

"Excuse me?" I managed.

"Your friend, Pierre I believe you call him, I'm afraid he won't be joining you today. Would you care to sit?"

The man was English and very well-spoken. He pronounced each word with absolute clarity, as though cutting the letters free from his tongue with a scalpel. I peered at him and the fragments of his appearance began to jog something in my memory. I'd seen him before. He was the gentleman in the linen three-piece suit with the radio who'd been sitting nearby when Pierre had hired me.

"That's right," he said, reading my expression. "You recognise me. Very good."

The man patted the space beside him on the wooden bench with the end of his newspaper. I gave the spot a wary look.

"Oh do sit," he said. "We haven't got all day."

Reluctantly, I lowered myself onto the bench. The man withdrew a gold pocket watch and consulted the time. I wasn't sure whether my punctuality pleased him or not. He closed the watch and dropped it into the pocket of his waistcoat, which was cut from the same tweed fabric as his tailored suit and fairly screamed London. He didn't have a moustache but he could have carried one off. All things considered, he looked every bit as if he'd just walked off the set of an Ealing comedy.

"You know, of course, that Pierre is not his real name," the man said, absently.

"Who are you?"

"Nathan Farmer," he told me, straightening his spine. "And you're Charlie Howard, the writer." He tapped my knee with his

newspaper. "At least, that's your better-known profession. I understand you're quite the lock man."

"Listen," I said, "I don't know who your source is but –"

"Tsk," he muttered, interrupting me. "Don't let's play that
game. I know things Mr Howard. That's my business. I suppose
one could call me an information gatherer."

I stared hard at him for a moment. "And just who exactly
would you be gathering information for?"

He gave me a wry look, eyes twinkling, as though my question
had pleased him greatly. "I have a number of clients, Mr Howard.
I'm rather good at what I do, you see. On certain occasions, their
interests coincide. That just happens to be the case with you. Or
rather, with the painting you were paid to acquire."

"You've lost me, I'm afraid."

Nathan Farmer inhaled deeply and crossed his right leg over his
left thigh. His brogues were a highly polished brown colour, like
freshly brewed tea.

"I find that very hard to believe," he said. "Almost impossible,
in fact. Why, when I spoke to your friend this morning, he was
more than willing to tell me what it was you'd discussed."

"You've spoken to Pierre?"

Farmer nodded. "At the police station. He's been detained, I'm
afraid. No formal charges just yet, though I dare say we can find
something if we need to. But that all depends on you, really."

"On me?"

"On how much you're willing to co-operate. Of course, you may
not be overly concerned for the welfare of your friend. In which
case," he went on, running his fingers along the distinct crease in his
trousers, "I have to say I don't think it would be too difficult for me
to give the police a more accurate description of your features. I
imagine if they were broadcasting your real appearance on the television, you could find moving around a good deal more tricky."

I thought about playing dumb about that one too but it was clear by now it wouldn't work. The man knew what he was talking about. I began to wonder if he'd also arranged some back-up – perhaps a few heavies were lurking among the shrubs behind us.

"Why don't we take a walk?" I said. "I'm not too keen on staying put just now."

"If we must."

"And you can leave the newspaper," I added, freeing the folded broadsheet from his hand and tossing it into a wastepaper bin.

"Whatever for?" he asked, frowning.

"Well, I don't know who you work for, but I've written enough crime fiction in my time to know how easily a wire can be hidden inside a newspaper. Let's see the lining of your suit too."

"I'm disappointed," he said. "A King's graduate. I expected such an educated chap."

"Just show me."

Farmer spread his arms wide in a listless manner and gestured for me to pat him down. I did just that, trying not to draw too much attention to the two of us.

"Would you care to check beneath my tongue for any cyanide capsules?"

"That's very cute," I told him. "Come on, let's go. You can tell me what it was you came here to say."

We began walking in the direction of the Eiffel Tower. I didn't mind in the slightest – the crowds of tourists at the base of the tower would offer me some protection and they'd make it harder for us to be followed, assuming Farmer had people with him. I didn't know about that. It could be he was by himself after all, but then, why make it easy if he wasn't?

"Do you have the painting?" he asked, as we passed a line of tour coaches and approached a queue of people snaking out from the right-hand leg of the tower.

"The scene of Montmartre, you mean?"

"Indeed."

"The one painted in oils? Signed Maigny?"

"Yes, yes."

"Then no," I told him. "I don't."

Farmer turned and leered at me, his lips peeled back over some expensive dental work.

"Don't take me for a fool, Mr Howard," he said, in studied calm.

"I wouldn't dream of it. In fact, I'll tell you the absolute truth. It was the damndest thing. The painting was already gone when I broke in to steal it."

Farmer's lips twisted, as though he'd sucked on something sour.

"Gone, you say."

"Oh yes. But there was a silver lining. I knew who'd taken it."

Farmer paused, aiming to control himself. "Pray tell."

"It was a guy called Bruno. Something of a charlatan. He'd had me break into the same apartment under false pretences two days before."

Farmer swivelled on his heel on the gravel square, his eyes filled with utter contempt. I could smell something sweet and pungent from a stall to our left – a mixture of sugared popcorn, strawberry crêpes and heated candyfloss. Beside the stall, a middle-aged man was lining up a photograph of his teenage daughters, their arms held aloft as though they were supporting one leg of the tower between them. I concealed my face with my hand.

"Honestly," I told Farmer. "I wouldn't invent something like this."

"Even supposing I believed you," he said, eyes narrowing, "I don't imagine you'd tell me where I could find this Bruno character?"

"Gladly, if only it were that simple. But I'm afraid he gave me a false name and I've drawn a blank so far in looking for him."

"And what was your next move going to be?"

I glanced over Farmer's shoulder, to where I could see a uniformed gendarme approaching, his peaked blue cap visible in snatches between the heads of the tourists surrounding us. The officer didn't appear to be looking at me directly but his proximity made me uneasy. I cupped Farmer's elbow and began walking him in the direction of the Seine. We reached the Quai just as a pedestrian crossing lit up in our favour and then we passed in front of the waiting traffic and onto the Pont d'Iéna. I could see a collection of Bateaux Mouches moored together along the river's edge, all of them looking too large and too angular for the setting.

"To answer your question," I said, returning my attention to my dapper companion, "I didn't have a next move. Or rather, you seem to have taken it from me. I was going to ask Pierre if he could give me any information about the woman I found dead in my apartment. You understand, I imagine, that her death has become something of a pressing concern for me."

"No doubt."

"I didn't kill her, incidentally. You didn't ask, but I thought you might care to know."

He met my eyes. "I see."

"How about you?"

"Excuse me?"

"Any chance you broke into my place and killed her?"

Farmer's lips puckered in evident distaste. "Absolutely not."

"What about one of these people you're working for?"

"No," he replied, in a terse voice. "I'm not a killer Mr Howard. And neither are the clients I represent."

He cast his gaze ahead of us, to where the grand façade of the Trocadero building loomed up from the end of a narrow reflecting pool. Foamy water was cascading from the decorative fountains but a few people were lounging on the grass banks around the pool's edge. A number of black salesmen tried to draw our attention to the mini Eiffel Towers and fake handbags they'd displayed on blankets spread out across the floor. The blankets had handles sewn into them, I noticed, so the traders could gather up their wares and flee if the police decided to hassle them. To the right of the salesmen, in-line skaters were weaving between rows of plastic cones that had been positioned at regular intervals on the smooth tarmac. Their bright clothes and oversized stereo headphones seemed wildly futuristic alongside Farmer's outfit.

"So what now?" I asked.

"I want the painting, Mr Howard. That's all."

"You mind me asking why? Pierre showed me a photograph and I have to say it's an ugly-looking thing. Not worth a great deal of money, I wouldn't have thought. But Pierre's client was willing to pay through the nose for it. And now you turn up, acting like some long-lost member of the Lavender Hill Mob, and I have to wonder what's so appealing about the damn thing."

"It's just a painting, Mr Howard."

"Really?"

He smiled. It was the kind of smile a teacher might offer a problem pupil. "Will you obtain the painting for me?"

"I already told you. I can't find this Bruno guy and –"

"Yes, yes, I know what you told me. But I dare say that was before I gave you sufficient motivation. Two days, Mr Howard. I want the painting at the end of that time. If you can't provide me with it, my contacts in the local police will charge your friend Pierre with receiving stolen goods. You may think that doesn't affect you. But the goods in question are the items you left Amsterdam with. And please don't insult me by saying you don't know what I'm talking about. I have contacts in the Netherlands too."

I frowned. "That was over a year ago."

"Yes, but that matters very little, doesn't it? After all, I imagine your friend will give the police your name and your description if the right pressure is applied. Just another complication to add to this unpleasant murder business you seem to have become caught up in."

"I told you, that wasn't me."

"And I believe you."

"You do?"

Farmer nodded. "I've met killers, Mr Howard, and you are a different breed. A wily thief, perhaps. But not a cold-blooded murderer."

"I guess I should be flattered."

I gestured towards the curved stone steps at the base of the Trocadero building and Farmer began to climb them alongside me. We didn't talk for a few moments and I used the opportunity to try and get my mind in some form of order. I didn't know what to say next. He knew about the documents hidden in the painting, I was sure of that, but there was no way I could mention them without making it obvious I'd lied about having the painting myself. Those documents surely connected to something big. Characters like Nathan Farmer weren't the sort of people I came across in the shallows of the criminal world I usually paddled in. He was a creature from the deep, something far more predatory than I was used to. Not a shark, maybe. No, he was more the type to lie in wait, tendrils outstretched and poised to ensnare anyone foolish enough to come within his grasp.

Was it Farmer who'd left me the message on my laptop, I wondered? Had he been in my apartment when Catherine was killed? If it wasn't him, and I asked him about the message, would that just throw up more complications?

"How do I contact you?" I asked, as we neared the top of the steps.

Farmer reached inside his jacket and removed a small business card. It was ivory coloured, with gold embossed text. The stock was thick and high-quality.

Nathan Farmer, the card read. *Confidential Services*. Beneath Farmer's name was a telephone number.

"I have an answering service," he told me. "You may call me at any time."

"I'll see what I can come up with."

"Please do," he said, and offered me his hand. "My car is waiting for me," he added, motioning over my shoulder to where a chauffeur-driven Jaguar had been parked. The car was steel grey, a mirror for the sky.

I felt my forehead crinkle. "But how did you . . ."

He smiled, waving my confusion aside. "Two days Mr Howard."

He began to walk off, leaving me to stare down at the business card in my hands. I pressed one of the corners into the flesh of my fingertip, then looked up and ran after him.

"Final question," I said, grabbing his bicep in a way he clearly didn't appreciate. "Are you for real? Forgive me for asking, but I met a guy a little like you not so long ago. He turned out to be working a con."

"Ah, yes – you did indeed. I read your little book, you see. Quite the escapade." He dusted down his arm and straightened his tie. "But I'm afraid this is wholly different, Mr Howard. And I am, as you put it, quite real."

This time, when he turned, I let him go. His uniformed driver had stepped out of the Jaguar and opened the rear door for him. I watched Farmer ease into the supple leather interior and sit with utter poise while the chauffeur closed his door. Farmer didn't give me a second glance as he was driven away.

TWENTY

I found my way to the Arc de Triomphe in something of a daze, roused only by the buzz of the Renaults and Citroëns swarming around the twelve-lane roundabout. I'd become entirely caught up in myself, preoccupied with the onset of events. I'd gone to the Champ de Mars to find answers and had come away with yet more questions. Who did Nathan Farmer represent? What did the shadowy people behind him want with the documents hidden in the painting? Was he really capable of manipulating the police in the way he'd suggested?

I simply didn't know and the frustration was grinding away at me. I could ignore the threat he posed, I guessed, though it didn't strike me as an altogether sensible approach. I didn't want to leave Pierre dangling for one thing – and not just because of the number of crimes he could connect me to. I owed him something, a form of loyalty I couldn't readily explain, and I only hoped he felt the same way about me. From what Nathan Farmer had said, I got the impression Pierre hadn't told them a great deal just yet, though I had no way of knowing for certain.

More pressing still was the murder investigation I'd become connected to and that was swiftly gathering pace. The painting was tied into it, that much was obvious, and even without the added motivation Farmer had applied, it was something I needed to be wary of. The French police might be many things but I was yet to find out if they were lateral thinkers. If not, they'd stick to the most obvious explanation for the crime. The owner of the apartment where the body had been found, the one who'd gone missing, had to be their killer.

Feeling jaded and luckless, I headed down and then through a dank pedestrian underpass that transported me to the beginning of the Champs-Élysées. I checked my watch. There was still more than an hour until I was due to meet Victoria. I decided to take a stroll along the wide boulevard in the hope the exercise might trigger something inside my brain that, in my more optimistic moments, might be called lucidity.

Who knew if it worked? I didn't, for one, because I zoned out of my surroundings entirely and only came to again when I nearly stepped off a curb at the Place de la Concorde in front of a tour coach. The driver of the coach leaned on his horn, making me jump backwards and then stand blinking for a moment, recomposing myself and doing my best not to look too embarrassed. I put my hand to my forehead and found I'd broken out in a sweat.

The elaborate topiary and neatly manicured lawns of the Tuileries gardens were just a short distance ahead of me, and on a normal day it was one of my favourite spots in all of Paris, but I didn't feel up to carrying on. Instead, I staggered down into the nearest métro station and took the underground for two stops, emerging again at the Palais Royal. A group of children were leap-frogging over the monochrome-striped pillars that had been installed in the courtyard beneath the palace and I veered through them and on into the peaceful, galleried gardens beyond. I made it nearly as far as the fountain in the middle, then collapsed on a metal park bench beneath a canopy of boxed lime trees, hugged my arms around my body, closed my eyes and fell asleep.

Something trickled down my ear canal; wet and slow-moving. Something else struck the side of my face, my earlobe, my nostril. My eyelids flickered open and a drop of rain fell smack onto my pupil. I blinked and then squinted as more rain came down. I peered out beyond the crook of my elbow and saw the gardens sideways on, another row of well-tended lime trees, and the circular pool below the ornate fountain dimpled with rain. Groaning, I eased myself upright and smeared some of the rain around my face.

"You were snoring," said a voice I recognised.

I looked to my left and found that Victoria was sat on a green metal chair with her feet resting on the end of the bench I'd been sleeping on. She was wearing a grey hooded sweatshirt and tan casual slacks. A black plastic artist's folio, roughly a metre square, was gripped between her knees. I glanced up at the brooding sky above the balconied apartments, raindrops cascading towards me as though I was peering into a grey-scale kaleidoscope.

"What time is it?" I asked, working my jaw around to loosen it.

"Forty minutes after we were due to meet. I decided you could do with the rest. Feeling better?"

I shook my groggy head, then lowered it between my knees. "Worse, if anything," I mumbled, gripping my hair. "Now all I want to do is sleep some more."

"You mean you don't want to know what's in the folio?"

"What's in the folio?" I said, speaking into the ground.

"I don't know. I haven't opened it yet."

I looked up. "You're serious?"

She nodded.

"You're telling me you've sat there for almost three-quarters of an hour and you haven't taken a single peek?"

"Not once."

"Wow. Maybe you're not cut out for this thieving lark after all."

I gestured for Victoria to slide the folio across to me but she shook her head, lowering her feet to the ground.

"Let's get out of this rain first. It's really going to let go in a minute."

"I think we should look."

"I think you should remember we're sat in a public park that just happens to be surrounded on all sides by residential apartments and restaurants. There might not be anyone down here but that doesn't mean no-one's watching us."

"That's scary – you're beginning to sound just like me. What do you suggest?"

"Follow me," she motioned, with a jerk of her head.

And so I did. I followed her beyond an inner quadrant of floral plants and miniature hedgerows, through an archway at the rear of the gardens and out onto a street that connected with Places des Victoires. I didn't know where she intended to take us. All I could see were boutique stores and pricey bistros, cramped patisseries and cafés. None of them would be any more private than the gardens and might very well leave us more vulnerable to prying eyes. Victoria had been right about the weather, though. The clouds were darkening into a grisly mass and the rain was becoming heavier. It didn't look as if it would ease up any time soon.

"Do you even know where you're going?" I asked, pacing along beside her.

"Patience."

"Want me to carry the folio?"

"I'm fine."

Without warning, Victoria swerved left, leading me over a glistening pedestrian crossing.

"There," she said, and pointed to a dark-stoned building up ahead.

"Clever girl," I told her, and received a backwards glare for my trouble.

The building Victoria had led me to was a church – Notre-Dame des Victoires. It was relatively squat and modest, a stark contrast to its namesake cathedral a few miles away. The oversized wooden doors at the front of the building were unlocked and Victoria went in ahead of me. The place was dimly lit and the temperature was noticeably cool. Smooth flagstones lined the floor beneath our feet, and the soles of Victoria's flat shoes tapped against them. I looked up above the rows of flickering votive candles in the atrium, past the stained-glass windows and on towards the vaulted stone ceiling, rainwater dripping off my eyebrows and my nose.

"Sanctuary," I said, in a hushed voice.

"Exactly."

"You want to sit down?"

"Why not?"

Victoria led me along the central aisle of the nave, in the direction of the altar. The altar was imposing and looked to be made of white marble. I could see a statue of Christ, prone on the Crucifix, as well as a collection of frescoes with scenes of worshippers looking heavenwards. There was nobody else inside the church. Every dark wooden pew was empty.

Victoria peeled off to the left and I followed her, both of us turned sideways and shuffling along between the pews. She neared a side annex lined with a vast number of marble plaques and then sat down, positioning the folio next to her. I sat down too and reached for the plastic clasps on the folio.

"Care to hazard a guess?" I asked.

"Just open it," she said, clearing the rainwater from her eyes. "It might not even be relevant."

If you're wondering where the folio came from, that's the easy part – it was inside Catherine's deposit box in the bank vault on Rue Quincampoix. But how did we get it? Well, that's a little more complicated. First, we needed Catherine's swipe card, and finding that was why I'd returned to her apartment the previous night. And the place where I found it? Well, that was kind of neat. Like I mentioned, once I saw the object the card was hidden inside, I knew I was right straight away. The fact is I'd found it at the back of the framed photograph of Catherine with the man with the ponytail, the one that had been resting face-down on the surface of her dressing table. When I'd been in her apartment the second time, looking for the painting of Montmartre, I'd assumed the photograph had been put face-down for an emotional reason, maybe because the man with the ponytail had upset her. By the time I returned to look for the swipe card, though, I already knew that Catherine had a tendency to hide things at the back of picture frames. So when my brain finally engaged and I clocked the photograph frame positioned like that, a judder ran through me and I knew without a shred of doubt that it was where I'd find what I was looking for.

After that, I had only to persuade Victoria to visit the Banque Centrale on my behalf. Oh, and to impersonate Catherine Ames. She was reluctant at first, and that was understandable, but once I'd got hold of Bruno on the telephone and he'd confirmed what the arrangements should be, she began to relent. After all, I told her, I really didn't think Bruno could be Catherine's killer now he'd agreed to help us. And there was no way I could possibly go to the bank myself, since even in my more metrosexual moments, I was hardly equipped to pass myself off as a French woman. The only real risk was whether the security guard at the beginning of the corridor leading to the bank vault would query Victoria's ID. As it happened, though, Bruno got his timing spot-on and Victoria found him chatting to his colleague when she arrived. Bruno had handled all of the talking, enabling Victoria to flash Catherine's driving licence before signing the name "Catherine Ames" in the visitors' ledger.

In all honesty, during the wait for our meeting, I still hadn't been certain that Victoria would go through with it or that the plan would pass off without a hitch. But I guess I should have had more faith because everything had worked beautifully and now I had the folio in my hands.

I pressed down on the clasps affixed to the lid of the folio and began to inch out what was inside. It turned out the object was a painting, oil on canvas, and the first glimpse of it very nearly blew my head off.

"Holy crap."

"Ssshh." Victoria nudged me and pointed towards a statue of Mary Magdalene to our right. "We're in a church, remember?"

I swallowed, then nodded and pulled the painting all the way out of the folio. I set the empty folio down on the floor and showed the painting to Victoria. When she still didn't get it, I whispered the artist's name into her ear.

"Shit me," Victoria said, then clamped her hand over her mouth.

I grinned. "Now do you understand?"

Victoria's eyes had become very large and her mouth was wide open behind her hand. She was shaking her head, utterly astonished.

"It's not real."

"You think?"

"It can't be."

We traded a look, neither one of us quite sure what to say next. I touched my fingertips to the canvas, feeling the layered imprint of the oils. The painting was a Picasso and it happened to be one of the better-known works from his cubist period.

I said, "The last time I saw this, it was hanging in the modern art museum in the Pompidou Centre."

"What's it called?"

"The Guitar Player."

Victoria pivoted her head and scrunched up her face. "Where's the guitar?"

"You don't see it? Here – this part is the hole in the middle of the guitar. And this is the player's arm. At least, that's what I've always taken it to be."

"It's pretty hard to make out."

"That's sort of the point. You could spend days looking at this thing and each day you'd find something new."

Victoria squinted some more, then gave me a defeated look. "You're the art fan, Charlie. How much is it worth?"

"Difficult to say. On the open market with good provenance . . . I don't know, tens of millions, perhaps."

"*Millions*," Victoria stage-whispered, way too loudly.

I checked behind us, then nodded and raised my hand in a cool-it gesture.

"But we're not talking about the open market. Selling something like this – if it's hot, it's not easy. A painting this famous draws a lot of attention. I don't know, behind the scenes, maybe one hundred, two hundred thousand tops."

"That's some drop."

"No kidding."

"And what are the chances it's genuine?"

I shook my head. "I think we have to assume it's a fake. I certainly haven't heard anything about the painting being stolen. It looks like a good reproduction to me but it's difficult to say without having something to compare it against."

Victoria nodded, absorbing my words. I reached for the folio and began to slide the painting back inside.

"One thing we do know," I went on, "is a woman was killed over it."

"Hey," Victoria began, "do you think this could have been the painting everyone was really after? Maybe there was a mix-up."

"No," I said. "Pierre had a photograph of the painting his client wanted stolen and it was definitely the scene of Montmartre."

"But this thing has to be connected to it, surely?"

"I agree. I just don't know quite how. And there's something else I haven't told you yet. Things have become even more complicated."

"In what way?"

"Pierre's been arrested."

Victoria's expression freeze-framed and she reached for my arm. "Arrested?"

"I'm afraid so. He wasn't there to meet me this morning. Somebody else was instead."

And at that point I told Victoria all I could about my meeting with Nathan Farmer. I explained what he'd said to me and what he'd threatened to do and then I told her that he was after the painting of Montmartre too. Victoria became confused by some of it, so I had to repeat myself for a time, but once we had everything straight all either of us could do was shake our heads and sigh.

"Do you think this man can really do the things he says?" she asked me.

"Yes." I shrugged. "And no. But I think it's safer to work on the basis that he can."

"Have you come across anyone like him before?"

"Luckily, no. He's a fixer, I'd guess you'd say. People with enough money pay him to get the results they want. From the looks of his clothes and his car, he's done pretty well by it."

"He manipulates people? That's his profession?"

"Absolutely."

"So he's a thug?"

"A cultured thug. With fingers in a lot of pies."

"And paintings."

"Evidently." I exhaled and let my shoulders drop. "Tell me, how did Bruno strike you?"

Victoria threw up her hands, as if it was difficult to say. "Nervous. Young. A bit lost, to be honest."

"Not like a murderer?"

"Hard to tell, isn't it? But I'm beginning to see where you're coming from."

"And he didn't try to look inside the folio at all?"

"Not even once. As soon as I returned his money, he seemed more than happy."

"Which suggests he was telling me the truth about the loan-shark. I don't suppose he gave you my rake back?"

"Incredibly, no. And I didn't ask him how long it took to get out of the handcuff either, before you ask."

Victoria gripped the back of the pew in front of her, then gave me a searching look. "Charlie, you know what I'm wondering? Scrap the bank heist idea. The documents we found hidden in the painting – do you think they could be tied into an art theft?"

"An elaborate plan to steal a Picasso from a signature gallery in the heart of Paris, you mean?"

Victoria bowed her head, clearly embarrassed.

"As a matter of fact," I told her, "that's precisely what I think."

TWENTY-ONE

The Place Georges Pompidou was a giant slab of rain-slicked concrete, infested with pigeons, street artists and the occasional pickpocket. We hurried across it with our heads bowed, me feeling conscious of the plastic folio in my hand, not wanting the painting inside to get wet. Ahead of us was the steel and glass edifice of the Pompidou Centre. The entire building was inverted, with coloured pipes and tubes adhered to the outside, carrying wastewater and electricity cables and clean air from one place to the next. Large see-through tubes containing escalators transported visitors up and down between floors. My initial reaction when I'd first seen the building came back to me again – the whole thing was like a scene from a Jetsons cartoon made real.

"This place is huge," Victoria said, pacing through the rain alongside me.

"Wait until you see the inside."

It was quite staggering. By fixing all the utility pipes and escalators to the outside, the architects had created a vast interior. The foyer itself was several storeys high and the floor was lined with a smooth, hard-wearing material smeared with shoe marks. The side mezzanines and main walls were hung with large, brightly coloured neon signs, oversized posters and suspended flat-screen televisions. A bank of sleek ticket counters faced us and there were shops and cafés too.

"We haven't thought this through," Victoria said, speaking from the corner of her mouth.

"How do you mean?"

"The painting," she said, nodding pointedly towards the folio in my hand. "We can't just walk around with it, can we?"

"First of all," I said, "quit talking like that – you look suspicious. Second of all, how about you buy us some tickets for the modern art museum and I'll deal with the painting?"

"But –"

"Trust me. I know what I'm doing."

Looking back, I'm not altogether sure that was true but for some reason Victoria seemed to accept it. I left her to air her school French once again and made my way over to the left-luggage stand. The smartly dressed woman behind the bright red counter gestured for me to pass her my sodden jacket but I shook my head and gave her the plastic folio instead. She paused, and for one horrible moment I thought she was going to check the contents, but it turned out she was just searching for a space to stow the folder. My confidence flooded back. They probably got this quite often, I thought. Perhaps artists who came to visit the gallery tended to bring paintings and ongoing work with them, even calling in for inspiration on their way to or from their studios. Maybe Catherine had done the exact same thing. Her apartment was little more than a ten-minute walk from the Pompidou Centre, after all, and the bank branch where she'd stored the painting was closer still. With every new discovery, things were beginning to make a bit more sense.

"Voilà," said the luggage attendant, handing me a numbered pendant. It was grey in colour, around the size of a one-euro coin, though wafer thin. I thanked her and slipped the pendant into my trouser pocket, then turned round to find Victoria coming towards me, pushing her wet hair away from her face. She was holding two ticket stubs and a paper brochure.

"I got a map. The Picassos are on the fifth floor."

"Good thinking. I've stashed the folio."

I gestured towards the left-luggage counter with my thumb. Victoria gave me a dubious look.

"Best place for it," I told her.

"Aren't you afraid they'll look inside?"

"Not in the slightest. Come on."

We took the external glass escalators up as far as the entrance to the modern art museum on the fourth floor and then climbed a flight of internal stairs towards the permanent exhibitions. Victoria consulted her map and turned left at the Rothko canvas in front of us, leading me alongside a glassed terrace at the front of the building, through which I could see a number of sculptures and, beyond them, the pale rooftops of Paris, the curved outline of the Musée d'Orsay, the distant shimmer of the Grande Arche and the knot of skyscrapers at La Défense, not to mention the blurred pencil stroke of the Eiffel Tower. The gallery walls were painted a brilliant white, in stark contrast to the honey tones of the wooden floors beneath our feet. Slatted benches were positioned here and there, inviting visitors to sit and ponder the works of art.

The Guitar Player was in the second gallery space on our left, hanging amid a collection of other cubist works by Picasso and Georges Braque. I hovered a few feet away from it with Victoria alongside me, the pair of us not speaking a word, just standing together in the cathedral silence. Sure, I couldn't hold the painting in the folio up beside the original for a true comparison but there was no denying how alike they seemed. I guessed Victoria was thinking the same way because she made a clucking noise with her tongue.

"My God," she said, under her breath.

"Similar, right?"

"I'll say. And to think, this one is worth millions. How much would you say the one downstairs could fetch?"

"Sold as a straight-up reproduction? I'm really not sure. A lot of the value is in Picasso's name, of course."

"Of course. You know, I'm starting to see what you mean about the painting now. Standing here, looking at it from a distance, I'm beginning to spot new things emerging."

"You mean like pound signs?"

She grinned, shook her head.

"Picasso was a pretty cool guy," I told her, crossing my hands behind my back.

"You mean he was a womaniser."

"That too. But really, I have a soft spot for him."

"Kindred spirits?"

I gave her a sideways look. "You don't know the half of it. Want to hear my favourite Picasso quote? 'If there's something to be stolen, I steal it'."

Victoria rolled her eyes. "I very much doubt he meant it in a literal sense."

"What other sense is there?"

She shook her head at me, as if exasperated, and I took the opportunity to approach the painting for a closer look. The frame that contained it was relatively plain but it appeared heavy, constructed from a quality timber that had been turned and varnished with great care. A sheet of protective glass had been inserted at the front of the canvas and possibly the back too. I couldn't see how the painting was attached to the wall. If it had been hanging on wires from the ceiling, I would have been fairly confident it wasn't alarmed. Instead, there was some kind of fixing behind the frame, which meant it could be suspended from an everyday hook or a complex pressure sensor or even bolted into position. I leaned my head to the side and tried to peer around the edge of the frame but I couldn't catch sight of anything. It might have been different if I could have pressed my cheek flat against the wall and used my pocket torch to illuminate the space but I had a funny feeling that might attract the attention of the female museum attendant who was sat on a black plastic chair beneath the main archway into the room.

Bearing the museum attendant in mind, I backed up and contemplated the painting once again; the muted browns and greys and blacks, the sharp, deliberate angles. By itself, each individual 'cube' appeared curiously meaningless but as soon as I refocused on the whole thing, the picture began to make fleeting sense. Kind of like the clues of the greater mystery I was caught up in, I guessed.

I swivelled to find Victoria gazing up towards the exposed ceiling space above our heads. She titled her head and chewed her lip, then turned a complete circle and scanned right around the perimeter of the room, from where halos of light were being projected by a collection of spot bulbs. I watched her walk to one side of the gallery space and poke her head out through an archway that led into an adjoining corridor. She returned to me with a glint in her eye.

"I forgot to tell you," she began, trying but failing to sound casual. "I got those photographs developed."

"The negatives from the back of the painting?"

"Uh huh. I put them into a one-hour place before I went to the bank. I think you might be interested to see them now."

"Really?"

"Think so."

She bowed her head and reached for her handbag, delving around inside until she came up with a glossy yellow envelope. She peeled back the envelope seal and removed six colour photographs. I didn't take the photographs to begin with – I was too preoccupied with what else I'd seen inside her handbag.

"That brown envelope," I said, fighting to control the strain in my voice, "tell me it's not the one from the back of the painting."

"Why?"

"Victoria," I said, wincing, "you should have left it at the hotel."

"I thought we might need it. And I thought it would be safer with us."

"What if your bag got snatched?"

"I've never had a bag snatched in my life. Why would it happen today?"

I just looked at her, unsure what to say next. I didn't want to come across as a control freak or have the museum attendant concentrate unduly on us, but I really wasn't happy about the situation either.

"Listen, don't take this the wrong way, but would you mind if I held on to the envelope?"

She scowled at me.

"Hey," I went on, "if I lose it now it's my own fault, okay? It's all down to me."

"Whatever you like," she told me, in a churlish voice, meanwhile pulling back the flap on her handbag and removing the rather crumpled envelope. She handed the envelope to me and I slid it inside my jacket pocket. I took a deep breath and gave her my best smile.

"So, can I see the photographs now?"

"I suppose."

I took the photographs from Victoria's hand and leafed through them. Moments later, I looked up and held her eye. We both smiled.

"Thanks for getting these. I forgot to remind you and –"

"It's no problem. I can be trusted, you know."

I did know. And now I also knew that the photographs were interior shots of the exact same room we were stood in. But instead of taking illicit photographs of the paintings, the photographer had focused on the uppermost corners of the room. In each of the angled shots, they had managed to capture the spotlights, the water sprinklers, the exposed ventilation shafts and metal beams, as well as the somewhat blurred image of the security cameras.

I followed the same route Victoria had taken to the edge of the room and passed out through the side archway into the narrow corridor beyond. The walls were hung with a selection of framed newspaper and magazine articles about Picasso and Braque. I glanced right and saw the floor-to-ceiling glass panels at the front of the building. I also saw a fire extinguisher, a fire hose and a red bucket full of sand. Beside the fire safety equipment was a pair of glass emergency exit doors that led out onto the terraced walkway beyond. From just above the doors, a security camera was pointing down at me. It matched one of the scenes in the photographs exactly. I turned and was about to say something further to Victoria when I noticed that the museum attendant was staring at me, her brow furrowed.

I smiled back as pleasantly as I could, then slipped the photographs into my jacket pocket along with the other documents. I approached Victoria and took her by the arm, leading her past the attendant, out through the central archway and into the main gallery corridor beyond. I didn't pause to admire the bronzed sculpture of a horse immediately in front of us or the oversized Picabia abstract hanging on the facing wall. Instead, I steered Victoria to the right, past the Matisse room.

"Let's get a coffee," I said. "We can talk this stuff through."

Victoria gave me a puzzled look, but I just winked at her and ushered her through the crowds of visitors in the direction of the museum exit. From there, we took the glass-encased escalators up to the sixth floor and made our way to the terraced café on the far right of the building. As we walked, I explained about the museum attendant and how we should be careful not to make ourselves appear too suspicious, especially given the photographs and the documents I happened to be carrying in my pocket.

"So we're agreed then, the documents are all part of a plan to steal The Guitar Player?" Victoria asked me.

"I guess. Although they're hardly the most comprehensive set of plans."

"It is pretty odd. But when you factor in the painting from the vault in Catherine's bank, it begins to make more sense. The idea must be to switch the original for the forgery."

"I agree. But what doesn't add up is why everyone has been trying to get hold of these documents," I said, patting my jacket pocket. "Without the forgery – well, they're useless."

"Maybe not useless. They could always just snatch the original without trying to conceal the theft."

"They could. But if they were content with some kind of smash and grab, I'm not sure they'd need any of these plans in the first place."

I guided Victoria towards a quiet table that was adorned with a single red rose and happened to be situated on the edge of the café terrace, beside a reinforced glass screen that looked out over the city skyline. Victoria settled into one of the white plastic chairs but I remained standing and consulted the printed menu card.

"You mind ordering me an espresso?" I asked. "I need to go to the gents."

"Won't you have anything to eat?"

"Not right now. Just find me an ashtray and I'll be fine."

She squinted at me. "You should eat, Charlie. You're looking pale."

"Maybe later. I need to go and throw some water over my face first. Wake myself up a bit."

I gave Victoria a tight smile and headed out of the café, beyond a temporary exhibition space to where I'd seen a sign for some toilets. The toilets were sleek and modern-looking, with grey walls and red floors that contrasted with the clinical white of the sink and the urinal. None of the stalls were occupied. I had the whole place to myself.

I stood before the urinal, thinking. It was more than a little odd to be inside such a famous building, admiring such a famous painting, and knowing all the time that some kind of scheme existed for a quite outrageous theft. It was the stuff of make-believe. Actually, come to think of it, it wasn't all that far removed from a plot strand in my first Michael Faulks novel.

In *The Thief and the Five Fingers*, Faulks is hired to steal a painting from an art gallery in central Berlin, but his plans are far more detailed and complex than the ones I'd apparently uncovered. Faulks enters the gallery during the day and hides out until late afternoon, then crawls inside the network of ventilation shafts that criss-cross the gallery building until he's above the area where the painting is located. He waits until the gallery has closed, at which point he lowers himself on a high-tensile wire after cleverly redirecting a network of laser sensors with some hand mirrors to prevent his entry being detected. Next, he confounds the pressure sensors that have been wired up to the painting and then he engages a motorised winch to raise himself and the painting back up into the ventilation shaft. He doesn't replace the painting with a forgery, though. Why hadn't I thought of it, I wondered? Then I answered my own question. It was because Faulks had carried out the theft after hours, when the gallery was shut, so he was long gone before the theft was discovered.

Did that mean the people hoping to steal the Picasso were planning to take it during the day? Was that why they needed the forgery?

I finished up at the urinal and moved over to the sink. I wafted my hands in front of the sensor fixed below the tap and then soaped and rinsed my hands. I triggered some more water and cupped it to my face, bathing my sore eyes. I ran my wet hands through my hair and washed the back of my neck. I reached for some paper towels and was just dabbing my face dry when the door to the toilets opened.

Two men walked in and I recognised them instantly. The first was Mike, the dreadlocked Mancunian hippy who worked at Paris Lights. He was wearing his one and only red jumper yet again. Alongside him was the Italian guy with the slick, coiffed hair with whom Paige had been getting cosy following my reading. What was his name again? Mario? Luigi? Paolo, that was it.

"Hello there," I said, extending my freshly washed hand.

The Mancunian didn't move to accept it. Instead, he pulled a gun from beneath his jumper and pointed it at my chest. The gun was very large and very dated, like a revolver from a Second World War film. It dwarfed the Mancunian's hand, the barrel looking almost cartoon-like in its dimensions. He wasn't wearing gloves, I noticed, and that made me think perhaps he didn't plan to shoot me. Then again, I'd forgotten to don my Kevlar vest before visiting the museum, so I wasn't all that keen to test my theory.

"What's going on?"

"Check him," the Mancunian said to the Italian, pointing at my jacket with his spare hand.

The Italian moved towards me, walking in a relaxed manner, like his joints were elastic. He was chewing gum, acting as if this was an everyday encounter for him. He gestured lazily for me to raise my hands and then he began frisking me. He found the spectacles case containing my picks and probes, as well as the brown envelope and the photographs. He passed them over to the Mancunian, who pocketed them, meanwhile keeping the gun trained on me.

The Italian was just about to drop to his knees and check my trousers when the door to the toilets opened for a second time. The Mancunian gave me a warning look and hid the gun under his jumper. The Italian wheeled round and I lowered my hands to my side, then quickly slipped them into my trouser pockets. None of us whistled, though I guess it wouldn't have been entirely inappropriate.

An elderly gentleman entered. He paused when he saw the three of us, as if sensing something was amiss.

"Bonjour," the Italian said to him, smacking his gum between his lips. He clapped me on the back, then gripped my shoulder tight.

"Bonjour," I added, stiff-jawed.

The elderly man nodded uncertainly, failing to react to the look I was giving him. He moved towards one of the stalls and as soon as he'd closed the door and slid the bolt across, the Mancunian removed his gun and pointed it at me once again. I put my hands back up in the air, concealing the left-luggage pendant I'd just removed from my trouser pocket between my fingers. I didn't want them to have the pendant but I couldn't see where I could usefully hide it either. I thought about letting it slip down into my sleeve but if I did that, I'd have no control over when it might fall out.

The Italian checked my pockets, removing my wallet, my cigarettes and Nathan Farmer's business card. He passed all three items to the Mancunian and then he pulled my arms down by my sides and nudged me towards the exit. The Mancunian came right up to my ear.

"You're coming with us," he said. "No funny business."

Not even a knock-knock joke, I wanted to ask, but instead I kept quiet. He jabbed the gun into my back, just below my kidney. I considered ditching the pendant but it was metal and likely to make a noise when it struck the floor. I was very conscious of having it stuck between my fingers but I was equally reluctant to try and return it to my pocket in case I drew their attention.

"You'll behave?" the Mancunian asked.

"Scout's honour."

"Good. Turn right out of here."

I did as he said and led the two of them through an open-plan museum shop and out through a swinging glass door positioned beneath a red neon down-arrow and onto the terrace beyond. Most visitors would turn left, back towards the escalators. The Mancunian steered me right, in the direction of the elevators and, beyond them, the metal emergency exit stairs that flanked the far end of the building. The elevators were on different floors, I noticed, but I wasn't encouraged to wait for them. Instead, I was guided towards the emergency exit doors up ahead.

Each door had an aluminium handle fixed horizontally across it and a sign in French and English reading, "*To be used only when the building is being evacuated*". As I neared the door, the Italian stepped ahead of me and reached for the aluminium bar.

"Don't," I said.

He turned and looked at me with a limited degree of interest. I pointed towards a sensor positioned at the top of the door.

"It's wired into an alarm. If you want to get me out of here quietly, we're going to have to take the main escalator."

The Italian absorbed my words, then grinned disconcertingly, his gum visible between his teeth. He pushed down on the bar and the door clunked open. I braced myself for the high-pitched wail of a siren but nothing happened. I looked up and saw that a lead plate had been fixed over the sensor attached to the doorframe. It was a neat trick.

The Mancunian prodded me with the gun once again, ushering me through the door and onto the metal stairwell beyond. I stood on the grilled platform and waited as the Italian expertly closed the door behind us, using a pair of long-nosed pliers to remove the dummy sensor plate at the very last moment so that the circuit was reconnected without triggering the alarm.

"A real craftsman," I said. "I think this is maybe the second time I've seen your handiwork. The first would have been when you picked open the locks to my apartment, correct?"

The Italian didn't respond. He was busy chewing his gum and peering down over the railings, towards the flights of stairs below. He pulled his head back and nodded an all-clear to the Mancunian. The Mancunian gave me a shove. The shove wasn't particularly hard but I made the most of it and stumbled forwards down the stairs. I wasn't planning on going for the gun or making a run for it or playing the hero. All I wanted was an excuse to bring my hand close to my face. I straightened, acting as if I was regaining my balance. Then I steeled myself and swallowed the left-luggage pendant I'd slipped into my mouth.

It went down real easy; like an ostrich egg.

TWENTY-TWO

"Stop coughing," the Mancunian told me.

"I'm sorry," I croaked. "Do you have any water?"

His eyes narrowed. "This some kind of a trick?"

"No trick," I said, and coughed again.

The pendant seemed to be stuck in my throat. I was pretty sure it wasn't. In fact, I was pretty sure it was on its way down to my gut already. But it sure as hell *felt* as if it was stuck in my throat and just the idea of it being there was enough to trouble me. I had an image of the pendant completely blocking my oesophagus, like a freakish valve. It was nonsense, I hoped, but I wanted to drink something to make certain.

"Pass us that can," the Mancunian said, to the Italian.

The Italian was driving. I was sat in the back of a beaten-up Peugeot 205 GTI with the Mancunian alongside me and his gun pointed at my hip. We were really motoring. You want the definition of danger? Try fighting not to choke while having a gun held on you and being driven through the most congested streets in Paris by a distracted Italian in an eighties pocket rocket.

The Italian downshifted and veered out around a taxicab onto the wrong side of the road. He accelerated, then swerved back in, meanwhile reaching for the can of Cola the Mancunian had pointed to.

I took the can from him and necked it. In that instant, my situation grew even more perilous. I had no idea how long the can had been inside the car but the coke was far from fresh. The stale, flat, syrupy mixture hit the back of my throat and I almost gagged.

"Where are you taking me?" I asked, grimacing as I swallowed.

"Don't worry," the Mancunian said. "It's not far."

They took me to the bookshop, as it happened. I guess I should have seen it coming but the truth is I'd had visions of being driven to a disused building on the outskirts of the city, bound and gagged and beaten half-senseless. No doubt that's what would have happened to Faulks if I'd been responsible for plotting the scene myself. Luckily for me, I wasn't, and I ended up in the room with the unplumbed toilet in it that adjoined the study Paige had asked me to access.

I had my cigarettes back too. The Mancunian had handed them to me along with an ashtray, a cup of milky tea and a straight-backed chair. I sat down and lit a cigarette, aiming to smoke until I'd neutralised the lingering taste of the gone-off cola. Granted, it wasn't the most extreme torture scenario I could have envisaged, but it wasn't exactly a dinner party either. The Italian had taken control of the gun and he was pointing it in my direction from his position slumped upon the toilet bowl. Though I tried not to, I kept finding myself staring into the barrel. The hole at the end was large and very black, almost big enough for me to crawl into. Maybe the thing didn't fire bullets after all – perhaps it was loaded with homing missiles.

I hadn't seen any sign of Paige. She wasn't in the back rooms I'd been led through and I couldn't make out her voice among the few I could hear from downstairs. I didn't know whether to expect her to be involved or not. She'd lied to me about knowing Bruno, but that didn't necessarily mean she was part of what was going on now. And what exactly was going on? I got the impression we were waiting for someone, though I wasn't entirely sure. Maybe the Italian was aiming to hold the gun on me until I smoked myself to death.

"Would you care to tell me why I'm here?" I asked.

The Mancunian looked up at me with a blank expression. He was sat in an area of exposed floorboards over by the window, sorting through the documents and papers from the brown envelope the Italian had taken from me. I'd watched him in silence for a while, his dreadlocked head on his shoulder, holding the blueprints up to the light or tracing his grubby finger over one of the circuit diagrams. He hadn't seemed surprised by the contents of the envelope, nor altogether shocked by the photographs of the security cameras in the art museum. I got the impression they were exactly what he'd hoped to find.

"Not even a clue?" I asked, when he failed to say anything.

"Just wait. You'll hear it soon enough."

Would I? It would have been nice to be able to believe him but I very much doubted what he said could be true. I got the feeling I was never going to uncover the answers I needed. I kept finding out new things and those things kept leading me towards further mysteries. I seemed to be moving away from solving the riddle of who had killed the woman in my apartment and how I might clear my name, becoming caught up in the plans for a wildly ambitious robbery. I didn't need any of it. All I wanted was for my life to be simple again.

I sighed at just the idea, stretching my legs out before me. The carpet beneath my heels was thick and ornate and expensive-looking. I might have called it ostentatious had it actually fitted the room we were sat in. Instead, it was threadbare at the edges and left patches of floorboard exposed. And who knew when it had last been vacuumed? Never, was my guess. The dirt and grime and hair the carpet was caked in was really quite something to behold and it made a complete mockery of the ashtray the Mancunian had provided me with.

I exhaled and tapped some ash from my cigarette into the ashtray. Each time I inhaled, my body quaked a little less, though I was still far from relaxed. I looked up at the clouds of cigarette smoke eddying above my head and wished I could just float away from it all. I was fed up with chasing around trying to solve puzzles and I was tired of feeling dead on my feet. I just wanted to sleep and once I'd slept I wanted to open my eyes and find that everything had magically resolved itself.

What was Victoria doing right now, I wondered? Would she think I'd bailed on her or would she know something was wrong? I guessed the former, and it wasn't great timing. Just as I'd begun to mend things between us, this had happened. I hoped I'd be able to explain myself eventually but who knew when or even if I'd be given the chance?

Just then, I heard footsteps from the study across the way. The locking mechanism on the door retracted and I caught sight of the door handle turning. An instant later, I found myself staring at a truly exotic individual.

"I gather from your expression you were expecting a man," the figure said.

Actually, I still wasn't entirely convinced I wasn't looking at one. The figure was dressed all in black: black leather boots, faded black jeans and a ribbed black vest top. I glimpsed the vaguest swell of breasts beneath the material of the vest and a delicate gold bracelet on her wrist. Her hair was unbrushed and had very possibly gone unwashed for as long as the carpet. Auburn in colour, it was more like a tangled mane really. She wore no make-up and her face was deeply lined with a maze-like network of wrinkles and creases. She appeared unhealthily thin and because her clothes and her jeans in particular were very tight, she reminded me somewhat of a lion tamer minus the whip. At a guess, I thought she was pushing seventy. Then she spoke again and I registered her deep, growling baritone of a voice and added a few more years.

"So you're Charlie Howard," she began.

"Guilty," I replied, stubbing my cigarette out in the ashtray.

She peered down at me through lidded eyes, then reached for her back pocket and removed some cigarettes of her own. She placed a full-tar number between her bare lips and fired it up, drawing a good cubic foot of smoke into her lungs.

"Younger than I was expecting," she said, in the deep, husky voice.

I shrugged. There wasn't a great deal I could do about it.

The woman took a rangy step into the centre of the room and stood right before me. She crossed one arm in front of her stomach and cradled the elbow of her other arm in her palm, keeping the cigarette ever close to her lips. She took another long, determined draw.

"I'm Francesca," she went on eventually, extending her hand to shake. Her nails were all bitten down and unpainted.

"Hello Francesca," I said, gripping her hand and finding that it was chafed and lifeless. "You're the owner of this place, correct?"

Francesca exhaled and waved her arm about the room in an expansive gesture. There was a hole in the armpit of her vest and I caught sight of a flash of pale skin.

"Since 1961," she told me, breathlessly. "A great many writers have stayed here, of course. Some wonderful books have been written inside these very walls."

"At gunpoint?" I asked, and gestured towards the Italian.

Francesca turned and her shoulders sagged.

"Paolo," she said, pronouncing the vowel sounds with all the energy and flair of a native Italian. "We're not barbarians."

The Italian lowered his eyes and set the gun down on the floor. It wasn't completely out of the equation, I supposed, but it was a step in the right direction.

"I told them not to harm you, I was very specific about that."

"That's good. You have them house-trained."

"Ha!" Francesca threw back her head and laughed heartily, much like a pirate in a children's film. She didn't slap her thigh when she was through but the move wouldn't have been entirely out of place.

"I knew you'd amuse me. I could tell from your book."

"You've read it then."

"I read everything that goes on the display table. It's a personal rule."

"I'm flattered."

"I didn't say I enjoyed it."

She stared at me, eyebrows raised. I waited for her to break into the pantomime laugh once again but it never came. Evidently, she wasn't my number one fan.

"I suspect your range is quite limited," she added.

"Depends how hard you throw me."

Francesca's eyes narrowed and she took another ragged draw on her cigarette. There was still a way to go until she reached the filter but she dropped the cigarette and ground it out on the carpet with the toe of her boot.

"Please don't exhaust my patience."

"I'll do my best. And in return, perhaps you could tell me why I'm here?"

"That's simple," she said. "The painting."

"Painting?"

"The one you stole."

"Stole?"

Francesca grimaced, then turned to the Italian and clicked her fingers in an impatient way. "The book Paolo," she said. "Go fetch."

At her prompting, the Italian stood up from the toilet and entered the study. He emerged a few moments later with a copy of *The Good Thief's Guide to Amsterdam* in his hands. He gave the book to Francesca, who opened it at the first printed page and then passed it over to me.

I recognised my handwriting immediately. "*To my protégé*," I'd written, before signing my name.

"Where did you find this?"

"Catherine's apartment," Francesca told me. "Mike found it on the morning I sent him and Paolo to collect the painting."

So that was how they'd made the connection to me. I cast my mind back and remembered Bruno removing the book from his backpack and leaving it on the kitchen counter. They must have found it and assumed I was the one who'd left it there. It was some assumption. Not even I was that careless.

"I wrote this inscription, but that doesn't mean I was in that apartment."

"So explain this," the Mancunian said, lifting the papers and documents in his hand. He stood and delivered them to Francesca. She thumbed through the documents, a smile beginning to form on her face.

"Excellent," she said, revealing a set of crooked, nicotine-stained teeth. "You are a clever boy."

I wasn't sure if she meant me or the Mancunian but I didn't imagine it mattered all that much. What mattered was steering the conversation back in a direction that might prove useful to me.

"So maybe it was me," I admitted. "But what about your boys here? I take it they're the ones who broke into my place."

Francesca looked up from the documents and winked, unabashed.

"And they left the message on my laptop?"

"Paolo's idea," she said, face clouding over.

"It didn't say who you were."

She rolled her eyes, as if she'd already been through all that with the Italian.

"So tell me," I went on, "did they also kill Catherine in my living room?"

"Ah," Francesca replied. "I'm afraid that had nothing to do with us."

"You expect me to believe you?"

"From what I gather from the radio, you're really much better-placed to know the killer's identity."

"It wasn't me," I said, inverting my thumb towards my chest.

"Indeed."

"I'm serious."

"Well, it's a serious situation."

"You fitted me up."

"Now, now. I've told you it wasn't us. I give you my word on that."

"Your word?"

"My word," she said, raising her voice and glaring down at me in a way that suggested she wasn't willing to be tested any further.

But if what she was saying was really the truth, then who had killed Catherine? And why? I'd assumed the culprit had to be the same person who'd picked the locks on my apartment door but Francesca was telling me that wasn't the case. Could someone else really have arrived after Francesca's goons had left and before I got home? How had they known they'd be able to get in and how had my concierge missed two groups of visitors? The situation was becoming ever more confusing and I was beginning to fear I'd never get to the bottom of it all. The more people who ruled themselves out of the equation, the smaller my chances of finding the real killer became. At this rate, I might have to reinterview myself.

"Where's Paige?" I asked. "Is she involved in all this?"

"That tramp," Francesca said, spitting the word from her lips. "I would have pictured you with better taste."

"So she's not involved?"

Francesca gave me a curious look. "What made you think that she was?"

I shrugged.

"She no longer works here, as it happens."

"Oh?"

"She was a thief."

I laughed, amused by the disgust with which she said it.

"Here at the bookshop," Francesca added, as if that somehow explained her attitude. "I gave her a roof over her head, a little food. All she had to do in return was sell books. But no, she stole them instead."

"Really?"

"From my office," Francesca said, with a flick of her head in the direction of the study. She reached for her back pocket again and lit a fresh cigarette. She took a hit, then exhaled. "She must have taken the keys from my bedroom, I suppose. She stole some of my oldest and most expensive editions and sold them for a pittance."

Well I never. Perhaps stealing was more common than I realised. Maybe everyone was at it. Enough people seemed to be happy to dupe me into doing their dirty work for them. First Bruno, then Paige had worked the same trick. You had to wonder who might be next. Was everyone into this thieving racket?

"The books weren't the worst of it, of course. She also used my telephone to place some international calls. That's expressly forbidden, you understand." She bunched her shoulders and cast her lit cigarette around in a circular motion. "So, you can see why I had to ask her to leave."

Francesca paused and returned her attention to the papers and photographs in her hand. She leafed through them and her face took on an affectionate expression, almost as though she had found a collection of pleasing mementoes from her past. I didn't interrupt. I just took the opportunity to gulp down some tea and try to think straight. I felt certain there were important questions to be asked. I just wasn't sure what they were yet.

"I assume you have the keycard," Francesca said, not looking up from the photograph she was studying.

"Keycard?"

"To Catherine's deposit box. It doesn't appear to be here."

"I haven't seen any keycard."

"It was in the painting with these papers. She told me so herself."

"I don't know what to tell you. There was no keycard inside the painting."

Francesca fixed me in the eyes, trying to gauge whether I was telling her the truth. She could try all she liked. I wasn't giving anything away.

"You have gout, I see," she said, from nowhere.

"Sorry?"

"Your fingers." She gestured at her own knuckles with the fingers that held the lit cigarette. "I've known many writers suffer from it."

"It's under control."

"Hmm. Mike?" she said, motioning to the Mancunian.

Before I could react, he had stepped behind me and wrapped one arm around my chest, clamping my left arm alongside my body. I bucked against him, trying to loosen his grip and meanwhile he reached for my right wrist, aiming to steady it. His red jumper smelled like a toxicologist's worst nightmare. I fought against him, grasping for his dreadlocks, then his face, but it had no effect. I was just about to push backwards on the chair and try to topple us both over when I heard a clicking noise and looked up to find the Italian had cocked the trigger on the bulky revolver and was pointing it at my kneecap. I stopped resisting, though my body was still tense. The Mancunian regripped my right forearm and held it out to Francesca. She took my hand, ran her fingers lightly over my swollen knuckles and cooed reassuringly. She raised my knuckles to her lips and gave them a smoky kiss. Then she slipped my middle finger inside her mouth and bit down as hard as she was able.

I screamed. I didn't care how loud or how wildly. I tried to snatch my hand back, pulling her rotten old teeth with it if I had to, but the Mancunian held my arm firm. I stamped my foot into the ground, meanwhile staring with wild eyes into Francesca's deathly grimace. She was gnawing fiercely, shaking her head from side to side and growling too. God, I wanted to kick her in the crotch, but just as I was about to try the Italian sensed it and pressed the gun muzzle into my thigh. The pain from my finger was a searing white light in my head. I thought I might black out but just then Francesca released my bloody digit from her teeth and raised the lit cigarette in her hand. She held the burning end above my mashed knuckle.

"The keycard," she said, pus smeared across her lips.

"I don't have it."

The pain was instant and excruciating. I could feel the heat in the very bone of my finger. I squealed, bracing my feet behind the legs of my chair. The smell of my burning flesh came up at me.

"Alright," I said, through gritted teeth. "I don't have it any more. I have the Picasso forgery instead. The Guitar Player."

Francesca pulled the cigarette away, looking deep into my eyes. I guess she believed what she saw because she released me and the three of them stepped clear. I clutched my hand to my chest and pivoted forwards from my hips, trying to smother the pain. My entire hand seemed to be throbbing. I glanced down; my knuckle looked like roadkill.

"You took it from her bank? How?"

"It was easier than you might imagine," I gasped. "Problem is, I don't have it any more."

Francesca glared at me. "Where is it?"

"Someplace safe. But I can get you it. Really."

"When?"

I thought about the pendant in my stomach, working its way through my intestines. I'd swallowed it more than an hour ago now, though I couldn't imagine it had progressed very far. And I was certain I'd need the pendant in order to retrieve the forgery. The left-luggage counter at the Pompidou Centre was permanently manned and constantly busy. Short of breaking into the entire complex after hours, using the pendant was my only option.

"Twenty-four hours," I said. "Assuming everything works in the regular way."

Francesca squinted at me, as though mistrusting my answer. "One day?"

I nodded, gingerly shaking my hand out. Electric pulses shot up my forearm and I scrunched my face against the pain.

"Then you may have your twenty-four hours. But I want that painting, Charlie."

"Right," I said, burying my hand in the crook of my armpit. "Because you're going to try and steal the original."

Francesca straightened. She didn't answer me but she didn't really need to.

"Just the three of you?" I went on.

She pouted, weighing her response. "Plus the others."

"Others? You mean from the bookshop?"

Francesca nodded and I laughed. I just couldn't help myself. The absurdity of what she was saying was more than I could take.

"You're kidding. You have to be. Who do you think you're up against here, the Keystone Cops?"

"My staff have skills."

"Oh really?" I said, gesturing with my healthy hand towards the Mancunian. "What are you going to tell me? This guy grew up in the circus so he's your wire man? And the girl working the till downstairs, she's ex-SAS?"

"We have a plan."

"No," I said. "You have papers, photographs, a circuit diagram. It's madness. You're booksellers."

"To the outside world."

"Oh right, but you each have a secret identity?"

Francesca sighed, as if I was exhausting her. She handed the brown envelope and the loose sheaf of papers to the Italian, meanwhile taking the revolver from him and emptying it of bullets. Once she'd removed all of the bullets, she showed me the chambers. Then she tossed the gun away across the room and reached into her pocket for a crumpled handkerchief. She stepped over and signalled for me to pass her my hand. Reluctantly, I held my hand out to her and she clamped the handkerchief against my bloody knuckle.

"Pablo was a friend," she went on. "When he lived in Paris. He wouldn't have wanted me to lose everything."

"Why would you?"

"Books," she said in a wistful tone, raising the handkerchief and looking at the pulped mess beneath it. "There's no money in books any more."

"So get a bank loan," I said, gritting my teeth. "You don't need to steal a Picasso."

Francesca gave me a sly grin, as if I'd caught her in a deliberate lie.

"Have you been to Cuba, Charlie?"

"What?"

"A wonderful place for a new bookshop. Paris isn't what it was any more."

"You have to be kidding me."

A change passed across Francesca's features and I swiftly removed my hand from her grip. She backed away from me and shook her head. I got the impression she was about to deliver a misjudged speech but before she had a chance the Mancunian interrupted her. He was holding out my wallet and my spectacles case. On top of the wallet was Nathan Farmer's business card.

"This worm," Francesca said, after scanning the name. "When did he get to you?"

"Earlier today. He wants the painting too."

"And did you agree to help him?" she asked, her voice rising.

"He didn't leave me much choice."

"No," she said, returning my things to me. "That's not the way he operates."

"You've met him then?"

"I know of him. He was in touch with Catherine too."

"And Catherine was what, getting you to bid against each other?"

"Not in the slightest," Francesca said, as though I'd proposed something altogether more sordid. "She wanted me to have the painting. She wanted to help the bookshop."

"Which is how come you sent Fido and Rover here to break into her place and take it."

"Things became complicated."

"Tell me about it."

Francesca took a deep breath and crossed her arms in front of her chest. She tapped her callused lips with her fingertip, thinking.

"You're a born thief," she said. "Surely you must want to be part of all this?"

"What, the biggest farce in the history of crime?"

Francesca gave me a cool stare.

"Now that you mention it," I said, "I think I probably do."

TWENTY-THREE

"Perhaps when I've explained the background, you may become a little more confident in our chances," Francesca said.

"I'm all for that," I told her.

We were on the roof terrace at the top of the townhouse that contained the bookshop, just the two of us. There were no climbing plants or painted trellises or homely touches of any description, but there was a set of cracked plastic patio furniture to sit on. A dented ashtray, branded with the name of a Belgian beer, was positioned on the table between our seats. I was holding a cigarette in my healthy left hand and found that I was smoking faster than normal, affected by Francesca's pace. Her habit was never to smoke her cigarettes close to the filter and it struck me as an odd quirk because as soon as she'd stubbed one out she would light a replacement. It made me think she probably got through half a packet a day more than she needed to.

"I'm trying to think of the best place to begin. It's not a straightforward tale," Francesca said.

"Just pick a point and go for it. We can jump back in time if needs be."

"Flashbacks." She screwed her face up. "Such a crude device."

"Best friend of the mystery novelist."

"Some, perhaps."

She took a long draw on her latest cigarette and vented the smoke through her nostrils. I spread the fingers on my right hand beneath the table, testing the pain. Yep, it was still there, like glass splinters were being ground into my knuckle.

"Lucky I'm not the sensitive type," I told her, trying not to grimace.

Francesca said, "You'll have heard of Catherine's husband, naturally."

I squinted at her, then shook my head. Francesca toked so hard on her cigarette it lit up like a stop sign.

"Gerard Ames."

I shook my head again, then rested the fingers of my right hand on my thigh. Better not to move them for the time being. That way, maybe the pain would begin to recede.

"Dear God," Francesca said. "And you class yourself as a professional?"

"I take it he's one of my competitors."

"No, he's quite out of your league. You're aware of the Group of Three, one assumes."

"Didn't they cover an old Stones' number?"

This time Francesca sighed and stubbed her cigarette out in the ashtray, which was vastly more preferable to my knuckle. She reached for a replacement with her spare hand, triggered her lighter and raised it to her face in an automatic gesture, waving the flame at the business end of the cigarette.

"May 1966," she went on. "Three Parisian security vans, all robbed at different points in the city at the exact same time on the exact same day. Almost one million francs in all. It became known as the Group of Three."

"Catchy."

"The man behind it was Gerard."

"Right. And this Gerard was Catherine's husband."

"Not at that time," Francesca said, pointedly. "Catherine would have barely been a teenager in 1966. Gerard, though, was already making quite a name for himself."

In the back of my mind I recalled the photograph in Catherine's apartment – the one of her and the older man with the pony-tail.

"A real Jack the Lad," I said.

"A genius, actually." Francesca held up her palm, as if she expected me to protest. "Oh I know, it's a word that gets used far too casually. But that's what he was. Imagine the technology he had at his disposal. Imagine the planning and the organisation it took. No mobile phones; everything done according to the time on a wristwatch and the co-ordinates on a map."

"Stop it. I'm welling up."

"He was handsome too. In Paris at that time, he became something of a celebrity. At least, he was prominent in the social circle I moved in."

"The art scene?"

Francesca scrunched up her nose, as though she'd just smelled something unpleasant. "I suppose one could call it that. It was really just a collection of like-minded people. Liberal, anti-establishment, Left Bank, avant-garde, call it what you like. But I met Gerard and," she hitched her shoulders, "we were a couple for a time."

I backed away from her and blew some smoke out of the side of my mouth. "Oh?"

"It wasn't the love affair of the century," she told me, flapping her hand. "But he was a very charming man. Dangerous too."

"So he floated your boat."

Francesca gave me a weary look. "We remained friends afterwards. He often came here to confide in me. He liked to talk through some of the jobs he was planning. I didn't mind that. It was fascinating to me. Alas," she said, with a shrug, "I wasn't the only one he was talking to."

"You mean he drew attention to himself?"

"Oh yes. And of course, there's nothing wrong with that, until one says the wrong thing to the wrong person."

"So what happened?"

Francesca took a sharp intake of breath and I heard a rattle of catarrh in her throat. "He was caught. The mid-seventies. Another strike on a group of security vans."

"Only this one didn't end up with a catchy title."

"They were waiting for him, you see. His whole gang went to prison, though Gerard received the longest sentence."

"I get it," I said, drawing in some more smoke from my cigarette and exhaling over Francesca's shoulder. My finger was still throbbing, I noticed, emitting regular pulses of pain. "So where does Catherine fit into all this?"

"Oh, that was much later. Five, six years ago. Gerard had been out a decent spell by then. The two of them met and found they were attracted to one another."

"Despite the age difference."

"Because of it, I imagine. I was the one who put them together, you see."

"You?"

Francesca gave me a devilish smile and tucked some of her hair behind her ear. She smoothed her fingers across the dried skin of her forehead.

"I was friendly with Catherine. I'd even acquired one or two of her paintings for the bookshop."

"Really?" I said, thinking how I'd never seen anything other than books lining the walls.

"I had to sell them," she explained, with a shiver.

"Right. But you knew her and you knew him and you played matchmaker."

"Indeed."

"And they had the kind of relationship Shakespeare could have written a sonnet about. And you had a wonderful feeling of fulfilment. And meanwhile cheeky old Gerard planned to knock off the Pompidou Gallery."

Francesca threw her head back with a gasp and then she showed me her nicotine-stained teeth once again. "Oh, I do like you," she said.

"Of course you do. It's love's young dream – the two of us discussing armed robbery together. So why don't you tell me the rest?"

"The rest?" Francesca pursed her lips. "Well, let me see. Catherine's a very talented artist."

"Was. But no argument here. I saw the paintings in her apartment."

Francesca nodded. She extinguished her cigarette and lit another. I stubbed my cigarette out in the ashtray too – it was filling up rapidly.

"And I saw the Picasso forgery she produced," I went on. "At least, I'm assuming it was her."

Francesca nodded again, though with a shade more caution this time.

"I imagine that was Gerard's idea."

"Oh no," she said, puffing away. "I think it may have been Catherine's. She'd hinted along similar lines to me in the past."

"She had? Why you?"

"As I said, I moved in the same circles as Gerard. My ambitions tended to be more modest but from time to time I found the people who worked here had certain abilities."

"Like your Italian lock man, you mean?"

"Precisely." She circled her lit cigarette, as if it were a thinking aid. "Or they could learn, given sufficient encouragement. On a few occasions each year, once I felt confident in the people around me, we might carry out a small theft."

I felt my forehead crease. "I don't get it. Don't the people who work here come to you because of the whole bookshop vibe?"

"Ah, but I only say yes to the select few. I'm a very good judge of character."

"I'll take your word for it."

"There's no need. I trust you, yes?"

She gave me a sideways smile and her eyes lit up. I got the distinct impression she was flirting with me.

"Back to Catherine," I said. "Why the Picasso?"

"Because of her job. She worked as an archivist for the Pompidou."

"Oh." I frowned. "But I heard she worked near Orléans?"

"But come Charlie, you must know how the major galleries operate."

I shrugged.

"Honestly." She ingested more smoke. "Well, let me see, they generally have far too much material to keep in one building, you understand. They don't have enough space, for starters, and it's also a fire hazard. Take the Pompidou. I imagine they have perhaps a quarter of their collection on display at any one time. The rest has to be rotated and stored."

"In Orléans?"

"All over France. The idea is to spread the risk. I know of at least three locations. There may be more."

"And Catherine worked at one of them?"

"Quite."

I raised my hand to my chin and stroked the stubble I found there. "But what difference does that make if the painting she was aiming to forge was hanging in the gallery?"

"Come now, a gallery doesn't simply acquire the painting when they buy a piece of art, Charlie."

Her eyes narrowed and she made the end of her cigarette flare once more.

"Go on."

"There may also be sketches, notes, pigment charts. It varies depending upon the artist concerned."

"Ah, but Picasso sketched, right?"

"Not always," she said. "But with The Guitar Player, he did."

"Okay. So Catherine was able to pay a lot of attention to his preparatory work."

Francesca nodded enthusiastically. "She copied his sketches, over and over again. The truth is, someone with Catherine's level of skill can soon adopt another artist's style."

"Even Picasso?"

"Cubism," Francesca said, turning up her nose. "It looks complicated, I grant you. It's certainly beyond you and me. But think of it as a series of lines. If you're a talented artist you really just need to break down each facet of the painting, one after the other, until you can build it back up again."

"That simple, huh?"

"After enough time practising the same painting, it could be."

"And you're saying it was for Catherine."

"You saw what she produced."

"I guess I did. So what happened next?"

Francesca was all set to answer when something appeared to catch in her throat. She swallowed, eyes blinking, and then she began to cough. She produced a dry, rasping sound – like a saw-blade cutting through dead timber. She hacked and she convulsed and she spluttered and still the blockage wouldn't clear.

"You want me to smack you on the back?"

She waved her hands no, her face reddening. Then she coughed with renewed fervour. Her lips bulged outwards. She turned her face away from me and spat a globule of God-knows-what onto the tar roof. Probably more tar.

"Excuse me," she said, placing her hand on her heaving chest and taking a restorative draw from her cigarette. If I didn't know any better, I could have believed I was in the middle of an anti-smoking campaign. "Where were we?" she asked, her voice an octave higher than before.

I smiled benevolently, as though charmed by her manners. "You told me about Catherine's forgery and I asked what happened next."

"Yes, of course," she said, swallowing a little phlegm. "Well, you may have noticed, the security at the Pompidou is not what it might be."

"I don't know about that. There are cameras, alarm sensors, attendants. Plus there are crowds."

"That's where Gerard came in," Francesca said, removing her handkerchief from beneath the elasticated sleeve of her vest and dabbing at her lips.

"Let me guess – he devised a cunning plan."

"There's no need to be so sceptical. I told you he was a genius. But I think even he was surprised at how easy it could be."

"Really?"

"Oh yes. By the time he'd worked it all out, he was quite cock-a-hoop."

"And you know this because he told you?"

"Me. Other people he knew. Too many people."

"Ah," I held up a finger. "Because Gerard liked to talk."

"Precisely."

"You mean he hadn't learned his lesson from when he got caught before?"

Francesca grinned. "In more ways than you might imagine. Right now, he happens to be back in custody."

I frowned. "Just for shooting his mouth off?"

"No, no," she said, shaking her head. "Temptation got the better of him, I'm afraid. Just as he was planning to put the Picasso theft into action, he became distracted by another opportunity. A contact was planning to hijack a security van. Just one this time. Gerard couldn't resist."

"You're kidding me. He got arrested?"

She nodded, a self-satisfied smile playing about her lips. "He's awaiting trial. Apparently the police are seeking eight years, though Gerard's lawyer is confident he'll be out in eighteen months. And he's served close to two months already."

"Eight years? For a robbery that didn't even happen?"

"Like I said, he's quite the celebrity. A serial offender. But he has the best lawyer in all of Paris."

"That may be so. But his plans for the Pompidou heist are ruined."

Francesca hummed uncertainly, displacing the cigarette fog that had enveloped her. "Gerard was prevented from carrying out the job, you're right. But his plans still exist."

"Ah. And a lot of people know about them."

"Precisely."

"So what, Catherine tried to get these other people involved?"

"I understand it was Gerard's suggestion. He knew he'd missed his chance but he told her they could still profit from it. She just had to find somebody to buy into the scheme."

"Someone like you."

Francesca shrugged and extinguished her cigarette. This time she didn't reach for another.

"What about Nathan Farmer?"

She shook her head. "Farmer is more of a gatekeeper."

"You mean he works for the gallery?"

"Insurance firms, generally. Not that any of them would admit as much. His approach is hardly something they'd care to be associated with."

I paused and turned over some of what she'd said. Lowering my left hand beneath the table, I couldn't resist testing my knuckle. It felt sticky and wet to the touch but the pain was beginning to lessen. That said, my joint felt curiously stiff and immobile, and even with the medication I had back at the hotel, I imagined it would be a while before I'd be flexing my finger with abandon.

"Even supposing I believe all this," I said, "why did you end up sending Paolo and Mike to break into Catherine's place?"

Francesca glanced away across the terrace, in the direction of the Île de la Cité. "She'd decided to sell to someone else."

"Who?"

"She wouldn't tell me. I couldn't allow it, of course."

I screwed up my eyes, fighting to concentrate. "So how many people wanted these plans exactly?"

"Your guess is as good as mine. More than five, I would have said."

"And these other interested parties might be prone to violence?"

She looked back at me, a keenness about her expression. "You're suggesting they could be responsible for Catherine's murder?"

"The idea had occurred to me."

"Come now Charlie, you can tell me the truth. I have a flexible sense of morality."

"It really wasn't me."

Francesca gave me a tainted smile, then leaned her head back and blew the residue of smoke from her lungs.

"So now," she went on. "I've told you everything I know, we have Gerard's plans downstairs and you claim you can get me the forgery. It seems to me we have everything we require to press ahead within the next day or so and you certainly deserve to be involved. What say I pay you ten per cent of whatever we sell the Picasso for?"

I glanced skywards, turning it over. "Ten per cent? That strikes me as a little light, considering the switch can't happen without me."

Francesca's eyes narrowed. "Fifteen. My final offer. And please don't be discourteous"

I looked off to the side, towards the two towers at the front of Notre Dame Cathedral. I could see a gaggle of tourists on the roof of the nearest tower, peering out at the city through telescopes and camcorders.

"Okay," I heard myself say. "You'd better explain how we're going to do this."

TWENTY-FOUR

Going through everything with Francesca delayed me for a further hour. By the end of that time, she'd outlined the approach she was aiming to take to steal The Guitar Player. It was pretty much as I'd expected, though no less audacious for that. And the truth is I didn't have the slightest appetite for any of it. I was a house burglar, not a gallery thief. Sure, I liked to think I was good at what I did, that I brought a certain talent and professionalism to my work, but I wasn't in the business of carrying out high-profile heists. There was too much heat and too many things could go wrong. It was the sort of job Faulks might go for, but not me.

Of course, I hadn't mentioned my doubts to Francesca. So far as she was concerned, I was the latest willing recruit to her madcap scheme. The reality was I'd agreed to take part because I needed the information she'd given me and I also needed as much time as possible to clear my name. Now, I just had to work out how on earth to set about doing that.

First, though, I made my way to a phone booth and dialled Victoria's mobile. It rang twice before she answered.

"It's me," I told her, my throat feeling dry and sore from all the cigarettes I'd smoked. "Don't be mad. It wasn't my fault."

"Oh Charlie, thank God. Are you okay?"

"Sure," I said, surprised at how forgiving she was being. "Things have become more difficult, but isn't that always the way?"

"Where did you see it? On your way to the bathroom?"

I felt my brow knot. "See what?"

"The television."

"Victoria, I haven't the faintest idea what you're talking about."

"Your picture," she said. "They're broadcasting the right one now."

I stopped talking and propped my forehead against the thickened glass of the telephone booth. I gripped the telephone receiver tightly, despite the fireworks that went off in my finger. Well, wasn't that wonderful? Finally, just as it felt like I'd begun to make some headway, my momentum had been stolen from me. With my real face broadcast in the French media, it was going to be almost impossible to move around unnoticed. Every single person I passed became a potential informant. And then there were the police to think about. Every officer in Paris would have been briefed on my appearance.

"I didn't know," I said, quietly.

"But I thought that was why you left the gallery?"

"Nope. That had a lot more to do with the gun that was pointed at my face."

"What?"

"Never mind. I'll explain later. Where are you right now?"

"On my way to the hotel," Victoria replied, her voice pinched.

"I'll meet you in your room. We might have to think about finding somewhere else to stay."

"Christ, Charlie."

I looked up to see a woman approaching the telephone booth, fumbling in her purse for a phone card. I turned my back on her and shielded my face with my hand.

"Stay calm," I said. "It'll be okay. I promise."

"How can you possibly promise me that?"

"What would you rather I said? I'm screwed?"

I laughed faintly but Victoria didn't join me. She was muttering something under her breath.

"Hey, stay with me," I told her. "I'm going to give you some-thing to do. It's important. I need you to visit a pharmacy and see what you can find to help me change my appearance. Hair dye, hair clippers. Anything like that."

"A wig?"

"No. I need to draw as little attention to myself as possible."

"What colour dye?"

"I don't care. Just so long as it's not peroxide blonde. I figure that would be a bit obvious."

"Alright," she said, as though resolving herself to it. "Anything else?"

"Laxatives," I told her.

"What?"

"I need some."

"Oh, come on Charlie. You won't lose enough weight to change your appearance that quickly."

I smiled, despite it all. "I'm trying to buy myself some time. My next twenty-four hours just got one hell of a lot shorter."

I was some way along the street before I was stopped. A hand reached out from behind me and gripped me by the arm. My body tensed and I cursed under my breath. I turned round slowly, my mind already rehearsing how I might break free and make a run for it. But it wasn't a police officer. It was Paige.

"Jeez," I said, bringing my palm to my chest. "You nearly gave me a heart attack."

Paige didn't respond. She just raised her swollen eyes and

chewed her lip. She looked washed-out; bloodless. Her hair was lank and her pupils dark and unfocused. If she'd been at all wet it would have made a whole lot more sense – she had the appearance of someone who'd just been rescued from drowning.

"Are you okay?"

Paige inhaled deeply, nostrils flaring. My words had stirred something in her. She stared hard at me, tight-lipped, as though she was struggling to concentrate. I was just about to add something more when I saw Bruno hovering behind her shoulder. He seemed unsure of himself too, though an awful lot more composed than Paige.

"You two want to talk?" I asked, and gestured towards Square Viviani behind me.

Neither of them responded so I took it upon myself to lead them towards the rear of the square. I found a secluded spot beneath a canopy of trees, in the shelter of the northernmost wall of the church and close to where I'd given my reading. There were a handful of stone benches and all of them were unoccupied. I sat down in the middle of one of them and Paige and Bruno sat either side of me. The air smelled of early lavender and cut grass. Bruno cleared a circle in the pea gravel in front of him with the toe of his shoe.

I could feel the tension in Paige. Her body was stiff and her movements awkward. I figured she could do with a reassuring arm being placed around her shoulders but I was sure she wouldn't welcome it from me. I guessed that was fair enough considering how I'd behaved the last time she'd seen me. Mind you, she couldn't exactly have the cleanest of consciences.

"I heard you got sacked," I said. "You tricked me into getting you into Francesca's study."

Paige nodded glumly, the first sign she'd heard anything I'd said.

"You make anything from the books you stole?"

She shook her head.

"I guess I made us quits by walking in on you two. I had to find out what was going on, though. You must understand that."

"What is going on?" Paige asked, in a faraway voice.

"It's complicated."

She nodded and looked down at her clenched hands. Her fingers were interlocked, twisting around one another. "Did you kill Catherine?" she asked.

I looked first at Paige, then at Bruno. I shook my head resolutely. "No," I said. "I'm trying to find out who's responsible. I didn't realise you knew Catherine too."

"She came to the bookstore," Paige said, as if that explained everything.

"She was a friend?"

"Just a nice lady."

I exhaled and dropped my hands to my thighs. "So why are you both here? Do you have something to tell me?"

I looked between them again, trying to decide whom I should focus on. It was hard to tell. Neither of them was entirely together and that made me nervous. I really didn't know what to expect. They seemed lost more than anything, though I already knew to my cost it could be a mistake to underestimate them.

"We want to know what this means for us," Bruno said, finally.

"I don't understand."

"Will you mention us if you get caught?"

I blinked and shook my head. "Is that really it? Because I have to say, you're not even close to being my main concern right now. However you two got involved in this thing, that's down to you."

"And the painting?" Paige asked.

I arched my eyebrow, waiting for her to continue.

She shrugged. "Bruno told me what you said to him. There was something about it, wasn't there?"

I shook my head, as though I was powerless to help. I held up my hand and saw Paige's eyes flicker when she registered my bloodied finger. "I'm not getting into this now," I said.

"The bank vault then. Tell us about it."

"Not happening."

Her face took on a hard cast. "Maybe we'll go to the police."

"Be my guest. I'm sure Bruno would be just thrilled about that."

I found my feet and crossed my arms in front of my chest, looking down over them both. They appeared dazed. I don't know; maybe they were.

"Listen," I said, "the best thing either of you can do right now is to help me find out what's going on here. Forget the police. If there's anything you know, anything at all you haven't told me, now is the time."

I looked between them, waiting for a response. They contemplated the floor, acting sheepish. I had the feeling there was more they could tell me but they weren't prepared to take that risk. I had no idea how to convince them otherwise, short of banging their heads together, and I somehow doubted that would work.

"Last chance," I said, and when they still didn't speak, I hitched my shoulders, then turned and went in search of the nearest métro station.

TWENTY-FIVE

I watched my cut hair collect around the edge of the plughole and then swirl counter-clockwise into oblivion. I'd started by trying to clip my hair myself but I'd given up once the clipping machine had slipped through the inert fingers on my right hand for the third time. Victoria, of course, had revelled in the task, and she'd been equally happy to don a pair of my plastic disposable gloves and apply the jet-black hair dye to my new grade-two follicles.

She stood over me with the shower attachment, rinsing my hair into the bath. I'd been sleepy before but already my fatigue felt much worse. The water was warm, Victoria's fingers were kneading away at my scalp in a pleasing way, and I found myself wishing the process would take a good deal longer.

Soon, though, Victoria stepped away from my bare back and turned off the taps. She passed me a fresh towel and I used it to dry my hair, my face and my chest. Drying my hair was much quicker than normal and when I removed the towel it was smeared an inky black. I threw the towel into the bath and ran my hand over my prickly scalp. I wiped a circle of fog clear from the bathroom mirror and contemplated the results of my makeover.

"A new you," Victoria said, from behind me.

I peered into the mirror, as though not entirely trusting my reflection. I looked leaner and perhaps meaner too. I'd refused to let Victoria dye my eyebrows and now I saw that it gave me a quirky, off-kilter appearance. It was something that most men wouldn't be able to put their finger on and that most women would spot immediately. Even so, I was drawing the line at my eyebrows.

One thing I was pleased about was that I hadn't had the opportunity to shave for more than a day. I raised my fingers to the stubble on my chin and upper lip and willed it to grow unnaturally fast.

"Oh, get over yourself," Victoria said.

I smiled back at her in the mirror, then looked down at the shelf behind the sink to where Victoria had placed the packet of laxatives she'd bought. I tipped four powder sachets out and handed the box to Victoria.

"You mind reading me the dosage?"

Victoria turned the box in her hand and meanwhile I filled a plastic tumbler with tap water and tore open the first sachet, adding the pinkish powder to the water.

"One sachet, every four hours," Victoria said. "I think."

"Right. I figure I might reverse it."

"You can't be serious."

"Afraid so," I said, ripping open the second packet and tipping the powder into the mix.

I swirled the contents with my finger, the water and powder effervescing in a lurid pink haze.

"Bottoms up," I said, and necked it. "God," I went on, shaking my head. "This stuff is rank."

"What did you expect?"

"I don't know," I said, flushing the last residues of powder from my tongue with a fresh slug of water. "But I suspect it's going to be worse the second time round."

I wasn't wrong. The granular consistency and the saccharine aftertaste of the follow-up dose almost made me gag. I wiped my lips with the back of my hand, grimacing into the mirror.

"Eugh," Victoria said, with a note of fascination. "Please don't tell me how this turns out."

"So long as I get that pendant back, I really don't care."

"You might not. But I imagine the poor woman who cleans my room might take a different view."

I turned round and held Victoria's eye for a few moments before she looked up at the ceiling and shaped to walk out of the bathroom. She pressed my T-shirt into my chest as she passed.

"Get dressed," she said. "Then you can tell me the rest."

The rest was not a quick tale. I'd already told her about how I'd been abducted from the Pompidou and what had happened following my arrival at the bookshop, including Francesca's assault on my finger. Then I'd interrupted things by asking for her help with my hair and, since she couldn't very well hear what I was saying with my head pointed down into the bathtub, we'd paused for a time. Now I had to remember where I'd got to.

I emerged from the bathroom pulling my T-shirt over my head, then raised my hand to my hair again and found myself toying with the fuzz at the back of my skull. It was an odd sensation, being able to feel the bumps and knots of my scalp so close. I wasn't sure it was something I'd be able to get used to.

"Quit fidgeting and tell me," Victoria said, passing me an anti-septic dressing and a bandage that she'd acquired from reception.

I sat down on the desk in the corner of the room, applied the dressing to my gummy finger and began to bind my two arthritic digits together with the cotton bandage. Down beside my feet and resting against one leg of the desk I could just glimpse the painting

of Montmartre, the root cause of all my problems. I glowered at
the thing and fought the urge to stamp down on it with my foot.
Knowing my luck, I'd only break a toe.

Victoria made an impatient clucking noise with her tongue. She
was sat on her bed with her arms folded in front of her chest, waiting for me to speak.

"Alright," I said, winding the bandage around and around.
"Where had I got to?"

"Francesca had just asked you to join in with their crazy heist
and, being a complete idiot, you'd agreed."

I shrugged. "Idiot or not, I had to say something. And this way
she explained a lot more about what has been going on. You want
the highlights?"

"Of course."

"Okay," I went on, nudging the painting of Montmartre with
my foot. "So the papers and the documents we found in the picture
relate to a plan to steal The Guitar Player."

"Which we already knew."

I finished applying the bandage and offered my hand to
Victoria. She reached for a roll of surgical tape on the bedspread
alongside her and tore off a strip to secure the bandage in place.

"Correction," I said, flinching as she applied some pressure.
"We thought we knew. Now we know for sure."

"Okay." Victoria smoothed the tape down at the edges. "And
where does that get us?"

"It gets us ahead of the curve for once. Or at least I thought it
did," I said, admiring our first-aid skills. "Here's the set-up: the
blueprints relate to the floorplans of the gallery – they're not a
huge advantage, I suppose, though it's better to have them than not.
The circuit diagrams are more important. They show the isolation
switch system for the security cameras in the vicinity of The Guitar
Player."

"Right. And one of Francesca's bookhounds is a master electrician, I suppose."

"So she claims."

Victoria raised an eyebrow.

"Then there's the codes," I went on, ignoring the look in her eye. "Apparently they relate to the pressure sensors that are wired up to most of the paintings in the Picasso room."

"What, and the codes are never changed?"

"Listen, I didn't say it was flawless. I'm pretty sure Francesca is a good few hardbacks short of a full library, if you know what I mean."

"Miraculously, I think I do."

I held up my bandaged fingers.

"There is one thing I'm impressed with."

"The forgery?"

"That too," I said. "But what I was really talking about was the photograph of the man with the side parting. The one holding hands with the young girl?"

"Oh yes. Which part of the master plan does that relate to?"

"Well, the girl isn't his daughter. And she isn't his wife."

"So?"

"So that isn't something he wants his wife to know. Oh, and he just happens to be one of the gallery attendants."

Victoria peered at me uncertainly. "So what, they threaten to tell his wife about the girl and he turns a blind eye while they steal a painting worth millions? Come on, that's crazy. And besides, there's nothing to say he'll be on duty at the time."

I threw up my hands, as if conceding the point. "He's already in the bag, apparently. That was something Catherine had arranged."

"Weird. So this plan was down to her?"

"No, as it happens. It was down to her husband. And believe me, you're going to love this part."

And at that point I went on to tell Victoria the background to the entire scheme. Her eyes went very wide at certain points in the tale, and that didn't altogether surprise me, since I'd had much the same reaction myself. It was a colourful story, to say the least, but that didn't mean I was prepared to discount it. Sure, some of the facts could have become embellished along the way and the aim of the plan was certainly ambitious, but it still struck me as plausible. I'd seen the forgery with my own eyes, after all, and it was without question a good likeness. If Catherine had been capable of that kind of work, who was to say the plan her husband had come up with wasn't every bit as impressive?

Well, Victoria apparently.

"I'm not sure I buy any of this," she said, in an offhand way.

"Why not?"

"We're talking about the Pompidou here, Charlie – a national institution. I just find it hard to believe that a bunch of crackpots from a bookshop could waltz in during the middle of the day and steal a Picasso."

"Put it like that and I admit it sounds crazy. But maybe it's not as extreme as you think."

"Oh?"

I toyed with my shaved head once again. "Galleries and museums – they don't have the kind of security most people would expect. Funding is tight and most of their cash goes on acquiring art. By the sound of it, the Pompidou is way ahead of most other places. Take the theft of The Scream from the National Gallery in Oslo a few years back – the gang who took it braced a ladder against a second-floor window, smashed the window glass and reached in and snatched Munch's masterpiece in under a minute. The museum authorities had been dumb enough to hang the painting right next to an unprotected window in a room without a single security camera. So admittedly, the Pompidou is a tougher prospect, but compared to a bank, say, it's still a soft target."

"You really think so?"

"Sure. Think about it: I got right up close to The Guitar Player the other day and nobody challenged me. If I'd had the inclination, I could probably have grabbed it and got out through the emergency exit before the museum attendant had even left her seat. That's the problem galleries face. They want visitors to have easy access to the works on display and their only viable protection is a bunch of attendants who barely make minimum wage."

"So you really think Francesca's plan is credible?"

"No, it's *in*credible. But if you're asking me if it can be done, the answer's yes, I think so."

Victoria paused and made a humming noise, then tapped out a quick ditty on her teeth with her fingernails.

"I'm assuming Francesca hasn't seen your mugshot on the television news yet. If she had, there's no way she'd let you take part."

"I wouldn't be surprised if the last time Francesca watched television, they were talking about a young man called Neil Armstrong enjoying a quick stroll on the moon."

Victoria shut one eye, then inhaled deeply through her nose.

"Tell you what – even though I think it sounds utterly absurd, I'll give the plan the benefit of the doubt. In which case, my question to you is this: Do you think Gerard could have had something to do with Catherine's murder?"

"It was the first thing that occurred to me."

"What, she double-crossed him and he took revenge?"

I lowered my head and lightly squeezed my bandaged fingers, testing the padding. It was surprisingly effective. Sure, I wasn't likely to take piano lessons in the near future, but at least I wouldn't be snagging my knuckles on anything either.

"It's possible. From what Francesca said, Gerard had a lot of connections, so he could have hired somebody to kill Catherine, even from behind bars."

"Why not just hire someone to steal the painting?"

"Maybe he did," I said, and wiggled my eyebrows.

"What? You think Gerard might have been your client?"

"Maybe."

"But if that's the case, why would he hire someone to kill Catherine too?"

"I don't know. But it's something to ponder."

"Hmm."

"You're not convinced."

"It's not that so much. I guess I'm frustrated more than anything."

"Frustrated?"

"Yes," she said, dropping her hands to her thighs. "The rules say the killer should be introduced early on."

"Rules?"

"In a mystery novel," Victoria replied, rolling her eyes as though I was a complete dunce. "That way, we have a fair chance to work out who the killer is."

I felt my jaw drop and shook my head. I held up my hands like a pair of weighing scales. "Real life," I said, lowering my bandaged right hand, "versus mystery fiction," I went on, raising my left.

"Oh I know. But I still feel kind of cheated, Charlie. We've been trying to figure out what happened and all the time we didn't have enough information."

"We have that information now, though."

"But it's still not the solution to your problems."

I laughed. "Not even close. First, I might need to prove that a guy who happens to be locked up in a French prison arranged for Catherine to be killed. And if I can't do that soon, then I might have to participate in Francesca's attempt to steal the Picasso without getting caught. Plus I have Nathan Farmer to satisfy."

"And his clients. Whoever they might be."

"More mystery."

"So what's next? Because I'm ready for some answers, Charlie."

"Me too," I said. "How about you pass me your phone?"

TWENTY-SIX

I dialled the number on Nathan Farmer's business card. A woman with a distinct French accent answered in studied English. I took a risk and gave her the number for Victoria's mobile, then broke the connection.

"I might have to get you a new number when all this is over," I told Victoria, with a shrug.

"Marvellous. Will you also notify my clients?"

"Isn't that what your assistant is for?"

Victoria grunted and shook her head. She reached for the mobile, as if to place a call of her own, but before she had a chance it began to chirp and I answered it.

"Mr Howard?" said a cultured voice on the other end of the line.

"Ah, Mr Farmer. That was prompt."

"Do you have the painting?"

I glanced down at the scene of Montmartre and nudged the gaudy frame with my toe. "I'm working on it."

"I do hope things are progressing."

"Oh, I think that's fair to say." I closed my eyes, concentrating on where I needed to take the conversation. "The only thing is, I'm afraid my task has become somewhat more challenging just recently."

"Oh?"

"My picture was broadcast on the television news a few hours ago. The saddest part is it even looks like me."

"I'll address it."

I frowned. "Excuse me?"

"It won't happen again."

I raised my hand to the back of my head. "You can really do that?"

"For the next day or so, it should be possible. After that, it will be out of my control."

I whistled. I was beginning to wish Nathan Farmer worked for me. "Some control. These clients of yours must be influential people."

"I very much doubt you have the time to speculate on such things. Was there anything else?"

"Plenty. I need to speak with Pierre."

Farmer became silent. I opened my eyes and gave Victoria a doubtful look. She held up her hands, fingers crossed.

"I'm quite sure that's impossible."

"Oh come now. A man who can change the television news? Surely you can work a telephone?"

"It's a far more complicated matter than you realise."

"Isn't everything these days?"

Farmer became silent again. I could imagine him turning my request over in his mind. I was afraid to let him think about it for too long – he'd only convince himself it couldn't be done.

"It's very important I speak to Pierre," I went on. "I want you to have the painting but I need to talk to him to make that happen."

"I'll see what I can do," he said. "But there will be conditions."

"You mean you'll listen in."

"Indeed."

"Fair enough," I told him. "Start dialling."

"Charlie?" Pierre said hesitantly, as though expecting a trick.

"Yes, it's me," I said. "How have you been?"

"Not so good, my friend. The food here, it is terrible, oui?"

I smiled. "And the company?"

"They ask many questions."

"About me?"

"Oui." He made a whining noise in his throat. "And my work. I tell them, I am retired."

"And they don't believe you?"

"I do not know. They ask only questions."

"They're listening to this call, you understand."

"Ah, in this case I will not say where the bodies are buried, yes?"

He chuckled but I didn't respond. So far as I could tell, he didn't know about Catherine just yet. I figured it was better to leave things that way. If I mentioned her death, it might panic him into saying something that could create problems for both of us. I shut my eyes for a moment and did my best to concentrate.

"Listen Pierre," I said. "I can get you out of this but we need to be straight with one another. They want me to give them the painting."

Pierre paused, thinking through the implications of what I was saying. "Do you have it?" he asked, in a hushed tone, as if somehow only I would be able to hear.

"No. But I think I can find it, so long as I can work out who your client was."

"But I do not know this," he whispered.

"Truthfully?"

"Oui. I already told you."

I exhaled and covered my face with my hand. "You said they sent the money to your post office box, correct?"

Pierre didn't confirm what I'd said but I guessed that was only because he knew the call was being monitored.

"I was thinking, maybe we can use that information to smoke them out."

"I do not see how. It will not work."

"Okay," I went on, trying to sound a good deal more patient than I felt. "What else? They contacted you by phone, right?"

"Oui."

"They didn't leave a number?"

"No." He paused for a moment. "Mais . . ."

"What?"

"My telephone, it has a screen, yes?" he said, his voice suddenly brightening. "On the screen, you may see the number that is calling. The last twenty numbers, in fact."

"You're saying it might still be on there?"

"It is possible, yes."

"Wonderful," I responded. "Give me your address."

There was another pause. I suppose Pierre knew precisely what I had in mind and it wasn't altogether surprising he was reluctant about it. I don't know, maybe he'd left his place in a state before the police had picked him up and he didn't want me to think badly of him.

"I'm not going to rip you off, Pierre. I'm trying to help you here."

"And help yourself too, yes?"

"Goes with the territory. But like you said, we're friends, right? You can trust me."

I glanced across at Victoria. She looked pensive. I gave her a wink.

"Rue Soufflot," Pierre said finally, in a gruff tone. "In the fifth arrondissement. Apartment 7, building 18. There is an electronic lock on the front doors to the building. The code is . . ."

"No worries," I interrupted him, conscious that Farmer was listening. "I'll figure it out. How many digits?"

"Five."

"And your apartment? What kind of locks do you have?"

"*Fortins*. Two of them."

"*Fortins*? That's all?"

"I only live there, Charlie."

I blew air through my lips. "Even so, when this is over, you should really install something more secure."

"When this is over," Pierre repeated. "And when do you think this may be?"

"Less than a day, I hope," I told him, putting my hand to my stomach. "But there's a lot to do and I'm going to have to press on."

"Then good luck, oui?"

"I'm going to need it." I cleared my throat. "Mr Farmer? Would you be so good as to call me back?"

I cut the connection and held Victoria's mobile in my palm for a few moments before it began to chirp once again. I put the telephone to my ear and told Nathan Farmer when and where I intended to return the painting to him. Once our conversation was over, I hung up and peered across at Victoria.

"You get most of that?"

"I caught the gist."

"Think it'll work?"

"Who knows?" she said. "I guess stranger things have happened."

TWENTY-SEVEN

I guessed so too. Take me, for example, preparing to break into an apartment that belonged to my fence. Until a few hours ago, I hadn't even known where Pierre lived. Now, I was stood opposite the double doors to the outer courtyard of his building, admiring the neighbourhood he had made his home. It was a fine location, no more than a minute away from the Jardin du Luxembourg in one direction and the Sorbonne in the other. It was the type of address where any successful Parisian would aspire to live and I must confess I was a little surprised that Pierre could afford it.

The doors that guarded the front entrance to Pierre's building were entirely suited to the area. Painted a lustrous royal blue, they were many inches thick and many feet taller than me. There was no keyhole to pick, because as Pierre had told me, the doors were secured by an electronic locking mechanism that was accessed via a digital control panel. I waited until the street was relatively quiet around me before stepping between the lines of parked and dented city cars and approaching the panel. I had my fingerprint powder with me as a way of discovering the code, but I feared the street was too exposed to employ that particular approach. And in any case, I didn't think it would be necessary. Five of the keys were recessed a little further than the remainder – as though they'd lost their spring from being compressed too many times. Sure, it would take me a while to enter variations of the numbers until I hit upon the right combination but it was still feasible. Then again, perhaps I would try something else.

If I was Faulks, I thought ruefully, I'd have some kind of handy electronic gadget in my pocket that I could simply insert into the digital panel. The device would flash and whirr and run through a series of random digits and only a few seconds later I'd hear the thud of the locking mechanism retracting, simple as that. I didn't have any such gadget, though, and truth be told I doubt it exists. And since I didn't have a ladder or a grappling hook or a utility belt on me, I wasn't about to scale the gates or the limestone walls. There wasn't even a drainpipe to shinny up.

With all those options ruled out, I went for the next best thing – I waited. And perhaps five minutes later, the nearside door opened magically of its own accord and I watched one of Pierre's neighbours step out. My accomplice was a young man wheeling a racing bike, wearing day-glo Lycra and a safety helmet, and he was only too grateful when I reached for the door and held it open so that he could manhandle his bike through the gap. Once he was outside, I passed through the doorway before it might occur to him to query whether I had any right to be there. Not that it seemed probable he would. At a rough guess, I thought the building was likely to contain something in the region of forty apartments, so there was no reason to assume that anyone living there would be able to recognise all of their neighbours. For that matter, the cyclist could have been a thief himself, though I'm not altogether sure he would have been able to stash much swag beneath the clinging fabric of his cycling shorts.

After swinging the large door closed behind me, I found myself inside a shaded, cobblestoned courtyard. I stood for a moment in the pleasing coolness, listening to the silence all around me and experiencing the sensation of having entered a well-ordered oasis in the middle of bustling St. Germain. There were a collection of terracotta pots off to my side, filled with climbing plants, and beyond them a wall-mounted fountain dribbled water into a wooden cask.

Directly ahead of me was an archway and beneath the archway were two opposing doorways. A series of numbers above the doorway on my right told me it was the route I needed to follow to reach Pierre's apartment, so I pushed through the painted wooden door and began to climb the stone internal staircase. I could hear my footsteps echo around me but that was all. The world beyond the courtyard walls was entirely muted.

I had a pair of disposable plastic gloves with me but I didn't slip them on. I might not have had a key but Pierre had pretty much consented to me cracking his locks and Farmer knew all about it, so I wasn't concerned about fingerprints. And the truth was I was glad to leave my gloves in my pocket. In order to put them on, I would need to remove the dressing from my fingers, and since the knuckle Francesca had attacked had swollen quite visibly, I wasn't sure I'd be able to slide my gloves over it in any case.

Of course, keeping my fingers bound meant I had less dexterity and less feeling in my hands, and if the locks I was about to tackle had been of a better standard, that loss of sensation would have been a problem. As it was, when I finally confronted the *Fortins* locks Pierre had warned me about they looked every bit as pliable as I'd imagined. I whistled and shook my head. Roughly translated, 'Fortins' means 'small fort', but in my experience they're about as tough to overcome as an addiction to chewing razor blades. It was incredible to me that Pierre could be so cavalier about his property. There was no way he could have believed the digital code on the courtyard doors offered him sufficient protection from a break-in and, to be honest, I was glad it was something I'd only just found out. If I'd known the kind of locks he had on his place before now, I'm pretty sure it would have put doubts in my mind about how much I could trust his professionalism. After all, if he was this careless about his own security, then how could I be confident he was capable of protecting me?

Mind you, complaining about such things seemed a little prudish considering how much easier the *Fortins* were about to make my day. I ran my fingertip over them, as though they might contain some kind of hidden message, but the only message they gave out was that picking them would be relatively easy. I knew from experience that there were only four pins on each lock and that the cam and the retracting mechanism were made of low-grade metals that could be forced if necessary. A beginner with a flick-knife could probably defeat them. And thinking about beginners made me think about Bruno and that, in turn, made me think about using one of my rakes. Being an impulsive type, I decided to go with my instincts, so I reached for my spectacles case and removed one of my rakes and a screwdriver, and in about the same time as it had taken me to do exactly that, I had both locks cracked and ready to turn.

I prodded the door open with my foot, stepped inside and was still putting my tools back inside my spectacles case when I suddenly realised I hadn't knocked. My assumption had always been that Pierre lived alone but as I stood at the threshold to his apartment it occurred to me for the first time that I had nothing on which to base that assumption. I guess I'd formed the opinion because whenever I'd called his number, Pierre had always been the one to answer, and I couldn't recall ever hearing any background voices. But what did that really mean? It could be that he had a separate business line that nobody else was allowed to pick up. Or it could just be that whenever I'd called in the past, his seven-foot, sixteen-stone Fijian bodyguard had happened to be out.

I stood still, door open, listening for any movement from the interior of the apartment. I couldn't hear anything but now the idea of somebody being there had occurred to me I was finding it hard to shake the notion. I really wanted to shut the door to prevent any passing neighbours seeing me but at the same time the thought of taking a few noisy steps and easing the door closed was far from appealing. I was stuck, unable to act for perhaps two entire minutes before sense finally took hold of me and I closed the door, then called out to see if anybody was home. After all, if Pierre did live with someone, chances were they knew what he did for a living as well as the situation he currently found himself in. So it struck me as unlikely they'd object to me being there, especially once I'd explained that I was aiming to help.

As it turned out, nobody responded to my call, and once I'd passed through the compact hallway and into the main living area I felt pretty certain I was by myself. Mainly that was because the apartment was very small and I couldn't imagine where anybody could be hiding. The living room was open-plan, with a glass desk positioned beneath two full-length windows, a sofa and an arm-chair in the middle of the parquet floor, and a wall of fitted shelving units set back beneath a mezzanine level towards the rear. A step-ladder led up to the mezzanine and I climbed the first few rungs and poked my head up for a look. There was a neatly made futon bed and a reading lamp and a *Paris Match* magazine and that was all. The ladder and the sleeping platform were a surprise to me because although Pierre was relatively fit he was getting on in years. Perhaps he'd chosen the apartment to defy the ageing process.

I poked my head through the other doors I could see in the studio. The first led into a small kitchen, the next opened onto an even smaller bathroom with a toilet, a sink and a corner shower, and the final door concealed a fitted wardrobe. I'd like to be able to describe the rest of the place but that's all there was. You could swing a cat if you happened to have one to hand, but it wouldn't thank you for it because it would bounce off just about every wall. I was beginning to understand why Pierre had seemed so relaxed when I'd spoken to him on the phone – it wouldn't have surprised me if the cell he was being detained in was bigger than his apartment.

Thinking of phones made me remember why I'd come in the first place. I turned round, scanning the space I'd found myself in, until I spied a sleek black telephone positioned on a low side-table beside the glass desk. I crossed over to the telephone and crouched down and peered at the display. It told me the time and the date. Lower down, I saw a column of speed-dial buttons and below them, a further button with the image of an address book printed on it. Beside the button was a flashing light.

I pressed the button and the digital screen updated to show a telephone number beside a date and a time. I began to cycle through the stored numbers for the most recent calls the telephone had received and soon found I could discount several of them because they related to the period since Pierre had first contacted me about the job. Once or twice, I saw my home telephone number and also Victoria's mobile number appear. Finally, I neared the end of the list and located five numbers that could have belonged to Pierre's client. I grabbed a pad of paper and a pen from Pierre's desk and wrote the numbers down. I read through them quickly, hoping to recognise one of them, but without any luck. Two of the calls were preceded by international dial codes – one from the UK and one from the States. The three that were left looked as if they were local.

I stood up from my crouched position and stretched my back,

meanwhile scouting around the side-table for any signs of a tele-phone directory. There was a low console unit against the wall and I slid the doors back and rooted around inside. There were flyers for take-away food outlets, clusters of paper receipts, reams of correspondence, discarded pens, cassette tapes, a spare light bulb and even a sleeping-mask branded with the logo of a national air-line. There was no telephone directory, though, and I was about to discount the idea altogether when it occurred to me to check the fitted shelving units beneath the mezzanine.

I crossed the room, bowing as I passed below the mezzanine even though it was a good foot clear of my head. The shelves con-tained all manner of items: DVD cases, CD cases, vinyl LPs, ornaments, framed photographs and books. Among the books I was pleased to see a collection of my Michael Faulks burglar novels, spines thoroughly cracked. I was even more pleased to see a Paris telephone directory. I removed the directory from the shelf, flicked it open to around the middle of the book and began shuf-fling back towards the glass desk and the pad of paper on which I'd scrawled the telephone numbers.

I was maybe halfway across the room before I heard the noise for the first time. It wasn't footsteps or the sound of a key in the lock or even the creak and muffled tick of a gun trigger being cocked. It was the ungodly squelch of my stomach. I paused, frowned, and clutched my hand to my guts. I could feel my insides turning over. My intestines weren't just cramping; they were clenching and unclenching as if a wrestler was trying to squeeze the very life from them. A bubble of gas escaped my backside and my stomach burped and gurgled like a blocked sink. I felt a muscle in my bottom quiver, dropped the telephone directory and clutched my hands to my buttocks. I raced towards the bathroom, knock-kneed, squeezing my cheeks together so hard they trembled. I reached for the handle on the bathroom door and was already visualising myself collapsing mercifully down onto the toilet seat when I realised I couldn't. The laxatives had done their job, but I'd be a fool to risk loosing the luggage pendant down the U-bend of Pierre's toilet.

Cursing, I turned from the door and lunged for the kitchen. I snatched open a kitchen cupboard, then a drawer, desperately trying to find some kind of receptacle. I spied a copper saucepan on the hob and I was all set to grab it and go right there and then in the middle of the kitchen before some inner resolve and sense of dignity took hold of me and I willed myself to hang on for just a moment longer. I opened another drawer and, God in heaven, praise be to Allah, I found a roll of clear plastic bags. I grabbed the roll and darted for the bathroom, meanwhile fiddling with the buckle on my belt, then ripping open the button-fly on my trousers, hauling my boxer shorts down and dropping onto the porcelain toilet seat. I tore a bag from the roll, blew on the opening, tugged the thing apart and stuffed it down between my legs. Then I let go, and believe me, it's really best for all concerned if I refrain from describing the nature of what followed.

Suffice it to say that when it was all over with, I was more than a little bit grateful to be able to slip a disposable plastic glove onto my left hand in order to search for the pendant. I found it soon enough, which perhaps isn't surprising considering what it was I was searching through, and once I had the pendant I washed it and soaped it and rinsed it in scalding hot water. Then I rewashed it and resoaped it and rinsed it before gingerly risking a sniff. Much to my relief, I remained conscious. Finally, I felt suitably ashamed of what had happened to give Pierre's toilet a thorough clean before slipping the pendant into my pocket and returning to the kitchen with the roll of plastic bags.

I put the plastic bags back where I had found them, then stood for a moment looking down into the kitchen drawer before sliding it closed. I shut the other cupboards and drawers that I'd pulled so frantically open and then I went back to the glass desk and consulted a number of entries in the telephone directory. Perhaps ten minutes later, when I was finally done, I closed the directory and put it back on the shelf where I had found it. Then I returned to the telephone and spent a good deal of time trying to work out how to delete my number and Victoria's number from the list of Pierre's recent calls. Unsurprisingly, I couldn't figure it out, and eventually I began to think it wasn't all that important.

So far as I could tell, there was nothing else I could usefully do, so I shut the front door of the studio apartment behind me, picked the *Fortins* locks closed and made my way onto the street and afterwards into the centre of the Jardin du Luxembourg. I found a sage-green metal chair near to a circular boating pond and sat watching groups of children prodding wooden sailing boats with sticks while I prodded ideas around my mind without a great deal more accuracy. My ideas drifted and ricocheted, bouncing off one another and tilting precariously, threatening to capsize. I was really struggling to think clearly and it was bothering me a great deal. Francesca's heist was scheduled for the following afternoon and I knew I'd need to be at the top of my game to avoid being arrested. More importantly, I had a wholly unexpected lead to address.

TWENTY-EIGHT

In her infinite wisdom, Francesca had decreed that the best time to carry out the Picasso robbery was late afternoon. By then, she assured me, visitor numbers would be low and the museum attendants would be less alert. I wasn't sure I believed her but neither did I think it mattered a great deal. If something was going to go wrong with her scheme, it wouldn't be because of the time of day she chose – it would be because the whole thing was so preposterous in the first place.

Before we could try our luck, though, I first had to retrieve the plastic folio from the left-luggage counter. It was something I'd been feeling increasingly unsure about. I had no idea what kind of policy the Pompidou operated, but it didn't seem too outlandish to assume they might check the contents of any items that were left for more than a day. Then again, I guessed visitors often forgot to collect coats and bags, so perhaps it wasn't all that unusual. If it was as common as I hoped, they might not have looked inside the folio just yet. I'd only left it there for one night, after all. And even if the counter staff had checked the folio, there was still a chance they wouldn't recognise the painting for what it was. Sure, they worked within the Pompidou complex, but the entrance to the art museum itself was four floors up and perhaps they weren't all that familiar with its contents.

In any case, nothing was said when I handed over the pendant. The scent of perfumed soap emanating from it wasn't even commented upon. The lady on the counter, who happened to be different from the day before, simply took the pendant and retrieved the folio for me without a second thought. I was almost sorry it was so easy. I'd prepared all manner of stories in my head and now all my work had been wasted.

Once I was back outside, I carried the folio away to the right, as far as an orange VW camper van parked just behind the Atelier Brancusi art museum, on the edge of the largely pedestrianised Rue Rambuteau. The camper van had a faded CND insignia painted onto its front panel and a swarm of campaign stickers adhered to its rear window. I swung one of the dented barn doors open and climbed inside the damp-smelling interior, squeezing myself down onto a bench seat beside a selection of Francesca's motley crew. The interior was dimmed because a collection of tatty plaid curtains had been drawn across each of the side windows. Nobody said anything until I'd undone the plastic clasps on the folio and slid the painting out for them all to see. At that point, smiles spread around me as if they were contagious.

"Very good," Francesca remarked, from behind a lighted cigarette. She reached out to touch the canvas but I flinched as her cigarette came towards the work.

"Sorry," I said, on catching her expression. "Go ahead."

Francesca gave me a level gaze, then smoothed her fingertips over the textured surface. She sighed with contentment.

"Catherine, Catherine," she said. "She was talented, no?"

I nodded, then checked the reactions of the others inside the van. Altogether, there were eight of us – Francesca, Mike, Paolo, the guy with the colourful skullcap and the beaded goatee beard and the girl with the multiple piercings I'd seen inside the brasserie following my reading, as well as two others I'd only just met. The guy with the skullcap was called Jan and he was supposed to be Francesca's electronics expert. Jan was Polish, from Krakow originally, and he'd told me he'd come to Paris seeking a job in the IT industry. I doubted that disarming a series of pressure sensors and rerouting a collection of security cameras inside one of the most famous modern art museums in the world was quite what he'd had in mind when he'd set off from home, but he seemed wildly enthused by the task.

"You have everything you need?" I asked him.

"Yes," he said, hefting a plastic toolbox in his hand and giving me a toothy grin.

"And you're sure you can do this?"

"Once Paolo the magician gets me inside, it will be easy."

I transferred my gaze to Paolo the magician. He didn't look much like a stage entertainer. In fact, like Jan and Mike, he was dressed in a regulation blue boiler suit. Francesca's theory was that the boiler suits would make them look like workmen or contractors, so nobody would query why they were walking around the service corridors they needed to access. To my mind, the outfits made them look like a gang of art thieves. Didn't robbers always wear blue boiler suits in the movies? But then again, maybe that was the point. Perhaps the very fact that the outfit and the ruse were so familiar would give it a chance of working. And hey, it was sort of novel to see Mike wearing something other than his grubby red jumper.

To tell you the truth, I was a little bothered by all the attention Paolo was getting. Yes, he could turn locks, but the fact he'd been tasked with getting Jan and Mike inside the building still annoyed me. A sense of professional pride made me believe I could do a better job, but even though I'd told Francesca as much, she'd stuck with what she knew. I guess the state of my bandaged fingers had a role to play in her thinking and there wasn't a great deal I could do about it.

So far, I'd resisted the temptation to quiz Paolo on what his approach would be. I knew they were intending to access the building via the same metal fire escape steps they'd led me down at gunpoint just a day before, and I also knew that Paolo was capable of defeating the security locks on the double gates at the bottom of the stairs and the alarm sensors above the glass doors on the fourth and fifth floors. I just believed I'd be neater and faster and less likely to make mistakes.

"You don't want to switch?" I asked Paolo, for maybe the third time.

He treated me to a contemptuous sneer and shook his head, meanwhile transferring a selection of picks, screwdrivers and pliers to the chest pocket of his boiler suit.

"I was thinking, you could use a couple of rakes on those locks. Hold them back to back and you could probably jog all the pins a lot quicker."

Paolo looked away and glanced out of a side window from behind one of the curtains, as though my suggestion was entirely inconsequential.

"Fine," I said, passing the folio to Mike. "It's all yours," I told him.

He nodded, then checked on Paolo and Jan once more. He consulted the time on his watch and gave Francesca a meaningful look. She stubbed her cigarette out on the floor of the van and gripped him firmly by the wrist.

"Go," she said, and with that Mike popped the door on the camper van and the three of them set the entire farce in motion.

*

We waited twenty minutes, first watching from between gaps in the window curtains as Paolo picked the locks on the gates at the bottom of the fire escape stairs, then following them with our eyes as they made their way up between floors. At the double doors on the fourth floor, Paolo took a good five minutes to disarm the security sensors but Mike and Jan crowded around him, making it seem as if they were just carrying out repairs to the doors themselves. Once they were through, they moved beyond our line of sight, heading off along the external glass corridor towards one of the emergency exit doors that led into the inner recesses of the museum. Jan had calculated that he would need ten minutes to do his job and after that they would retrace their steps and make their way to the fifth floor of the building.

Francesca smoked her way through four cigarettes as we waited and pretty soon the air in the camper van became too acrid for my liking. The girl with the piercings seemed unfazed by the smoke and the two others, a red-haired girl from Battersea and a tanned South African rugby fanatic, were sat in the front of the van with their windows wide open. The South African was Francesca's driver and his instructions were to stay with the van at all times and only to move if it became absolutely necessary. I doubted he had any experience as a getaway driver but I didn't think that really mattered considering the camper van would struggle to get above walking pace. Francesca's plan didn't account for a madcap dash from the scene of the crime and if it ever became about that, we were almost certainly doomed.

I saw Francesca consult her watch and stub out her latest cigarette. She leaned forwards and rubbed the South African's shoulders.

"Wait here for us, Boyd."

"Sure thing," he said.

"Good boy."

She opened the barn doors on the side of the van and ushered me and the two girls outside. We gathered on the pavement next to a rack of rental bicycles, blinking in the sunshine. I placed my hands on my hips and squinted up at the inside-out exterior of the building. All the primary colours and the glass and the pipe-work made it seem so cheerful, like a children's play area. So why did it suddenly feel so daunting?

TWNETY-NINE

We purchased tickets for the museum in separate queues and headed upstairs in staggered intervals so as not to look as if we were part of a group. By the time I handed my ticket to the attendant at the entrance to the museum on floor four, I could already see Francesca climbing the wooden stairs towards the more permanent exhibitions one floor above. I chose to go up in the lift, then strolled as casually as I was able alongside the glass-lined corridor in the direction of the Picasso room.

To be fair to Francesca, the museum was quieter than I had expected. Even so, there were still plenty of visitors. Most were ambling between the linked display rooms, hands clasped behind their backs, fingers gripping glossy brochures. Others were sneaking flash photographs of the art, only to be reprimanded by the numerous museum staff. There were a few kids running between rooms or hanging off modernist sculptures and there was also the occasional art student sat with a sketchbook and a pencil, copying elements from some of the more obscure works.

Although the cubist room was situated towards the opposite end of the gallery, it didn't take long for me to reach it. Francesca and the girl with the piercings were already inside, admiring a pair of compact Picasso portraits on the left-hand wall. Like me, I got the impression they were finding it hard to act as if they were absorbed by the paintings. All I wanted to do was to stare at The Guitar Player. It was right there, smack in the centre of the wall that faced the main entrance to the room, and it was by far the most distinctive canvas. I gave it the merest glance, then circled over to the right and waited for the redhead to arrive and do something similar. Once she was with us, the girl with the piercings gravitated back out into the main corridor and hovered beside the bronzed horse sculpture. Behind the horse was an opposing wall and hanging on the wall was the large Picabia called Udnie. The fact it was there was fundamental to the heist – the room where The Guitar Player was situated was one of the few areas in the museum that was faced by an opposing wall rather than another viewing gallery.

There were only three entrances to the room: the large archway from the main corridor where the girl with the piercings was keeping watch and the two much smaller side archways. As I already knew from my previous visit, one of the side archways led into an adjoining corridor that was fronted by the expanse of glass running along the exterior of the building and a pair of emergency exit doors. Behind those doors, if all had gone to plan, Paolo, Mike and Jan would be waiting.

The security camera in the service corridor was just one of the many in the vicinity that Jan had been tasked with looping for a ten-minute period. I guessed we were already something like three minutes in so Francesca would have to call it soon or risk missing our window of opportunity.

There was one more factor, of course, and that factor happened to be a middle-aged man in a sober grey uniform who was sat upon the plastic chair beneath the main archway into the room. I recognised the museum attendant as Jean-Patrick Deville, the smart-looking chap from the photograph with the centre parting, the young girlfriend and the questionable morals. He was wearing a white ID badge on his lapel that exactly matched the one I had found at the back of the painting of Montmartre. Francesca was holding his eye, I noticed, and hers was certainly a knowing gaze. So long as it was only us and him in the room, and so long as Jan had been able to rejig the security cameras and disable the pressure sensors, and so long as Paolo succeeded in picking the locks on the emergency doors without triggering an alarm or drawing unnecessary attention to himself, then we would be home and dry. Was it just me, or did that seem like one hell of a lot of provisos?

I tensed and glanced for a moment towards The Guitar Player. I felt the museum attendant watching me. His hands were gripping the side of his chair, knuckles whitening as though he was bracing himself for a surge of 50,000 volts, and I could see beads of perspiration on his forehead. Francesca looked over to me and I was all set to give her the go-ahead when I decided to check on the girl with the piercings one last time. She was tugging on her earlobe, signalling that someone was approaching. I shook my head to Francesca just as a group of schoolchildren invaded the space.

The group were shepherded by a middle-aged woman with a frazzled expression who held a metal aerial above her head with a yellow ribbon attached to it. The woman moved to the space directly in front of The Guitar Player and craned her neck until she was certain her entire group were present. Then, in a hoarse, scraping voice, she began to lecture them in what I thought was probably Spanish. The group seemed disinterested and distracted by one another. They were chewing gum or peeking at the displays on their mobile telephones, and at least one kid was listening to an iPod. I rose up on the balls of my feet and peered across the heads of the schoolchildren towards Francesca. Her jaw was set hard and she was staring daggers at the female teacher. Just then, a male teacher arrived and shuffled towards the rear of the group. He offered the museum attendant a casual wave that seemed as though it might carry enough force to topple him from his chair.

The teacher droned on and on. More than once, I felt certain she'd reached the end of her presentation, only for her to take a deep breath and begin a new thread. Time was ticking away. I had to assume that Paolo, Mike and Jan were hovering outside the emergency exit, trying their best to appear inconspicuous and meanwhile looking searchingly towards the redhead, willing her to give them the all-clear.

Two of the schoolgirls seemed very interested in my appearance. They were openly staring at me and conferring with one another. I wondered for a moment if they'd seen my picture on the television news but I thought it unlikely. It was probably just that they'd spotted the discrepancy between the colour of my hair and my eyebrows. After all, they both seemed familiar with the finer points of hair dye – one of the girls had blonde highlights running through a dark bob and the other had lurid pink locks. I tried to ignore the way they were whispering to one another but I was finding it tough. I began to think about sticking my tongue out or sneering at them, which wouldn't have been my smartest move ever.

Mercifully, the teacher chose that moment to clap her hands and I got the impression she was asking if anyone had any questions. I was tempted to thrust my hand into the air myself: "*Please Miss, may we get on with our million-dollar heist?*"

Eventually, the group began to shuffle out of the room, with just the two girls who'd been staring at me continuing to linger. I did my best to behave as if I was completely absorbed by the Braque piece in front of me. I scratched my head and rubbed my chin, eruditely assessing the work with all the concentration of a gnat. From the corner of my eye, I glimpsed the male teacher return and herd the girls out of the room. I checked on the museum attendant, if only to make sure he hadn't been reduced to a puddle of sweat and anxiety, and then I looked back towards the girl with the piercings. She gave me a solemn nod and I passed the signal onto Francesca. Francesca gestured towards the redhead and less than a minute later, Paolo, Mike and Jan burst in.

As soon as they entered the space, I hurried across to The Guitar Player and whipped it off the wall, setting the heavy wood and glass frame face-down on the floor in a way that spared my fingers too much discomfort. I stepped aside and Mike moved in with a battery-operated screwdriver to remove the four Phillips screws that were securing the glass backing in place. The moment the screws were out, Jan levered the glass free with a long-bladed knife and I very carefully removed the canvas. Meanwhile, Paolo popped the clasps on the plastic folio and eased Catherine's canvas into the picture frame. Jan replaced the glass backboard and Mike began to screw it into position. Before he was done, I slipped The Guitar Player into the plastic folio. Once the last screw was tightened, I handed Jan the folio and signalled for the three of them to go. As they left, I heaved the frame up from the floor and set it hanging once more on the wall, trying my best to get it as straight as possible.

The entire procedure was over in less than two minutes and even though I say so myself, it was beautifully choreographed.

Stepping back from the painting, I raised my hand to the back of my head and scratched my skull. I turned to Francesca and she winked at me before heading for the corridor. I was all set to give the attendant the thumbs-up when a middle-aged couple entered the space. They walked right over to The Guitar Player and stood perhaps two feet away, admiring the painting. I did the same myself. I could have looked at it a hundred times more and still been unable to tell if it was any different from the painting with which Jan was hurrying down the fire escape. I wasn't sure whether that said more about my eyesight or the quality of the reproduction and I didn't altogether care. The painting was gone. Francesca was gone. The girl with the piercings and the redhead were beginning to make their way out too. I had only to follow.

Except I didn't. I stayed where I was and waited for Nathan Farmer to arrive.

THIRTY

Farmer entered the Picasso room alongside a short, balding man. The balding man wore a dark V-neck sweater over a crisp white shirt and carried a pigskin briefcase in his hand. They were flanked by a team of security guards who worked efficiently to seal off the room and evacuate any visitors from the end of the gallery we were occupying. Deville, the museum attendant, remained in his plastic chair, staring mournfully at the floor. Farmer and the balding man didn't trouble themselves with him or even with me. They simply approached The Guitar Player and then the balding man fixed a jeweller's loupe into his right eye socket and scoured the canvas.

While the balding man worked, Farmer tapped the soles of his tea-coloured brogues in a nervous quick time, awaiting his verdict. I did the same thing in my scuffed baseball trainers. It didn't speed the man's work at all but it at least gave me something to do beyond wringing my hands and muttering soundlessly.

The balding man pressed his face right up against the glass of the picture frame, trawling over the canvas inch by inch. His nose was twitching, I noticed, as though he were a bloodhound tracking an elusive scent. Or perhaps he just had a head cold. Whatever the reason, the twitching and the inspection continued, as did the silence in the room.

"You were able to watch it all?" I asked Farmer, aiming to break the tension.

"Yes," he said, in a distracted way. "We reinstalled the cameras the moment your Polish friend finished with them."

"So you saw me attach the tracking device to the canvas before it was put in the folio?"

Farmer gave me an arch look. "You're beginning to doubt yourself?"

"Just nervous, I guess."

"Well, I dare say I can understand that."

I dare say he could. After all, he'd come away with by far the better end of our deal, and that was only provided my logic was sound.

"You have someone following the camper van?"

"Yes, yes," he told me. "Don't fret. We won't lose them."

"Both our heads would be on the line if you did, I guess."

"Oh, do be quiet and allow this gentleman to work."

The gentleman did just that. He was focusing on the bottom right-hand corner of the canvas, where an artist's signature might normally be found. There was no signature on The Guitar Player and there wasn't one on the forgery either – Picasso had never signed the work. Even so, Farmer had assured me the balding man was expert enough to determine the efficacy of the canvas.

The balding man inhaled and removed the loupe from his eye. I readied myself for his opinion but instead he pulled a handkerchief from his pocket and cleaned the lens of the loupe. He fixed the loupe into his eye once more and re-examined the bottom right-hand corner of the painting. Then he motioned for Farmer to join him and encouraged him to look at one greyish-brown facet in particular. He was speaking French in a low, hushed tone and I was unable to make out what he was saying.

"What's he think?" I asked Farmer.

Farmer turned to me, removed his gold pocket watch from his breast pocket and consulted the time. Whatever he found on his watch face didn't appear to please or displease him in the slightest. Eventually, he said, "It seems you were right."

"Yes." I punched the air. "I knew it."

"Which would explain why you were quite so nervous, I imagine?"

I let that one slide.

"Admit it," I told him. "You're impressed."

"I'm neither impressed nor disappointed," he said, putting his pocket watch away. "I'm simply pleased to have done my job."

"Oh come on, don't I even get a thank-you?"

"Why don't you just follow me?" he said, crooking his finger. "Your friend is waiting upstairs."

"That's really it? Lighten up, guy. You could at least shake my hand."

Farmer crossed his arms in front of his chest and studied me for a moment. He drew in a calculated breath. "Very well," he said, before treating me to one of the most formal and uninspired hand-shakes I've ever had the misfortune to experience.

The moment I entered the security room behind Nathan Farmer and Victoria saw me for the first time, she stepped away from the bank of colour monitors she'd been watching and placed her fists on her hips.

"Will somebody please tell me what the hell's going on?"

"That's the idea," I told her. "You saw it, right?"

"I saw you and the bookshop crowd take that Picasso," she said, gesturing at the monitors. "I don't understand what it means, though. Mr Farmer here wouldn't tell me a thing other than that you wanted me to be your witness. But witness to what, Charlie? I can't clear your name because I was stood here watching you help them."

"That was kind of the point."

She glared at me, stiff-jawed, and I reached over and placed a hand on her shoulder.

"I wanted you to be able to confirm that I was involved."

"Why? So you can get a few extra years behind bars?" she asked, shaking my hand loose.

"No. So that the people who matter acknowledge that I played a role in returning the original to the gallery."

Victoria's forehead became a cluster of frowns. "You might have wanted to think about that before you let those clowns steal it in the first place."

"Look," I said, moving towards one of the television monitors that was screening back the image of the Picasso room and pointing to The Guitar Player. "*That's* the original."

Victoria gazed at me as if I was mad. She bared her teeth. "What?"

"Francesca's gang stole Catherine's forgery."

"I don't understand. Are you saying you'd switched them?"

"No," I said, reaching for her shoulder once more. "The truth is Catherine's forgery has been hanging in the gallery for some months. The original was in her bank vault. A day ago, you were carrying it in your hands."

Victoria stared at me for a few moments, the colour beginning to fade from her cheeks. She dropped onto the swivel chair positioned to her side and raised her hand to her forehead. "Tell me this is a joke."

"It's no joke," Nathan Farmer said. "At least we don't believe it is. X-ray and forensic tests will be able to confirm it. But for now, the opinion of the gallery expert seems quite conclusive."

"Along with my reasoning," I added.

Farmer nodded without another word, as though punctuating what I'd said in an attempt to stave off any praise I might be seeking. Perhaps he was afraid I would try to secure a reward. I knew when not to push my luck, though. Quashing the investigation into my involvement with Pierre's activities was more than sufficient for me.

"Would either of you care to share this reasoning?" Victoria asked, looking between us as if she was uncertain whom she loathed more.

"Sure," I told her. "It all came back to Pierre's client."

"Catherine's husband, you mean? The armed robber?"

"No, as it happens. I know we discussed that theory but I was never all that comfortable with it. I mean, what was the guy's motive?"

"Revenge. Catherine was trying to sell the plans to the heist out from under him."

"That was our idea," I allowed. "But it didn't add up. We had no way of knowing whether they'd really fallen out. And if they hadn't, what was to stop him sharing in any money Catherine might make from selling the plans?"

"Um, how about the fact he's locked up?" she said, with heavy sarcasm.

"But he's only going to serve another sixteen months if his lawyer is to be believed."

Victoria glared at me, frustration seeping from her every pore. She looked ready to pounce on any error I might make. It wasn't that she wanted me to be wrong; she was just annoyed because I'd kept her in the dark until now.

"Okay," she said, in a level tone. "So if Catherine's husband wasn't Pierre's mystery client, who was? Was it Bruno?"

"I don't think so. And I have to admit, I didn't exactly work all this out for myself. I had to find a clue first."

"A clue. Fancy that. Clues can be good."

"Clues can be excellent. Especially when they tell you something important."

"Such as?" she said, rolling her hand as if to wind the information out of me.

"Such as the telephone number that belonged to Pierre's client."

"Wait a minute. You're saying you recognised one of the numbers you found on his telephone?"

"Not to begin with. But I narrowed it down to three possibilities and then I cross-checked those numbers against the city telephone directory."

Her eyes went wide. "You went through the entire telephone directory?"

"No-o. I just checked some numbers for the people who could have been involved in this thing. I checked Bruno's number, the number for the bank he worked at, the number for the bookshop, the number Mr Farmer here had given me. Everything I could think of, in fact."

"And?"

"And I found a hit."

"Christ, Charlie. Will you please just tell me who Pierre's mystery client was?"

"It was Catherine," I said. "She hired me herself."

THIRTY-ONE

"Gah," Victoria said, clutching her temple. "Now I'm really confused. You're saying Catherine hired you to burgle her?"

"No. Catherine hired Pierre to find someone to burgle her. In return for twenty thousand euros."

"But that's insane."

I backed off from her. "Why?"

"Well, duh, why would anyone want to be burgled?"

"I have a hypothesis."

"Is that the same thing as a hunch?"

I gave her a doped smile, then shook my head. "I hope it's a little more than that. At least, it was good enough to persuade Mr Farmer here to trust me."

"I don't know about that," Farmer cut in.

"Either way," I went on. "There's logic to my thinking. Want to hear it?"

"Gosh, like you wouldn't believe."

I grinned and showed Victoria my hands and my forearms, like a magician demonstrating to an audience that he has nothing concealed up his sleeves. "To begin with, we know that Catherine and her husband had come up with a detailed plan to steal The Guitar Player."

Victoria nodded, bright-eyed, like a setter awaiting a treat.

"We also know that Catherine had studied Picasso's work at the gallery archive near Orléans and she'd produced an excellent forgery." Victoria went to speak but I held up a finger and stopped her. "Meanwhile, Gerard had done some legwork of his own and he'd come up with various pieces of information. The most crucial piece was the museum attendant. Once they were in a position to coerce him, they had a much better chance of switching Catherine's forgery for the original."

"Sure. But then Gerard was arrested before his plan could be put into practice."

"Not necessarily. I think that's what they wanted people to believe."

"Huh?"

"In fact, I'd go so far as to say Gerard planned his arrest. Think about it: Francesca's take was that Gerard had never learned to stop shooting his mouth off, even when it got him sent to prison the first time round. But let's suppose he hadn't just learned his lesson – let's suppose he'd also worked out exactly what it could do for him."

"I'm not sure I follow you."

"Well, Gerard couldn't ever be suspected of carrying out the heist if someone else did it first, right?"

"But you said they didn't."

"Yeah, but no-one was supposed to know that. The way I see it working, Gerard put his plan into effect weeks ago. He switched Catherine's forgery for the original Picasso and then Catherine stored the original at her bank. After that, Gerard got himself arrested. Of course, dumb old Gerard had been talking for months about how he'd planned the perfect heist. And pretty soon, Catherine began letting it be known that she was fed up with her moron of a husband and she was willing to sell his plans for a reasonable sum. After all, she couldn't be expected to carry out the theft herself."

"This is sounding beyond far-fetched, Charlie."

"I know. But not impossible."

She grimaced. "You think?"

"Well, stealing the Picasso certainly wasn't. I'm willing to bet Deville, the museum attendant, will be able to confirm he was there when they did it. And what better way to throw the authorities off the scent than by having somebody steal the very plans everyone's been talking about before anyone gets to put them into practice?"

"Even though they were useless by then."

"Exactly. It's all smoke and mirrors. Catherine gets me hired to steal the painting of Montmartre from her apartment. Maybe she even lets it be known that her forgery was taken at the same time. So it seems the heist can never go ahead."

"Oh, okay. And if the heist can never happen, the last thing anyone would suspect is that it's already occurred."

"Precisely."

She screwed up one eye. "I think I'm still confused."

"I can understand that. But even if you don't follow my thinking all the way through, you can't ignore the fact that the person who hired Pierre contacted him from Catherine's apartment."

"That doesn't necessarily mean it was Catherine. Didn't Pierre say he was contacted by a man?"

"Well – there is that. But even if I don't have all the answers, it's still a theory that works. Plus there's the fact that the painting that's hanging there now," I said, jabbing my finger at the television monitor near Victoria's elbow, "looks as if it really is the original."

"Subject to the necessary tests being carried out," Farmer added.

"Of course."

Victoria turned to him. "And where exactly do you fit into all this Mr Farmer? Do you work for the gallery?"

Farmer squared his shoulders and inhaled deeply. "As I told Charlie, I have a number of clients and in this particular matter their interests just happened to coincide."

"By which you can take it he works for the gallery, the insurance company and the local authorities," I said. "Any I missed?"

"I don't see a reason for me to confirm it," Farmer told me.

"I guess I don't either. Provided I'm in the clear."

Farmer shook his head and slipped his hands into his trouser pockets. "I'm really not sure we're there just yet."

"But I got the Picasso back. That was what you wanted, right?"

"Originally. But there's also the small matter of Catherine Ames' body being found in your apartment. I'm afraid it's going to be rather difficult to simply ignore."

"Yeah right," Victoria said, finding her feet. "As though Charlie wouldn't have solved that too. Come on Charlie, tell him who you think the killer is."

"You must have an inkling," I said, with a tilt of my head.

"Pierre?"

"I agree," I told her. "Happen to know why?"

"Not really. Although I find it kind of suspicious that he didn't notice how his client's telephone number matched the number of the person he was asked to have burgled."

"He did notice. The number was circled in the telephone directory I found in his apartment."

"Well, there you go then."

"And there's more. When I was inside Pierre's apartment, I happened to look inside his kitchen drawers. He had a roll of plastic bags. The bags looked very much like the one that was used to suffocate Catherine."

"Plastic bags," Farmer said, in a dubious tone.

"Plus a roll of electrical tape. Black – the same colour as the tape that was used to secure the bag round Catherine's neck."

"You're basing your accusation on plastic bags and electrical tape? These are common household items."

"It's also a feeling I have. Plus motive. Catherine and Gerard would have needed to sell the Picasso, yes? They'd have needed a fence. There's nothing to say they hadn't already lined Pierre up. And I'm guessing he would have been pretty steamed when he heard Gerard had got arrested and Catherine was looking to hire someone to steal those plans."

"Hmm," Farmer said, and rocked forwards on his toes. "I do hate to be the bringer of bad news but aside from pointing out that what you've just said makes almost as little sense as your quite pathetic and entirely ineffective disguise, I'm afraid there's a rather large hole in your theory."

"Oh?"

"The police have had your fence in custody since the afternoon he hired you. There's no way he could possibly have killed Catherine Ames."

THIRTY-TWO

"What now?" Victoria asked me, once Nathan Farmer had ducked out of the room, dodging any shrapnel from the bombshell he'd so casually dispatched.

"I don't know," I said, in a distracted way. "I think I might be screwed."

I was staring at the television monitors, as if the various gallery scenes they were screening might trigger something in my mind. My best explanation for who had killed Catherine and why they'd done it had just been blown and I was finding it hard to let go. I kept trying to fit the pieces back together in a way that would make sense but it simply wouldn't work. Evidently Victoria was going through the same process.

"Pierre being in custody doesn't necessarily wreck everything," she said. "I mean, he has a whole list of contacts, right? He has other burglars on his books. What's to say he doesn't have killers too?"

I frowned. "A hitman, you mean?"

"Why not?"

"I don't see it," I said, shaking my head. "And I didn't find any evidence of that in Pierre's apartment. Plus, there's something else I'd forgotten."

"Oh?"

"Pierre didn't know where I lived. At least, I don't think he did. So even if he hired someone, he wouldn't have known where to send them."

"But if he did hire someone, they could have followed you from the moment Pierre hired you to do the job."

"All of that just to set me up?"

"Absolutely. Do you think we should mention this to Farmer?"

"No," I said, and dropped into a swivel chair across from Victoria. I pivoted backwards over the cushioned backrest and pressed the heels of my hands against my forehead. "I think we need to ditch the whole Pierre idea."

"But why? He had those bags and that tape."

"But no cable ties. And Farmer's right – if he was the killer, why would he leave them lying around his home?"

"The telephone number then. He had it circled in his telephone directory."

I sat upright and faced Victoria, doing my best to appear contrite. "No he didn't."

"But you said –"

"I know what I said. But the truth is I put the circle there myself. At the time, I really did think Pierre could be the killer but I also knew the evidence was pretty thin. So I figured I'd add another piece to the puzzle."

Victoria whistled and rolled her eyes. "I'm not sure I'm comfortable with that, Charlie."

"I'm not sure I'm comfortable with it either. But having it on my conscience seemed a hell of a lot better than serving time in a French jail for a murder I wasn't guilty of."

Victoria crossed her arms in front of her chest and inhaled deeply. I gave her a sheepish look, as though I knew I'd overstepped the line, but still not feeling ready to apologise for it either.

Trying to work out what could have happened was beginning to drive me a little nuts. It was as if I'd been picking away at a really secure lock in my head and no matter how many pins I thought I'd shifted or how much progress I thought I'd made, the damn thing was still refusing to yield. Maybe the truth was I'd been tackling the lock in the wrong way. In my eagerness to have the mystery resolved, I'd been going at it like an oaf, trying to force the thing instead of taking a more considered approach. Maybe what I needed to do was to step back and think about the problem afresh.

"Forget Pierre," I said. "Scrub the whole idea. Where does that leave us?"

"You won't like it."

"Try me."

"Okay." She pressed her hands together and raised them in front of her mouth, fingers steepled. "Like I said before, the killer has to be someone you met early on."

"Oh crap. Not this again."

Victoria lowered her hands and twisted her lips.

"I'm sorry," I told her. "But that doesn't get us anywhere new. None of the people I met early on could have done this."

"Bruno could have."

"But why? He sold the painting of Montmartre cheaply. He didn't know anything else was going on."

"He didn't have to. Maybe he just wanted to kill Catherine."

"In my apartment?"

"Why not?"

I shook my head and stood up from my chair. I moved over to the corner of the room and pressed my palms flat against the wall. I lowered my head and growled.

"Paige then," Victoria suggested.

"No," I said, into the wall.

"You don't know that."

"I do," I said, turning and forming my left hand into a fist, then grinding it into my right palm. "I'm sorry. I know you're only trying to help but Paige didn't have any reason to do it."

"Francesca then. Or one of the crowd from the bookshop."

"I didn't meet Francesca until yesterday."

"So ignore the rules. Ignore everything I've said up to now. It has to be someone tied into this thing and Francesca did know about the significance of the painting. She knew all about the heist."

"And that's all she was interested in. She didn't need to kill Catherine."

"Even if she found out she'd been tricked?"

"But she didn't find out. If she had done, she wouldn't have nicked the forgery from down there."

I pointed at the television monitor, then threw my hands into the air. I turned on the spot and cradled my forehead, trying to free up my mind. I really needed to undo that damn mental lock. Either that, or go crazy trying. Losing my temper with Victoria wasn't really on but my frustration was getting the better of me. I was beginning to think I'd never find a way through.

"Farmer then," Victoria whispered, nodding her head towards the door he'd just left by.

"No."

"You won't even consider it? Charlie, you can't rule people out like this."

"It wasn't him," I said, under my breath.

I met Victoria's eyes and held them for a moment. Then I dropped my head and ran my hand over my inflamed knuckles. I almost welcomed the physical pain; at least it was some form of distraction.

"Anyone else?" I asked, fighting to regain my composure.

Victoria shook her head. "Me?" she offered, with a thin smile.

"Definitely not."

"Then I'm all out of suspects. Unless it was that girl at your reading. Or the catalogue model in the back of your Faulks novels."

She laughed faintly and I smiled at her, raising my bandaged fingers to scratch my temple. I closed my eyes and inhaled deeply and in that moment it felt as though Victoria had just handed me a golden key to the lock in my mind. I inserted the key and turned it and the lock sprang open as easy as that. I grinned widely, relief flooding my system.

"Do you have your handbag with you?"

"Yes," she said, cautiously.

"And your mobile?"

She showed it to me.

"Come on," I said. "I've had an idea."

THIRTY-THREE

I telephoned Bruno at the Banque Centrale and told him we needed to meet. I asked him to contact Paige and he rang me back in under five minutes, saying they would come to the brasserie we'd gone to following my reading. Neither of them had taken much persuading, and I suppose I could have been worried by that, but the truth is I wasn't surprised. My best guess was they were anxious about how the investigation into Catherine's death might impact on their lives and they seemed willing to do whatever it took to end their uncertainty.

As we made our way across the Pont Notre Dame and along Rue de la Cité, Victoria begged me to tell her what was on my mind but I asked her to stay quiet and give me a chance to think. I still had a few things to straighten out and I couldn't do it while she was yammering on. It was hard enough not to get distracted by the kind of thoughts that afflicted me when I caught sight of the city's police headquarters up ahead or the dark-stoned exterior of the Conciergerie, the former prison where Marie Antoinette and the French Revolutionaries had been detained. Fortunately, by the time we neared the brasserie, it seemed to me like it all fitted. Of course, only Bruno and Paige would be able to tell me if I was right.

I directed Victoria to an outside table beneath an unlit patio heater, where we selected a pair of wicker seats that afforded us a view of the approach Bruno and Paige were likely to take. I signalled the waiter for two espressos and set about lighting a cigarette. Victoria didn't say anything, though she did waft her hand in front of her face the first time I exhaled. I blew more smoke off to the side, then killed the cigarette. Our coffees arrived and we sipped them in silence. I listened to the purr of vehicle engines from the Quai and the occasional car horn. In the lulls between the vehicle noise and the chatter of the café patrons, I could just catch the background hum of a commentary track on a passing Bateau Mouche. A couple near to us were sharing moules frites and the tang of the lemon juice the woman was squirting over her dish caught in my nostrils. I covered my nose with my finger and tried to concentrate. I was still probing and testing the logic of my theory when I finally saw Bruno and Paige hurrying over a pedestrian crossing in our direction.

"Sit down," I told them, kicking two wicker chairs out from under the opposite side of the circular table.

"Who's she?" Paige asked, nodding at Victoria, but declining to make eye contact with her.

"A good friend," I said. "Bruno has met her before. At the bank."

Paige turned slowly and treated Victoria to a sour look. She crowded over the table towards me, her eyes protruding out from their sockets and threatening to caress my face.

"What is this? Are you setting us up?" she asked, casting an intent gaze over my shoulder and around the terraced eating area.

"Now why would you think that?"

"It's pretty sudden, this meeting. Bruno wouldn't say what you wanted."

"Because he doesn't know," I told her. "But it's nothing for the two of you to be concerned about. All I need is for you to look at a picture."

"The painting?" Bruno asked, jutting his head into our inner circle.

"No." I turned to Victoria. "Do you still have Catherine's driving licence?"

Victoria held my eyes for a moment, her pupils crammed with question marks. Then she lunged towards the floor to gather her handbag. She lifted the bag onto her lap and undid the buckle that secured the leather flap on the front. Reaching inside, she removed a small plastic card, around the size of a credit card. On the front of the card was Catherine's name and address, alongside her digital image.

I took the licence from Victoria and handed it to Bruno. He spent a good few moments looking at the image before glancing up at me, an uncertain expression on his face.

"But this is not Catherine," he said, blinking.

I gestured to Paige and she snatched the card from Bruno's hand and subjected it to a close examination.

"You know who this is?" she asked, jabbing her finger at the picture.

"Tell me."

"It's Sophia."

"The Estonian lady? The one you said left the bookshop with Francesca's keys?"

"Uh huh."

"You happen to know her last name?"

Paige shook her bloodless face. I studied her for a moment longer, then reclaimed the card and slipped it into my trouser pocket.

"What's happening?" she asked.

"Never mind," I told her, rising from my chair and pulling Victoria upright by her elbow. "Excuse us. We have to go."

"Go?" Bruno said. "But you cannot just leave."

"Watch me," I told him. "And don't look so nervous. Like you said, you guys weren't involved in all this. So you really shouldn't have anything to worry about."

I led Victoria away from the café and across the Quai towards the River Seine. We descended a flight of stone steps beside a second-hand poster stall and found an empty bench overlooking the marine-green river, not too far from a gaudy floating restaurant. I glanced back in the direction we'd come from and then all around us to make sure we hadn't been followed. It seemed safe enough. Even if someone managed to watch over us from above, the wall we were sat against was very high so we couldn't be overheard.

"Will you tell me what on earth's going on?" Victoria asked, when I was through working my neck like a marionette's.

"I'll try. I'm still figuring some of it out myself."

"But you have figured it out."

I nodded. "I think I know who our killer is."

"So tell me."

"It's Catherine."

Victoria looked at me as if I was insane. She searched behind my eyes for whatever it was she couldn't quite place.

"I thought you said it wasn't suicide."

"I did. And I was right. But the dead woman in my apartment wasn't Catherine Ames. It was the Sophia woman Paige just mentioned."

Victoria cradled her forehead with the fingers of both hands. "You'd better explain."

"It's a little complicated."

"You don't say."

I smiled in a tired way and glanced sideways at the glistening waters of the river. Further upstream, an industrial barge was approaching the nearest bridge span. The barge was loaded with mounds of aggregate and it looked almost too big to steer. As I faced up to explaining everything to Victoria, I began to think I knew something of what the skipper of the barge was going through.

"It's difficult to know where to begin. But how about this? To the outside world, Catherine worked as an archivist for the Pompidou, right?"

"Right."

"But she was also a skilled artist, and more than that, she was a forger."

"Sure. We know she faked the Picasso. I'm with you on that."

I arched an eyebrow. "Yeah, and maybe she faked a lot more besides. When I searched through the canvases in her apartment, I didn't have that in mind. But there were a fair number of different styles now I think back on it and I'd say there's a chance at least some of them were copies of other works."

Victoria pouted, as though the information was inconsequential.

"That's the background," I went on. "Catherine's a forger – it's in her nature. It's also something she's good at. So what's to say she can't manipulate other images?"

"Like?"

"Like the photo ID on her driving licence. I went through her things twice and during that time I only found two photographs of her. Number one, the driving licence. Number two, the framed photograph that was face-down on her dresser."

"There could have been others."

I shook my head. "Believe me, I would have found them. And that's kind of odd. I mean, here's someone who's really into the visual arts . . ."

"So what's your thinking?" Victoria asked, interrupting me. "She doctored both images? Why would she do that?"

"Preparation. With a modern computer, it wouldn't have been hard to take an old photograph of herself with Gerard and impose Sophia's head in place of her own. I'm assuming they look fairly similar in the first place, you understand, or else it wouldn't have worked."

Victoria raised her hand and made a huffing noise. "What wouldn't have worked, Charlie?"

"Killing Sophia and making it seem as if it was Catherine. That's why she suffocated her with the bag. All the discoloration of her skin and the swelling, it would have disguised her appearance, blurred their differences to some extent. She didn't just fake a Picasso, Vic – she faked her own death."

Victoria backed away from me and screwed her eyes tight shut as if she'd just smelled something unpleasant. "But the police aren't fools. They'd check dental records and the like, wouldn't they?"

"Not necessarily. Dental records are often a last resort. It's not a perfect science, no matter what we're led to believe. So in the first instance they'd go for something much more straightforward."

"Such as?"

"ID on the body. Things in her purse, for instance."

She peered at me. "Which you're saying Catherine could have planted."

"Yes. But that's not all. They'd also want someone who knew Catherine to positively identify her."

"So then you're screwed."

"Uh uh," I said, wagging a finger. "Who's the first person they'd contact?"

"The spouse, I suppose. But Gerard's in prison."

"So? He's still Catherine's next of kin. And if he's in on the scam, all he has to do is say it's her and turn on the waterworks. Chances are, the authorities won't look any further, especially if the real victim is a foreigner who happens to have been working as a volunteer at a nutty bookshop in the centre of Paris. Most of the people who stack shelves at Paris Lights are free spirits. It could be months or even years before anyone they know back home raises an alarm. And this Sophia was early fifties, probably single. Maybe there is no-one back home."

"I don't know, Charlie . . ."

"It's audacious, I admit. But so was stealing a Picasso in the first place. Why have alibis that are any less daring?"

"Alibis, plural?" she asked, squinting.

"Absolutely. Gerard gets himself arrested after letting as many people as possible know he hasn't put his masterplan into effect. Soon after, Catherine looks as if she's been killed by somebody trying to get their hands on Gerard's grunt work. So they're both in the clear."

"But if what you're saying is even half-right, it sounds like more than just smoke and mirrors."

"Not really. First they create the impression that a heist that went ahead without a hitch never happened. Then they make it seem as if they're both out of the picture. Now all they have to do is wait, what, another sixteen months for Gerard to get out of the clink before they reclaim the Picasso and sell it for a small fortune, funding new lives somewhere else."

"But hang on, the Picasso was in the vault at Catherine's bank. And if everyone thought she was dead, she wouldn't exactly be able to wander in and claim it."

"I thought of that. But then I realised, who would she have left her things to in her will?"

Victoria sighed. "For your explanation to work, it has to be her husband."

"Spot on. So when Gerard gets out of prison, he has every right to go and collect Catherine's belongings."

Victoria leaned back against the blackened masonry behind her and shook her head from side to side, as though trying to dislodge the doubts that were forming inside her mind. It didn't seem as though she was having much success.

"If what you're saying is right," she began.

"It has to be."

"Then how do you explain the swipe card to Catherine's safety deposit box being in the back of that photograph frame? It's not something she'd want to leave just lying around."

"It wasn't just lying around. It was hidden."

"Not terribly well."

"Only because the person who went searching for it happened to be a burglar with sufficient motivation to find what he was looking for."

"I don't know. It would make more sense if Catherine had kept the swipe card herself. I mean, she couldn't very well access her apartment once she was supposedly dead, especially considering the police might be checking for any clues as to who killed her."

"But the police weren't looking that closely – the idea was to set me up for the murder at the same time as making it seem as though the infamous heist plans had been stolen. I guess Catherine and Gerard figured their apartment would be pretty much untouched until he was released. And like you said, Catherine couldn't have accessed the bank vault before then because she was meant to be dead."

Victoria crossed her arms in front of her chest. "Why not just sell the Picasso ahead of time?"

"And risk a leak? An informant? No, this way it was relatively secure. They could maybe risk a leak once Gerard had his freedom and they could trade the painting for enough cash to help them hide. But not before."

Victoria stood from the bench and walked towards the water's edge. She looked away after the barge, as though it held some secret answer that might convince her of what I was saying. I guess it was a lot to take in. It had already taken me days to put together. True, maybe Victoria or I would have handled things differently, but that didn't mean Gerard and Catherine hadn't done just as I'd said.

"Supposing you have it sussed," she said, turning back to me. "Supposing I don't find any holes in all this."

"You'll find holes. You always do."

"Yeah, but supposing you can cover them. Where does that leave you? All you have is a theory and a truly wild one at that. If you're right and Catherine stays hidden, and Gerard doesn't confess, you're still the prime suspect – even if they do happen to identify this Sophia woman."

"That's why I need to talk to Nathan Farmer," I said, delving into my pocket for his business card. "I have to convince him I'm right."

"And what about proof?"

"Proof's overrated," I told her, extending my hand and clicking my fingers for her mobile telephone. "At least, I've always thought so."

THIRTY-FOUR

Farmer agreed to meet with us at Place de la Bastille. We emerged from the Bastille métro station to find his sleek Jaguar parked just away from the National Opera House. I tapped on his window and he folded the newspaper he was reading and signalled for his chauffeur to admit us without bothering to acknowledge our existence. We climbed into the cream leather interior at the rear of the Jag, and I was instantly overcome by the new-car scent that enveloped us. The leather beneath my backside was soft and wonderfully sprung and the walnut inlays and panels on the doors and the dash were polished to a high sheen. I bounced on my seat and ran my hand over the leather, making an appreciative noise in the throat.

"Only the very best for you, Mr Farmer," I remarked.

He eyeballed me.

"Don't worry. It's a good thing," I assured him. "The nicest car, the finest suits, hand-crafted shoes. And to top it all, you deserve the most refined explanations available."

"You sound as if you're going to sell me a new home appliance," he said, dryly.

"It's just the satisfaction I get from a job well done. It's the same with my novels. Right, Vic?"

Victoria nodded. "It's exactly the same, Charlie."

"Shall we have a drink?" I asked, gesturing to a cut-glass decanter of whisky set into the moulded leather console ahead of us.

"Why don't we just talk," Farmer said. "Let's see what you have."

"All business, huh?"

"I'm afraid the situation rather demands it."

Farmer made a deft gesture towards the rear-view mirror and his chauffeur slipped the automatic transmission into drive and began to pull away from the kerb, turning left onto Rue Saint Antoine and continuing in the direction of the Louvre. I waited until we were passing the glass pyramid at the heart of the museum before really getting to the crux of my theory. I told Farmer that the dead woman in my apartment was an Estonian called Sophia and that her murder had been part of an elaborate cover-up of the Picasso heist that Catherine Ames and her husband Gerard had masterminded. I explained the motives behind their actions and the methodology they'd employed, and I was glad to see that in the second telling, the story sounded even more convincing to my ears.

As I unburdened myself of the tortured logic of it all, we glided up and down the broad, sloping avenues of the Champs-Élysées, circling around the Arc de Triomphe at one end of the boulevard and the Place de la Concorde at the other. We passed glitzy motor-car showrooms, expensive perfumeries and extortionate restaurants and cafés. We passed throngs of tourists. We passed every make and model of French car you could possibly imagine. And the over-whelming sensation I had was one of space. Not just space to think clearly now that my brain was beginning to shed some of the junk that had been swirling around it, but also a real appreciation of the wide expanses at the very heart of the city, all of it a welcome counterpoint to the confusion and fatigue I'd endured for the past few days.

I'd almost reached the end of my explanation when Farmer interrupted me with his first question. It was one I hadn't anticipated.

"How did Catherine access your apartment?"

"Excuse me?"

"How did she get in? You had good locks, correct? I believe you thought the Italian bookseller had picked them open."

I blinked. "He had."

"But according to you, he's not the killer."

"Nope."

"Then how did Catherine get in?"

I felt my eyebrows switch places. I fumbled for an answer.

"It's obvious," Victoria said, from just off to my side. "The Italian didn't lock up, so Catherine was able to get in once the group from the bookshop left."

"She can't possibly have known that would be the case," Farmer said.

Victoria shrugged. "Maybe she did. Maybe it was just luck."

"Or maybe Gerard had taught her to pick locks," I suggested.

Farmer gave me a despairing look. "So you had two break-ins, one after the other, both within a matter of hours, and the concierge at your building didn't see either of them."

"Could happen."

Farmer grunted.

"You haven't met my concierge," I told him. "Anyway, you don't want to get bogged down in the details. Just test the body in my apartment and see if you can prove it isn't Catherine. Or better still, that it's this Sophia woman. If I'm right about that, you can track Catherine down and get the confession you need."

"You're being rather simplistic."

"That's true. But believe me, after the way I've been feeling for the past few days, I can't rate simplicity highly enough."

Farmer pulled a silk handkerchief from his trouser pocket and coughed into it. The cough was an effete number. I sensed it was a delaying tactic, a move to give him time to run back through my argument and decide how he felt about it. I checked on Victoria's reaction. It didn't strike me as too reassuring.

"Outline your theory again," Farmer said, mopping his lips. "From the very beginning. Be specific. I need to think about this in more depth."

I started twittering away once more, all birdsong and sunlight and first-degree murder, and I was perhaps three minutes into my monologue when the telephone in the rear of the chauffeur's seat began to ring. Farmer answered, listened intently, then muttered a few curt responses before setting the receiver back into its cradle and telling me the news.

"We've been monitoring your friend Pierre's telephone line," he said. "Someone just left a message on his answering machine. It was a woman. Asking if he'd obtained the painting."

I felt a nerve twitch in my cheek. "Sorry?"

"The painting of Montmartre," he said, his fingers splayed and denting the leather seating beside his leg. "And that poses an interesting problem. I have to say I was inclined to go along with your theory. It's outlandish, naturally, but I could live with that. The problem now is where does this fit in with your thinking? You imagined the theft of this painting was just a mechanism to get you arrested and make everyone believe the Picasso heist could never proceed. But if this phone message is genuine, it contradicts all that."

I stared at the damn telephone that had scuppered me and rubbed my bandaged fingers against the side of my face, the cotton webbing catching in my stubble. "It has to be Catherine."

"Possibly. But you do see my point."

"So what are you saying exactly?"

"The woman left a telephone number," he went on. "There's something we can try but I imagine we'll only get one shot at it. I say we have your fence call her back and set up a meeting. I'll have men at my disposal. If we can, we'll detain her."

"And if she doesn't come?"

Farmer withdrew his pocket watch and contemplated the time, unwilling to meet my eyes. "Pray that doesn't happen."

THIRTY-FIVE

Boy, was I praying. Hands clasped together between my knees, brow knotted, I found myself repeating a silent mantra over and over in my head. Please be here. Please be here. The damn phrase was going to drive me nuts. Perhaps I needed to vary it. Maybe a different mantra would lead to better results.

It was later the very same evening and I was sat on a concrete bench in Place de la Défense with Victoria and Nathan Farmer on either side of me. Ahead of us loomed the Grande Arche, a marble and glass composite of impossible angles and towering dimensions. I could see an oblong of evening sky through the archway. The sky looked bleached, as though the colour had been drained from it. Shreds of cloud were being reflected over and over again in the windows of the arch; like a desktop image that had been endlessly repeated on a stack of computer monitors.

Pierre was stood at the bottom of the flight of stone steps in front of the mammoth structure, a pale blue sweater draped round his shoulders. He wore a white polo shirt, tan trousers and navy espadrilles. From where I sat, it was impossible to tell if his time in custody had affected his appearance. I guessed he wouldn't have had much sleep for the past few days and maybe that would show around his good eye. I'd heard he'd been allowed to shower and shave before he was driven to the arch and no doubt it had helped to make him feel a little more human. In his left hand he held the painting of Montmartre, wrapped once again in brown paper and string. His right hand gripped his leather manbag.

I didn't speak with Victoria or Farmer but they didn't seem to care. We were each of us absorbed in the wait, wondering if she would show. I didn't know quite what to do if she didn't. There'd be some move I could make, there always was. But the thing that concerned me was how long Farmer could keep the authorities waiting. My thinking was that if events stretched on for more than a few days they'd become jittery and my face would begin to look like a good fit for the television newscasts all over again. And if that happened, the chances of anyone investing time in my theory would be slim at best.

I was unclear what was motivating Farmer. Perhaps he felt some kind of loyalty to me for returning the Picasso to the gallery or perhaps he was old-school enough to believe he should help out a fellow Brit abroad. Either way, I had to respect him for giving me a chance to prove my innocence, even though I knew he couldn't indulge me for ever. Soon, it might become inconvenient for him to fight my corner or a new crisis might require his attention. Losing Farmer wasn't a scenario I was eager to confront. She simply had to show.

Just as the thought ran through my mind, Farmer raised a pair of compact binoculars to his eyes. The binoculars weren't compact enough for my liking. Sure, we were a good distance away from the arch and we were obscured by a low wall and a collection of shrubs, but we were hardly invisible. And binoculars were exactly the kind of equipment that would send her running if she happened to catch sight of us. We'd assumed she'd emerge from the métro station situated towards the far side of the plaza, or arrive via the boulevard that ran round the back of the arch, but there was no guarantee. She could just as easily approach on foot from behind us, and if she did, everything would be ruined.

Victoria gave me a tired smile and bunched her shoulders. She mouthed the word "Okay?" and I nodded my head, then looked towards the arch once again. I didn't want to miss a thing.

"She's late," Farmer said, lowering his binoculars.

"Maybe she clocked your spy gear. Not exactly discreet."

Farmer coughed and slipped his binoculars back into a suede carry-case. He consulted his pocket watch. Why didn't he just buy a wristwatch like everyone else? It was such an annoying mannerism: *hand to chest, fingers into pocket, remove watch, pop clasp, check time, close clasp, return watch to pocket.* I guessed the whole procedure might add up to an entire wasted day by the end of his life and I thought that perhaps I would buy him a watch when we were through – a cheap digital number from one of the street markets near my apartment. It would be worth it just to see his expression when I handed it over. I imagined it would be like I'd passed him a soiled tissue.

"Maybe we should wait somewhere else," I said. "In you car, even."

"We won't be able to see her from the Jaguar."

"She won't be able to see us."

Farmer made a clucking noise with his tongue and shook his head. He was about to reach for his pocket watch again but I gripped his wrist.

"Thirty seconds since you last checked," I told him.

Farmer shrugged and pursed his lips. He dropped his hands and drummed his fingers on his thighs. I looked at Victoria and offered her a tight smile. Then I looked back at Pierre.

Pierre was turning on the spot, gazing up at the centre of the arch immediately above him, to where a white, canvas-like structure had been suspended on metal cables. He looked bizarrely small in comparison to the cloud-shaped canvas and the arch itself; as though he'd ingested a magic potion that had shrunk him many times over. If it had been the middle of the day, he would have been surrounded by a mass of people – workers hurrying to and from the branded glass skyscrapers that crowded the area, tourists waiting to ascend to the roof of the arch inside the glass-capsule elevators. Right now there were only a handful of visitors contemplating maps and guidebooks, a scattering of pigeons and a group of hooded teenagers on skateboards, leaping down the stone steps, landing with a clap of plastic on concrete that echoed around the space. The noise might have been a gunshot, it was so loud. Not that any of Farmer's troops were carrying guns. At least, I didn't think they were. The police officers were stationed out of sight, on the rooftops of the nearby buildings, in the entrance to the IMAX cinema positioned off to the side. I'd tried looking but so far I'd been unable to spot any of them. I knew that was a good thing but I kept checking anyway, as if it was some kind of compulsion. What did I really want? Maybe to be able to blame someone other than myself if the meet never happened, I suppose.

Just then, Pierre raised his hand to his eyes and glanced over at us. It wasn't the smartest move ever but there wasn't much I could do about it. I couldn't speak to him because he wasn't wearing a wire or an earpiece or any of that nonsense. He stood there, holding my eye. I lowered my head and contemplated my feet. If ever I got out of this mess, I swore I was through dealing with him.

I heard more trundling noises and looked up to find that the skateboarders were circling Pierre, acting territorial. The circle got tighter, faster. Then one of the kids swerved abruptly and barrelled into Pierre and I thought for one horrible moment the kid was about to snatch the painting. He didn't. Instead, the kid groped for Pierre's waist, like the crudest of pickpockets, and then he backed away and began to skate off. His buddies followed. I waited for Pierre to realise that his wallet was gone but instead I saw him unfold a scrap of paper and study it. He looked up and held my eye once more and then he turned and swiftly climbed the steps in the direction of the glass elevators.

She was up there, had to be. And if she was looking down from above then she would have seen Farmer's men on the rooftops and probably us too.

"What's he doing?" Victoria asked.

"They gave him a note. Did you see that?" I said, turning to Farmer.

"You told me to put my binoculars away."

"But you can see what she's done, right? She's changed the meet."

"Or your friend is leaving us."

"You're crazy. You really think he's going to try and flee from the top of that arch?"

"Do you think she's going to?"

I threw up my hands, then pushed up from the bench and began running after Pierre.

"You'll jeopardise everything," Farmer called. "You'll have only yourself to blame."

"At least I'm doing something," I yelled back. "For Christ's sake, where are your men?"

Coming towards me from the left, as it happened. It dawned on me then that maybe the officers in the IMAX cinema had been briefed to make sure I didn't launch an escape bid. Under normal circumstances, I might have felt a bit aggrieved about that, but right then I was just glad of the back-up.

I lowered my head and ran as fast as I could, aiming to reach the steps at the base of the arch before they got too close to me. I made it in good time and took the steps in pairs, then leapt for the crest and continued my run in the direction of the exposed elevator shafts. There was no queue at the ticket booth for the elevators and no sign of Pierre either. I turned on the spot, looking this way and that, but it seemed for all the world as if he'd disappeared. He wasn't in the elevators; he wasn't on the opposite side of the arch; he hadn't doubled back on himself. I glanced over my shoulder and saw the bobbing heads of the onrushing police officers. Time was running out. I checked to my side and in that instant I snatched a glimpse of the back of Pierre's head. He was passing through the glass vestibule of the government offices that occupied the left-hand limb of the arch. I darted after him, bundling through the revolving doors at the entrance to the vestibule and finding myself in a modern, air-conditioned foyer.

Aside from a waif-like cleaner who was polishing the marble floor with a noisy, vibrating machine, the foyer was empty. The cleaner wore a pair of ear-protectors and a glazed expression. I bypassed her and hurdled a metal turnstyle positioned next to the deserted reception desk. Two stainless-steel elevator doors confronted me. I glanced up at the electronic displays above them. Neither elevator was anywhere close. I cast my eyes around for alternatives and caught sight of a nondescript door off to my left. I crashed through the door just as Farmer's troops entered the vestibule.

On the other side of the door was a flight of stairs leading upwards, but no sign of Pierre. I supposed it was possible there had been other options I'd missed back in the foyer but I didn't have time to find out. I looked once more at the door I had come in through and noticed a steel bolt at the top. I slid the bolt across just as someone barged into the door from the opposite side. The wood of the door seemed to bulge in the centre, like a drum skin being struck. There was a pause and then a police officer started to hammer on the door and shout loudly in French. I backed away and made for the stairs. I ran up the first flight, then the second. At the top of the third flight I stopped dead in my tracks.

Pierre was slumped on the floor, clutching his right hand to a dark, glistening spot on his chest just below his left shoulder. Poking out from between the fingers of his hand was the rubber shaft of a knife. Blood was pulsing over his fingers, smearing amid the hairs on his bare wrist. I looked from the wound to Pierre's face. He was grimacing, breathing sharply through his teeth. His eyes were narrowed, as if trying to shut out the pain. I fished in my pocket and removed a handkerchief. I pressed the rag against his hand, then between his fingers and into the gaping wound. The cloth turned red, staining my fingertips. I looked at the knife and thought about pulling it out but I feared it would just make thing worse. Instead, I freed the blue sweater from around Pierre's neck and compressed it around the blade.

The banging was getting louder downstairs. I could hear splintering noises too. The police were forcing their way through the door and it was sure to give in just a moment.

I looked to either side of Pierre. His manbag was there but the painting was gone.

"She took the painting?" I asked.

Pierre nodded, and I could see that it hurt him to do it.

"Where'd she go?"

He gestured upstairs with a tortured heft of his chin.

"The police are coming," I said, getting to my feet. "They'll look after you. Stay with us, okay?"

I didn't wait for his response. I just stood from the floor and reached for the stair banister with my bloodied fingers. I yanked on the banister and sprang for the first steps as the door broke through below me. I moved fast, drumming my legs. I could hear heavy footsteps from below – as though an army was coming. I kept moving as quickly as I could, trying to ignore the acid burn in my lungs. Did she have any other weapons or would the knife have been it? I didn't know and there was only one way to find out. As I reached the next floor, I craned my head up between the stairwell and saw a blur of flesh two flights above. Shouts came at me from below – a jumble of assertive French. They were ordering me to stop. I sucked in more air and ran on.

I can't tell you how many floors there are inside the Grande Arche but I do know I ran up most of them like a madman on fire. It was only as I neared the top that I began to wonder if I'd made a mistake. Why would she head for the roof? She had to have planned her escape route and I doubted the roof could form part of it. Security guards and tourists would be clogging the space and the only viable exits were the central glass elevators and what I guessed would be a matching set of stairs and elevators on the opposite side of the arch. By now, Farmer would have police stationed at the bottom of them all.

I glanced out of a window in the stairwell. I was what, a dozen floors from the top? When would she break off? Had I already gone too far?

I paused for what felt like a maddening few seconds, straining to hear her above of me, but I couldn't distinguish her footfall from the noise of the officers down below. They were getting closer. They had to be fitter than me and it was beginning to show. I went up one more floor and then I chanced my luck and dived through an internal door into the dim-lit office corridor beyond.

Catherine Ames was ahead of me, doubled-over, the painting gripped in her hand. It was surreal to see her at last. For so long, I'd associated her name with the dead body I'd found in my apartment, and now the differences in her appearance seemed almost vulgar, they were so stark. She looked older than I'd expected, heavier too. Her broad face was flushed and her forehead and flat nose glistened. She had on a pair of grey slacks and a plain pink

T-shirt, the material stained with patches of sweat and flecked with traces of Pierre's blood.

Catherine turned when she heard the door smack open and I glimpsed a cussed determination in her eyes. I called out her name but she didn't respond – she just wiped a thread of saliva from her lips and stumbled into a run once again. I thought she was going to fall but she regained her balance and kept on. Her progress was laboured and she was clutching her side, as if she had a stitch. I bowed my head and pursued her through the abandoned corridor, passing forlorn work cubicles and photocopy rooms, slumbering printers and water fountains. I caught my toe on a metal filing cabinet and veered wildly to the right, striking the partition wall with my shoulder. I yelled out in frustration and the noise was enough to make Catherine glance back at me in a panicked way.

"Stop," I yelled. "Arrête! Catherine."

Maybe the din I was making was enough to spook her; maybe she thought I was quick enough to catch up. Whatever she was thinking, she kept checking over her shoulder and it was slowing her down. I shouted some more, conscious that I was gaining on her and starting to believe I'd be able to dive for her ankles on the other side of the internal door she was heading towards. She lunged for the handle and whipped the door back. I reached out and hollered, aiming to startle her. It worked. Catherine shrieked and hurled the wrapped painting towards me, the sturdy door swinging closed behind her. The painting twirled towards my head, spinning over and over. I was moving too quickly to avoid the collision. A corner of the dense frame connected with my temple and knocked me clean off my feet.

The last thing I can remember is the back of my skull striking the floor.

THIRTY-SIX

From what I could gather when I put things together later on, it was around twenty minutes before the first police officer found me. I was sat with my back against the wall by then, gingerly prodding the swollen gash around my temple. I didn't try to stand by myself because I was feeling too giddy but I was obliged to find my feet when the officer hauled me up by the armpit and roughly cuffed my wrists behind my back. He marched me to one of the elevators, my feet occasionally giving way beneath me, and then he transported me outside to where Farmer was waiting.

"Did you catch her?" I asked, squinting out through the shards of pain piercing my head.

"Just," he replied, gesturing some distance away towards a marked police van with its emergency light flashing. "Looks as if she'd done all her running by the time she got down here."

"That's wonderful. Do you think you could let me go now?"

I turned and showed Farmer my cuffed hands. He motioned to the officer to release me and once I was free I stood leaning against an outside panel of the glass vestibule, rubbing first at the chaffed skin on my wrists and then at the swollen area above my eye. I gulped air, trying to steady myself.

"Charlie," Victoria said, stepping close to me. "Are you okay?"

"Will be," I managed.

"Are you concussed?"

"Oh, I think so."

"What did she hit you with?"

I pointed to the wrapped painting the officer was clutching in his hand.

"Ouch."

"Tell me about it. Better than getting stabbed, though. How's Pierre doing?"

"On his way to the hospital," Farmer said.

"And then back home, I hope."

"We'll see."

I held his eye but I didn't learn a great deal. I decided to ask the question I really wanted answered. "Where does this leave me? Am I in the clear?"

Farmer gestured for the officer who'd arrested me to leave us alone. Once he was halfway down the stone steps and out of earshot, Farmer leaned towards me and spoke to me in a confidential tone.

"I've talked to my clients. They're amenable to keeping you out of this."

"That's the very least they should do," Victoria said, one hand on her hip.

Farmer gave her a cool stare, then focused on me once again. "You'll have to leave France, naturally. You may be watched in the meantime."

"How long do I have?"

"A day. They expect you to be gone by then."

"And just where is he supposed to go?" Victoria demanded.

"It's alright," I told her, squeezing her hand. "You can help me decide."

THIRTY-SEVEN

It wasn't until the following afternoon at Charles de Gaulle airport that I had an opportunity to talk with Victoria. In the meantime, I'd slept for ten hours straight and had largely recovered from my man-versus-picture frame incident, and I'd also squared things with Farmer so that I was able to return to my apartment and collect the last of my things, albeit under police supervision. At the airport, I paid for takeaway coffees for myself and Victoria and then we sat down beside one another in a pair of leather-backed seats, our luggage by our feet.

"So this stinks," Victoria said, to no-one in particular.

"You think?" I asked, bringing my Styrofoam coffee cup to my lips.

"Well, duh. First, you recover a priceless Picasso that could easily have been lost for ever. Then you solve a murder mystery. And how does the French state repay you?"

I swallowed my coffee. "I confessed to burglary, Vic. I couldn't very well expect them to ignore that and let me carry on."

"I don't see why not."

"Sure you don't."

"Well," she said, tapping her finger on the lid of her coffee cup. "I still think it's shoddy."

"What were you hoping for? The Legion of Honour?"

She pursed her lips. "A thank-you might have been nice."

"Overrated. Not going to prison is good enough for me."

"And being chased out of their country?"

"Not chased," I said, pointing my two bandaged fingers at her. "Just invited to leave. And anyway, maybe it was time to move on."

"But you're not even close to finishing your book."

"I can take it with me, you know."

"Well, you're more forgiving than me, that's for sure."

I shrugged and imbibed through the plastic lid of my coffee cup again. Victoria did the same and when she looked up she had a milk-froth moustache. I reached out to clear the smear with my thumb. Victoria flinched, then relented. I ran my thumb over her lips, wiping the foam onto my trousers.

"Thank you," she said.

"No. Thank you. For everything."

"You're welcome."

"I mean it. You did a hell of a lot for me. And I'm really not sure I deserved it. After what I did . . ."

"Oh, stop it. You're forgiven already. I thought we were moving on."

I smiled and glanced up at our surroundings. The airport was an oddly futuristic space, filled with muted greys and blacks, steel and glass. I knew from previous visits that some of the different areas were linked by tubular escalators that reminded me of the Pompidou Centre. It was more *Jetsons*-style architecture; like a seventies vision of a space station.

Above us, a bank of four monitors displayed a list of departure destinations. I still hadn't figured out quite where I was going to go. Hopefully, inspiration would hit soon because I really didn't want to dwell any longer than necessary. I'd enjoyed almost all of my time in Paris and part of me was a little sore to leave. The other part knew just how fortunate I'd been.

"Charlie," Victoria said. "I know you don't have much time but can we talk some more about what happened?"

"What's eating you?"

"A few things."

"Uh oh."

I drank some more of my coffee, then set it down on the floor and reached for a cigarette. Victoria seized my wrist and shook her head, pointing to a no-smoking sign.

"We could go outside," she suggested.

"Nah. It's okay. We're fine here."

"Sure?"

"Absolutely. I've been thinking about giving up. So I'll just sit here and drink my coffee and you can ask me whatever you need to."

"Anything?"

"Anything."

"Okay." She took a breath. "Did you sleep with Paige?"

I stared at her, mouth open, and she blushed.

"Forget it," Victoria said, raising her hand and turning her head away. "I don't know why I asked that. It wasn't what I meant to say."

I placed my hand on her knee. "She's not my type."

"She's exactly your type."

I smiled, shook my head. "Never happened."

"Right."

"It's the truth. Believe me?"

"If you say so. Like I said, I really don't know why I asked in the first place."

"Well, you did, and I told you. So what else?"

Victoria lifted her shoulders and sighed. She cleared some hair from her eyes and tucked it behind her ears.

"Well," she went on, "with everything that happened, there's one thing we never really dealt with. Pierre said his client was a man. But if the call came from Catherine's apartment, that man couldn't have been Gerard."

I sucked on my lips. "It wasn't."

"So who?"

"Could have been anyone, I guess. But if you want my best bet, I'd say Bruno."

"Really?"

"Uh huh. We know he'd been in Catherine's apartment before and it could be he was sleeping with her, like he claimed. But even if that's the case, I think it might have been because she wanted a man to make that telephone call."

"Just to confuse Pierre?"

"It was an extra layer of protection, I suppose. And it would explain why Bruno wanted to steal the painting of Montmartre. I mean, for one thing he would have known it was valuable, but even more than that, he would have known that Catherine wouldn't be all that bothered if the thing was taken."

"I guess that adds up."

"I think so," I said, taking another mouthful of coffee.

"And was it Bruno who told Catherine where you lived? Or was that Pierre? Someone must have told her or she wouldn't have known where to kill poor Sophia."

I glanced up at the ceiling, considering the point. "I don't think it was either of them."

"Why not?"

"Look, this part confuses me, okay? And I'm not sure I've cracked it just yet. I figure it can't have been Bruno because he wouldn't have wanted to admit that he knew me, and he had no idea I was also the thief Catherine happened to have hired. And it wasn't Pierre. I really should have trusted him more. Plus, he doesn't know where I live."

"So?"

"So I think there are two possibilities. One is that after contacting Pierre, Catherine kept an eye out for someone breaking into her place. If she saw me go in, she could have followed me until I went home."

"But you didn't go home. You went to the bookshop and then you went searching for Bruno. The first time you got home, the body was there."

I frowned. "Oh. Right."

"So who else did you figure it could be?"

"Paige," I said, wincing.

"Thank goodness."

"Excuse me?"

"Well," Victoria said, "I really didn't like her attitude back at that café. I kind of wanted her to be involved somehow."

"The truth is she's the only person I can remember giving my address to. When she asked to organise my reading, I wrote it down for her in case she needed to get in touch."

"That's it?"

"That, plus the way she and Bruno have been behaving. They both seem to have something playing on their conscience."

"So it's a hunch."

I pointed my finger at her and cocked my thumb, as though I was aiming a pistol. "You got me."

"Not that I suppose it matters a great deal."

"Doesn't change a thing," I said, pulling my imaginary trigger. "The authorities will focus on building a case against Catherine and Gerard."

"You think they'll succeed?"

"With Farmer working for them, I'd say the chances are pretty high. He might even get a confession."

Victoria nodded and glanced down at her coffee. "I

hope someone has contacted that poor Sophia woman's family."

"It's not something they're likely to overlook."

"Actually," she said, eyebrows forked, "now I think about it, what happens to Francesca and the crowd from the bookshop? Presumably they're going to be arrested?"

"Not the impression I got."

"Oh?"

"I guess they could be spoken to, cautioned if you like. Farmer could handle that. But maybe the Pompidou won't be too bothered if they let things run their course."

"How come?"

"Art theft is huge, Vic. Internationally, I mean. People think it's just movie stuff but it's really not. After all, it's low-risk compared to drug trafficking or arms trading, and if you steal the right painting you can make a lot of money."

"So?"

"So Francesca is going to try and sell the painting she stole to somebody. Maybe she already had a buyer lined up and maybe the Pompidou don't care very much if that person spends a fortune on a fake. Let's say they wait six months and release some kind of story about how they've had the Picasso room valued and authenticated as a routine insurance procedure. Whoever bought the fake is going to have to look into it and when they find out they've paid a lot of money for a forgery, they won't be happy. They might even get out of the game for good."

Victoria adopted a pained expression. "But if that happens, they might come after Francesca. That doesn't sound very fair."

"True, but she's hardly your average pensioner. Besides, she told me she was going to Cuba if the heist came off."

"Just like Faulks. You're joking, right?"

"Cross my heart."

Victoria reached for my forearm. "Hey. You put that tracking device on the painting, didn't you? Maybe the authorities will be able to find whoever buys it."

"Nah," I said, shaking my head. "I think the range would have been pretty limited. And Francesca would have been smart enough to check for things like that when she had enough time. It wasn't hard to spot and she must have been suspicious when I didn't make it back to the camper van."

"Hmm. You really have an answer for everything."

"Except for where I'm going to head next. You have any ideas?"

Victoria contemplated my luggage. "Well, how about –"

She was interrupted by her telephone chirping inside her handbag. She reached for her bag and gathered the phone, then scrunched up her face when an unfamiliar number appeared. I watched her answer the call, then sigh and hand the phone to me.

"Charlie," Pierre began, in a hoarse voice. "You were going to leave without saying goodbye?"

I checked over my shoulder to be sure I wasn't being monitored. "I didn't have a great deal of choice, Pierre. How are you feeling?"

"They tell me I will live."

"Well, that's something."

Pierre offered me a faint, wheezing laugh. "I wanted to thank you," he said. "You were right – we should not have done this one, oui?"

"I went into it with my eyes open," I told him, standing up and scanning the area. I didn't see anyone suspicious, not even the two police officers who had followed us to the airport in a marked squad car. "Did you get the package I sent to the hospital?"

"It is why I called. There was no need."

"I would have felt bad about keeping it. It wouldn't have been right."

"Well, maybe I will buy an airplane ticket, yes? Come and find you."

"They've told you to get out too?" I asked, resuming my seat.

"No. I can be useful to them, yes? To Mr Farmer, I think so."

"He'll have you running errands for him as soon as you're discharged."

"He already does, my friend." Pierre cleared his throat. "This Guitar Painting, it was not the only thing Gerard and Catherine stole."

"Really?"

"They told you she worked near Orléans?"

"I heard she was an archivist."

"They have checked the papers she worked on only yesterday. There are three sketches by Picasso. All gone."

"Gone?"

"Replaced with fakes. You did not see these?"

"No," I said, and whistled. "I wish I had. But listen, I'd better go, Pierre. I'm worried my friend might send me her phone bill."

"Ha. So long, Charlie."

"Take care."

I ended the call, pressing the telephone against my closed lips for a moment while I thought around the implications of what Pierre had said. Victoria opened her palm to my side and I dropped her telephone back into it.

"What package?" she asked.

"Excuse me?"

"You asked Pierre if he'd got the package you sent him."

"Oh," I said, avoiding her eyes. "I couriered over his share of the ten thousand euros Catherine paid us."

"You're joking."

"Nope. I figured she wasn't likely to pay the second instalment."

"But Charlie, that's crazy."

"Actually, me asking for the whole ten thousand up front was the crazy part. I've felt bad about it ever since."

"But hang on," Victoria said, raising her palm, "if you sent Pierre half, doesn't that mean you still paid for the painting of Montmartre out of your own share?"

I nodded, somewhat glumly. "That's true."

"So you're left with what, a thousand euros? For all this trouble?"

"Give or take a bit. Plus the five hundred Bruno paid me right at the beginning."

"But that's terrible. It might not even be enough to cover the cost of your flights out of here."

"At one stage, I thought it was barely going to cover the cost of our airport taxi."

I smiled, but Victoria didn't reciprocate. She shook her head and gave me a stern look.

"I don't think you should take this so lightly. You got a really raw deal, Charlie."

"Oh, I don't know about that."

"You think fifteen hundred euros is good? You're cheaper than I thought."

I stared meaningfully at her, dropped my head on an angle. I couldn't help but grin.

"Something to show you," I said, and with that I fished around in the smaller of my two holdalls until I found my box of disposable gloves. I slipped one of the gloves onto my left hand and then I rooted around some more before coming up with a scroll of yellowed paper. I checked behind and in front of us again for any prying eyes and then I unrolled the paper with my bandaged fingers for Victoria to see. The sheet was a little bigger in size than a hardback novel.

"What's this?" Victoria asked, reaching for the edge.

I snatched the paper away. "Sorry. Don't touch. At least, not without gloves on."

"Why? What is it?"

"A Picasso."

Victoria's face became a tangle. "I don't get it."

"There are two more in my bag. They're original sketch works, preparatory drawings for The Guitar Player. Here – look at the lines."

I pointed to some angular, charcoal outlines. Victoria lowered her head towards the paper, then looked up at me with her mouth wide open.

"Explain."

"Catherine took them, from the archive in Orléans. Pierre was just telling me they discovered some fakes among the Picasso originals she'd been responsible for. She did the same thing she did with the painting in the end. First she produced some forgeries and then she switched them for the real thing."

"My God," Victoria said, covering her mouth with her hand. "Are they valuable?"

"All three of them? Should be worth a few tens of thousands, I imagine."

"And you're taking them?"

"Absolutely. So you see, I've not had such a bad deal after all."

"But when did you even get these?" she asked, searching my face. "You never mentioned it."

"Because I haven't had them long. Only since yesterday, as it happens."

Victoria backed away from me, squinting, as though trying to process it all in her mind.

"These are the reason Catherine showed up for the painting of Montmartre," I said. "I figured there had to be something to make it worth her while. At first, I thought maybe she'd found out that I'd taken the swipe card from her apartment. Or maybe Bruno had been in touch with her. I didn't know. But I guessed there had to be something more to that ugly oilwork."

"But we checked the back of the painting. That's where you found the plans."

"Yes, but we didn't check the frame itself. Look, when she threw the painting at me yesterday, I was out cold for a while, just like I said. But when I came round I had maybe ten minutes before I was found. So I opened the packaging and I had a good look at the painting. Something I hadn't noticed before was a slight indentation all along the top edge of the frame. I poked at it with one of my burglar tools and guess what? It was wax, painted over to look like the rest of the gilded wood. I dug out the wax and found there was a cavity with these sketch works rolled up inside. That's why the frame was so damn big. She needed the space."

"I can't believe it."

"I'm struggling with it myself. And I figure Farmer must have guessed by now. Once I got that wax out, I couldn't very well put it back. All I could do was wrap the painting again and act concussed when I was found. But they must have opened the painting up pretty much right away and seen that gap. And Farmer knows as well as I do that there had to be a compelling reason for Catherine to show her face yesterday."

"So why didn't he come after you?"

"Maybe he will. Or maybe he figures I deserve a break. Either way, I guess he told Pierre something about it because that's what his phone call was about. He was warning me."

Victoria studied my face intently. "So that's why you're so relaxed about leaving."

"That's part of it. I need to go somewhere I can sell the damn things."

I cast my eyes up to the bank of departure monitors above my head and scanned the names of the destinations on offer. Some in Europe, some across the Atlantic, some even further afield.

"Can you get the drawings through customs?" Victoria asked.

"Hope so. In fact, I might even follow Catherine's example. If you straighten these sketches out, they're small enough to fit inside the back of the frame I keep my Hammett novel in."

"Seriously? You think that'll work?"

"Only one way to find out."

Victoria pressed the heel of her palm against her forehead. "But where are you going to go?"

"Ah, well I sort of thought you might choose."

She peered at me. "You did?"

"Come with me. At least for a little while."

"Uh uh." She shook her head. "I have a job to go back to. A mortgage to pay."

"All of that can wait."

"Oh really. And what about my other clients?"

"They'll understand. You need a holiday, Vic."

"Ha. Let you get me into even more trouble, you mean?"

"Maybe," I said. "But don't you think it might be fun to find out?"

USEFUL INFORMATION

HOW TO PICK A PIN AND TUMBLER LOCK

First, see how a traditional key opens a lock. Note that the pins are preventing the cylinder or "plug" from turning. Once the key is inserted, the indentations on the key raise each individual pin to the correct height. Sideways force is applied through the key and the cylinder can turn.

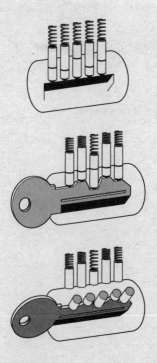

Now, see how a pick is used in place of a key to raise the pins to the appropriate height. Clockwise tension is applied via a tension wrench or a screwdriver. As each pin is "jogged up" it rests on the ledge of the shear line (the ledge is created as a result of the sideways pressure applied via the tension wrench/screwdriver). Once all the pins are raised to the appropriate height, the lock "plug" can turn. The plug is connected to a cam that, in turn, is connected to a door bolt.

By using a raking tool instead of a traditional pick, simple locks can be opened much faster.

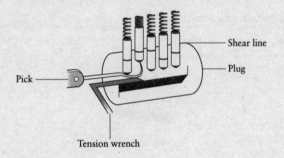

ANNOTATED FLOORPLAN
Centre Georges Pompidou – Fifth Floor

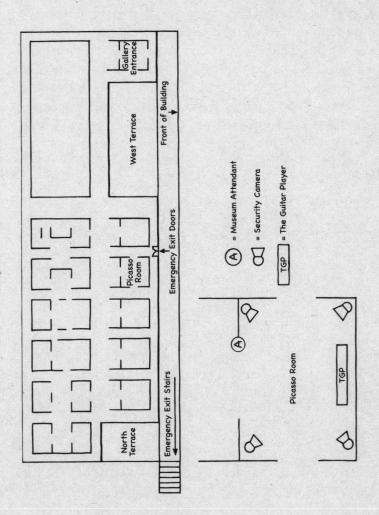

FRENCH WORDS AND PHRASES

Basics and Greetings

Yes	*Oui*
No	*Non*
Good day	*Bonjour*
Goodbye	*Au revoir*
Thank you	*Merci*
I don't understand	*Je ne comprends pas*
Do you speak English?	*Parlez-vous anglais?*
Men's/women's toilets	*Hommes/Femmes*

Other Essentials

"Hello. I'm here to visit Mr/Mrs . . . Please can you let me in?"
"*Bonjour. Je rends visite à Monsieur/Madame . . . Est-ce que vous pourriez me laisser entrer s'il vous plaît?*"

"I seem to have lost my keys."
"*Il m'apparaît que j'ai perdu mes clefs.*"

"No, you're mistaken, this happens to be my apartment."
"*Non, vous avez tort. Ceci est bien mon appartement.*"

"Oh, do you live here? I'm sorry, I must have become confused."
"*Ah, vous habitez ici? Je suis désolé, je me suis confondu.*"

"Please can you direct me to the nearest hardware store?"
"*S'il vous plait, pour aller à la quincaillerie la plus proche?*"

"Can you give me the number of your local fence?"
"*Vous pouvez me donner le numéro de telephone de votre receleur locale?*"

"How much for this jewellery/these coins/this painting?"
"*Combien pour ces bijoux/cette pièce de monnaie/ce tableau?*"

"You've made a mistake. This door was open when I got here."
"*Vous avez tort. Cette porte était ouverte quand je suis arrivé.*"
"I demand to see a representative from the British Embassy."
"*J'exige que je vois tout de suite un réprésentant de l'Ambassade Britannique.*"

Equipment

"Do you sell . . . ?"
"*Est-ce que vous vendez . . . ?*"

Picks, probes, rakes, screwdrivers
les outils, les sondes, les râteaux, les tournevis

Fingerprint powder*la*
poudre à empreints

Disposable Latex Gloves
les gants latex jetables

Lint free cloth
sle chiffon non pelucheux

Hair dye, hair clippers
le teint pour cheveux, les coupeurs

False passports
les passeports contrefaçons

ACKNOWLEDGEMENTS

I would like to acknowledge Jeremy Mercer's *Books, Baguettes and Bedbugs*, a terrific memoir of life in the Shakespeare & Co. bookshop, on which the fictional Paris Lights bookshop is based.

The annotated floorplan of the fifth floor of the Pompidou Centre is based on the map contained in the free museum pamphlet *Musée National D'Art Moderne*. Copyright: Centre Pompidou, Conception graphique Atelier de création graphique, 2007

Thank you to everyone who read the completed manuscript and provided feedback, to Jane and Oxford Designers & Illustrators for the Pin and Tumbler illustrations, to Kaushik for his help with the French translations and to Linden for her watchful eye. Special thanks to Jo, for everything else.

POCKET
BOOKS

J. A. Jance
Web of Evil

Ali Reynolds is travelling the blistering, lonely highway,
from Palm Springs to Los Angeles to finalise her divorce and
confront the television network that callously fired her. As she
passes the site of a horrifying accident, she thanks goodness
it's no longer her job to report the news. But suddenly Ali
finds she is the news . . . For the victim is none other than
Ali's cheating husband, and soon she'll find herself the
prime suspect at the centre of a terrifying web of evil.

ISBN: 978-1-84739-047-9
PRICE £6.99

Hand of Evil

Ali Reynolds is grieving. The newsreading job she once loved
is gone and so is the unfaithful husband she thought she knew
so well. But she's roused from her misery by a startling call:
a friend's teenage daughter has disappeared. Ali offers to help
but, in doing so, she unknowingly begins a quest that will
reveal a deadly ring of secrets, at the centre of which
stand two indiscriminating killers . . .

ISBN: 978-1-84739-048-6
PRICE £6.99

POCKET
BOOKS

Joy Fielding
Heartstopper

Welcome to Torrance, Florida. Population: 4,160. A safe place where residents leave their doors unlocked and allow their children to run freely. But that was before the disappearance of popular, pretty Liana Martin. As Sheriff John Weber digs up more questions than answers and the body count rises to three, one truth emerges: it's the prettiest girls who are being targeted, the heartstoppers. And English teacher Sandy Crosbie must do all she can to unmask a ruthless killer before it's too late. . .

ISBN: 978-1-84739-045-5
PRICE £6.99

Charley's Web

When columnist Charley Webb receives a letter from Jill Rohmer, a young woman on death row for the murders of three small children, she soon finds herself in great danger.

Jill wants Charley to write her biography so that she can share the many hidden truths that failed to surface during her trial – including the existence of a mysterious man she calls Jack. But as Charley becomes more involved, she starts receiving anonymous letters threatening her own children. Jill is safely locked away – but could the elusive Jack still be out there?

ISBN: 978-1-84739-046-2
PRICE £6.99

POCKET
BOOKS

Noah Charney
The Art Thief

Rome A magnificent Caravaggio altarpiece
disappears at dead of night.

Paris In the basement vault of the Malevich Society,
curator Genevieve Delacloche is shocked to discover
that one of its greatest treasures has vanished.

London The National Gallery's newest acquisition is
stolen just hours after it was purchased for £6.3 million.

As three separate investigations get underway,
Inspector Jean-Jacques Bizot in Paris and Harry Wickenden
of Scotland Yard begin to suspect that what at first appears
a spate of random thefts is nothing of the kind. Pursuing a
dizzying trail of false leads, bizarre clues and double-crosses
across Europe, the detectives' only chance of uncovering the
truth is to band together to outwit an ingenious criminal
mastermind with his own mysterious agenda.

ISBN: 978-1-84739-141-4
PRICE £6.99

POCKET
BOOKS

Charlie Howard also appears in Chris Ewan's
brilliant debut novel

The Good Thief's Guide to Amsterdam

In Amsterdam working on his latest novel, Charlie is
approached by a mysterious American who asks him to steal
two apparently worthless monkey figurines from two separate
addresses on the same night. At first he says no. Then he
changes his mind. Only later, kidnapped and bound to a chair,
the American very dead, and a spell in police custody behind
him, does Charlie begin to realise how costly
a mistake he might have made.

The police think he killed the American. Others think he
knows the whereabouts of the elusive third monkey. But for
Charlie only three things matter. Can he clear his name? Can
he get away with the haul of a lifetime? And can he
solve the gaping plot-hole in his latest novel?

ISBN 978-1-84739-127-8
PRICE £6.99

**POCKET
BOOKS**

This book and other **Pocket Books** titles are available from your local bookshop or can be ordered direct from the publisher.

Free post and packing within the UK
Overseas customers please add £2 per paperback.
Telephone Simon & Schuster Cash Sales at Bookpost
on 01624 677237 with your credit or debit card number,
or send a cheque payable to Simon & Schuster Cash Sales to:
PO Box 29, Douglas, Isle of Man, IM99 1BQ
Fax: 01624 670923
Email: bookshop@enterprise.net
www.bookpost.co.uk

Please allow 14 days for delivery. Prices and availability
are subject to change without notice.